Stories of Crime & Detection

VOLUME ONE

The Britling Stories

JAMES RONALD

Edited by Chris Verner

 Moonstone Press

This edition published in 2023 by Moonstone Press
www.moonstonepress.co.uk

The Green Ghost Murder originally published in 1931 by William Collins.
Too Many Motives originally published in 1930 by Odhams Press
Find the Lady originally published in 1930 by William Collins.
Six Were to Die originally published in 1932 by Hodder & Stoughton.
Blind Man's Bluff originally published in 1929 by the *Daily Mail*.

ISBN 978-1-899000-66-1
eISBN 978-1-899000-67-8

A CIP catalogue record for this book is available from the British Library
Text designed and typeset by Moonstone Press
Cover illustration by Jason Anscomb
Printed and bound by CPI Group (UK) Ltd, Croydon CR0 4YY

Royalties from the sale of this book will be donated to MND Scotland,
who fund ground-breaking MND (motor neurone disease) research and
world-class clinical trials to combat an uncommon condition that affects
the brain and nerves, and causes weakness that gets worse over time,
eventually resulting in death.

Contents

INTRODUCTION

In addition to James Ronald's first published short story involving crime, this inaugural volume of *Stories of Crime and Detection* contains three pulp fiction novelettes and one novel featuring Police Surgeon turned amateur sleuth Daniel Britling. The unassuming—but missing nothing—Police Surgeon is cast in the great tradition of Golden Age Detective Fiction sleuths. These stories make up a first-ever Daniel Britling collection. They were published between 1930 and 1932.

> Police Surgeon Daniel Britling was a small man with a large head. Disgruntled Scotland Yard officials who were forced to concede him credit for astuteness in criminal investigation (which was not a part of his professional duties) sometimes made pointed remarks about his large head, which they attributed to conceit, but other less prejudiced officials admitted that when Daniel put his interfering finger into the pie of criminal detection, he not infrequently pulled out the plum which the detective in charge of the case had groped in vain for. To not a few people, Britling was known as 'Dapper Dan'. He was always meticulously dressed in well-cut, dark clothes, and he wore a pearl-grey soft hat at a jaunty angle upon his head. His Vandyke beard was trimmed daily, and his moustache was graded to a nicety on each side.

In the first Britling story, *The Green Ghost Murder,* Daniel and his prim twin sister Eunice have travelled to Carstow, a large but pleasing town near the mouth of the Mersey, where the air is bracing and the climate mild, in order for him to recuperate after a severe attack of pneumonia. The story opens with Eunice knitting a sock:

> Although she would be sixty years of age on her next birthday, her eyesight and hearing were exceedingly good. At the moment her eyesight told her that the door into the next room had moved slightly, so gently that only a draught could have stirred it, and her ears told her that the window in the next room had been raised cautiously from the outside.

The Green Ghost Murder was first published in Hush magazine, Vol 2, No. 11, April 1931. As this publication date is actually after the second Daniel Britling story date, I think there must have been a preceding publication somewhere, or the story sat on the shelf. Hush was a crime and mystery magazine published by William Collins for the Detective Story Club. It was purported to be edited by Edgar Wallace, but was actually edited by George Dilnot, a journalist who wrote books on true crime as well as fiction. The magazine contained new and reprinted stories that ran from June 1930 to June 1931, comprising only 13 issues. Contributors included authors Marjorie Bowen, Agatha Christie, Sidney Horler, and Edgar Wallace; the last three issues contained novelettes by James Ronald.

The phrase 'locked room mystery' or 'impossible crime mystery' refers to a criminal action —usually murder—that on the face of it could not have happened, because there is no evidence to explain it. Usually, a dead body is found inside a room that has been sealed somehow from the inside. The reader is then presented with the puzzle and all of the clues, and is encouraged to solve the mystery before the solution is revealed in a dramatic climax. *Locked Room Murders* is a bibliography by the late Robert Adey containing a description of the problem and, separately, the solution to locked room and impossible crime stories with insightful comments. Adey's book includes four novels by James Ronald and *Too Many Motives,* a 7500-word novelette, the second story to feature Police Surgeon Daniel Britling. Though technically not a locked room murder, it does appear to be an impossible crime until Daniel solves the puzzle wearing two hats; divisional surgeon and amateur sleuth.

The story takes place in London and introduces stock characters Lord Clavering and Inspector Evans. Business tycoon Mark Savile celebrates his 54th birthday by perversely inviting four men to dine at his home who hate him and then goads them until one of them punches him. The motives of the party are the mystery that holds the reader.

Too Many Motives was first published in 20-Story Magazine No 94, April 1930. Published 1922-1940 by Odhams Press, 20-Story Magazine was a monthly pulp fiction publication with an emphasis on adventure and mystery stories. Authors included W.E. Johns, Agatha Christie, Edgar Wallace, and James Ronald. *Too Many Motives* later appeared again in Hush magazine Vol 3, No.13, June 1931.

Daniel Britling's twin sister Eunice, Lord Clavering, and Inspector Evans, reappear as characters in the third Daniel Britling novelette, *Find the Lady,* which is concerned with the disappearance of Lord Clavering's cousin, Lady Frances Dorian. The story was published in Hush magazine Vol 2 No.12, May 1931.

Daniel Britling's fourth and final outing is in the novel *Six Were to Die,* an impossible crime story first published in January 1932, as a Yellow Jacket Original by a much-improved class of publisher, Hodder and Stoughton. The synopsis suggests plenty of scope for murder and misdirection:

Seven financiers had indulged in illegal practices and were about to be dealt with by the police. Six of them decided to put the blame on the seventh, who went to prison for a long term. When he came out, he prepared his revenge, and five out of the six died suddenly and unpleasantly.

The version presented here is transcribed from a serialised account in the Atherstone News and Herald (UK), July to December 1933. There are minor punctuation and text differences between these and other versions. It was also serialised in the Hawick News and Border Chronicle (UK), the Goulburn Evening News (Australia), and in other newspapers under the pseudonym Peter Gale. Under the pseudonym Kirk Wales, Ronald later sold *Six Were to Die* again in 1941 to Mystery House, an affiliate of Arcadia House Inc, New York.

The final story is *Blind Man's Bluff,* Ronald's first published crime fiction. Written in two days after a year-long hospital stay—and according to him, sold on the third day, no doubt making good use of his newspaper contacts—*Blind Man's Bluff* was first published in the *Daily Mail*, 5 October 1929. but also appeared in *The Australasian*, Melbourne, Victoria, Australia, 16 June 1934, the *Falkirk Herald*, Scotland, 13 March 1935, and the *Linlithgowshire Gazette*, West Lothian, Scotland, 15 March 1935; all three under the pseudonym Mark Ellison. This pattern of publications and pseudonyms will appear time and time again, which means that trawling for lost stories catches a few, but many may escape the net. Each version of the story is slightly different. This version is a hybrid of all of them, restoring cut text where possible.

ABOUT THE AUTHOR

James Jack Ronald, to give his full name, was born 11 May 1905, in North Kelvinside, Glasgow, Scotland. He was the son of James Jack Ronald, a Chartered Public Accountant, and Katherine Hamilton Ronald. He was educated at Hillhead High School, Glasgow, established in 1885.

Until he was five, James Ronald says he was chubby, happy, and irresponsible, but in 1911, his sixth year, he was run over by an automobile causing a very real morbidity to creep in. For ten years following the accident he suffered recurrent dreams about a wheel that became larger and larger as it turned faster and faster. He was invalided over a long period during which, with his mother Catherine's encouragement, he enjoyed a prodigious amount of reading. He later claimed he owes his literary gift, and resultant career, to this near-fatal automobile accident, which caused him to change from a sunny little extrovert to a cloudy introvert.

When he was fourteen, he wrote an account of the accident, setting down all the details in a somewhat light vein, not forgetting to note that the candy he had purchased with such delight on that foggy morning was found sticking to the wheels of the car as he was being carried off. The piece won him first prize for composition and congratulations from the masters at the school and even the headmaster wished him well, but that did not prevent corporal punishment for his appalling handwriting. He was called into the headmaster's office, but kept waiting so that everybody knew that he, James Ronald, was going to receive a beating from the headmaster. This injustice obviously affected him very deeply, because it remained with him all his life, and crops up in interview after interview:

> After all, I taught myself to read before going to school and could see no reason for accepting a beating because they failed to teach me how to write, so I bolted.

In a spirit of rebellion against repeated punishments for bad handwriting for compositions for which he invariably got an 'A', Ronald came home from school one day announcing he would never return. It was time to leave. His mother Catherine was understandably distressed, concerned her elder son leaving school at such a young age would diminish his career prospects. Aware of the scarcity of jobs just then in Glasgow, she told him he could only stay away from school if he remained active in some useful employment, making it clear she would not condone an idler in the family.

Within three days James Ronald was an errand boy for the *Glasgow Evening News*, a paper into which he had smuggled a poem some months earlier. But there was 'no writing, nothing editorial' in his set up and he thoroughly disliked it and lost the job. He found another post immediately with the *Glasgow Sunday Mail* and kept this one until he printed his own rival paper on the office mimeograph. He broke the machine and, failing to cover his tracks by leaving a sheet in the copier, he was fired. Then came a dozen jobs, including one with an art dealer for whom he gilded statues and washed windows. His mother told him, 'It is no disgrace to wash windows, James, but it is a disgrace to wash them like that.'

By the age of seventeen, James Ronald had run through all prospective employers in Glasgow, including every newspaper.

He felt the need of open space—'a lot of it'—and after various and sundry abortive departures, finally won grudging permission to seek his fortune in the New World.

For some reason, Chicago stuck in the mind of the young Ronald as a magic word. He became determined to travel to the United States of America. The main method of crossing the Atlantic Ocean in the 1920s was by steamship and ocean liner. The passengers aboard the *SS Saturnia* included seventeen-year-old James Ronald, who arrived at his destination on 6 December 1922, at the Port of Québec, an inland port located in Québec, Canada. From there he continued his journey across the Great Lakes to Chicago, Illinois, United States. He managed to survive in Chicago, the fastest-growing city in world history, with a flourishing economy approaching three million people, attracting huge numbers of new immigrants from Eastern and Central Europe. Ronald stayed in Chicago for five years, wanting to write, but unable to afford the time because he was forced to earn money to live. He was taken on and fired from a variety of jobs with monotonous regularity. Like his experiences in Glasgow, he exhausted all potential employers, dabbling in some forty jobs ranging from short-order cook and dishwasher to muslin salesman; from dance promoter and theatre manager to washing dishes again in a Greek restaurant. He edited ten trade journals at one time for a Chicago publisher; and gave new life to a women's religious magazine. A chain-smoker, he confessed slyly to have worked for the Anti-Cigarette League, his excuse being 'a man must eat don't you know'—at that time eating being the only philosophy he could afford to practise. It was in the Windy City that he learned about life.

Working in the U.S as 'a visitor' to avoid immigration may have caught up with Ronald because, in 1927, he returned to Britain on a more permanent basis, and secured a well-paid job with an English newspaper chain, and a promise of future advancement. However, during his first holiday in the job, a car accident disrupted this promising career trajectory. Whilst driving a small open two-seater Rover 8, Ronald was struck by a two-ton truck and thrown out against the radiator of another vehicle. Left with a broken hip and temporarily crippled (and without the newly acquired job), he settled down to write.

Ronald's writing developed in three stages. First, he hammered out serializations and short stories which were syndicated in newspapers, both at home and abroad; and a number were also published in obscure pulp magazines. Some stories then became lost and forgotten and this has unfortunately contributed to a lack of recognition for an impressive body of work. These early narratives were very difficult to track down, but searching has provided me with an enjoyable and rewarding task—a treasure hunt for lost tales. This was not made any easier because many of these stories were published under pseudonyms; Peter Gale, Mark Ellison, Kenneth Streeter, Alan Napier, and even women; Cynthia Priestley and Norah Banning—in addition to known pseudonyms Michael Crombie and Kirk Wales. Those I have discovered have all been gathered together for republication in this series.

A second writing stage followed; the full-length mystery stories which have made him so popular with Golden Age of Detection aficionados. They are out-of-print, elusive to find, and first editions are very expensive.

Finally, late in life, James Ronald embarked on his Dickensian-style life drama novels. He received enthusiastic praise for his ingenuity, freshness, and sharp sense of humour, by many critics and writers of the time, such as August Derleth. Orville Prescott, the main book reviewer for *The New York Times* for 24 years, called James Ronald 'a born novelist,' and that he 'has in full measure the two basic drives which inspire a writer of fiction—the urge to create characters and to tell stories about them. Mr. Ronald does both naturally, directly and well.' His work received praise and has been compared to William de Morgan, H. G. Wells, Rudyard Kipling, J. M. Barrie, and Somerset Maugham.

James Ronald is a writer who has not gained the long-term recognition he deserves. His work has received high praise for his ingenuity, freshness, and sharp sense of humour by many critics and writers of the time and current enthusiasts, highlighting him as one of the leading storytellers of the day, yet barely anything has been republished since his death in 1972. I hope the reader will enjoy these imaginative and entertainingly written stories as much as I have collecting them.

Chris Verner
Berkhamsted, Buckinghamshire, UK
April 2023

THE GREEN GHOST MURDER

MISS EUNICE BRITLING looked up with a start from the half-finished mauve-coloured sock which she was knitting. Although she would be sixty years of age on her next birthday, her eyesight and hearing were exceedingly good. At the moment her eyesight told her that the door into the next room had moved slightly, so gently that only a draught could have stirred it, and her ears told her that the window in the next room had been raised cautiously from the outside.

It seemed evident that an intruder was about to enter the little house by stealth, a fact which in no way amazed Miss Britling; it pleased her rather or would please her when the danger attendant on the intruder's presence was past, for she had prophesised burglars from the moment she had set foot in the house. It was hardly a house, more a cottage, consisting as it did of two bedrooms, a dining-room, a tiny sitting-room, kitchen, scullery and bathroom. In size, it was ideal for the Britlings, whose menage consisted simply of Doctor Daniel Britling, his twin sister Eunice, and a young servant girl who 'lived out'; but the sitting-room and adjoining bedroom at the rear on the ground floor, the windows of which were only three feet from the ground, were a direct invitation to enterprising burglars.

The Britlings had taken the place furnished for a month, to allow Daniel to recuperate after a severe attack of pneumonia, for it was situated in Carstow, a large but pleasing town near the mouth of the Mersey, where the air is bracing and the climate mild. Only the convenient size of the house had overcome Miss Britling's qualms, for she felt sure that so tempting a means of entrance as the unbarred windows offered would draw burglars as cheese draws mice.

As usual, she was right. A burglar was breaking in at this very moment, and she was alone in the house. Daniel was not there even to listen to her triumphant 'I told you so!' far less to expel the intruder. The little maid-of-all-work was out. Under the circumstances, most elderly ladies would have screamed loudly and long, but Miss Britling was made of sterner stuff. She took a full water-jug from a table in the corner and carried it into the bedroom.

The intruder pushed the window up half-way, and was climbing in. Miss Britling swung back her arm in preparation for heaving the contents of the water-jug over him.

Then a familiar voice said: "Don't be alarmed Eunice. It's only me."

Miss Britling started. 'Daniel, you utter fool!' she exclaimed and switched on the light.

Dr. Britling, who was thus revealed with one leg in the room and the other out, completed his unusual entrance and shut the window.

"Sorry if I startled you," he said, "but I didn't want the blighter to know I live here. I dodged him neatly at the end of the road and slipped over the garden wall."

"What blighter?" was Miss Britling's not unnatural inquiry.

"The one who at this moment is probably marching up and down the avenue, wondering where the dickens I've got to," he said. "I'll go and have a look."

Miss Britling stared in bewilderment at her brother. He was a police surgeon and, since his duties lay in the West End of London, not unfamiliar with crooks. In addition, he was an ardent student of crime, and had played an active part in unravelling more than one mystery.

Nothing of his association with crime or the police was suggested by his appearance. He was short and slim, and his large head made his body look more tadpole than human. It had been said by more than one Scotland Yard official that his large head was due to conceit, but other less prejudiced officials had been known to admit that when Daniel put his enterprising finger into the pie of criminal detection, he almost invariably pulled out the plum that the detective in charge had groped for in vain.

He was always meticulously dressed in well-cut dark clothes, and he wore a pearl-grey fedora at a jaunty angle upon his head. His Vandyke beard was trimmed daily, and his moustache was graded to a nicety on either side.

Criminology was his hobby and almost his profession.

His sister, who infinitely preferred romance to mystery, was inclined to be contemptuous of her brother's activities. At the moment, however, she was impressed by his manner. He tip-toed through to the dining-room, the windows of which looked out into the street, drew back the curtain slightly, and peered out. Miss Britling followed and looked over his shoulder.

A young man, dressed in a fawn-coloured raincoat and a grey felt hat was walking up and down outside, looking up at the houses in the row, and his face wore a puzzled expression.

"He has been following me for the best part on an hour," said Daniel in an annoyed tone. "Twice I thought I had shaken him off, but in a few moments there he was at my elbow again. It's very annoying, for I shall have to stay in the house until he is gone, and I particularly wanted to go out this evening."

"Then why not open the door and ask him what he wants?" asked Miss Britling, not unreasonably.

"Because I know what he wants," replied Daniel in so dark

a tone that his sister started nervously. "He is a humble member of a vast organisation; an organisation like a giant octopus, that is spreading its tentacles throughout the country."

Just then the young man looked directly at their dining-room window, and recognised Daniel. Like a flash he darted up the front steps and began to ring the doorbell furiously.

"What are we going to do?" whispered Miss Britling.

"Nothing. We are in a state of siege until the young man tires or the doorbell breaks. I think I'll just have a glass of port and a biscuit in the interval."

"Hadn't we better call the police?" suggested Miss Britling.

"My dear Eunice," he replied. "One does not call in the police to cope with an organisation of this kind. Have a glass of port, and compose yourself, my dear. He'll go away when he's tired."

Almost as he uttered the words it appeared that his prophecy was confirmed. The ringing, pounding and rattling ceased, and they heard the sound of footsteps retreating down the front steps.

"Excellent!" said Daniel heartily, after a brief pause. "It seemed too good to much hope that he would be so easily discouraged." He looked out of the window. "No, dammit," he added peevishly. "Look!"

Miss Britling looked. The young man was climbing over the back garden wall!

"What on earth shall we do?" she gasped.

"I don't think we can better your own plan of campaign in a similar emergency," said Daniel grimly, grasping the water-jug as he spoke.

The young man's face appeared at the window. Laying the water-jug at his feet, Daniel pulled up the window quickly.

"I say—" began the young man.

That was as far as he was allowed to go. With lightning rapidity, Dr. Britling threw the contents of the water-jug in the young man's face, and banged down the window. The young man spluttered and shook his fist angrily at Daniel, then retreated over the wall.

"Now that the coast is temporarily clear," said Daniel. "I shall go out and resume my walk. I shan't be late; not later than ten at the most."

He opened the front door cautiously and peered to right and left of him. The street was deserted. Carefully adjusting his hat, he stepped out, closed the door after him, and strode briskly away.

Before he had gone a hundred yards, he heard the patter of running feet behind him, and the young man came racing up, mopping his face with a large coloured handkerchief. They stood eyeing each other for a moment, while the young man shook a miniature fountain of water from his hat.

"I say, I don't think you understand who I am—" the young man began reproachfully.

"I understand perfectly," retorted Daniel sternly. "You are a reporter!"

"That's right. On the *Carstow Morning World*, I wanted—"

"A persistent, snooping, sneaking, bell-ringing, wall-climbing reporter," Daniel pursued remorselessly. "And a very poor reporter at that."

"You're right again," agreed the young man, less cheerfully. "I'm a rotten reporter. But how did you know?"

"Know?" snorted Daniel. "Why, man, it's obvious. You've been following me with a blessed notebook all afternoon. A notebook dammit! No reporter worth his salt carries a notebook."

"I suppose that's so."

"But what I can't understand," continued Daniel aggressively, "is why you should follow me at all."

"I thought an interview with you might give me some bright

copy for the paper," replied the reporter readily. "Our star man on the *World* used to be a crime reporter on Fleet Street, and he gave me the idea. He recognised you as you left the station yesterday. He's heard of your remarkable—"

"I am deeply indebted to your star man for having heard of me," said Daniel raising his hat. "Good day."

"Oh, but look here," he said. "You must listen to me. Dash it all, I'm soaking, and it's all your fault."

"I contest that statement," replied Daniel calmly. "But continue, why must I listen to you?"

"Well, confidentially, I'm in the soup. I was given a fortnight's notice yesterday, and unless a miracle happens, I'll be out of a job in a couple of weeks, and I won't get another in a hurry. It's deuced bad luck, because my mother's a widow, and we both rely on my screw. My name's Angell, by the way, Gordon Angell. Healy—that's our star man—says that although officially you are only a police surgeon, actually, you are the best brain at criminal detection in London. He says that when you're called in to examine the body of a murdered man, you nose about for yourself and often unravel the mystery while the regular police are scratching their heads. Now, if you could give me some details of your cases it would make a rattling good story, show the boss what I can do, and I might not lose my job after all."

Daniel listened to all this impatiently, shifting his weight from one foot to the other as his impatience increased. He stared aggressively into Gordon Angell's face.

"And if I allowed you to tell your readers how much cleverer than the police I am, do you suppose the police would ever allow me to 'nose' about the scene of a murder again?" he demanded. "If you do, you're mistaken. They'd simply point to the body, allow me to make my examination, then lead me gently but firmly to the door. I'm sorry, but I have nothing to say."

He walked off briskly towards the centre of the town. Angell hurried after him with breathless anxiety.

"But it means so much to me—" he expostulated.

"It means a great deal more to me," retorted Daniel firmly. "You are in danger of losing your job, but I should lose my hobby. You can find another job, but I should never find another hobby."

His attention was attracted by a tall, powerfully-built man with dark hair and piercing black eyes, who passed them at that moment.

"I know that face," he murmured reflectively, going off at a tangent. "Now, where have I seen it before?"

"He's a music-hall actor," replied Angell in a dejected tone. "One of the Bodoni Brothers—acrobats. The art editor showed me his photograph this morning. Playing at the *Gaiety* this week."

"Memory plays strange tricks," Daniel reflected aloud. "In some ridiculous way, that man is associated in my mind with the name 'Rosa', but that is absurd—Rosa is a woman's name."

"If I can't get anything out of you," said Angell mournfully, "I may as well go to the theatre. It's one of my jobs to report on the show every Monday night."

"Don't let me detain you," said Dr. Britling. "Good evening!"

2

At breakfast the following morning, Miss Britling was distinctly acid of manner.

"Goodness knows how I've managed to live with you all my life without going mad," she said. "You are the most irresponsible, light-headed human being I have ever met."

"If you are not reading the paper," said Daniel gently, "I should like to look at it myself."

"I daresay you would," she commented with asperity. "And then you'd go rushing out without finishing your breakfast to investigate this ridiculous ghost. But I brought you here for a rest, Daniel Britling, and a complete rest you'll have."

"If there's something of interest in the paper, you might as well show it to me now. I'll see it in the long run anyway."

Miss Britling sighed and passed the paper across the breakfast table. Daniel propped the paper against the marmalade dish.

A two-column heading on the front page attracted his attention to the following article:

GREEN GHOST WALKS AGAIN!
CENTURIES OLD WRAITH APPEARS

Last night at a late hour, Mrs. Henry Chalmers, of 21 Odgen Road in the Heaton district of Darstow, was startled to see a tall figure, dressed in luminous green clothing standing in the garden at the rear of her house. Her surprise was the greater when she discovered that she could see right through the figure, making out a rosebush behind it. The figure raised a shining hand and began to walk towards her. Mrs. Chalmers screamed, and as she did so, the figure abruptly vanished, leaving no trace of its presence. The constable on the beat was called in, but could find no sign of a human intruder.

Our representative interviewed Mrs. Chalmers, and found that she was convinced she had seen a spectral figure. Colour is lent to her story by a legend which used to flourish in the Heaton district. Where the suburb now stands was at one time a dense forest, where, in the bad old days, robbers lurked and preyed on defenceless travellers. Legend has it that almost three hundred years ago a handsome youth dressed in green was foully murdered in the forest, and that afterwards his spirit returned to earth and wreaked vengeance on the murderers. As late as sixty years ago, the forest was shunned by those who lived near it because of its reputation for evil, and the belief that a green-clad spectre haunted it.

"This at least is certain," the report concluded, "no one who has discussed the matter with Mrs. Chalmers can doubt that she has had an unpleasant and shocking experience. Is it possible that the Green Ghost of Heaton Forest, famous in local legend, has come back from the grave to protest against the houses which now stand where its forest, dark and impenetrable, once stood? Most people will scoff at the theory, but there are some who will support it, mistaken though they may be."

"Nonsense and balderdash!" exclaimed Miss Britling vehemently. "The foolish woman was haunted by her own rosebush!"

"Perhaps you are right," said Daniel complacently, rising from the table. "Or, perhaps there is another explanation. I rather think that there *is* another explanation."

"Of course, I'm right," retorted Miss Britling. "I—Where are you going?"

"To number twenty-one Ogden Avenue," he replied. "There are some questions I should like to put to Mrs. Chalmers."

"You'll do nothing of the kind! Going off there on a fool's errand when you ought to be resting! For once your overbearing curiosity must remain unsatisfied. Do you hear me, Daniel?"

But Daniel had gone.

Number twenty-one Ogden Avenue was a square, comfortable house with no pretentions to architectural beauty, but with a large, rambling garden which saved it from actual ugliness. It had an untidy hospitable air, but the expression on the face of the short, stout man who opened the door to Daniel was anything but hospitable.

"Well, what is it?" he demanded in an unpleasant tone.

"I should like to speak to Mrs. Chalmers—"

"I dare say you would, but she's not at home to anyone this morning," snapped the short, stout man indignantly.

"—A word or two about her distressing experience last night—"

"I thought so," said the other, putting his hands on his ample hips. "Another spook chaser, eh? All morning one person after another has wanted to see my wife about this ridiculous newspaper article. Ghosts!" He snorted again. "I ask you, does my garden look like the sort of place where ghosts would hang about?"

"To be quite frank, it doesn't," said Daniel. "It looks rather a wholesome sort of garden."

"The roses ain't bad," said Mr. Chalmers in a mollified tone, but added fiercely, "but they won't be up to much if these idiots come about, trampling them down. Ghosts, my granny! There's no more green ghosts in that garden than there is greenfly—and I'm *death* on greenfly."

"It would seem that someone has been exercising a lively imagination," suggested Daniel.

The short, stout man leaned forward and tapped Daniel on the chest in a confidential manner.

"There you've hit it," he said. "Imagination is my wife's curse. She can see just four times as much as anyone else—especially in the dark. I dunno just what happened. Maybe she saw a rosebush moving with the breeze, and thought it was a man lurking out there. She certainly got a bit nervous and being alone in the house called in the constable on the beat, but she didn't mention any green ghosts to *him*. A reporter turned up a little later and it was then that she began to really imagine things. Mark my words, *he* put her up to it. Just a hint to my wife that she saw a real live ghost and mountains wouldn't shake her belief that she *did* see it. Of course, it made a good story for the reporter. But this is the last you'll hear of the Green Ghost, because there ain't any ghosts about here."

But the events of the next few days proved Mr. Chalmers to be a false prophet. Carstow heard a great deal about the Green Ghost during the next week. After centuries of lying quietly in his grave, the Green Ghost became very active in the suburb of Heaton if one could believe the many who swore they saw him.

A servant girl and her swain were the first to see the spectre. He appeared suddenly to them on Heaton Common when they were in the act of embracing fondly on the precarious seat afforded by a fallen tree. His appearance was sufficiently uncanny to make them fall backwards simultaneously, landing with painful force upon their respective spines. He was dressed in luminous green, and was weird, ghostly, and awe-inspiring. When they picked themselves up tremblingly, he had vanished as mysteriously as he had appeared.

Then a certain Miss Dove saw him as she returned home from her Wednesday evening Dorcas Meeting. If her story is to be believed he popped out of the solid earth at her feet, fixed her with an evil, ghoulish stare, and disappeared in a puff of pungent smoke. Her legs 'went from her,' and she collapsed with equal suddenness.

Phlegmatic, unimaginative women saw him, children saw him, drunk men saw him; even one man who was not at all drunk saw him, took to his heels, ran all the way to the nearest public house and promptly proceeded to become drunk enough to satisfy anyone. The Green Ghost became the topic of the hour, and curiosity-seekers from all over Carstow made pilgrimage to Heaton to see the places where he had appeared. Every day the *Carstow Morning World* had a full column on the current activities of the Green Ghost. The *Carstow Morning World* organised a ghost hunt, gathering together bands of large men who went about whacking hedges with large sticks, and causing more commotion than a dozen Green Ghosts put together.

One morning, when the excitement was at its height, Daniel met Gordon Angell and a tall, shrewd-looking man in the main street of the town. Angell was effusively friendly. "I've been looking forward to meeting you again, doctor," he said. "This is Healy, our star man on the *World*. Healy, this is Doctor Britling."

They liked each other at once, and not unnaturally the three men gravitated quite soon to the *Mitre,* a cosy little inn on a side street. There they met Billy Hannaway, Carstow's leading bookmaker, who was being morosely thoughtful over a pint tankard of bitter beer.

"What's the matter, Billy?" asked Healy jovially. "Seen the Green Ghost?"

The bookmaker laughed harshly. "The Green Ghost," he jeered. "Be damned to that for a tale! I'd like to meet him! I'd pull him inside out, and wrap his guts round his neck. Maybe that joker can scare a lot of hysterical women and children, but he'd meet his match if he tried to haunt me."

"When he does," said Healy, "I'll write a column and a half about it."

"Not on your life," retorted Hannaway. "When he does, your paper will run a three-line paragraph about it—in the obituary column!"

A prophecy which was not long in coming true—

"Speaking of the Green Ghost, doctor," said Healy. "This young man is doing himself proud over it. He was in the sub-editor's room when the scare started, and the boss has allowed him to handle it ever since. He's making a good job of it, too. Spends his evenings scouring Heaton for a sight of the ghost. He's usually first on the scene after a haunting, too."

"That's interesting," said Dr. Britling with a shrewd glance at Gordon Angell. "Very interesting—"

3

The telephone bell in the little house occupied by Daniel and his sister rang that evening at eight o'clock. Daniel answered it and heard Conrad Healy's voice speaking at the other end of the wire.

"This is Healy of the *Morning World*," he said excitedly. "You remember Hannaway—you met him in the *Mitre* this morning? Well, he's dead! —Murdered! No, I'm not joking. He's been murdered by the Green Ghost!"

Daniel called a taxi-cab, and was conveyed to the suburban house of the murdered bookmaker. He found no difficulty in picking out the house, although the taxi was forced to stop at the corner of the street owing to a large crowd of people which thronged the pavement and overflowed into the road. News of the murder had spread quickly in the neighbourhood, and it was all that the police could do to keep the gaping mob from crowding into the house. The police were there in force; a score of them formed a cordon round the house and garden.

Fortunately, Healy, the reporter, was standing on the steps of the house watching for Dr. Britling. Noticing Daniel's plight, he spoke a few words to a police sergeant who was standing near him and the two came across and rescued the little police surgeon.

"I've been cracking you up to the Inspector in charge," Healy whispered, "and he's willing to give you the run of the place. As a matter of fact, he's a good sort, and he'll only be too delighted to accept your help."

"What an unusual policeman!" commented Daniel drily, following the reporter into the house.

In the kitchen they found two men and a stout middle-aged woman who had 'cook' written all over her. She was slumped down in an ungainly attitude on a kitchen chair. Her hands were red, in contrast to her face which was ashy in colour, and they trembled spasmodically. Her well-padded body was shaken with spasms of shivering. A glass which had contained brandy stood on a kitchen table beside her, and one of the men was pouring a second liberal dose of the stimulant into it.

Daniel was introduced to the two men. Inspector Milliken was tall and spare, with shrewd grey eyes and an alert expression on his long, clean-shaven face; his hair was greying at the temples, but thick and black at the crown of his head. He spoke in short, crisp sentences. "Heard of you, doctor," he said. "Glad of your help. Look round as much as you like."

His subordinate, Sergeant Keating, was of average height but heavily built, with a large, stolid-looking face and phlegmatic, unemotional eyes. He stared owlishly at Daniel, and touched his forehead with a plump finger in acknowledgment of the introduction.

Sergeant Keating handed the replenished glass of brandy to the cook. Her hand managed to be steady enough to convey it to her lips and hold it there while the fiery liquid trickled down her throat, without spilling a drop.

"The murder was committed in the garden," Milliken explained to Daniel in a whispered aside. "The constable who sent in the alarm took charge at once and nothing has been disturbed. Bright lad, the constable. First thing he did was examine the ground for footprints. There are flowerbeds all-round the walls, so that anyone climbing over or getting into the garden by any way except from the house, would be bound to leave his prints. There was only one set. I haven't been out there yet; I wanted to hear this woman's story first."

Gradually the stimulant began to take effect. The colour returned in a flood to the woman's cheeks, and she sat up in her chair.

"I want you to tell me, as simply as you can, what happened tonight," said Inspector Milliken gently.

"It would be about half-past seven," she began nervously. "I was standin' at the scullery window washin' up the supper dishes. Mr. —Mr. Hannaway was sittin' in a deckchair out in the garden listenin' to the music from his portable wireless set. I could see him from the window—I had it open so's I could listen to the wireless. It was real lively music, and I got along fine with the washin' up. I happened to look up—" she began to tremble again at the recollection.

"Tell me what you saw," said Milliken in a sympathetic tone.

"A figure dressed in shining green was standin' by the wall," continued the woman jerkily. "It didn't look nowise human. It glowed green in the dusk like it was lit up behind. As I watched, it crossed the garden and stood right behind Mr. Hannaway's chair. I let out a yell and ran through the house and out of the front door. Down the street I met a policeman, and he came back with me and went out to the garden. I was scared to move a step over the front door. Then he came back and told me that Mr. Hannaway was dead! Stabbed in the back! The next I remember is sitting in this chair, with this gentleman handing me a glass of brandy."

She looked gratefully at Sergeant Keating.

"You're sure the figure was dressed in green?" asked Milliken. "You didn't just imagine it from reading the papers lately?"

"Of course, it was dressed in green," the cook replied hoarsely. "I saw it as plain as I see you. Green flowing draperies and a green mask."

Her voice sank to a whisper. "It was the Green Ghost!" she said.

"How long had Hannaway been sitting in the garden?"

"Alf an hour at the most," she replied.

"You saw no one else enter the garden during that time?"

"No one at all, jus' the Green Ghost!"

"Could anyone have entered the garden without you seeing him?"

"No sir, not while I was at the window, and I was there from the moment Mr. 'Annaway went out."

Milliken turned to Daniel with an expressive gesture. "Looks as though this Green Ghost is our man, all right," he remarked.

They went out into the garden. A uniformed policeman was there, staring up at the moon, which had just risen, in order to keep his eyes as far as possible from the deckchair and the limp body which lay in it. An uncanny effect was created by the gay music which the wireless set was still picking out of the air.

A smartly-dressed man of medium height was standing by the deckchair. This was the local police surgeon. Inspector Milliken leaned across and switched off the wireless set. "Made your examination, doctor?" he asked.

The other nodded briefly. "Death was instantaneous," he replied. "The knife was plunged into his back with terrific force and the murderer knew what he was about, for one lunge was sufficient. Poor chap," he added looking down at the limp, grotesque figure in the deckchair. "It was all over with him in an instant. I've left the knife in the wound."

Inspector Milliken walked to the rear of the chair, followed by Daniel Britling. The large wooden handle of a long knife was sticking out at the back. The blade was buried to the hilt in the dead man's body. The blow had been quick and direct, through the canvas back of the chair and the murdered man's clothes into the small of his back.

Using a silk handkerchief to prevent smudging any

fingerprints which might be on the handle, Milliken gently drew the knife out of the wound; blood welled out as the knife was withdrawn and trickled down the canvas back of the chair.

The two men examined the knife closely. It had a long wide blade with a very sharp point, and the handle, almost as long as the blade, was made of plain varnished wood. In all, the weapon was almost two feet long.

"A common type of knife," remarked Milliken. "Sold by the gross."

Daniel requested permission to handle the knife. He took it carefully, and weighed it reflectively. "An uncommon type," he replied, returning it to the inspector. "In this case, bought by the dozen."

"I can buy a knife like this for half a crown in several shops in the town," objected Milliken.

Daniel nodded cheerfully. "A knife like it," he agreed. "But not *quite* like it."

"Well, maybe it looks different to you," grumbled Milliken. "You probably see more than I do. I've only got two eyes."

"On the contrary," replied Daniel gently. "I see exactly what you see. The difference is not in the appearance of the knife."

Milliken looked reflectively at his small-bodied, big-headed companion, then shook his head philosophically. "I don't get you at all," he grunted. "However, that's neither here nor there. The case seems clear enough. This practical joker they call the Green Ghost has gone too far this time. I don't quite figure out why he should kill Hannaway—"

Healy started suddenly. "This morning several of us were in the Mitre," he exclaimed. "Hannaway was present, and when some joking reference was made to the Green Ghost, he boasted that the Green Ghost couldn't scare him. He said— Good God!—he said that if he ever met the Green Ghost, the *World* would run a three-line paragraph about it in the obituary column!"

There was a brief, ominous silence.

"Well, he was right!" said Milliken grimly. "But that doesn't explain his murder exactly, unless the whole Green Ghost business was started as a preliminary to the murder."

"What a story this will make!" remarked Healy, almost gloatingly.

With the aid of a flashlamp, Inspector Milliken and Dr. Britling examined every inch of the moist soil of the flowerbeds which lined the wall. They found two sets of the same footprints, one set leading to the deckchair, the other returning from it.

"Well, there's not much more I can do here, tonight at least," said Milliken. "I can't interview Mrs. Hannaway at present, because she's suffering from a nervous breakdown."

Daniel looked up at a window on the first floor and saw a white face peering out. "Who's that?" asked Daniel in a tense voice.

"That's the lady herself—Mrs. Hannaway," the Inspector replied. "Looks ill, doesn't she?"

"Good heavens!" said Daniel suddenly. "That is Rosa!"

4

Inspector Milliken, Dr. Britling, and Conrad Healy went into the house again. The police official turned to Daniel with a deferential air.

"It's my opinion, doctor," he said, "that the first step in this case is to establish the identity of the Green Ghost. When we lay hands on him, the case is over."

"If that's what you want," replied Daniel, "I can tell you his name at once."

The Inspector stared incredulously. "You're joking!" he exclaimed.

"Not at all," said Daniel. "I'm afraid he's bolted, though, or he'd be here now. "He's one of the *Morning World* reporters."

"Which one?" demanded Healy sharply.

"Gordon Angell," replied Daniel calmly.

Healy brought his fist down with a bang on the kitchen table. "And the boss withdrew his notice because of his intelligent handling of the story!" he exclaimed. "He was actually considering raising his salary! And Angell was the Green Ghost all the time! Well, I'll be—" For a brief space he became completely incoherent.

"You're quite sure?" asked Milliken doubtfully.

"Quite sure," replied Daniel. "On the night the Green Ghost first appeared, Angell was desperate. He had been given two weeks' notice and was terrified that he might not be able to find another job. He tried to get an interview with me in the hope that a bright story might make the editor alter his decision. I refused to be interviewed, and he was at his wits' end to know what to do. I'm afraid I put an idea into his mind. I suggested, jokingly, of course, that he should burn down the town hall, or murder his editor. I never dreamed, of course, that he'd take me seriously. That night he was sent out to interview a woman who had sustained a slight fright at something which she fancied she saw moving in her garden. Probably she saw nothing, but seizing the opportunity, Angell persuaded her that she had seen a ghost. He amplified the ghost into the legendary spook of the neighbourhood. The woman was of a neurotic, imaginative disposition, and she swallowed the bait whole. That gave him a good story, and he decided to keep it up. He haunted the district himself, playing on the fears of people who should have known better than to be frightened by a young man attired in a few yards of green silk and a dab of phosphorous paint. Naturally he spent his evenings scouring the district for the ghost, for it gave him an excuse for being in the district. Naturally he was always first on the scene, with his notebook in his hand, for all he had to do was to slip off his disguise behind a tree, and appear in the role of sympathetic investigator."

"He was in the *Mitre* this morning!" said Healy in a hushed voice. "He heard Hannaway bragging about what he would do if he met the Green Ghost! But surely, he can't have murdered the man just for a story!"

"Perhaps someone else masqueraded as the Green Ghost and did the job?" said the Inspector.

"If my theory is correct," Daniel replied, "it was Angell himself whom the cook saw. Yes, Angell thought that haunting Hannaway would be a good joke and make a good story. Tonight, at half-past seven, or thereabouts, having made certain that the street was deserted, he put on his green draperies and mask and stealthily climbed the wall—"

"Excuse me doctor," said the Inspector suddenly. He turned to Conrad Healy. "Do you happen to know whether this chap Gordon Angell wears rubber soles?"

"Yes, he did. Why?"

Without a word, Milliken led the reporter out to the garden. When they returned, in a few moments, the inspector was jubilant.

"Your theory is right, doctor!" he exclaimed triumphantly. "Healy has identified the footprints in the garden as Angell's. Maker's name and a lion rampant on the sole. Eight-pointed star on the heel. Angell's our man all right. Maybe he had another motive for killing Hannaway besides the desire for a good story. We needn't worry about that now. Time enough when we catch him. I'm off to get the search underway. Thanks for your help. Healy didn't blow your trumpet half loud enough. See you later."

"Which way are you going, doctor?" asked Healy. "Can I give you a lift in my car?"

"No thanks," replied Daniel. "I'm only going as far as the theatre, and I really enjoy walking."

Daniel went to Carstow's big new music-hall, but not as one of the audience. He went to the stage door and interviewed the stage manager, a curly headed, bored-looking young man who was shouting orders in a hoarse voice to the weary-eyed scene-shifters, who were preparing the stage for the second house. It was almost nine o'clock, and the performance was due to begin, but a ten-shilling note deftly passed persuaded him to answer a few questions.

"Funny that you should ask about the Bodoni Brothers," said the stage manager, after he had answered several of Daniel's questions. "They had a bit of a dust-up this evening. Seems they're fed up with the big fella with the black hair and the nasty eyes. He's a rotten acrobat—seems he was doin' somethin' else before he joined up with them a month or so ago. He was an acrobat with a circus years ago, but you've got to have continual practice if you're going to make good in that line. The others in the team are talking of giving him the push."

"Then they aren't brothers?"

The stage manager laughed. "Not they. No more'n their name's Bodoni. Only it's the custom with acrobats to bill themselves as brothers, with flashy names."

"What is the big man's real name, do you know?"

"Search me," the stage manager replied with a shrug of his shoulder. "Smith, he calls himself, but you've only got to look at him to see that he's an Eyetalian."

"Did you ever know of an act called 'Gaspari and Rosa'?" asked Daniel.

"'Gaspari and Rosa'? Can't say that I did. But this theatre's only been open for a year. What are they? Acrobats?"

"No," said Daniel. "Not acrobats."

5

On the morning after the murder, the Carstow *Morning World* had sensational fare to offer its readers. The front page was plastered with large black headlines:

WELL-KNOWN CARSTOW BOOKIE MURDERED!

GREEN GHOST UNMASKED!

POLICE CAPTURE ALLEGED MURDERER!

The giant presses at the *World* Building swallowed miles of white paper, chewed it, then spat it out in the form of thousands of copies of the newspaper. Thousands of copies? Hundreds of thousands!

In the main, the *Morning World's* story was a truthful, if highly-coloured account of the events of the previous evening, or as nearly truthful as that bright and efficient newspaper was ever permitted by its editor to be. It is true that the *Morning World's* apology for permitting one of its reporters to hoax the public for almost a week was compressed into a brief paragraph and crowded into an obscure corner on the last page but one, there to be lost in the excitement of more grippingly-written matter.

There was a police cordon drawn round the murdered man's suburban house, and unless one lived in the road, or was a butcher's boy or a postman, or a detective, or a similarly privileged person, it was impossible for one to pass the end of the street in which the house was situated. Reporters, of course, are allowed to go anywhere. Conrad Healy was allowed not only into the street, but into the house itself. The uniformed constable who stood on guard on the front steps opened the door for him. He found another policeman drinking a cup of cocoa in the kitchen, who informed him that otherwise the house was deserted, Mrs. Hannaway having gone to consult her doctor, and the cook-general having decamped to her sister's late the previous night.

Healy strolled out to the garden and surveyed the scene of the crime.

The body had been removed to the local morgue, but otherwise the garden was precisely as it had appeared the previous evening. The bloodstained deckchair still stood in the same place, and bedside it was the portable wireless, now decently silenced. There were footprints everywhere. It seemed that everyone who had entered the garden on the previous evening had done his level best to tramp every flower and plant into the earth.

"Good thing the constable thought of looking for footprints," mused Healy. "It would be a hopeless task now."

He walked up and down with his head bent. "Now why," he mused, "why on earth should Angell kill Hannaway?"

It was really a ticklish problem. Of course, Angell *had* killed Hannaway. Angell was the Green Ghost. The Green Ghost had been seen standing behind Hannaway's chair just before the bookmaker had been found dead—stabbed in the back. No one else had entered the garden; for that they had the cook's evidence and the undeniable fact that there had been only one set of footprints. Everything was quite clear—excepting the motive.

There had to be a motive. Murderers do not kill without reason, unless they are mad, and Angell was certainly not mad.

Unless—could it be that Angell was in debt to the murdered bookmaker? For a sum which he could not pay?—the idea was possible, but not probable.

"Good morning," said a quiet, cultured voice, and looking up, Healy saw Dr. Britling sitting on the garden wall.

"Poaching on my preserves?" asked Daniel, with a twinkle in his eye. "I'm supposed to be the unofficial Nosy Parker in this case, you know? I'm having a bird's eye view of the scene of the crime. The view that Angell had last night."

"Then it *was* Angell who came over the wall last night?" asked Healy quickly. "In spite of the youngster's footprints, I had a vague hope that it might have been someone else, masquerading in the Green Ghost attire."

"It was Angell," said Daniel definitely. He looked down at the smooth surface of the wall on the garden side.

"There's a recently cut foothold on the other side," he said. "Angell used it last night, and it enable me to climb up here this morning. But I don't fancy the drop into the garden. Do you mind opening the back gate?"

"I'd be delighted—" Healy opened the gate, and Daniel entered the garden.

"I suppose you know they've collared Angell," the reporter remarked. "Got him as he was doing a guy, which rather strengthens the case against him. He denies killing Hannaway, but so far, he's refused to say another word. I don't blame him. In his shoes, the less he says the better it will be for him."

"That is evidently what he believes," agreed Daniel. "I suppose he feels that if he admits to certain things, the rest will be taken for granted."

"Not much to see here," said Healy. "The place is like a ploughed field. Too many feet last night."

Daniel nodded reflectively, then walked towards the house

with Healy a pace or two behind him. They entered the kitchen where the constable, having finished his cocoa, was enjoying a quiet smoke. He hurriedly put his pipe away as they entered the room.

"Please give my card to Mrs. Hannaway, and tell that I should like to speak to her for a few moments," said Daniel, proffering an oblong slip of pasteboard.

"'Fraid that's impossible, sir," replied the constable. "Miss 'Annaway went out an hour ago to visit 'er doctor. Nerves all upset."

Dr. Britling turned very white. "Do you mean to say that idiot of a woman has actually left the house?" he demanded, in a hoarse, strained voice.

"That's what I said, sir," replied the policeman phlegmatically. "Gone to consult a doctor, so my mate told me. I didn't see 'er myself."

Without another word, Daniel wheeled, marched through the house, and threw the front door open. Healy heard him address a brusque remark to the constable on duty on the steps.

"Just under an hour ago it was, sir," the constable replied. "She went in a taxi."

"Was she carrying anything?" asked Daniel sharply. "A suitcase or a kitbag, for instance?"

The policeman tilted his helmet forward, and scratched the back of his head. "Now that you come to mention it, sir, she was," he asserted. "A pretty 'eavy suitcase, too. She was staggering with the weight of it, before the cab driver took it from 'er."

Daniel glared at the man. "Didn't it occur to you to wonder why she should take a heavy suitcase with her to consult a doctor?" he snapped.

"Can't say it did, sir. 'Course it does seem odd, now that you mention it, but I didn't think anything of it at the time. The Inspector said we were to be considerate, and not bother Mrs. Annerway, 'er being ill."

With an indignant snort, Daniel closed the door with a bang. "Do you know if there's a telephone in the house?" he demanded of Healy.

"In there," replied Healy, pointing to the door of a room at the rear of the hall.

Daniel went into the room, lifted the telephone receiver, and jiggled the hook impatiently. Healy followed him, with a puzzled look on his face.

"What's up?" he inquired while Daniel waited to be put through to the police headquarters.

"A great deal," replied Daniel angrily. "A very great deal indeed. That stupid, stupid woman, leaving the one place where she was safe!"

"But she's only gone to consult her doctor!" Healy objected.

"Doctor be damned!" retorted Daniel. "Hullo, is that police headquarters at last?" he continued in the same irate tone. "Put me through to Inspector Milliken at once, please...that you, Inspector...This is Daniel Britling...I'm at Hannaway's house...I want you to meet me at the station at once...Yes, the railway station...Oh, don't waste time, and...This is no joke. I don't want you to see me off for anywhere...If you don't hurry, you'll have another murder to worry about...Yes, I said murder...I'm taking a taxi to the station at once...For heaven's sake hurry. I tell you; a life depends on it!"

6

In a taxi, on the way to the station, Healy wisely refrained from questioning Dr. Britling, for he could see that the little police surgeon was extremely anxious and nervous. Dr. Britling spoke once, to ask a brief question about the train services from

Carstow to London, and the reporter answered briefly, with the information that the only morning train to London went at half-past eleven. It was now within a quarter of an hour of that time.

Inspector Milliken, Sergeant Keating, and a third plainclothes man awaited them in a police motorcar which was parked outside the station. The inspector quickly alighted when Dr. Britling's taxi drew up, and came forward to meet Daniel, who seized his arm and hustled him to the station.

"Not a word, not a question!" was Daniel's greeting. "We've no time for explanations now."

He led the inspector to the booking-office, and there inquired whether a woman answering to the description of Mrs. Hannaway has taken a ticket that morning. The booking-clerk, consulting his time sheet, told them that she had taken a ticket for London at twenty-eight minutes past ten.

"She had an hour to wait," remarked Daniel. "The waiting-room, of course."

It was deserted, except for the waitress in charge, who informed them, however, that the woman they sought had been in the waiting-room for fully half-an-hour, but had left in the company of a tall man.

"That's her suitcase in the corner," the girl added. "She asked me if she could leave it there. 'Course it wasn't regular, seeing as there's a left luggage office cross the station, but it don't do no harm to oblige people, I always say."

"What did the man look like?" asked Daniel brusquely.

"I really couldn't say. He wore a felt hat pretty far down his forehead, and his coat collar was tuned up. He was pretty tall, and dark-complexioned. The lady seemed quite surprised to see him."

"Did she say anything?"

"Well, now you mention it, she did. She jumped up from the bench she was sitting on when he came in and said, 'You didn't expect to see me, my dear?' Then he took her arm, and says to me, 'The lady and I are going for a walk. Do you mind if we leave her suitcase here for the present?' Of course, I had no objection, though it wasn't quite—"

Daniel cut her short with an abrupt gesture. "Did the woman make any objection to going with him?"

The girl shook her head. "Not she! She didn't say a word after she jumped up and cried 'Hugo!' She seemed to be sort of dazed, as though she hadn't seen him for a long time, and was quite overcome with surprise."

The little police surgeon turned to Inspector Milliken. "I'm afraid no insurance doctor would pass Mrs. Hannaway as a good life at this moment," he said. "I am very much afraid that we'll be too late to save her. Our only chance is to go to the *Gaiety* Theatre as quickly as we can."

They went out of the station and entered the police motorcar.

"The *Gaiety* Theatre," said Inspector Milliken to the driver. "Make it snappy, there's no time to be lost."

Through Carstow's crowded streets the car sped, touching sixty miles an hour at times, and taking corners on two wheels. The police emblem on the radiator cleared the way like magic. They soon drew up outside the *Gaiety* Theatre.

They piled out quickly, and Daniel led the way to the stage door. Just inside was a little wooden erection like a sentry-box in which the doorkeeper sat.

"Anyone in the theatre?" asked Daniel.

The doorkeeper removed his pipe from his mouth with aggravating deliberation. "One of th' Bodoni Brothers, with a woman," he replied at length. "Rehearsing."

First impressing the need for quietness on the others, Daniel tiptoed down the passage to the wings at the side of the stage, followed by the three police officers, and the inquisitive doorkeeper. They halted in the wings. An amazing sight met their eyes.

Propped up at the opposite side of the stage was a large, thick wooden board, to which Mrs. Hannaway, stripped to her underwear, was strapped with her arms spread out so that her body formed a cross. Eleven knives, seemingly identical with the one found in Hannaway's body, were stuck in the wood about the woman, under her armpits, above her head, within a fraction of an inch of her ear, touching her fingertips, outlining her body on the board, so closely that they seemed to touch her.

"Twelve knives, Rosa," said the man in a cold, purring voice. "The twelve we used in our music-hall turn in the old days, my dear. My hand has not lost its cunning. I have planted each of them exactly as I used to do. Quite like old times." His voice hardened. "But this time, you see, I have a thirteenth knife. We never used thirteen before. An unlucky number, eh? Can you guess, my dear, where I am going to place this thirteenth?"

The woman was deathly pale; her lips parted, and an agonising moan came forth.

"Yes, I think you can guess," the man continued. "The thirteenth knife is for your heart, Rosa. Your black, treacherous heart."

With a little articulate cry, the woman's head fell forward. She had fainted.

The man raised the knife… As he did so, the pipe dropped from the doorkeeper's mouth and clattered to the floor. With a hoarse cry, the knife-thrower wheeled and glared at his unexpected audience. His eyes flashed suddenly, and he poised the knife to throw it at them.

With amazing agility, Daniel dived and drove the point of his umbrella into the pit of the knife-thrower's stomach. The man groaned and collapsed in a huddled heap.

7

Two of the police-officers released Mrs. Hannaway and carried her, still unconscious, to one of the dressing-rooms. Dr. Britling prescribed brandy, which was hurriedly procured. The knife-thrower was handcuffed, and his arms were strapped by one of his own straps.

Some minutes passed before Mrs. Hannaway regained consciousness. At last she opened her eyes and looked about her with a terrified expression on her white face. She sat up with a wild cry, but became more composed when she saw Milliken and Daniel standing beside her.

"Hugo—" she began in a tense voice.

"You are quite safe from him," said Daniel soothingly. "He is in custody."

"Thank God!" she exclaimed. "Oh, thank God!"

Later she told them an amazing story. She and the man who had attempted to murder her had at one time toured the British and continental music-halls under the names of 'Gaspari and Rosa'. Gaspari was her partner's real name; he was a knife thrower, and at the climax of their performance, when she stood against the board, Gaspari outlined her figure on it with knives. They had done it a thousand times, and Gaspari had never once even scratched her, so perfect was his aim. They were married—unhappily married, for Gaspari had the temper of a fiend, and was unreasonably jealous of every man upon whom her eyes rested. While they were engaged at a theatre in Blackpool, her husband hurt his arm and was unable to appear. It was necessary for him to have massage treatment and Rosa was free from his surveillance for several hours a day. She met Hannaway and fell in love with him; in the end, she eloped with him. That was five years ago, and since then she had never seen or heard of the knife-thrower until he appeared that morning in the waiting-room.

"But I knew he had found us at last," she continued brokenly, "when the policeman told me that Billy had been knifed in the back. That knife! —it was Hugo's trademark! And I knew that my turn would come, too. I tried to run away, but he caught me this morning at the station, and made me go with him to the theatre. I was too frightened to attempt resistance. At the theatre, he knocked me down with his fist, and when I regained consciousness—ugh! —I was strapped to the board which we used in our performance, and he was standing before me with his devil's smirk on his face and thirteen knives in his belt…"

She covered her face with her hands, and trembled convulsively.

8

"But what beats me," said Inspector Milliken in a puzzled tone, "is how you fathomed it out. Perhaps you will explain."

Hugo Gaspari had been safely lodged in the cells, and now Milliken, Dr. Britling and Conrad Healy were sitting comfortably in the inspector's office, enjoying three of the inspector's excellent cigars.

"To a certain extent it was pure luck," replied Daniel, eyeing the long ash of his cigar with satisfaction. "From the beginning, I had a shrewd suspicion that Gordon Angell was at the bottom of the Green Ghost scare. When Hannaway made his boasting reference to the Green Ghost, I saw a flicker in Angell's eye which told me that he was thinking what a good story he could get out of 'haunting' the bookmaker. I was fully prepared, after that, to hear that Hannaway had seen the 'ghost' but I was not at all prepared to hear that he had been murdered. I was certain that

Angell was the Green Ghost, but even more certain that the young man was incapable of murder. At the beginning of the week, I had seen the music-hall performer Gaspari in the street, and his face was very familiar to me. I could not remember just where I had seen him before, and the name he was acting under at the time—Bodoni—conveyed nothing to me. Still, the feeling that I knew his face persisted…and he was associated in my mind with the name 'Rosa.'

"When I examined the weapon with which Hannaway was killed, I realised that it was exactly the type of knife used on the stage by knife-throwers. It looked like a very ordinary knife, but it was balanced perfectly, which is not necessary for the type of knife used by butchers and the like. Then I saw the face of Mrs. Hannaway at the window. The name 'Rosa' sprang to my lips, and I remembered suddenly where I had seen the knife-thrower before. Six years ago, I had gone to Coliseum in London on several occasions to see a turn called 'Gaspari and Rosa'. Gaspari was a knife-thrower and his performance interested me exceedingly.

"By putting two and two together, I decided that Gaspari had killed Hannaway for some reason—probably jealousy. He had done it without mounting the wall, and throwing his knife across the intervening space, into Hannaway's back. Later Angell, in his guise as the Green Ghost, had mounted the wall, probably in the same place, using the niche Gaspari had cut for the purpose, with the attention of attracting Hannaway's attention, and seeing what effect the 'apparition' would have on the bookmaker. It was becoming dark, but to his horror, Angell must have seen the dark red patch on the back of Hannaway's deckchair, and the long handle of the knife protruding from his back. He went into the garden to investigate, and was seen by the cook-general who gave the alarm. Realising of what he would be suspected if he remained on the scene, Angell bolted, leaving his footprints to bear witness against him—the only footprints in the garden.

"This morning I intended to fill up the gaps in my theory by questioning Mrs. Hannaway—after that, I should have come to you Inspector and told you the whole story—but the stupid woman had bolted from the house where she was safe, into the arms of the man she feared. The rest you know."

With a sigh, Daniel knocked the long ash of his cigar into the ashtray. It had become too long for safety.

THE END

TOO MANY MOTIVES

M OST PEOPLE GIVE dinner parties to their friends. Mark Savile displayed his grim sense of humour by giving a dinner party to four men who hated him. It would have been impossible for him to find four friends to be his guests; indeed, it is doubtful whether he had made one single true friendship in his entire fifty-four years of life. That did not trouble him. It would almost seem that it pleased him to be hated.

The book of Savile's life held a lengthy reckoning of the misery to which he had brought others in his meteoric rise to a position of power in the world of finance.

When Eldoradian Concessions Limited failed, there were those who said that the investigations of the receiver would result in prison for Savile. They said that he had gone just a little too far. And had overstepped the shadowy division between robbery legal and illegal. These were false profits. Thousands of small investors lost their savings in the crash of his bubble company, but Savile went his way the richer by one hundred thousand pounds.

At the age of fifty-four he was reputed to be enormously wealthy; he was despised even by fellow-financiers, which is degradation indeed; and he had not a single friend—excepting the women who flocked to him like flies to a jam pot.

He celebrated his fifty-fourth birthday by a dinner-party to four men of the many who hated him. Why Savile's invitation was accepted each of the four would have found difficulty in explaining. Perhaps his audacity piqued them.

Of the four, Borrow was the only one whom Savile had never directly injured. Financially, John Borrow was too sound an opponent for Savile to cross swords with. But Borrow's best friend had shot himself, driven out of his mind by the ruin that Savile had brought upon him, and that was a score John Borrow intended to settle one day.

Harold Denholm came to Savile's dinner-party because he was afraid to stay away. Savile had a powerful hold over him, and in the invitation to dine Denholm read a fugitive hope that the financier intended to make things easier for him.

Lord Clavering accepted the invitation to dine because of his uneasiness over Fortunas Copper of which he was a director, and because Savile was the only person he knew the real condition of the company's affairs.

Dennis Barclay was drunk when Savile's invitation came. For a week he had scarcely drawn a sober breath. When he read the letter and realised from whom it came, he tore it into shreds.

All four came to dinner at Savile's flat.

As each of the guests arrived, he was shown into the tastefully furnished library of the flat. When all four were present, dry Martinis were served, and it was not until they had finished their cocktails that their host made his appearance. He did not offer to shake hands with them, but bowed slightly to each in turn with just a hint of mockery in his eyes.

Borrow nodded gravely in return. Denholm muttered something in a low voice. Lord Clavering shrugged his shoulders philosophically. Dennis Barclay flushed and took a single step forward, but was just sufficiently sober to hold his peace.

Savile smiled suavely.

"I am informed that dinner is ready to serve," he said. "You will excuse the informality? I have only a single manservant."

They followed him in silence to the dining-room. The table,

which had a plate-glass top, was tastefully laid. A single alabaster electric light bowl directly above the centre effectively illuminated the table but left the remainder of the room in darkness.

A soft-footed man-servant left the room by another door as they entered.

"My man Simpson, is both cooking and serving tonight," said Savile in his rich, silky voice. "It has been necessary therefore to arrange a simple menu. I hope that you will enjoy it."

The meal, while not an elaborate one, was deliciously cooked. Each of the four courses of which it consisted had been chosen with the discrimination of a connoisseur.

Savile's dark, sinister eyes were all that showed his grim enjoyment of the jest he had perpetrated. He knew that they hated him and it pleased his grotesque sense of humour to dine and wine them as though they were the finest of good friends. Otherwise, he was a perfect host.

Savile's manservant came into the room and walked to his master's chair. Savile nodded. "You may go now, John," he said.

To his guests he remarked: "It is one of my peculiarities that I prefer my servant to sleep out. I value privacy." In a smooth, even tone, he continued his discourse upon vintage wines.

It is impossible to talk of wines without talking of countries and to a man like Savile countries meant capitals. The conversation drifted to Berlin, Vienna, to Budapest and Madrid. Gradually, Savile's guests took part in the conversation and it became almost animated, for they had all travelled.

Lord Clavering mentioned Venice as the city which appealed to him most of all the cities in the world. He had spent a year there; the happiest year of his life.

They had come now to coffee, brandy, and cigars. Savile pierced the end of his cigar with precious care and lit it without permitting the flame actually to touch the cigar.

"Venice is a city of beautiful dreams," he remarked, exhaling a cloud of fragrant blue smoke, "but there are two things that must be remembered about Venice. If one goes alone, it is a city of ghosts. One must be accompanied by a beautiful woman—and one must not go twice with the same woman."

There was an awkward little silence.

Dennis Barclay flushed angrily. "You have ugly ideas—about women, Savile," he said harshly.

Savile shrugged his shoulders. "Ugly? Perhaps—to you, who regard a woman as a goddess, to be placed upon a pedestal. I have my own ideas of everything. They do not often please others but they frequently amuse me." His eyes travelled to the face of each of his guests in turn. It amused him to see contempt written plainly on each. The artificial atmosphere which he had created was gone, and open hostility had replaced it.

"This dinner is one of my ideas," Savile continued in a calm, even voice. "It is even more amusing than I had anticipated. I wonder what would be said if it was known—publicly—that we five men dined together. I think there are many who would share the exquisite humour of my jest with me."

No one answered him. Dennis Barclay was white with fury, but he restrained himself.

Savile smiled, and continued slowly. "It would probably be said that if the object of the dinner was to discuss finance, Barclay would not be here, and that if the finance was—shall we say 'shady'? —Borrow would not be with us."

Denholm leapt to his feet, his eyes blazing. "Look here, Savile," he cried, "you've gone too far. What rotten suggestion are you making against Clavering and me?"

Savile met his eyes squarely. "Does it matter?" he parried with a sardonic smile. "Do you particularly mind what I say? I think not."

Denholm's face was set and grim, but he sat down in silence.

"It would seem that I am quite alone in the enjoyment of my joke," went on Savile smoothly. "Perhaps you have all too much on your minds to see the humour of this situation. Clavering is wondering how he will answer the questions the police will put to him when—"

Lord Clavering blanched and his hands clutched the arms of his chair so tightly that his knuckles showed white. "My God, Savile," he gasped. "Then the rumours about Fortunas Copper are true?"

Savile spread his hands in a deprecatory gesture. "How should I know? I am not even on the board."

"You took damn good care of that!" Clavering whispered hoarsely. "But if there's anything wrong with the company, you're responsible."

Savile laughed harshly. "My dear fellow, I'm only a shareholder," he replied, "and I'll have to bear my loss philosophically. The directors must do the explaining. But don't worry about the police, Clavering. They're notoriously easy to hoodwink. All they are fit for is laying traps for speeding motorists. The—er—higher branches of crime are beyond them. Think of the murders that go undetected my dear chap! And murder is the kingpin of crimes."

There was silence for a moment, save for the stertorous breathing of Lord Clavering, whose face was as colourless as putty. There was something diabolical about the way Mark Savile had piled on the agony that astounded the others, even with their knowledge of Savile's vileness.

John Borrow was the first to speak, and his voice, sharp and harsh, cut the silence like a knife. "There are times when murder is commendable, Savile," he said.

Savile's expression was bland, even a shade amused. "And those times?" he asked.

John Borrow took a deep breath. "To kill a man who has ruined a friend who trusted him," he replied slowly, "would be no more reprehensible than to decapitate a snake."

"You think so, do you?" replied Savile. "I too have ideas about murder. It is a fascinating subject. Not as a vehicle for revenge—but as an art. It can be an art you know, when a man of intelligence turns to it. But when the police investigated your hypothetical murder, it would be too easy to trace the motive, my dear Borrow. The undetected murder must be motiveless— there must be no traceable strings to lead to the murderer. Kill your wife, or your aunt or your enemy, and you are instantly suspected. Kill, for instance, someone you do not know—stab a stranger in an Underground crowd, or push a passer-by under a bus—and there are no traceable motives to lead to you. What do you think, Denholm, or do you shrink from the topic? You are looking very white."

Denholm leaned across the table and stared as one fascinated into his host's saturnine eyes. "I will tell you what I think," he retorted in a voice filled with emotion. "When a damned Shylock gets hold of a man and makes him repay a debt half a dozen times, and still holds it like a whip over him, and makes his life a living hell till he can't call his soul his own, I think that death is too merciful a punishment."

Savile's eyes were filled with ironic amusement at the other's vehemence. "But the motive is damning," was his only comment. "What do you say Clavering?"

Lord Clavering looked up. His ashy face wore a tortured expression. "I have nothing to say," he replied slowly, rising from his chair as he spoke. "Excuse me please—I cannot stay any longer."

He stumbled towards the door, a broken, beaten, man. Savile's voice held him back. "But won't you add your opinion to this very enthralling discussion? I am sure that it would be interesting."

Lord Clavering did not turn to face his tormentor. His voice, when he replied, was toneless. "If Fortunas Copper is a swindle, and you have shifted the blame to men whose only crime is—stupidity, you will discover my conception of a guiltless murder," he said.

Dennis Barclay, whose supressed fury had come to fever pitch, sprang to his feet, upsetting his chair. His fists were clenched and his eyes menaced Savile. "You swine! You unmentionable cad!" he raved. "I don't know why you invited us here, unless it was to gloat over us in your filthy mind. I don't know why I came. The thought of eating your food makes me sick. Savile, you rat, you defiler of women, I'll kill you if I hang for it!"

He sprang at Savile, and his first wild swing struck the financier on the temple, dazing him. Barclay's hands were at Savile's throat, squeezing the life out of him, when Borrow and Denholm interfered and dragged the infuriated young man back. Savile lay unconscious in his chair. His breath was coming in short gasps.

"Leave me alone!" cried Barclay, struggling desperately. "Let me get at the swine and finish him off!"

John Borrow's grasp on Barclay's arm did not relax. "We had better go," he said quietly. "He's not worth it, Barclay."

Somehow, they got Barclay out of the flat. By the time they were in the street he was calmer and he went off alone, leaving the others to go their several ways.

It was fully five minutes before Mark Savile opened his eyes with a groan. He looked about him wildly, until his glance fell upon the debris of the dinner and he remembered what had happened.

His neck was raw and sore and his head was throbbing

viciously. He put up a hand and rubbed his neck ruefully. He eased himself out of his chair and staggered rather than walked to the sideboard, where he mixed himself a stiff brandy and soda. Remembering the grim humour which had prompted him to hold his amazing dinner party, he smiled a twisted, bitter smile.

He went to the library and turned on all the lights. The brilliant illumination gave him courage, for he was a coward at heart. Now, although he had enjoyed his joke, he shivered with fear.

He sat down at his desk and produced writing-paper and an envelope. In a shaky hand he wrote an inscription on the envelope. It ran: "Should anything happen to me, this envelope must be handed to the proper authorities."

Then he drew the paper towards him and commenced to write. Just then the doorbell rang, and he rose and went to answer it.

2

Dennis Barclay did not arrive at his home in St. James's Street that night until half-past ten, although he had no engagement following the dinner which broke up so abruptly. He fumbled with his latchkey, placing it everywhere but in the lock, until his valet, hearing the scrapings at the door from the kitchen, where he was entertaining a friend, came and let him in.

Consternation was written on the valet's face when he beheld his master. Barclay was dead drunk and swaying on his feet. His clothes were rumpled and muddy and his tie was gone.

The valet had been employed by Dennis Barclay for some years, and he was very fond of his master. He helped him in and got him to bed where Barclay immediately lapsed into a sleep that was akin to stupor.

Herbert, the man servant, returned to the kitchen with a long face. His guest, the butler from next door, looked up at his entrance. "What's up?" he asked.

Herbert shook his head dolefully "It's Mr. Barclay—he hasn't been quite himself lately," he responded.

The butler nodded sympathetically. "I know. Is he—"

Herbert nodded. "You won't let it go further," he said. "If I thought you would, I wouldn't tell you—"

"You know me, Herbert," replied the butler. "'Aven't we been the best of friends for years?"

Herbert smiled. "The very best, old boy," he agreed. "Have another drink?" He poured two glasses of his master's rare old port. They sipped the wine gratefully in silence—in their own way they were almost connoisseurs.

"Mr. Barclay's been terribly upset lately," Herbert began at last. "He had a nasty shock some time ago. His young lady jilted him for another man—a man named Savile. Mr. Barclay took it hard. You know how it is when a thing like that happens; he's been drinking a lot, and hardly eating a thing. One night I came across him with *her* picture in his hand, and I could see that the way he's been treated had knocked the stuffing out of him, so to speak. But he's a mild type of man, Mr. Barclay is, though one of the best, and he took it quietly. I never heard him utter a word against the other man—drunk or sober."

The butler nodded sympathetically.

Herbert looked up; his face very grave. "He's been to dinner tonight with the other fellow—the man who pinched his girl," he said earnestly.

"Go on!" gasped the butler incredulously.

Herbert nodded. "The swine wouldn't let him alone. He wrote to Mr. Barclay and invited him to dinner. When the guv'nor got the letter, he took on something awful. It was the first time

I've ever seen him violent. I was scared he would do something crazy. You can imagine my surprise when at the last moment he decided to go. Go he did, and now he's back as drunk as a lord and with his clothes in a rare mess. Gawd, I hope he hasn't been up to anything—"

The butler put down his glass, and leaning forward, pressed Herbert's arm sympathetically. Herbert nodded gratefully. "*You* can understand, old pal," he said. "He's always been a gentleman to me."

The following morning two men called at Dennis Barclay's flat and asked to see him. Barclay was in bed, sound asleep, but the callers were so insistent that Herbert grudgingly wakened his master.

When Dennis Barclay entered the small sitting-room where the two men were waiting, one of them rose and said: "I am Detective Harris, of the Criminal Investigation Department, Mr. Barclay, and I must ask you to accompany me. Mr. Mark Savile has been killed and your presence at his flat is urgently requested by the inspector in charge."

Dennis Barclay looked queer for a moment, then he laughed shakily. "Dead, is he?" he remarked. "Then the world is a better place. If you will wait for a few minutes gentlemen, I will be ready to accompany you."

His face was very white, but he mounted the stairs to his room steadily.

3

Doctor Britling arrived at Mark Savile's flat fully an hour after the police. His delay was due to the fact that he had been consulting works of reference and piles of old clippings for information about the dead man, knowledge of which was none of his concern as a police surgeon. A policeman was on duty at the door of the flat, which stood open. Daniel crossed the hall quickly and entered a room in which there were six men—and the body of Mark Savile. Taking the occupants in with one swift glance, he nodded briskly to the inspector in charge.

"Ha, Evans! Good morning," he added cheerfully. "Glad to see you. *You* won't cramp my style, hey?"

Without waiting for an answer, he crossed the room to the fireplace, and knelt down beside the body, which lay on the hearthrug. His examination did not take long. Mark Savile had been dead for hours, and the cause of death was obvious; he had been shot in the right temple. The shot had been fired at close quarters, for the wound was blackened with powder marks.

"Well, the man's dead alright," remarked Daniel, rising to his feet. "He's been dead from between eight to twelve hours. Death was instantaneous, of course. What is it, Evans, suicide?"

Evans shook his head. "Quite impossible, doctor," he replied. "There's no trace of a weapon anywhere in the room. It is quite obviously murder."

Daniel nodded gravely. "Humph! Who are all these people?" he demanded suddenly.

Evans permitted himself a little smile. "This is Lord Clavering," he said, indicating one of those present. "And this gentleman is Mr. Dennis Barclay. Both of them dined here last night. The man in uniform is the commissionaire of the building who was on duty last night. That chap over there is the dead man's valet, and that completes the list."

The Inspector explained that they were awaiting the arrival of the other two guests of the previous evening's dinner. Daniel nodded briskly. "You don't mind if I look round a bit on my own?"

"Not at all. I'll be glad of your help, doctor," Evans replied easily. "But the case looks pretty obvious. Look here!" He produced a note in the dead man's handwriting. "I found this under the blotting pad on the desk."

He read it aloud: "'I have reason to fear that one of the men who dined with me tonight has designs on my life. Should anything happen to me, he is responsible. His name is—' You see, Mr. Britling, he was probably in the middle of writing this when he was interrupted—doubtless by someone at the door. He was alone in the flat, so he answered the summons himself, first slipping the unfinished note under the blotter. His visitor killed him before he had the opportunity of finishing the letter."

Daniel nodded slowly. "And his visitor was?"

The Inspector smiled. "One of his guests," he replied, "which one we will know shortly. The commissionaire here was on duty last night and saw all four leave. He was absent from the hallway for a time after that, but returned in time to see one of the four—he didn't know his name—coming downstairs. He had left with the others—but returned later."

"He will recognise the man again?"

"Yes, he's positive of that. It wasn't either Lord Clavering or Mr. Barclay, so it rests between the other two" —he consulted a piece of paper— "Mr. Borrow or Mr. Denholm. I've sent for them, of course. They should be here shortly."

Daniel nodded. "Who found him?" he asked.

The dead man's valet moved uneasily. "I did, sir," he said.

"Did you disturb anything?" The valet shook his head decisively. "Everything's exactly as I found it, sir," he replied in a tremulous voice. "Gave me a turn, it did, finding him like that. I could see he was dead, and I didn't wait to see anymore. I went in the other room quickly and 'phoned the police."

"What time was that?"

"About eight o'clock, sir. I don't sleep in the flat, and I arrived this morning at my usual time, half-past seven. I didn't come in here, and it wasn't until I had started on Mr. Savile's breakfast and had his bath running that I found out there was anything wrong. I went to call him and found that his bed hadn't been slept in. I came in here—and that's what I found."

He pointed a shaky finger at the body. Daniel nodded, but did not look at the body.

"What sort of master was Mr. Savile?" he asked.

The valet hesitated. "Well, you know how it is, sir. He wasn't bad—paid me on the nail and all that. Maybe he was a bit mean, but lots of guv'nors are."

"Locked up the cigars and liquor?"

The valet ventured a shaky smile. "Yes, sir, that sort of thing. He splashed the drink about when he had a party, but he always made sure I didn't get a little nip on the quiet."

Daniel smiled. "Did he have many friends?"

"Well, no sir, not many. Mostly women. Lots of *them* came here. He didn't have many gents calling."

"Have you noticed anything unusual about him lately?"

The valet reflected for a moment or two, then shook his head. "No, sir, I can't say I have. I *did* think it queer that he should invite four gentlemen to dinner last night. I didn't think—"

"That he had four gentlemen friends?"

The valet did not answer, but it was obvious that Daniel had read his thoughts. "That was all?"

"Now I come to think of it, sir," replied the valet seriously, "there was one thing that struck me as being unusual. Last night, when I was replenishing the brandy decanter, Mr. Savile, who was watching me do it—he always watched—says: 'A fresh bottle, John—you can pour what's left in that decanter into an empty bottle.' Then he laughs, sort of queer, and says: 'On second thoughts, John, you can drink it yourself, after you're off duty.'

Well, I was quite taken aback, sir, but he rally meant it. It was as good a glass of the real stuff as I ever tasted."

The strained atmosphere in that room of death relaxed. There were smiles on the faces of all those present, except the valet, who was very serious, and the commissionaire, who was overawed in the presence of murder.

"That is all John," said Daniel gravely. Then, turning to the others, he added: "An amusing little detail, gentlemen. But those things are often important, eh, Inspector?" Without waiting for an answer, he started on a painstaking tour of the room. His first objective was the single large window, which investigation proved to be efficiently locked from the inside. Foot by foot he examined the flooring, moving furniture, and opening such drawers as were not locked. His investigation brought him back again at last to the body of Mark Savile.

The body lay very stiff and straight upon the rug before the fireplace. The trunk and legs were stretched out in an orderly fashion as though already arranged for burial. The feet were pointing to the window and the right arm was outstretched towards the fireplace, the fingers curved but not clenched. The left arm was pressed close to the body and the hand was clenched tightly.

"What about the explosion?" Daniel asked, rising to his feet. "Did anyone hear it?"

Inspector Evans smiled ironically. "There wasn't one—or the whole building would have been roused," he replied. "The occupant of the flat next door says that he heard a 'plop' like the sound of a cork being drawn, at about a quarter to ten. That, of course, is the noise made by an automatic which has a silencer attached."

"Death instantaneous—no time to dispose of a revolver—and no revolver found," said Daniel reflectively.

"Answer, 'murder'," responded Inspector Evans. "And, by the

way, 'about a quarter past ten' is the time the commissionaire saw one of the murdered man's guests leave the building—for the second time."

At that moment the door of the flat opened, and four men entered. Two of them were detectives, and the other two were John Borrow and Harold Denholm. As they advanced into the room, the commissionaire clutched the inspector's arm.

"That's 'im, sir," he said in a hoarse penetrating whisper, pointing to Denholm. "That's the gent as I saw last night."

Inspector Evans nodded briskly. He advanced to meet the newcomers. Their eyes had already fallen on the thing which lay on the hearthrug and they were looking pale.

"Mr. Borrow or Mr. Denholm?" Evans asked, addressing Harold Denholm.

Denholm gave his name in a jerky voice. The sight of the corpse had shaken him. Evans submitted him to a searching scrutiny.

"Well then, Mr. Denholm," he said brusquely, "as you can see for yourself, there's been murder done here. It was done, as near as I can make out, at a quarter past ten last night. At approximately that time you were seen to leave this building, although you had previously left it half-an-hour earlier with the other dinner guests. Why did you return?"

Denholm hesitated, and his eyes travelled round the room. He flinched when the body of Mark Savile came within his line of vision. He half turned so that the sight was hidden from him.

"I—I came—on purely personal business," he said at last, in a slow, husky voice.

"What business?" insisted the Inspector.

"Nothing that can possibly concern this affair."

The Inspector's lips tightened. "That is for me to judge, sir," he snapped.

Denholm shook his wearily. "I am afraid that I must refuse the information," he replied shakily.

Inspector Evans gave him a hard look. "In that case," he said grimly, "it is my duty to place you under arrest—and to warn you that anything you say may be taken down and used in evidence against you!"

Harold Denholm's face had been white. Now it turned ash-grey. "You are going to arrest me?"

Inspector Evans moved impatiently. He pointed a stubby finger at Denholm. "Can't you understand your position?" he snapped. "You dined here last night with a man whom you dislike, you leave with your fellow guests in an agitated condition, you return afterwards, and at the appropriate time when you are in the building your host is murdered. Can't you see that the circumstantial evidence against you is damning?"

Denholm glowered defiance suddenly. "And what about Barclay," he demanded. "He was in the building, too, after we had all left it. I saw him leave. He tried to strange Savile last night. Are you going to arrest him as well?"

The Inspector's jaw dropped. His face was a picture of astonishment. He wheeled round and stared at Dennis Barclay.

"Is this true?" he demanded.

Barclay nodded. "Yes," he said simply.

Inspector Evans stood stock still for a moment. His large red face wore a perplexed expression. The case which he had seen forming against Denholm was crumbling, and a new line had opened up before him.

"Sit down—all of you," he said suddenly. "There's a lot in this affair that wants explaining. Mr. Denholm—you first. Tell me why you returned here last night, and exactly what happened."

They all found chairs, except the valet and the commissioner, who felt it in keeping with their positions to remain standing.

Daniel, who seemed engrossed in an inspection of the corpse, and the Inspector, who perched himself upon the desk.

"Well, Mr. Denholm," he demanded.

Denholm licked his lips nervously. "I came back last night," he began slowly, "to have it out with Savile about—about a loan which I had repaid several times over. I was desp—worried—and determined to put an end to paying him, no matter what it meant. I rang the bell, but there was no answer. That's the truth—I swear it. I rang several times, but the flat was quite silent. Savile was probably dead already. I saw Barclay leaving the building as I approached it. He didn't see me, because he went the other way."

The Inspector considered this, nodding his head heavily at each point which he turned over in his mind.

"There's something else you should know," Denholm continued, with a sidelong glance at his fellow guests of the previous night. "Barclay was engaged to a girl whom—well, Savile persuaded away from him. Last night, Barclay half-killed Savile and left him unconscious in his chair—if we'd let him, he'd have finished the job there and then."

Inspector Evan's eyes did not waver from Denholm's face. "You think Barclay killed Savile because of this girl?" he suggested evenly.

Denholm glanced nervously at Barclay, who neither stirred nor spoke. "I don't suggest that—quite," he said, in a tone that testified to his feelings of shame. "But I didn't do it. I think that Savile was dead before I arrived—and Barclay left the building as I arrived."

There was a silence after he spoke. Those who were present knew perfectly knew perfectly well that he was implicating Dennis Barclay to save his own skin, but it was undeniable that no matter what the motives were that prompted his indirect accusation, there was no lack of justification for it.

All eyes were turned on Dennis Barclay, except those of Daniel Britling, who was gazing with marked interest at Lord Clavering. Behind the tired-looking eyes of the peer, Britling read something more than merely horror of the murder, or even concern for his friend.

John Borrow was the first to break the silence. "Look here," he said crisply. "In the interests of justice—and common decency—it is only right that you should know, Inspector, that none of had any great liking for—er—the deceased. In fact, I think we each had a motive for wishing his death."

Inspector Evans wheeled round to face him. "And those motives were?" he demanded.

Borrow returned his gaze calmly. "On my part, friendship for a poor young fellow whom Savile ruined, and who shot himself." He was silent for a moment, then continued: "Yes, I think I would have killed Savile for that."

He recounted simply and briefly the conversation of the previous evening, when Savile had given his views on murder, and the others had been provoked into adding their opinion of justifiable murder—and had given their own motives for wishing ill to their host. He spoke without bitterness, as one should speak of the dead, but the impression of Savile which he gave to those who had not known him was not a pleasant one.

"He seems to have been a thoroughly nasty customer," commented Evans. "But that doesn't alter the fact that murder has been done. He was right too, mind you, about his motiveless murders. I should say that the motive is the greatest factor in tracing a murderer. But with four motives! Well, let's hear from you, Mr. Barclay. What happened when you returned here last night?"

Dennis Barclay moistened his lips. He glanced around at the others and was encouraged by a look of sympathy from John

Borrow. He smiled gratefully. "To be frank I came back to kill him," he commenced, with a gesture towards the corpse, which Daniel Britling had thoughtfully covered with a rug. "I meant to kill him in cold blood, then give myself up to the police. He deserved death if ever a man did. I rang the bell, and he was alive then, for he answered my ring. He wouldn't open the door, though. He spoke to me from the other side, and told me to go to hell. I rang several times but he didn't answer after the first ring. At last, I came away and—well I fancy I must have got drunk, for I don't remember anything after leaving the building."

Harold Denholm rose to his feet and pointed an eager finger at the Inspector.

"Don't you see," he cried, "Barclay admits that Savile was alive when he arrived. I rang the bell only a few minutes later, and there was no answer. Savile must have been dead when I rang, so—"

Daniel interposed smoothly. "You overlook the fact that Savile may have assumed that it was still Mr. Barclay who was ringing the bell," he pointed out, "and I must remind you that if Mr. Barclay had murdered Mark Savile he would not have admitted that Savile was alive, and answered his ring. He would have said, as you have said, that Savile did not answer."

Denholm whitened and sat down abruptly. He tried to speak, but the words would not form themselves. As though he had lost all interest in Denholm, Daniel turned to Lord Clavering and gave him a benevolent smile.

"Won't *you* tell us why *you* returned here last night?" he asked politely.

Lord Clavering started as though he had been shot. "How did you know?" he gasped.

Daniel shrugged his shoulders. "I didn't—that was a chance shot, but it is obvious that you did return. Why?"

"I suppose I should have made a clean breast of it," Lord Clavering replied steadily. "Yes, I returned. I was worried about the condition of a company of which I am director and I intended to force the truth out of Savile. My experience was the same as Denholm's—Savile didn't answer when I rang the bell."

On Inspector Evans face there was an expression of extreme perplexity. It was almost the expression that a prize fighter wears directly after he has been the recipient of a punch in the solar plexus. His case was running away with itself and opening up so many possibilities that they bewildered him.

He almost glared at John Borrow. "Well, sir? What about you?" he demanded.

John Borrow smiled apologetically. "I'm not in this, Inspector," he replied. "I went straight home last night and went to bed."

"You can prove that, of course?"

Borrow reflected for a moment or two. "Why, no, I'm afraid I can't," he said at last. "I have no servant and I didn't meet anyone who knew me. I'm afraid—"

Evans cut him off short with a wave of his hand. "Alright," he said bitterly, "we'll count you in."

He turned to Daniel. "What on earth do you make of this?" he demanded.

The doctor shrugged his shoulders philosophically. "We must use the things we know as a basis for learning the things we should like to know," he replied.

"Well, what *do* we know?" the Inspector snapped. "We know that murder has been done. That is proved by the complete absence of a weapon which might have been used for suicide. A man who dies immediately has no time to dispose of an automatic, and there is not one in the room."

The doctor nodded gravely. "We know that three of the dead man's guests returned to this building after leaving it last night, that the fourth cannot prove his alibi, and that all four had strong motives for murdering Mark Savile," the Inspector went on.

Daniel crossed to the body and kneeling down pulled the covering rug back and made a careful examination. He prised open the clenched hand, which was empty, and examined the curved fingers of the other hand which trailed across the fender of the fireplace.

The cuffs of the dead man's shirt seemed to interest him intensely; also, the type of his cuff links. His examination was thorough, extending as it did even to the soles of his shoes.

"Did you ever play 'Red Indians' as a child, Inspector?" he asked casually, speaking over his shoulder.

Inspector Evan's jaw dropped. For a moment he wondered whether the little surgeon had lost his senses.

The doctor smiled. "It was a long time since *I* was a child," he remarked, "but I can remember how artistically I used to 'die' when pierced by an imaginary arrow of the enemy. I would spin round, fall on my back, and lie stretched out very stiff, and very neat—just as the body of Mark Savile is lying now. But when a man is really shot and has dropped in his tracks, his attitude is more ungainly. His arms and legs are sprawled out. Now why did the murderer leave his victim's body so tidy? Why take time to adjust the limbs? And why spoil the job by leaving one arm sprawled out to call attention to the preciseness of the rest of the body?"

He rose to his feet, and turned to the dead man's valet. "Among your duties, you assist your master in dressing?"

The valet nodded.

"And you put the studs and cuff links in his shirts?"

"Yes, sir, always."

Daniel's next remark was addressed more to himself than

to the valet. "Then why, I wonder, did Mark Savile change his dress shirt last night?" he mused. "If you will look at the cuffs, Inspector," he continued, "you will see that they are quite soiled with fingerprints. No capable servant would do that. Therefore, Mr. Savile must have changed his shirt after dinner—or perhaps rolled up his sleeve and had trouble readjusting his cufflinks." To the valet he added: "Suppose you see whether you can find a soiled shirt."

As the valet left the room, Daniel picked up the dead man's last epistle, and read it aloud: "'I have reason to fear that one of the men who dined with me tonight has designs upon my life. Should anything happen to me, he is responsible. His name is—'"

"Having written so far," remarked Daniel, "why not continue?"

Inspector Evans made a deprecatory gesture. "The doorbell rang, he went to answer it, and was killed before he could finish the letter," he urged.

The little doctor gave him a mildly reproving glance. "One word, Inspector, was all that he need write. One word— 'Borrow' or 'Barclay' or 'Denholm' or 'Clavering'. Wouldn't you have written that one little word before answering the doorbell?"

Evans did not answer.

"With his pen in his hand," Daniel continued, "it would have been natural for Savile to add the name that gave value to his letter—but he didn't. Why?"

He paced up and down the room slowly. There was a suggestion of a schoolmaster lecturing his class as he talked. "Mr. Borrow said that Mr. Savile was a man of grim humour," he remarked. "Perhaps his humour was the humour of lunacy. He must have been a wicked man, at least—as wicked as the blackest imp of hell. Giving a dinner to four enemies was only the beginning of his joke. Working his four guests into a fever against him was only a preparation.

"To unravel the mystery of his death we must use guesswork to connect our links. One guess I shall make is that Mark Savile's affairs had reached a crisis. Perhaps, Lord Clavering, your fears about Fortuna Copper were well founded, and perhaps Savile had been unwily enough to implicate himself for once. At any rate the time had come when Mark Savile must commit his greatest crime. He chose to add others to it.

"Had he wanted to live, he would not have dined four enemies and inspired them with the desire to kill him. That would have been suicide—or shall I say that *was* suicide?

"At all events, he trapped his guests into their several threats and half-threats, and when they had gone he wrote his letter, which would implicate whichever one was rash enough to come back. Probably he had considered the possibility of more than one coming back—that would add spice to the jest. His murder could not be proved against one of them—but it would be suspected against them all.

"Four men with admitted motives, Inspector—and you could never get a strong case against any one of them to bring him to court. But the public would try them. They would be marked men wherever they went. The newspapers would display their photographs. The sensation-loving public would gloat over every particular about the private lives of these four men who were suspected of murder. Private lives! —they would have no privacy. The pointing fingers would follow them everywhere. Worst of all, these four men would suspect each other. Convict a murderer and hang him and his punishment is over, but cast a doubt which cannot be proved or disproved against a man and his trial goes on forever.

"Mark Savile knew the hell to which he was condemning

his four enemies. Death came to him on the wings of his last hellish joke.

"He lay down on the hearthrug, as he is lying now. His legs were straight and pressed together, but he had forgotten that a man who is shot and falls to the ground and does not lie neatly. His left hand was clenched tightly to give him courage. He pulled the trigger of his automatic pistol and, almost as the shot that killed him was fired, the weapon vanished!"

He halted in his stride, and beamed benevolently at Inspector Evans. "The weapon vanished!" he repeated softly.

The valet, who had previously returned to the room but who had hesitated to interrupt the little surgeon's discourse, now advanced and handed him a dress shirt which he identified as the one his master had worn at dinner on the previous evening.

"But the weapon?" said Inspector Evans in a tone of bewilderment. "Where is it?"

Daniel exposed the sleeve of the shirt. Almost to the shoulder it was soiled and grimy. "In a well-kept room there is only one place where such dirt is allowed to gather," he remarked.

"But we've already looked in the fireplace!" expostulated Evans.

"Not *in* the fireplace," responded Daniel quietly. "*Up* the chimney."

In a moment Evans was on his knees and was turning the rays of a flashlight into the gloom of the chimney. Then he thrust an arm up and, after considerable tugging and pulling, brought down a stout piece of wood which had been wedged in the chimney.

To it was attached a length of strong elastic and attached to the elastic was an automatic pistol with a Maxim silencer.

Evans stared at the apparatus in silence.

"When the shot was fired the weapon vanished," murmured

the little surgeon softly. "Tugged out of the dead man's unresisting hand and whisked up the chimney by the elastic. A simple device beloved by conjurors."

He picked up his pearl-grey hat and placed it on his head at a jaunty angle.

"I think that's all for the present, Inspector," he said pleasantly, drawing on his gloves. "I'll see you at the Yard later. Good morning gentlemen."

THE END

FIND THE LADY

"THERE'S A TELEGRAM for you on the mantelpiece, behind the clock," remarked Miss Britling when her brother was lighting a cigar after a breakfast of gargantuan proportions.

Doctor Daniel Britling glanced suspiciously at his prim twin sister, coughed, and walked to the fireplace.

When did it come?" he asked, fumbling behind the clock.

"About an hour ago," replied his sister calmly.

"You're quite impossible, Eunice," Daniel exclaimed irritably. "Why didn't you let me have it at once? It may be important."

"I expect it is—that's why I didn't give it to you," said Miss Britling placidly. "I know you, Daniel Britling. If I'd given it to you before breakfast you'd have dashed off to some ridiculous place on some absurd errand, without a bit to eat."

"As it happens, you're quite wrong," retorted Daniel, tossing the telegraph form to her.

With a great show of indifference, Miss Britling glanced at it. It had been handed in at the post office of a village in Surrey at an early hour that morning. "Shall call on you at nine a.m., concerning an important matter. Clavering," she read aloud, and added contemptuously: "An important matter! If it's something in your line, Daniel Britling, it will be more messy than important."

"Something with a dash of prussic acid in it?" suggested Daniel with a droll smile. "My dear Eunice, Lord Clavering is the head of one of the oldest families in the country."

"Even the oldest families have scandals," commented Miss Britling, who religiously read the Sunday newspapers. "Or rather, *especially* the oldest families, I should say." She glanced over her glasses at her brother. "One day you'll get more excitement than you want, Daniel Britling!"

Although they were twins, and nearer to sixty than either of them cared to admit, she persisted in regarding her brother as a mischievous child who needed continual watching and frequent scolding. She had been very annoyed when he tired of his quiet practice and became a police surgeon, and was still more annoyed at his inability to attend strictly to the routine tasks of that calling, and his persistence in doing what he termed 'a little sleuthing,' when called to the scene of a murder.

Police Surgeon Daniel Britling was a small man with a large head. Disgruntled Scotland Yard officials who were forced to concede him credit for astuteness in criminal investigation (which was not a part of his professional duties) sometimes made pointed remarks about his large head, which they attributed to conceit, but other less prejudiced officials admitted that when Daniel put his interfering finger into the pie of criminal detection, he not infrequently pulled out the plum which the detective in charge of the case had groped in vain for.

To not a few people Britling was known as 'Dapper Dan'. He was always meticulously dressed in well-cut, dark clothes, and he wore a pearl-grey soft hat at a jaunty angle upon his head. His Vandyke beard was trimmed daily, and his moustache was graded to a nicety on each side.

At precisely two minutes to nine a trim maid relieved Lord Clavering of hat, stick, and overcoat, and ushered him into the tiny sitting-room where his host awaited him. Daniel and his visitor shook hands genially, and seated themselves in comfortable arm-chairs before the fire.

"Please excuse this intrusion on such short notice," said Lord Clavering in a cultured voice. "The fact is, I'm rather worried, and I've a feeling that you can help me. We met, if you remember, the morning after Mark Savile's suicide. Only your shrewdness on that occasion prevented me—and three of my friends—from being entangled in a most unholy mess. A the time I was very much impressed by your remarkable insight into human nature, and that must be my excuse for requesting your assistance again."

Daniel produced a platinum cigarette case, inscribed inside with four names, of which Lord Clavering's was one, and extended it to his guest, who selected and lit a cigarette with a distracted air, and held it absent-mindedly between his fingers, so that it shortly went out.

"The delicacy of the matter prevents me from going to the police, or one of the regular private enquiry agencies," continued Lord Clavering in a hesitant tone. "There may be nothing at the bottom of it—or everything—one never knows with Frances. My aunt, Lady Agatha Dorian, is frightfully worried, and insists that we ought to find her. I suppose she's right."

The puzzled peer stared gloomily into the fire, and his restless fingers toyed with his cigarette until it snapped suddenly and spilled a cascade of golden tobacco shred on the carpet. With a muttered apology, he threw it into the fire.

Since you have decided to consult me," responded Daniel with a shrewd glance at his visitor, "suppose you come to the point and tell me what is causing this agitation on the part of Lady Agatha and yourself."

2

Lord Clavering coughed and stared gloomily into the fire. "Frances has always been difficult," he said, speaking slowly and deliberately. "She never looks before she leaps—and usually lands head over heels in a mess. That is why we are on pins-and-needles until we hear of her. Good Lord, she may have eloped with the head-waiter, or started to swim the Channel and drowned, or—or anything. Then again—" he coughed, and his grave face flushed with embarrassment. "Well, confound it all, Britling, she may have had her own reasons for disappearing. She's had all sorts of affairs with the most outlandish men, and this may be another of them. If she's simply gone off somewhere with someone, we want to know where, and either Lady Agatha or I will bring her back."

"I see," commented Daniel. "I seem to remember reading scraps of gossip about Lady Frances Dorian in the papers from time to time. Doesn't she drive at Brooklands? And didn't she also slap someone's face at a reception given by the Spanish ambassador?"

"She did," replied Lord Clavering gloomily. "The Marquis of Calliento was the unfortunate young man. It caused quite a flood of publicity. She was kidnapped and held to ransom by bandits in Morocco a few years ago. There is a scar on her left shoulder, a souvenir of a narrow escape from death at the hands of a jealous woman in Naples last spring. She is an extraordinary woman, even in this age of extraordinary women, and a deuced uncomfortable relative to have more or less on one's hands. She is an orphan, has a large income, and does exactly as she pleases."

"And now, I gather, she has disappeared," murmured Daniel. "Tell me, where, when, and how?"

"She was last seen at the Royal Lancaster Hotel in Brighton. She loathes Brighton, but had gone there to be near her fiancé, Viscount Ellantree, who is in business in London but has a week-end place a mile or so from Brighton. Four days ago, Frances paid her bill and announced her intention of leaving the hotel that afternoon. How and when she left no one knows. She was never seen to leave, and she is certainly not there now. That is all we know."

"The Royal Lancaster Hotel? That huge place on the front? Surely someone must have seen her leaving? —the place teems with employees of one kind and another."

"No one did see her," replied the peer distractedly. "Frances had been living at the hotel for some months—her place in Norfolk is in the hands of builders—and was presumably settled for another month at least—not that Frances ever settled. My aunt called there yesterday expecting to find her, and was informed that she had left for London on Monday. The information worried Lady Agatha, for she has set her heart on Frances marrying Ellantree, and this abrupt departure from Brighton seemed to suggest a row of sorts. She 'phoned Ellantree, and found that he was quite as surprised as she was, since Frances had said nothing to him about leaving the place, and they had been on excellent terms when he last saw her, the day before she left the hotel. So that was that... And there is a certain man in London whom Frances had agreed not to see again, after a contretemps which occurred some time ago.

"Lady Agatha was informed that my cousin's trunks had been sent to London according to Frances' instructions, to a hotel in Bloomsbury, of all places. After some frantic telephoning, Lady Agatha discovered that Frances had not arrived at the hotel, but that her luggage had been delivered there, and later had been removed by an unknown person—a man. That seemed to indicate that Frances had broken her word, and was carrying on a liaison with the chap I've mentioned—Caffrey's his name, by the way, Reginald Debenham Caffrey. My aunt got through on the 'phone to Caffrey's flat in Half Moon Street, and was informed by his man that Caffrey was out of town. That seemed fishy, to say the least.

"Aunt Agatha is a sleuth of sorts, however, and from inquiries she made at the Royal Lancaster Hotel, she began to fear that something even more peculiar had happened. No one had seen Frances leave the hotel, although, to do so, she must have passed at least half a dozen employees who were all familiar with her appearance. None of them had seen her go—they are all emphatic about that. After telegraphing and telephoning everywhere that Frances might reasonably be expected to be, Lady Agatha rang me up at my place in Surrey last night and told me the whole story. She was full of the grisliest fears and suspicions. She wanted me to go straight to Scotland Yard, but to avoid publicity I persuaded her to let me consult you first."

"What do you wish me to do?" asked Daniel.

Lord Clavering fumbled with his shirt-cuffs. "I—I really don't quite know," he said, a little uncertainly. "I thought perhaps you might go down to Brighton and see if you can discover anything fresh."

"I'm not a detective," replied Daniel.

"I know that, of course," agreed his Lordship dejectedly. "I knew that it was infernal impertinence to trouble you in the matter, only I hoped—but I can see that it is impossible."

"Not entirely impossible," said Daniel with a smile. "But I warn you that my claims to distinction in the field of criminal investigation are slight. I can only nose about in my own way, and the result of my nosing may be nil. Frankly, you would probably obtain quicker results by applying to Scotland Yard."

"That's the last thing I want to do," replied Lord Clavering quickly. "If you could possibly get away—"

"As it happens, that's easy," said Daniel. "There's a young man round the corner who does my work when I'm away, and he's simply dying for experience. If you really want me to go down to Brighton and see what I can discover, I'm quite able—and perfectly willing."

"That's very good of you," exclaimed Lord Clavering warmly. "Please go in my car—I'll send it to the door for you. And, of course, any fee you care to name—"

"Please!" said Daniel, with a deprecatory gesture. "I love to dabble in these things, but I have no wish to profit by my hobby. By the way, what's this man Caffrey's address? And the address of the hotel in Bloomsbury where the trunks were delivered? And have you a photograph of Lady Frances?"

"As a matter of fact, I have," replied Lord Clavering. Dipping into his breast pocket and producing a photograph clipped from the *Tatler*.

There were two people in the photograph, a pretty woman with dark hair, and a tall, slim young man with a handsome peevish face, both in evening attire. Underneath was printed, "Lady Frances Dorian and Mr. Reginald Caffrey, two of the distinguished audience at the first night of Noel Coward's new play." Daniel placed the clipping in his notebook, and jotted down Caffrey's address, and the address of the Bloomsbury Hotel.

"You'll dine with me tonight at my club?" suggested Lord Clavering as he departed. "I'd like to know the result of your investigations as soon as possible. Half-past seven suit you? Splendid. Ashton's, you know, in Albemarle Street."

3

Lord Clavering's smart Daimler took Doctor Britling to Half Moon Street, where he called at Mr. Reginald Debenham Caffrey's flat. The valet who answered his ring told him that Mr. Caffrey was out of town and would not return for a week or ten days at least. The valet parried Daniel's questions in a bland, suave manner, without giving him the slightest information. On interviewing the caretaker of the building, however, Daniel elicited the information that Mr. Caffrey had departed on Monday afternoon at four o'clock in a taxi with a single suitcase, and had not returned since.

Monday afternoon at four o'clock—and Lady Frances had disappeared on Monday afternoon! It would be strange indeed if there was no connection between the two departures. This was Friday morning; they had both been gone for the best part of four days.

He went to the Midway Hotel in Bloomsbury, and found it less than midway between the respectable and the shady. There were more married couples registered in the book at the reception desk than Daniel cared to see. The prosperity of the hotel was denied by the down-at-heels appearance of the lounge, but proclaimed by the diamond rings which scintillated on the fat fingers of the proprietress.

"I don't know no Lady Frances Dorian," said the proprietress irritably, in answer to Doctor Britling's questions. "I told Lady Agatha Dorian that when she rang me up yestiddy. I don't do no business with the peerage—not much, anyways. This ain't the Savoy."

"But you received certain luggage which was forwarded from the Royal Lancaster Hotel in Brighton?" suggested Daniel.

The woman made an impatient gesture. "That damned luggage!" she exclaimed. "I 'ad no end of trouble over it yestiddy, with the old girl ringing up from Brighton every five minutes with a new set of questions. Most impertinent she was. I 'ad to 'ang up on 'er, or I'd never 'ave got no peace. Good 'eavens, Mister whatever-your-name-is, that luggage belonged to a Mrs. Sims what occasionally comes here when she's in town."

"When did it arrive?" asked Daniel.

"A minute or two after six o'clock on Monday evening," she replied wearily (Lady Agatha had evidently strained her patience). "It was only on the premises about 'alf an hour. At 'alf-pas' six Mr. Sims rung up to see if it was 'ere, an' a few minutes later 'e called with a keb an' took it away. Any more questions, mister? This ain't an information bureau, you know—it's a hotel."

"Does Mr. Sims come here often?"

"'E comes when Mrs. Sims comes. And that's on'y an occasional week-end."

"Can you describe the couple?"

"No, I can't, and if I could, I wouldn't," she snapped angrily. "I've told you all I'm going to, so good-day."

That was that!

4

The Royal Lancaster Hotel in Brighton is lavish with plate-glass and long mirrors and gold paint, its architecture is Georgian, but it has been renovated and remodelled and brought up to date until it resembles nothing so much as an elderly roué who has produced an appearance of decayed youth on his flabby body and withered cheeks and corsets and paint. It has featured in more than once delicious society scandal, and seen the conception of many divorces.

The manager, a dapper little Frenchman, inclined to rotundity, received Doctor Britling in his office with an air more of apprehension than cordiality.

"There is little I can tell you," he said when Daniel had explained his mission. "All that I personally know is that my telephone-clerk came to me on Monday about half-past one o'clock and informed me that he had been speaking to Lady

Frances on the telephone; she had 'phoned down to say she was leaving that afternoon and wished her bill made up at once. Her departure seemed very sudden, m'sieu, so I telephoned to her suite and inquired whether she had found the service lacking in some respect, but she said she had received an urgent message and must go to London at once. She would probably return later, but could not say definitely when that might be. Well, I cannot keep my guests against their wills, m'sieu, I can only do my best to make them comfortable so that they will stay. There was more to be said, Lady Frances paid her bill, and gave instructions that her luggage was to be collected by the porter in an hour, and put on board the three o'clock train for London."

He frowned, and drummed his fingers nervously on the desk before him. "It transpires that the lady has disappeared since Monday afternoon, that she was not seen to leave the hotel, which is strange. But, m'sieu, there must be some quite simple explanation. She is certainly not here now. Every corner of the hotel has been thoroughly searched."

"How many means of exit have you?" asked Doctor Britling.

"Two only, m'sieu," replied the manager. "The front door which, as you have seen, opens to the street from the grand hall and the tradesmen's entrance. To the left of the front door is the reception desk, where three clerks are at work all day, and on the other side is the head porter's box, and the bench where the page-boys sit between errands. Beside the head porter's box and the page-boys' bench is the magazine stall. All of these people know Lady Frances, and, in addition, there is the commissionaire who stands always outside the door, and who could not have failed to see her if she left by it. No one saw her go. I am puzzled, m'sieu. I am mystified. I have questioned everyone. Lady Agatha has questioned everyone—the chambermaid, the porters, the pageboys, the commissionaire, the telephone clerk—and we have learned nothing. If they are telling the truth, Lady Frances must still be in the hotel, but that is impossible, m'sieu, I have assured myself of that. It is all very strange, but surely there is some explanation. These things are so bad for a hotel!"

"The tradesmen's entrance?" suggested Daniel.

The other shrugged his shoulders hopelessly. "There is always a porter on duty at the tradesmen's entrance, m'sieu. He saw her ladyship's maid leaving the hotel, but her ladyship, no."

"Her maid?"

"Another mystery!" responded the manager, with something akin to a sob in his voice. "No one knows where she has gone. She, at least, is known to have left the hotel. Lady Agatha says that she has murdered her mistress! I ask you, m'sieu, is that not an incredible suggestion? But people listen to these things. Lady Agatha tells everyone that her niece has been murdered in this hotel. Mon Dieu, she will have the place ruined, if we do not find her niece!"

"I will do my best," said Daniel with a smile. "Where is Lady Agatha?"

"In the drawing-room," replied the manager. "I will show you."

5

They went out of the manager's office, which was to the left of the reception desk, through which a charmingly-furnished, well-lighted room could be seen. The manager pointed a plump finger to a little group of women who were gossiping round the fire. "There is Lady Agatha," he said in a tired voice. "The lady with the large nose."

Daniel looked. Lady Agatha's huge nose, like the beak of a hawk, made identification easy. She was a formidable-looking woman, with a dominant chin, and a wide, thin-lipped mouth. It did not surprise him that the little Frenchman drooped at the mere mention of her name.

"I think we will leave her where she is for the present," he said. "She looks quite in her element."

"What a talker, that woman!" exclaimed the manager. "My staff will leave if she does not leave them alone. And when she is not questioning them, she is always my guest. M'sieu, I would do anything to get rid of her."

If I may go up to the suite vacated by Lady Frances—?" suggested Daniel.

"Nothing is simpler, m'sieu," declared the manager, beckoning to a pageboy. "It is still empty. You wish me to go with you?"

"Perhaps it would be better for me to look round alone," replied Daniel. "I shall want to interview certain members of your staff," he added. "There is a telephone in the room? Supposing I 'phone down when I want them, and you can send them up one by one?"

"Very well, m'sieu." To the pageboy the manager said: "Obtain the key to suite twenty-four, and conduct this gentleman to it."

After a nervous glance through the glass door at the talkative Lady Agatha Dorian, and a polite bow to Daniel, he scuttled back to the friendly shelter of his private office.

6

Alone in suite twenty-four, Doctor Britling commenced a careful, unhurried survey of the bedroom, sitting-room and bathroom which it contained. The rooms were spick and span, and at first sight appeared to contain no trace of their late occupant. Not even a hairpin or a smudge of face-powder had escaped the vigilant eye of the chambermaid. The furniture looked new, and every polishable surface shone brightly, except a corner of a table in the sitting-room which presented an odd contrast. It was slightly dented, and its surface was dull and discoloured.

There were radiators in every room, unobtrusive in design, and heated through hot-water pipes from a furnace in the basement. There was a fireplace in the sitting-room, a relic of the hotel's early life, which was no longer in use. An ornamental screen stood on the hearth before it, effectively concealing the grate.

Daniel drew the screen aside and looked behind. The grate was heaped with coloured paper, probably intended to support the camouflage of the screen. He took it out, and heaped it on the hearthrug. Underneath, he found some small pieces of charred wood, about a quarter of an inch thick, to which thick blue paper, like wallpaper, and badly scorched, was glued. He gathered up all the pieces of wood, wrapped them in a large silk handkerchief and placed them in his overcoat pocket, then replaced the coloured paper in the grate, and placed the ornamental screen back in position.

His survey of the rooms completed, he removed the dainty wax-doll attired in a crinoline which camouflaged the telephone, picked up the receiver and requested the telephone-clerk to send the chambermaid to him at once.

In a very few moments she came into the room. He tried to put her at her ease to begin with by complimenting her on the efficiency which was evident in her work, but she stared at him as though half expecting him to eat her—the result of Lady Agatha's previous questioning, he decided.

"I shan't take up much of your time," he remarked pleasantly. "Will you tell me please, what time you came into this room to tidy it up after Lady Frances Dorian left on Monday afternoon?"

"I don't know when Lady Frances left," replied the

chambermaid hesitantly, twisting her fingers on her apron. "It'd be shortly after four when I came in here, and she was gone then."

"Was there anything unusual about the appearance of the room?"

"Yes, sir!" The girl's tone was one of mild indignation. "I found the corner of that table in a proper mess. It was all white, as though something had been spilt on it, and cleaned up with a rag and warm water. Warm water to a table like that, sir! Why, it took the polish right off! I've waxed it and rubbed it and rubbed it and waxed it until my arms ache, and I can't get it to take on a polish again. It'll have to be French-polished to get that stain out, sir!"

Daniel nodded; he had noticed the corner of the table. "You say that washing with warm water did that?" he asked.

"I don't know anything else, sir, as would do it. And there's a dent on the wood, too, sir—you can see it if you look close—I'll take my oath *that* wasn't there 'til the day Lady Frances left."

"Hm. Someone's been pretty careless, eh?"

"Yes, sir. But you can't keep things proper in a hotel, sir. People haven't any respect for things that don't belong to them. They use clean towels to mop up anything they spill, or take the dust off their boots. They just don't care.

"Speaking of towels, sir, there was one missing after Lady Frances left!" She made the statement triumphantly, as though she had caught Lady Frances red-handed in a major theft. "A bath towel!"

"Is that usual? I thought—"

"Well, it isn't unusual, in a way. We often miss towels. People take 'em to wrap up wet toothbrushes or shaving things or boots or hair brushes. But a bath-towel, sir! There aren't many things so big that you'd want to wrap them in a bath-towel."

"I see. An odd theft, certainly. Not the sort of thing one would be likely to pack by mistake?"

"Oh no, sir! Much too big."

"How often do you clean the fireplace?"

"I tidy the hearth every day, sir, and then clean the front of the grate once a week. It's never used, you know, sir. Every six weeks or so we change the coloured paper in the grate."

"How long is it since you changed the paper last?"

The girl thought for a moment. "About a week, sir. Lemme see... this is Friday...Yes, sir, it was exactly a week, last Friday, it was."

"You're sure of that?"

"Yes, sir, quite sure."

Daniel's next question was a delicate one. He put it as tactfully as he could. "Please don't be offended, but in your employment, you often find out things about the guests that a less privileged person wouldn't know, don't you? Without spying on them, I mean; just in the ordinary course of your duties?"

"Well, that's true, sir." The girl's tone was perfectly frank. "You can't help it."

"I wonder if you can tell me anything about the relations between Lady Frances and her maid? Did they appear to get on well together?"

"No, sir, they didn't. As a matter of fact, I happen to know that Sadie—that's the maid's name, sir, Sadie Harper, was under notice. I used to talk to her told me that quite often—they'd been here for months—and once or twice we went out together, but she wasn't my sort. She seemed to think of nothing but men. There was a gentleman who came here once or twice to see Lady Frances, and Sadie told me that he was hoodwinking her mistress properly. She said that all the time he was supposed to be coming after Lady Frances he was really carrying on with her. I don't know whether she was telling the truth or not—I didn't find her especially truthful—but I've heard Lady Frances going for her something terrible, yes, and Sadie answering back, too!"

"Do you happen to know the gentleman's name?"

"I heard it once, sir, but I don't know's I can remember it." The girl wrinkled her forehead, and tapped her chin with a slim, tapering finger. "It was something like 'coffee.' Oh, and his first name was Reginald."

"Coffee? Do you mean Mr. Reginald Caffrey?"

"Yes, sir. I remember now, Mr. Caffrey!"

"Do you suppose you could describe this girl, Sadie Harper, for me?"

"Well, she was quite good-looking, in a bold way, sir. About average height for a woman, I should say. Oh, and she had golden hair, sir. Real gold, with a reddish tint in it. Very distinctive hair, sir. Striking."

7

There was nothing else the girl could tell him, so Doctor Britling dismissed her and sent for the telephone-clerk, a keen, smart-looking youth with intelligent eyes, who was not long in presenting himself at the door of suite twenty-four. His name was Gerald Winthorp. To put him at his ease, Daniel gave him a cigarette and motioned him to a chair.

"I want you to tell me, as fully as you can, about the telephone call from this suite on Monday afternoon, when Lady Frances told you she was leaving at once, and asked to have her bill sent up," said Daniel.

"To tell you the truth, sir," replied the clerk, "there were two telephone calls from this suite on Monday afternoon. I've only mentioned one before, for the other didn't seem to matter, and Lady Agatha—she's a terror, sir—rather got my back up. But the manager's told us to do our best to help you, and I think I ought to tell you about the first call. I hope you'll put me right with the manager, for I didn't even tell him about it. It—it—well, it didn't seem to amount to anything, that I could see."

"I'll make it right with the manager," said Daniel brusquely, "if you tell me the whole truth now."

"Thank you, sir. *You* may make something of it. *I* couldn't. At three minutes past one the light on the switchboard flashed for this number. I plugged in and heard Lady Frances saying something that sounded mighty like 'Help!' I wasn't sure, but I said quickly; 'Is there anything wrong, my lady?' There was no answer, but the receiver was still up at this end, so I repeated the question. After a pause of a few seconds, I heard hoarse breathing, and Lady Frances said; 'No, thank you. It's perfectly all right. I felt a little queer, but I'm all right now.' I offered to call the resident doctor, but she said no, she was as right as rain, and hung up. Well, it sounded a bit funny, but, working in a hotel, you soon find out that there's no understanding women—they're not rational beings—so I thought no more about it, until—"

"Did her voice sound normal?"

"No, sir, it didn't. It was shaky, as though she had had a bit of a fright."

Doctor Britling mentally digested this information. "You're sure it was the voice of Lady Frances?" he asked.

The young man stared at him uncomprehendingly. "The call came from this room, sir," he replied. "Who else could it be?"

Daniel shrugged his shoulders. "Lady France's maid would have access to the telephone in this room," he pointed out.

"I never thought of that, sir," Winthorp admitted.

"Well, it's a possibility. The point is, can you say definitely that it was Lady Frances's voice you heard?"

Winthorp thought for a moment, then shook his head. "I couldn't swear to it, sir. It might not have been."

"Then tell me this: are you certain that the voice you heard saying 'help' or something of the sort was the same voice that assured you a few minutes later that nothing was wrong?"

The eyes of the elderly police surgeon and the youthful clerk met; Dr. Britling's eyes were calm and expressionless but the eyes of the young man held a startled inquiry. He drew hard on his cigarette and there was a puzzled expression on his face. "No, sir," he said at last. "I'm not. There was a change in the tone of the voice. It might simply have been that the—the lady had her voice under better control when she answered me—or there might have been two voices."

"And either of them might have been the voice of Lady Frances, or neither—or it might have been Lady Frances who spoke all the time, only more composed when she answered you. Is that it?"

"Yes, sir. That's as near as I can come to putting it definitely."

"I see. Now, we come to the other telephone message, when you were told that Lady Frances was leaving the hotel. What time was it?"

"Twenty-eight minutes past one, sir?"

"Was it Lady Frances who spoke to you the second time?"

The young man rubbed his chin reflectively. "I thought it was, sir, but I'm not so sure now," he replied in a dubious tone. "One woman's voice sounds pretty much like another over the telephone. And there was something odd about that voice. I remember thinking at the time that the speaker was excited."

"So that it, too, might not have been the voice of Lady Frances?" suggested Daniel. "Or am I simply putting ideas into your head? You must try to be honest with yourself, you know. Don't let me create doubts in your mind that have no basis for existence."

"No, sir. I'm doing my level best to keep my impressions clear," replied Gerald Winthorp earnestly. "But I honestly can't say that the person I spoke with the second time was Lady Frances. I thought it was at the time, because the call came from this room."

"What was the message?" asked Daniel.

"The voice said: 'This is Lady Frances Dorian. I have been called out of town, and shan't require my rooms here for some time. I am leaving this afternoon. Please send up my bill as soon as possible.' I replied that it would be attended to immediately, then I went and told the manager. Lady Frances was regarded as a permanency, more or less, and I thought he would wish to know at once that she was leaving so suddenly."

"I suppose the bill was presented in due course?"

"Yes, sir," the young man replied. "I brought it up myself, as a matter of fact. That isn't a regular part of my duties; the assistant manager, or the head reception clerk usually does it, but they were both at lunch. I didn't enter the suite. Lady Frances's maid met me at the door and left me to cool my heels in the corridor while she got the money."

"A—a—ah! The maid!" said Daniel Britling. "Tell me, did *she* appear quite calm and collected?"

"I couldn't really say, sir," replied Winthorp uncertainly. "She didn't open the door very wide, and her arms were heaped high with dresses and that sort of thing. I remembered thinking what a whale of a lot of packing she and her mistress must be doing if their departure was as sudden as it seemed."

"Her voice," said Daniel. "How did it strike you?"

"I'm afraid I didn't notice it," Winthorp admitted. "She

was—well, perhaps I'm a bit of a snob—she's just the maid. I didn't notice her voice particularly, or anything about her. Oh, except that she was wearing a hat, instead of her uniform cap."

"That's hardly usual, is it?"

"No, sir, but I didn't think anything of it. I thought it might be one of her mistress's hats which she was packing and had put it on her head because she hadn't room for it in her arms."

"Might she have been the woman who spoke to you on the telephone?"

"Why, yes, sir, she might have been."

"She paid by cheque, of course?"

"No, sir," replied Winthorp without hesitation. "She gave me the exact amount in notes and silver. I was mildly surprised, for Lady Frances usually paid by cheque."

"Is there anything else you can think of which might have a bearing on the matter?"

The telephone-clerk reflected for a few moments. "I don't think so, sir," he said at last.

"Very well," replied Daniel. "You may go now, and please send up the porter who removed the luggage from this room and took it to the station."

"Certainly, sir. Good-morning, sir."

"Good-morning."

8

After Winthorp had withdrawn and before the porter made his appearance Doctor Britling scribbled a few notes in pencil of the important features of the chambermaid's and Winthorp's revelations.

In a few minutes there was a discreet tap on the door, which

Doctor Britling opened to admit a short, stockily-built man of about forty, who wore a blue uniform with brass buttons and leather shoulder pads.

"You wish to see me, sir?" he said, touching his forehead with a grubby finger.

"You are the porter who removed the luggage from this suite on Monday afternoon?" asked Doctor Britling.

"Yes, sir, me and the young lad 'oo 'elps me," replied the porter.

"At what time was that?"

The porter rubbed his chin reflectively. "I couldn't say to a few minutes, sir," he said at last. "But we only caught the three o'clock train with the luggage and no more, so it wouldn't 'ave been much before three. About ten to, I should say."

"And the suite was tenantless then?"

"Yes, sir," responded the porter, blinking his eyes a little. "I took a bit of a look around in each of the rooms first of all; it's a thing I always do, to make sure that there ain't no bags or cases hidden in corners. The rooms were all empty, except the sitting-room, here, which 'ad a pile of luggage in the middle of the floor."

"How much luggage was there?"

"One wardrobe-trunk, one steamer trunk, one 'at box, two large 'ide suitcases, one 'ide kit-bag, one attaché case," replied the porter, checking them off on his fingers.

"A fair amount, eh?" Doctor Britling commented. "The trunks would be pretty heavy?"

The porter shrugged his shoulders philosophically. "'Eavyish, sir. But then, wardrobe-trunks usually are," he responded. "They're built like blinkin' battleships, sir, and they 'old a sizeable lot. The other pieces were pretty well crammed, too. I was afraid one of the suitcases might burst, so I fastened it more securely with an old strap I 'ad in me room."

"What was the address on the labels?"

"Now, there was an odd thing, sir," said the porter. "While I was lookin' about, the lad I 'ad with me was examinin' the luggage. Suddenly 'e cries; ''Ere, Bill! We're in the wrong suite!' I laughed and tells 'im 'e's balmy. 'E gets quite 'uffy, and says: 'Oo's sweet is this, then?' I says: 'Why, it's Lady Frances Dorian's, o'course, stooped.' 'Oho,' ses'e. 'Then take a look at the luggage, an' see for yourself 'oo's name's on it.' I takes a look, and blowed if the kid ain't right, sir. The name on every one of those labels is Mrs. Sims, the address, Midway Hotel, Bloomsbury, London."

"What did you do?" inquired Doctor Britling.

"Looked at the number on the door, sir," replied the porter without hesitation. "Sure enough I'm right, we're in the right sweet, all right. So I ses to the lad: 'It's none of our ruddy business where Lady Frances is sendin' 'er luggage, or wot name it's addressed to. All we've got to do is to get this stuff to the station. So lend a blinkin' 'and and look lively and try to earn your bloomin' wages,' I ses. Just the same, it was a bit queer, wasn't it, sir?"

"Perhaps it looked queer," said Daniel indifferently, "But it simply means that Lady Frances was sending her luggage to a friend, a Mrs. Sims, I should think. There's nothing unusual about that."

"No, sir, there ain't, I see that," admitted the porter in a crestfallen tone.

"You put the luggage safely on the train?"

"Yes, sir."

"Did you notice Lady Frances at the station?"

"No, sir," replied the porter, then, brightening a little, he added: "But I did think I caught a glimpse of 'er maid, gettin' into a third-class carriage. The lad saw 'er first, an' ses, ''Ere

Bill, ain't that 'er Ladyship's maid, gettin' into that carriage over there?' I looks, and sure enough, it does look like 'er. Got gimlet eyes, that lad 'as—an' a ball-bearing joint to 'is tongue."

"That's all you know? You didn't speak to the maid?"

"No, sir, I didn't."

"I see; well, you needn't discuss what you've told me with anyone." Doctor Britling's eyes twinkled, and he added: "Not even the lad."

The porter smiled. "Very well, sir, I'll do my best—though he's a rare 'un for wormin' things out of a chap, that lad is."

"You might ask the head-porter to come up, please."

9

The head-porter was tall and burly, with broad shoulders which he held squarely; about sixty years of age, with grey hair and snowy moustache and eyebrows.

"You know, of course, that Lady Frances Dorian is missing?" was Doctor Britling's first question.

There was a flicker of ironic amusement in the head porter's steady blue eyes. "Her Ladyship's aunt, Lady Agatha, made that quite plain to all of us, sir," he replied drily.

"From your box to the right of the front door you would have seen her had she left that way?"

"There isn't a doubt of that, sir."

"But she did not leave by the front door?"

"No, sir," said the head-porter in a positive tone. "I'm certain of that. To be quite frank, sir, I was watching for her Ladyship. My department had been of considerable service to her during the months she had been in the hotel, and we naturally expected that she would not forget us when she left. We had heard from the reception-clerk that she was leaving that afternoon, and, well sir, it was only business for me to keep my eyes open."

"You mean that you expected a gratuity in acknowledgment of your services?" suggested Daniel.

"Something like that, sir."

"You were on duty all of that afternoon?"

"Yes, sir, from twelve o'clock noon to six in the evening without a break. I'll take my oath that Lady Frances didn't leave during that time, and the second porter, who follows me, swears she didn't pass him—he was on duty until twelve p.m."

"There are usually one or two page-boys sitting on the bench beside your box?" asked Daniel.

"Yes, sir, and I've questioned each of them, but they are all quite certain that Lady Frances did not leave the hotel on Monday afternoon, sir."

"There is the back door—" Daniel demurred.

"Yes, sir, but she wouldn't leave that way!" The head-porter was shocked at the suggestion.

"That remains to be seen."

IO

A few moments after he had dismissed the hotel-porter, Daniel admitted a frightened-looking girl into the room. She was carrying a number of garments over her arm.

"My name is Elsie Crewe. The housekeeper sent me, sir," she said tremulously. "She said I must show you these things, and tell you how I came by them. They belonged to Lady Frances, sir. Her maid gave them to me."

"That's interesting," said Daniel. "Extremely interesting. Please place them across the back of that chair."

The girl complied, and stood away from them, as though afraid that they would contaminate her.

"Don't look so nervous," said Daniel soothingly. "Sit down somewhere for a moment, while I examine them."

The girl sat down on the edge of a chair, looking as though she would have liked to take to her heels and run.

Doctor Britling picked up the first garment, a fur-trimmed coat which looked quite new. He felt in the pockets, found that they were empty, and dropped the coat over the back of the chair. Next, he lifted a skirt and jacket in grey tweed, examined them, and placed them on top of the coat. The remaining garments matched each other; they comprised what is known as a 'three-piece suit,' consisting of skirt, jumper, and coatee.

"Very smart," he commented, when his examination of the garments was complete. "And hardly worn at all, any of them."

Elsie Crewe started up with a frightened little cry. "I came by them honestly, sir," she said hoarsely. "I swear I did!"

Doctor Britling smiled and laid his hands on her trembling shoulders, gently forcing her back into the chair she had vacated. "You've no need to be alarmed, my child, I am quite prepared to believe you. Just tell me in your own way how they came into your possession."

The girl looked at his pleasant grey eyes, and took courage. "Her Ladyship's maid sold them to me!" she said, in a more composed tone. "Not for what they were worth, or anything like it, sir, just for a few shillings."

Watching her closely, Daniel was aware that she was telling the truth. Her timid eyes were frank and honest. "Did she explain how she was in a position to sell them?" he asked.

Elsie Crewe nodded. "She said that her mistress had given them to her, sir."

"I see," commented Daniel gravely. "Tell me how the transaction came about—and when it took place."

The girl thought for a moment. "It was on Monday afternoon, about two o'clock, or a few minutes past," she began. "I came off duty at two, and went straight up to my room. It's in a corridor on the eighth floor—the Maid's Corridor, they call it—where nine of us chambermaids have our rooms. There are ten rooms in the corridor, and I know that her Ladyship's own maid had the first one, for one of the other girls told me. The door of the first room was ajar, and as I went to pass I saw her Ladyship's maid in the room, packing a suitcase. I had never spoken to her before, for I only came to this job ten days ago, but I was lonely and I knew that none of the other girls would be upstairs at that time, so I said: 'Hello' She looked up sharply, and asked who I was. I said I was the new chambermaid, and she told me that she was Lady Frances Dorian's private maid—though, of course, I knew that. I had seen her about the corridors once or twice. She said that she was leaving that afternoon. I asked her if she'd got the sack, and she laughed and said yes, she and her mistress had had a rare old row which ended up with her being told to go. She said her mistress was leaving the hotel too. 'And would you believe it," she said, 'the shabby cat's gone off, leaving me to pack her things, after giving me the sack not an hour ago! It's taken me a full hour to throw her rags into her luggage,' she said. 'And this is the first chance I've had to pack my own things.' Well, sir, she seemed to have quite a lot to pack, and I said so. 'You're about right,' she said, sir. 'I'll never get everything in. Her Ladyship's always giving me clothes she's tired of—I'll miss that now.' Well, sir, she folded everything neatly, and tucked things down into corners, and crammed in all she could…and still these things there were left. 'It's no use,' she said at last. 'They won't go in.'

"'If you had another suitcase—' I suggested, trying to be helpful, but she shook her head and said she couldn't be bothered with another case. 'Here,' she said suddenly, 'You can have them,' and put these things over my arm. Well, sir, I didn't like to take them, but she insisted, so I made her take a pound for them. Of course, they're worth a lot more, but I didn't feel so bad, giving something for them."

"And then?" suggested Daniel gently.

The girl was now completely at her ease. "Then, sir, she locked the suitcase and said good-bye and went off down the back stairs," she replied.

"Isn't there a lift for the servants?" asked Daniel sharply.

"Oh, yes, sir," replied Elsie Crewe quickly. "But she said she couldn't be bothered waiting for it, it was so slow. And it is, sir—a poky old thing."

"Better than walking down eight flights with a heavy suitcase in your hand, though?" said Daniel.

"I should have thought so, sir," she agreed.

"Very well, you may go."

He saw her glance rest longingly on the garments which were dropped over the chair, and he smiled. "I think you may take them," he said. "But I shouldn't wear them just at present if I were you. They may be wanted for examination by the police."

"The police!" —her cheeks paled— "Oh, sir! I won't get into trouble? I didn't do wrong in buying them?"

Daniel shook his head with a benign smile. "Just tell them the truth, if they question you," he replied. "You have nothing to fear. Now, please, before you go, show me the back stairs."

The girl led the way out of the suite and down a long-carpeted corridor to a door marked 'Emergency Exit Only,' which gave access to the back staircase. There Daniel thanked her, bid her goodbye, and went down the stairs alone.

II

The stairs were of uncarpeted concrete, and the walls that flanked them were of the same solid and undecorated material. On each floor there was a wide concrete landing, and a door which opened to the bedroom corridors.

He saw no one on his way downstairs. At the bottom, he found a hall about twenty feet square, with large double doors opening off it to an alley. To the left of the hall, which was also constructed of undecorated concrete, was the shaft of the service lift, and a cubby-hole in which sat a middle-aged man of medium height, dressed in a shabby blue uniform, who was smoking a discoloured clay pipe which he hastily stuffed into his pocket when Doctor Britling appeared. He rose from his chair at the back of his little office, and came forward to the half-door which masked the lower part of the entrance to his little sanctum.

"Lorst yer way, did yer, sir? He asked with an ingratiating grin. "Easy enough to do, if you don't know yer way abaht the hotel. If yer go back up them stairs to the fust landin', an' open the door ahead of yer, y'll find the front 'all strite ahead, sir."

"As it happens," replied Daniel, "I came down here expressly to see you."

The man's jaw dropped, and his lips fell apart at the information. "Ter see *me*, mister?"

"Yes," said Doctor Britling. "I want to know whether you saw Lady Frances Dorian's maid leaving the hotel on Monday?"

The man was obviously relieved. "Wot, *'er*, sir?" he responded in a contemptuous tone. "Yus, I saw 'er. Monday afternoon, it was, abaht a quarter pars' two. She came dahn them steps luggin' a great 'efty suitcase."

"Did you speak to her?" asked Daniel.

"Speak to a 'igh an' mighty piece of goods like 'er? Not me, sir," the man replied emphatically. "I was through speaking to 'er the fust day she come into the hotel. Gave 'er a civil 'good-arternoon,' I did, an' I got me answer, strite, I did. Parsed me wiv 'er 'ead in the air, like I was so much dirt. Too big for 'er boots she was, sir. Arter that, she could 've gorn in an' out that door all day, an' I wouldn't 'ave let on I noticed 'er. I've got me pride, I 'ave, sir."

"You didn't happen to see Lady Frances leaving by this door on the same day?" asked Daniel.

The man assumed an attitude which expressed that he was 'struck all of a 'eap' at the question. "Wot, Lady Frawncis, sir?" he gasped.

"Yes," said Daniel patiently. "Lady Frances."

"Go out at this door?"

"Yes, at this door."

"Out at this door—Lady Frawncis?"

"That's what I said," retorted Daniel, losing patience. "Please answer my question."

"Yes, sir," said the man apologetically. "But—excuse me, sir—but wot a question! Why, sir, toffs like Lady Frawncis don't never use this door."

"Then you didn't see her?" said Daniel irritably.

"No, sir, I didn't," replied the doorman. "If I 'ad I wouldn't be 'ere talkin' to yer now. It'd be too much for me, sir. I'd 'ave 'ad a stroke, or sumpin."

"Were you on duty all Monday afternoon?" asked Daniel.

"Yes, sir. From twelve o'clock to nine p.m., sir, wivout a break. Me grub's brought in 'ere to me."

There was nothing more to be learned from the man, so Daniel retraced his steps to the first landing and opened the door which gave access to the main hall of the hotel. As he went through the door, he heard the man he had left repeating in a dazed tone: "That's a good 'un, that is. Lady Frawncis goin' out at this door! Lumme! That's a rare 'un!"

12

Daniel knocked at the door of the manager's private office and went in. The little Frenchman was sitting at a large walnut desk in the middle of the room, writing busily, but he jumped up at once when Doctor Britling entered. His shrewd little black eyes searched the investigator's face.

"You have good news for me, yes?" he said eagerly. "You are at the bottom of the whole affair? You have discovered the simple explanation of her Ladyship's disappearance?"

Daniel smiled. "I'm afraid you're asking a little too much," he replied good-naturedly. "I am far from being at the bottom of the whole affair, and it's by no means as simple as you hope. What I have learned makes it look rather sinister, indeed, but I can say nothing definite at the moment."

The Manager wrung his hands. "I hope you are wrong," he said anxiously. "These things are so bad for an hotel. And with Lady Agatha spreading the most horrible rumours, mon Dieu! —it is too much."

"I shouldn't worry too much at present," said Daniel. "It'll be time enough when you've something definite to worry about. After all, Lady Frances may have had her reasons for leaving the hotel as quietly as possible."

"Yes, but how?" The manager spread his hands expressively. "How could she do so without being seen?"

Daniel lay back in his chair and closed his eyes. In his mind he visualised Lady Frances leaving the hotel unseen.

"It is possible," he said at last. "Almost easy, for a woman. A day or two before she was going to leave, she might disguise herself slightly while *outside* the hotel. A different kind of hat from the type she usually wore, perhaps a tight-fitting hat, which concealed her dark hair, but permitted a stray curl or two of false golden hair to escape and be noticed; a dress with flowing lines to make her look taller; entirely different facial make-up; a suitcase in her hand, and there you have her, a different woman, presenting herself at the reception-desk and booking a room. Her disguise is not detected, and for a day or two she contrives to play the twin-roles of Lady Frances and the new guest. When the time comes, she leaves suite twenty-four, admits herself unnoticed to the other room, puts on her disguise and walks out of the hotel, a different woman. A woman, moreover, who is known to the employers of the hotel as a recent arrival, of whom they would take less notice than of a complete stranger. They would never dream of associating her with Lady Frances."

As he spoke the door suddenly swung open without warning, and Lady Agatha Dorian came into the office like a tornado. There was a grim look on her face, and the light of battle in her eyes.

"Why was I not informed that this Britling person had arrived?" she demanded imperatively; then becoming aware of Daniel's presence, she swung round and stared at him belligerently. "You are the investigator whom Clavering insisted on sending down!" she snapped. "You should have consulted me immediately on your arrival, my man. Nor that I suppose for a moment that you will be of the slightest use. This is a matter for the police! My niece has been murdered!"

13

At half-past seven to the minute Doctor Britling arrived at Ashton's Club, in Albemarle Street to keep his appointment with

Lord Clavering. His host met him in the hall and led him to a private room where dinner was laid for two. The conversation was confined to impersonal topics throughout their excellent repast. When coffee and liqueurs were served, Lord Clavering passed his cigar-case to his guest, then chose one himself and lit it with exquisite care.

"Lady Agatha dropped in on me a couple of hours ago," he remarked, exhaling a cloud of fragrant blue smoke. "She had a lot of unpleasant things to say about you, but, of course, I didn't listen to them. The deuce of it is that she had just come from Scotland Yard, where she had evidently been making things hum." He glanced sharply at Doctor Britling. "She says that Frances has been murdered. Do you think so, too?"

Daniel shook his head. "I do not like to presume murder without a body on which to base the presumption," he replied.

Lord Clavering sighed. "Well, murder or no, it's a dashed awkward situation. Now that the police are in it, the papers will have the whole story, and if Frances has simply disappeared for reasons of her own, the reasons are almost certain to be shady ones. There's bound to be a scandal, whatever happens."

14

Two days later Detective Inspector Evans of the C.I.D. called upon Doctor Britling. A large man with a large red face, he was one of the most thorough and efficient officers of Scotland Yard, and a personal friend of the dapper little police surgeon.

"Workin' on the case of Lady Frances Dorian," he said laconically. "Understand you've nosed over the ground a bit yourself. Queer case, isn't it? What do you make of it?"

"Tut, tut," replied Daniel reprovingly. "I don't expect you to come to me for advice. Why, I was going to ask you that very question myself."

"You're a deep one," said Evans admiringly. "I'm willing to bet you could unravel the tangle right now. But you won't until you're ready—look out I don't beat you to it."

"I'll tell you this," responded Daniel, "you can't do much until you find the maid."

Detective Inspector Evans smiled broadly, and closed one eye knowingly. "You're behind the times, old man," he said, regarding his boots with an extravagant display of interest. "We found her yesterday."

"Good work!" commented Doctor Britling approvingly. "I didn't know you had it in you."

"There's one or two things you don't know," scoffed Evans. "I'll bet you don't know why she dyed her hair."

"*Did* she dye her hair?"

"She did. A beautiful jet black. For the purpose of disguise, or course—they tell me she had rather distinctive golden hair. The Liverpool police found her living in second-rate lodgings in a suburb of the town. Living with a man—a seedy specimen, evidently—under the name of Mister and Missis Agnew. They'd never have stumbled on her, only her landlady became suspicious; had a look through her things, I suppose, and decided that there was something fishy about her lodgers. The landlady informed the police that her woman lodger dyed her hair and was living under a false name. The police investigated, and there you are. She admitted her real identity, of course, when they found a bottle of hair dye and some of her personal effects with her name on them, but the man's a mystery. Says he's a commercial traveller, and travels in soap, but won't say what soap, or for whom. According to the Liverpool Chief of Police, he's no advertisement for his product. The woman's story is that she was dismissed by Lady Frances after a bit of a row, and hasn't seen her mistress since she left on Monday. Doesn't know where her mistress is now. Damned lie, of course. The point is, what can we do?"

"I should think the answer is simple," replied Daniel, "now that you've got your hands on her."

Evans frowned. "Not half so simple as you'd think," he said. "We haven't sufficient evidence to arrest her."

"Arrest her for what?" asked Daniel.

The Scotland Yard man turned a look of disgust upon his host. "Please don't pretend to be dense," he snapped. "For the murder of Lady Frances, of course."

"I shouldn't be too sure that Lady Frances has been murdered," Daniel demurred.

"Good Lord, man," retorted Evans irritably. "You know what happened at that hotel as well as I do. Lady Frances was murdered by her maid, and her body was placed in one of her own trunks. I can't prove it yet, but I know it."

"And where are her trunks?" Daniel inquired with an innocent air.

"I don't know," Evans scowled. "We can't trace 'em."

Doctor Britling leaned forward and tapped his visitor on the knee. "Don't do anything for a day or two," he said. "I'm almost certain that Lady Frances will turn up."

15

The following day proved him to be right. Lady Frances Dorian, whose disappearance had caused such a stir, turned up as abruptly as she had disappeared. Or, rather, she wrote to her cousin.

Lord Clavering came to call on Daniel, bringing the letter, which had been posted from Paris. "DEAR TEDDIE," it began (the first of his Lordship's seven names was Theodore), "Reggie has been making discreet enquiries, and he finds that you and Aunt Agatha are making the dickens of a fuss about your little lost lamb. Sorry to have been the cause of such concern, but, really, you shouldn't be so stupid as to worry about me. I'm perfectly capable of taking care of myself. I've merely been to Paris with Reggie for a last fling before settling down to a dull-as-dishwater married life with my loving but tedious husband-to-be. We had a wonderful time. And now I'm coming back—I'm going down to Grey Gables tomorrow—I suppose I'm to be soundly spanked by my loving relations. Well, let's get it over. Lunch with me at Grey Gables on Wednesday, and tell me what a naughty, wilful girl I am. I'm inviting Aunt Agatha too. Might as well face the music and be done with it. But don't be too hard on me, or I might fly away again with Reggie. Love, "FRANCES"

Lord Clavering coughed dryly as he folded the letter and put it in his pocket. "Frances all over," he commented. "I've been round to Scotland Yard to call off the police. Inspector Evans seemed almost disappointed to find that Frances was alive and well after all."

"He had worked up rather a neat murder charge against her maid," replied Daniel with a smile. "Naturally he's annoyed when his corpse comes to life again."

"I shall have a few things to say to Frances when I see her on Wednesday. Fortunately, the police were able to keep the affair out of the papers. By the way, would it interest you to meet the young woman?"

"It would," said Daniel. "I should think she'd make an interesting study."

"For a brain specialist!" agreed Lord Clavering drily. "Well, drive down with me on Wednesday, won't you?"

"I shall be delighted."

16

Lady Agatha was in an extremely bad temper when she lunched at Grey Gables, her niece's house in Norfolk, on the following Wednesday. For one thing, the destruction of the plan on which she had set her heart—the marriage of her niece with Viscount Ellantree—had been only narrowly averted. For another thing, she had been made to look like a fool by practically shouting murder from the house-tops, and her dignity was very dear to her. Only the presence at the table of Doctor Britling prevented her from abusing her niece all through the meal. As it was, she sat and glowered in silence at the others, nursing her wrath until the family discussion which was to take place directly after lunch.

Lady Frances chattered gaily while luncheon was in progress. From her manner it appeared that she had not a care in the world. She was at her best, and at her best she was beautiful.

During luncheon the butler informed Lady Frances that the foreman in charge of the building operations, which were still going on in the house and grounds, would like to speak to her. He was shown into the room while they were lingering over their coffee.

"Just wanted to say, y'r ladyship, that no one had better go near the stables this afternoon," he said, twisting his hat between two work-roughened. "We've had to stop work there for the present while we're waiting on materials coming from Norwhich, and the new roof timbers are practically unsupported.

If anyone was to go blundering in, your ladyship, there might be a nasty accident."

"Very well, Harker," agreed Lady Frances. "I'll give instructions that no one is to go near the stables."

17

After luncheon, while the family conference was in session, Doctor Britling went for a stroll in the grounds. Although the place was in the hands of gangs of workmen, the garden, jealously guarded by her ladyship's gardeners, was quite lovely. Exploring what appeared to be an enchanted path, he came upon a bridge across a little stream which danced in a succession of miniature waterfalls over boulders cunningly placed in its bed. One of the gardeners, a short, stockily-built individual with a round red face, and a beard which fringed his chin and jaws, was standing on the bridge, smoking a short clay pipe and spitting into the water. He put his pipe away hastily when Doctor Britling approached, but Daniel insisted on him lighting it again. The two stood together on the bridge, smoking and commenting on the weather, the neighbourhood, and the garden.

"'Tis a good garden, zur," said the rustic, spitting reflectively. "But it doan't get a chance with th' present owner. 'Tis time and work that makes a garden, an' leavin' things alone, not pullin' them up to see how they're growin'. 'Er ladyship is queer in 'er ways. She don't understand gardens. Allus wantin' to change things about, in season and out. Shiftin' flower-beds about, as though they was on wheels. Y'see that there sun-house, zur" —he pointed a stubby finger— "believe it or not, that there sun-house was in a good half-dozen places before 'er ladyship was suited. And like as not she'll want it moved again tomorrow."

"A changeable disposition, evidently?" said Daniel agreeably.

"Changeable as the wind, zur," replied the gardener. "Why, when the workmen fust came she wanted th' old stables turned into a garage. An' bless me if she didn't change 'er mind afore they war half-finished an' decided that she wanted what she called a guest'ouse there instead." He spat. "You'll have noticed a sundial in the lower garden, zur? There weren't no sundial there a week ago—even a couple of days ago. Th' workmen were makin' a lily-pond there, accordin' to 'er ladyship's express instructions, but the very day arter she come home she sent for the foreman erly in the morning an' said she'd changed 'er mind. 'Fill that gurt hole in,' ses she, 'an' put me a sundial there instead.' No use arguin', 'ee 'ad to do it. Durn sight easier job fillin' it in than diggin' it, the men said, zur. Didn't seems that th' hole was half as deep as when they'd left it th' night before."

The gardener had other tales to tell about Lady Frances, her wilfulness and eccentricity, but Daniel paid little attention to him. Soon he tipped him half a crown and strolled slowly up to the house.

18

Lady Frances came upon him on the terrace outside the house half an hour later. He was leaning upon the brickwork of the terrace, smoking a cigar, with his eyes fixed on the sundial in the centre of the lawn.

"You're looking very solemn, Doctor Britling," said Lady Frances gaily. "A penny for your thoughts!"

Doctor Britling replied without looking up. "I was thinking that I should like to investigate under your sundial, Lady Frances."

A slim white hand flew to her throat, and an involuntary

gasp escaped her. "What—what on earth do you mean?" she demanded.

He turned and regarded her gravely. "It really isn't worthwhile to pretend to me," he said. "I know what is hidden under the sundial."

Lady Frances looked swiftly about her. There was no one else in sight. She grasped Doctor Britling's arm with painful force. "What do you mean?" she asked again, searching his face with her eyes.

"If I must put into words," replied Daniel with a sigh, "I mean a wardrobe trunk containing the dead body of your maid."

With a shuddering cry, Lady Frances groped her way to one of the wicker chairs which stood on the terrace and sat down limply.

There was nothing that Daniel could say. He turned away and resumed his quiet inspection of the lawn to allow her time to regain her self-possession. For some minutes Lady Frances sat huddled-up in the wicker chair, fighting for control of herself. Her slender body was shaken by spasms of shivering, and her breath came in long gasps, like the sobs of a frightened child. Gradually, however, she fought down the hysterical terror which possessed her. She sat up and dabbed at her face with a tiny lace handkerchief, then powdered her nose. When she spoke, her voice was almost calm. "I didn't mean to—kill her," she said.

"I know," Daniel replied simply. "It was an accident."

She stared at him with wonder in her eyes. "Do you know, you are rather a remarkable little man," she said. "I almost believe you know exactly what happened."

"I only wish I didn't," responded Daniel. "It isn't pleasant knowledge to share with a woman, Lady Frances."

"With a murderess, Doctor Britling," she said bitterly.

He shook his head. "You didn't intend to kill her."

"God knows I didn't," whispered Lady Frances in a hushed

voice. "We quarrelled, and, losing my temper, I struck her. In falling she hit her head violently against a corner of the table. She slipped to the floor and lay quite still. It was a terrible shock to me when I realised that she was dead. I hadn't meant to hurt her. She drove me to it. She attempted to blackmail me by threatening to tell my fiancé some things she knew about me—discreditable things."

"Within half an hour of arriving at the hotel," said Doctor Britling, "I knew that either you or your maid had been killed in that room. Which one, was the problem. It solved itself when I saw the corner of the table. No maid would ever use warm water and soap to remove a stain on a polished table. She would know it would also remove the polish. But you weren't likely to think of that. I knew, of course, that the killing was accidental. The fact that you ran to the telephone immediately and called for help proved that. Then, with the telephone in your hand, you realised what would happen, that the police would be called in and that the publicity which would result would damn you for ever in the eyes of the world. Until then you had frankly enjoyed publicity, but you realised that for a mistress to kill her maid, no matter how unintentionally, would make a particularly unsavoury story, one that you could never survive. Perhaps you were afraid that your story would not be accepted—that you would be charged with murder. So, when the telephone-clerk asked you if anything was wrong, you made up an excuse on the spur of the moment, and hung up the receiver.

"The body on the floor was bleeding badly from the head. You fetched a bath-towel and swathed the head in it, then began to plan some way out of the mess you were in. You realised that for your maid to disappear then, even if you were able to dispose of the body, would start enquiries which could only have one result. But if she could be made to disappear a week or so later, a hundred miles away, no one would be likely to connect her disappearance with you, her former mistress. How was it to be done? That was the problem. You decided to impersonate her.

"Among your luggage was a large wardrobe trunk, absolutely air-tight, in which the body could be hidden for weeks, if need be, without arousing suspicion. To make room for the body, you smashed up the wooden partitions which divided one side of the trunk and burned them in the fireplace in your room. After cutting off some of her golden hair, and removing her uniform dress, you placed your maid's body in the trunk and locked it securely. The blood on the table and on the carpet you mopped up with warm water and soap. Fortunately for you, the carpet was red, and did not show the stains.

"Having removed the obvious evidence of what had happened," continued Daniel, "you telephoned to the office, said that you had been called to town and were giving up your suite, and asked for your bill to be sent up. Then you hurriedly put on your maid's dress and a tight little hat. You crammed all your own hair into the hat, and over each ear you put a lock of your maid's hair. Then it was only necessary for you to make up your face a little differently, and to the casual glance you were not Lady Frances Dorian, but her ladyship's maid. When the telephone-clerk came with your bill you snatched up an armful of clothing, which aided your disguise. The young man is a bit of a snob, and didn't spare you a second glance. Having disposed of that part of the plan, you packed your things. It wasn't easy to cram the clothes which should have been in the wardrobe trunk into your other luggage. You crushed in everything you could, and still several of your heavier garments were left.

"On one or two occasions you had spent a week-end with Mr. Caffrey at the Midway Hotel in Bloomsbury, under the names of Mr. and Mrs. Sims, so you addressed the labels so that they would be forwarded there by the luggage-porter. After a careful survey of the room to make sure that you had left no damning evidence of what had happened, you made your way cautiously to your maid's room, arriving there without being seen. When you were packing her suitcase, a girl passed the door, and for a moment your heart must have been in your mouth, but luck was with you. The girl was a newcomer to the hotel, who had only seen your main once or twice, and never before at close quarters. It wasn't difficult for you to play your part so that she didn't suspect your identity.

"It wasn't safe to go downstairs in the servants' lift, for you might have been recognised, so you walked down and passed the porter at the tradesman's entrance with your head averted. A wire summoned Caffrey to meet you at Victoria, and when you told him what had happened, he agreed to help you. He collected your luggage from the Midway Hotel, and disposed of the wardrobe trunk in some way."

"He put it on the rear seat of his Bentley," said Lady Frances tonelessly. "And left the car in his private lockup at the West End Garage.

"I see. The pair of you went to Liverpool in disguise and obtained rooms in a second-rate lodging house under the names of Mr. and Mrs. Agnew. But it was necessary that the landlady should later be able to identify her lodger as Sadie Harper, Lady Frances Dorian's former maid, so you left your maid's clothes, marked with her name, and her letters lying about so that she would see them. You couldn't wear a hat all the time, so you bought a bottle of black hair-dye, which would later account for the 'change in colour' of 'Sadie Harper's' hair.

"The one thing that you had failed to take into consideration, however, was that in making it appear that your maid had left the Brighton hotel alive, you had also made it appear that you yourself had not. That unforeseen factor almost upset your plan, for you came very near to being arrested for murdering yourself! The police traced Sadie Harper (as they thought) to Liverpool, owing to the suspicions you had aroused in your landlady's mind. They didn't arrest you, however, for they weren't quite sure of their ground.

"You realised that Lady Frances must appear as soon as possible, so you wrote a letter to Lord Clavering and probably sent it in another envelope to a friend in Paris, who posted it there. Lord Clavering called off the police, and you and Caffrey went to London, collected your trunk, and brought it here. The workmen were digging a large hole on the lawn to make a lily-pond, and the night you arrived you and Caffrey carried the trunk to the hole, threw it in, and shovelled in enough earth to cover it. Then, early the following morning, before the workmen had started the day's work, you went to the foreman and told him that you had changed your mind and wanted a sundial on the lawn instead. You have a reputation for wilfulness and eccentricity, so your change of mind caused very little comment. The workmen filled the hole, and when several feet of soil and the brick foundation of the sundial covered up the body of Sadie Harper you felt that you were safe."

"Yes," said Lady Frances in a dull, hopeless tone. "I thought I was safe."

Her eyes wandered across the lawn to the sundial which marked the last resting-place of Sadie Harper. "What are you going to do?" she asked.

Doctor Britling shrugged his shoulders. "Nothing," he replied. "I'm going to leave the solution of the problem to you. I should suggest that you leave the country and lead a new life under a new name. A life of atonement."

Their eyes met, and a look of understanding passed between them.

"Thank you," she said, rising slowly to her feet. "I will do my best to atone."

It was a warm day, but she shivered slightly.

19

The atmosphere at teatime was scarcely less chilling than it had been at luncheon. Lady Agatha was still on her high horse, and her acid comments dried up the sporadic attempts at conversation that were made by Doctor Britling and Lord Clavering. Lady Frances was absent from the meal, and her absence incensed her aunt, who took it as a personal insult.

"Perhaps Frances didn't hear the gong," Lord Clavering suggested mildly.

"Frances hears what she wishes to hear, no more and no less," was the frigid rejoiner.

While Lady Agatha was pouring out her third cup of tea, there was a startling crash. Her hand shook, and she almost dropped the teapot.

"What on earth was that?" she gasped.

"It came from the garden, I think," said Daniel, hurrying through the French windows to the terrace outside.

He saw a workman running across the lawn. "Summat's up at th' stables," the man cried, halting for a moment.

With Lord Clavering at his heels, Daniel raced as fast as his short legs could carry him in the direction of the stables. They found a crowd of labourers hauling bricks and timber from the interior. The foreman came up to them with his face as white as a sheet.

"I warned her, your Lordship," he said. "You heard me warn her."

"What has happened?" demanded the bewildered peer.

The foreman passed a shaky hand over his eyes. "It's Lady Frances," he replied. "The whole roof's come down on top of her. I told her the supports weren't safe."

Daniel stepped over the debris into the stables. The workmen had cleared away the largest of the fallen timbers, and exposed the limp body of Lady Frances Dorian. The little police surgeon knelt down and took her wrist. After a few moments he rose, to find Lord Clavering eyeing him apprehensively.

"She's dead," he said.

"Good God!" cried Lord Clavering. "What a terrible end for a woman like Frances!"

"I warned her," the foreman was repeating in a trembling voice. "You heard me warn her."

"Yes, you warned her," said Daniel gently, and for a moment, tears glistened in his eyes.

THE END

SIX WERE TO DIE

Dr. Britling receives a Package

IN THE ACT of flicking dust from the top picture frame, Miss Eunice Britling paused with a feather duster in her hand, and listened. A vaguely familiar, faintly unpleasant noise was disturbing the tranquillity of the little flat in Orchard Street which Miss Britling shared with her brother. High above the domestic clatter of china and cutlery from the kitchen, high above the subdued hum of traffic from Oxford Street, it rose and fell, monotonously, unmelodious, rising like a bird—a rather clumsy bird—soaring toward the sky; dropping to the faintest of bass mutters. With it mingled the splashing and gurgling of water.

Miss Britling frowned. She had identified the noise. Her brother was singing in the bath.

She was already annoyed with Daniel. He had remained drowsily in bed beyond his usual hour for rising, keeping breakfast late and retarding the other work of the household. He had answered brusquely—and very much to the point— when his sister had remonstrated with him. It was adding insult to injury that he should cheerfully sing and splash in his bath.

Pursing her lips, she went into the tiny hall of the flat and knocked imperatively on the bathroom door.

"Hullo?" responded Daniel Britling's voice.

"That atrocious row is giving me a headache," said Miss Britling sharply, "and you're keeping breakfast late."

The singing and splashing ceased for a moment.

"Can't hear you!" called Daniel.

"I said, YOU'RE KEEPING BREAKFAST LATE!"

"Oh!" More splashing. "Shan't be a minute!" shouted Daniel cheerfully.

There came the corroborative sound of the bathwater gurgling away. Miss Britling returned to her feather duster, muttering something—not quite beneath her breath.

In a few minutes Daniel Britling, looking pink, fresh and well-groomed, entered the living-room briskly and sat down to the breakfast table. "Good morning," he said pleasantly.

"Huh!" was Miss Britling's ungracious reply.

Breakfast was eaten in grim silence on Miss Britling's part, and with hearty appetite on the part of her brother. Daniel read his morning paper throughout the meal—a habit of which his sister had strived unavailingly to break him.

Although they were twins, and nearer to sixty than either of them cared to acknowledge, she persisted regarding her brother as a mischievous child who required constant watching and frequent scolding. She had been extremely annoyed when he tired of his quiet practice and became a police surgeon, and was still more annoyed by his inability to attend strictly to the routine duties of his calling, and his persistence in doing what he termed a 'little sleuthing' on his own when called to the scene of a crime.

Divisional Surgeon Daniel Britling was a small man with an exceedingly large head. Disgruntled Scotland Yard officials, who were forced to concede him credit for astuteness in criminal investigation (which was *not* part of his professional duties), sometimes made pointed remarks about the size of his head, which they attributed to conceit. Less prejudiced officials had been heard to admit that when Daniel put his interfering finger into the pie of criminal detection, he not infrequently pulled out the plum that the detective in charge had groped for in vain. This did not enhance his popularity with certain of his colleagues.

It was his belief that the detection of crime was a matter for psychologists rather than policemen. Criminology was his hobby and almost his profession.

Nothing of his association with crime and the police was suggested by his appearance. He was always meticulously dressed in well-cut dark clothes and, outdoors, wore a pearl grey hat at a jaunty angle on his head. His Van Dyke beard was trimmed almost daily, and his moustache was graded to a nicety on both sides of his upper lip. Lines of humour radiated from the corners of his shrewd grey eyes.

Towards the end of the meal, Daniel looked to find his sister's eyes sternly focussed upon him.

"A parcel arrived for you this morning," she said stiffly.

"Then why haven't I received it?"

"Because you had already kept breakfast waiting long enough."

"But it may be important!" Daniel protested.

Miss Britling smiled scornfully. "If it is something in your line, Daniel Britling, it will more messy than important," she retorted, pursing her lips. "Nothing interests you but a sordid, unpleasant murder!"

"Art is never sordid," said Daniel. "And murder is one of the arts."

A single crushing syllable was Miss Britling's only reply. She swept out of the room and returned in a few minutes with a brown paper parcel about three inches in area, and two inches deep, which she placed on the table at her brother's elbow. She resumed to her own chair again, although she had finished her breakfast and had urgent duties perform. Although she would not for worlds have admitted it, she was filled with lively curiosity regarding the contents of the parcel and was eager to see it opened. To her intense annoyance, Daniel pushed it aside without as much as a glance at the label, and crossing the pleasant living room to a humidor which stood in a corner, selected his first cigar of the day.

With precious care he rolled the cigar between his long, thin fingers, placing it to his ear to listen to something or other (Miss Britling never knew what), to his nose to sample the rich aroma of the choice leaf; pierced the end cautiously, and lit it, holding the match so that the flame did not come in direct contact with the cigar. This morning, it seemed to Miss Britling, he was even more finicking than usual in the details of this ceremony. She watched each part of the ritual with mounting exasperation.

When the cigar was drawing to his satisfaction, Daniel exhaled a cloud of fragrant blue smoke. Still ignoring the parcel, he dropped into a comfortable armchair beside the fire and buried himself in the pages of his morning newspaper.

Miss Britling's curiosity had now reached fever pitch. Discarding all pretence of indifference, she said: "Aren't you going to open it?"

Daniel looked at her with raised eyebrows over the top of his paper.

"The parcel!" she snapped. "Aren't you going to open it?"

Daniel folded his paper carefully, and laid it aside. "The parcel," he repeated. "I had almost forgotten it."

Was his sister mistaken, or did his grey eyes twinkle with malicious amusement?

The dapper little police surgeon picked up the parcel and examined it carefully before opening it. The address was crudely lettered in block capitals on both sides, and the warning, 'Fragile. Handle with care' was inscribed in large letters in two places.

There were four stout knots in the string which secured the parcel, and Daniel untied each of them laboriously while Miss Britling's fingers itched to seize scissors and cut them quickly. Doctor Britling was not normally the kind of man who wastes time in order to save a small piece of string, but this morning he was thoroughly enjoying the exasperated curiosity which was consuming his twin sister.

To Miss Britling it seemed to be an endless age before the wrapping paper was removed, revealing a neat cardboard box beneath. This was fastened by strips of gummed paper. An ominous glint in his sister's eyes warned Daniel to slit the lid open with a knife rather than annoy her by further delay.

The first thing which met his eyes when he removed the lid was a small square envelope on which a few words were typewritten. He lifted it out and read the following sentence: "You are warned to read this letter before investigating further!"

Daniel's eyebrows went up and a puzzled look came into his eyes. He tore the envelope open, and extracted the single sheet of notepaper which it contained.

"Dear Doctor Britling," commenced the typewritten letter, "the small ivory casket which is enclosed contains a rubber ball filled with cyanide gas. When the lid is opened, a simple but ingenious mechanical device squeezes the ball and expels the gas through a spraying nozzle which faces the aperture. I need not remind a physician of your standing of the deadly properties of cyanide gas. If I had not warned you of the contents of the casket you would now be a dead man. I send you this grim souvenir as a warning. This morning one Jubal Straust will call upon you and request your aid on behalf of himself and five associates. Take my advice and do not listen to him. You are not a professional detective, and there is no reason why you should allow yourself to be drawn into an affair which is none of your concern, and which would only end disastrously for you. If you do not accept my advice, you will receive no warning with the next deadly message which is sent to you. You will die, swiftly and suddenly, without knowing from what quarter death has come."

The letter was unsigned. Daniel re-read it slowly, then folded it and placed it in his inside breast pocket. His expression as he did so was thoughtful. The message was grim, bizarre, unreal— but it carried conviction. It did not read like the ravings of an unbalanced mind. If Daniel was not mistaken, the writer meant exactly what he had written.

It was typical of Daniel Britling that no trace of concern betrayed itself in his facial expression. There was not the slightest strain of cowardice in the little police surgeon's composition.

Suddenly he wheeled, uttering a startled exclamation. Miss Britling had been unable to restrain her curiosity. She had picked the ivory casket which the cardboard box contained, and was examining it with delighted interest.

"How beautiful!" she breathed rapturously, feasting her eyes on the carving with which it was ornamented.

"Eunice!" cried Daniel sharply. "Put it down at once!"

With an inarticulate sound expressive of extreme indignation, Miss Britling replaced the casket on the table. "How dare you speak to me like that!" she retorted.

"My dear Eunice," said Doctor Britling more gently, "I have no wish to lose you just yet—and I have every reason to believe that sudden death is contained in that pretty little ornament!"

Miss Britling stared at her brother. "Nonsense!" she exclaimed scornfully. "Too much dabbling in crime is going to your brain, Daniel!"

Her brother shrugged his shoulders. "You were complaining the other day that we require a new mousetrap," he remarked. "You said, if I remember rightly, that our present one is a cumbersome affair which captures mice alive, thus presenting the twin problems of execution and disposal. Do you suppose there will be a mouse in that trap this morning?"

"I don't for a moment doubt it," snapped Miss Britling. "The place is overrun with them."

"In that case," said Daniel, picking up the casket, "I shall try a little experiment."

He led the way to the kitchen, where the astonished maidservant, in response his request, produced a large wire contraption which contained a small and bewildered mouse. Opening the kitchen window, Daniel placed the trap on the window sill, and beside it laid the ivory casket. He gingerly unfastened the small gold catch which secured the lid of the casket.

Miss Britling watched over his shoulder with the disapproving eyes of a parent who is giving her child plenty of rope, but will shortly pull him up with a jerk. The mouse began to scuttle apprehensively back and forward along the wire mesh floor of its prison.

Rummaging in a drawer, Daniel found a long thin strip of metal. He inserted one end of it beneath the lid of the ivory casket, taking care not to raise the lid sufficiently to set the deadly device inside in motion, and placed the other end on the window sill; then closed the window suddenly. Levered upwards by the strip of metal, the lid of the casket flew open—and the mouse which had been running backwards and forward dropped in its tracks.

Miss Britling stared from the deflated rubber ball which the casket contained to the wire trap in which lay the body the dead mouse. She was hardly able to believe that its life could have been snuffed out with such breath-taking suddenness.

"Well!" she gasped. "Well!"

"H'm," muttered Daniel reflectively, stroking his chin.

It was obvious that the warning letter was to be taken seriously!

Jubal Straust Explains the Situation

JUBAL STRAUST LEANED forward in his chair and handed a pink slip of paper to Doctor Britling.

"Does that interest you?" he asked, watching Daniel's face shrewdly.

Daniel glanced at it casually. It was a cheque for five hundred pounds. He raised his eyebrows slightly, and handed it back. "No," he said calmly, "I'm afraid it doesn't."

Jubal stared. People who displayed such calm indifference to money were rare in his experience.

"You say that you have a case for me," continued Daniel blandly. "My reply is that I am not a detective. Your personal cheque for ten times as much would not buy my services. But an anonymous person has threatened me with death if I aid you. I don't like to be threatened. I regard it as challenge. Therefore, Mr. Straust, although I am completely indifferent to your money, I am prepared to listen to whatever you have to say."

He sat back in his chair with his fingertips pressed together and waited for his visitor to explain his errand.

Jubal brought out large silk handkerchief and mopped his brow with it. "The cunning devil!" he muttered. "How the dickens did he know I was coming to consult you? Damn him—he's in touch with every move we make!" He shot a curious glance at Doctor Britling. "And in spite of his threat, you're prepared to listen to me?"

"Not in spite of it," corrected Daniel. "Because of it."

That was the literal truth. Since he had received the warning letter and the casket with its deadly contents, Daniel had spent some time investigating the personal history of Jubal Straust. He had decided that any harm which came to that prominent young financier would be no less than his just desserts. Nothing would have persuaded him to consider any offer that Jubal Straust might be prepared to make, had it not been for that threatening letter. Daniel did not intend to be intimidated.

Jubal Straust was the cleverest young man in London—in the opinion of Jubal Straust. In the opinion of those who had transacted business with him, he was one of the crookedest members the London Stock Exchange. And even if his own estimate of his cleverness is not accepted it must be admitted that he was wily enough to keep on the right side of the law.

Pretty women found him a fool. For the most trivial of favours—a kiss in the dark; the brief pressure of a slim, warm hand; the veiled promise of delights to come—he was prepared to pay with diamonds and pearls. Women who valued their honour lightly sold it at top price to Jubal Straust. He was, as Gideon Levison once remarked, the answer to a chorus girl's prayer.

Putty in the hands of pretty women, he was like stone to the rest of the world. In his luxurious offices in Throgmorton Street he was like a large, suave spider, spinning endless webs to trap the unwary; like a spider he devoured his financial victims without mercy. At the age of thirty-five he had accumulated over half a million pounds, and the contempt with which he was regarded even by his fellow financiers testified to the means whereby he had acquired it.

His forehead seemed enormously high, largely because he was bald from the brow to the crown of his head; a large, aquiline nose divided his plump face sharply; his thick lips were red and sensual, and, when he was with women or thinking of them, his lower lip hung open and his mouth was unpleasantly moist. He was tall and heavily built, but soft; layers of fat instead of muscle gave him an impressive girth. The curling brown hair on his temples was shot with silver threads.

His clothes were made in Savile Row; his shoes cost five guineas a pair; his cigarettes were Turkish, at a fabulous sum a hundred. Apart from the pursuit of women and the enjoyment of food, his only recreation was the amassing of money, which was his hobby and religion as well as his profession.

Jubal hitched his exquisitely-cut silver grey trousers, and producing an enamelled cigarette case, selected and lit a cigarette without the formality of asking permission. Doctor Britling observed that the hand which held the platinum cigarette lighter was trembling slightly. There were other indications of the visitor's agitation—a certain uneasiness in his dark eyes, the slight dampness of his forehead on a particularly cool afternoon, the twitching of a nerve beneath one of his eyes. It was apparent that, for all his self-possession, Mr. Jubal Straust was in a blue funk about something.

"You're supposed to be one of the cleverest criminologists in the country, Doctor," he said. "That's why I'm here. I have need of such a man." From his cigarette case he produced a folded slip of paper. Spreading it flat, he handed it to Daniel. "What do you think of that?" he asked.

Doctor Britling examined it with interest. On the paper was drawn two crosses, one above the other, and a crude representation a skull and crossbones.

"As a sample of art," he replied, "atrocious. As an attempt at intimidation, childish."

Jubal blew out cloud of steel-blue smoke, watching Daniel through half-shut eyes. "What would you say if I told you that five of the shrewdest financiers in the country were thoroughly alarmed upon receiving a paper like that?"

"I should say that financiers are easily frightened," responded Daniel thoughtfully. "Or, that they had an intimate knowledge of the man who sent the papers."

Jubal nodded. "It is apparent, Doctor, that you know something about human nature." He glanced at his watch. "Three o'clock," he remarked.

From a waistcoat pocket he produced a glass vial of white tablets and put one of them in his mouth. "I am a martyr to indigestion," he explained, replacing the vial. "I have to take one of these little tablets every hour."

Daniel thought, but did not say, that all the medical preparations in the world would not cure the financier's jangled digestive organs as long as he continued to stuff himself with rich food several times day.

"Six of us received these papers," said Jubal slowly. "My father, Israel Straust, of the Fortunatus Investment Trust Company; Gideon Levison, of Levison & Stern, the bankers; Mark Annerley, the theatrical promoter, and his wife; Hubert Quail, the diamond merchant, and myself. I am not authorised to go into details with you now, but we cherish no illusions regarding the meaning of these crude drawings. They are a definite threat of murder. I, Doctor, am to be the first to die!"

There was a faint tremor in his oily voice which betrayed the emotional stress under which he was labouring. "We received these warnings a week ago, and not one of us doubted that they were intended seriously. A clever and unscrupulous man, Doctor Britling, intends to kill each one of us. We gathered immediately at my father's country house near Leighton Buzzard to decide what steps to take. We are all living there now and the place is guarded like a fortress. But that is not enough. The man who intends to kill us is sufficiently clever to penetrate any system of defence. We must fight him, not with brawn, but with brains. We are important men, Doctor Britling. We believe in buying the best brains available for whatever purpose we may require them. My father has heard of you, and insisted that your services should be secured. We are prepared to pay you whatever you ask if you will help us to frustrate the villain who has threatened us."

Again, he wiped his forehead with a large expanse of silk handkerchief.

"Last night I received a further message," he said shakily. "It was lying on my bed. It said simply: 'You die at five o'clock tomorrow evening.'"

His composure deserted him, and he stared wide-eyed at Doctor Britling, his face contorted with sudden spasm of fear. "To die at five o'clock this evening!" he repeated hoarsely. "Two hours from now! It is terrible that such things can be possible in a civilised country!"

Daniel watched the financier keenly through half-closed eyes. His fingertips were still pressed together like the fingers of a praying child. His face was expressionless as a mask. "You believe, then, that this—this melodramatic villain will make good his threat!"

Jubal shook his head—but fear lurked in his eyes. "No, I don't," he said tonelessly. "If did I should go mad. I can't believe it possible. I am armed, and at five o clock I shall be in my car, with an armed bodyguard in the rear seat, returning to father's house. How can I be killed in such circumstances? And yet, the uncertainty is fraying my nerves. He will try—l have no doubt of that—and if it is possible to succeed, he is clever enough to do it."

He leaned forward with a strained expression on his face. His fingers were restlessly tying themselves in knots.

"I have tried to think how it can be done," he muttered, his voice sinking to a hoarse whisper. "That is why I delayed coming here until this afternoon; so that by five o'clock I shall be on the return journey. My car is fast—there are few cars that could hope to overtake it on the road. It would be impossible for anyone standing by the roadside to aim an effective shot at me. Every detail of the mechanism has been thoroughly examined and overhauled, so a sudden failure of the brakes or steering gear is out of the question. How is it possible to kill in such circumstances?"

"A time bomb," suggested Daniel.

"I thought off that. It is out of the question. Every inch of the car has been carefully examined."

Daniel rose and paced the room with short, jerky strides. "Why come to me," he demanded suddenly. "Why not go to Scotland Yard?"

"Because we have no faith in the ability of Scotland Yard to save us," replied Jubal simply. "We must rely upon our brains— and on yours."

"Who is the man who has threatened you?"

"I'm sorry, but I've told you all I can for the present," said Jubal. "If you will return with me to my father's house you will learn all there is to know, but I can't tell you anything else without the agreement of my associates."

Daniel looked thoughtful. "If I go, it must be clearly understood that I am at liberty to withdraw later, if I choose to do so," he stipulated.

"I agree," responded Jubal eagerly. "Will you come?"

Daniel hesitated for a moment, but he had already half-formed his decision. He was completely indifferent to the fate of Jubal Straust and his fellow financiers—but the threatening letter he had received had roused his curiosity, and his fighting spirit. It was a challenge which he was unable to ignore.

"I will come," he agreed at last.

"Good!" exclaimed Jubal.

There were some things to be arranged before Doctor Britling could accompany the financier. It might be some days before he would return, so it was necessary for him to telephone the young doctor who attended to his duties while he was out of town and arrange for his services in case of necessity. Daniel made a clean breast of the whole story to his sister (he had learned from experience that it was not wise to attempt to deceive her) and listened patiently to her disapproving comments and dark forebodings. Eunice was of the opinion that the death of five financiers would do the world no harm—she had once lost three hundred pounds in a bogus company—and that her brother would certainly get into trouble once he was out of her sight.

It was four o'clock before Daniel seated himself beside Jubal Straust in the front seat of the financier's sleek Hispano-Suiza and the car moved off up Orchard Street. There was a large man in the rear seat of the car who bore the unmistakable stamp of an ex-prize-fighter, and who kept one hand in a jacket pocket which bulged ominously.

As they glided northward along Baker Street, Jubal glanced at his wristwatch and put another white tablet in his mouth.

That the financier's imported car was speedy was proved when they were beyond the surging traffic. Jubal stood upon the accelerator, and the car ate up the road, the speedometer needle quivering between sixty and seventy miles an hour. At that speed, the huge car was steady as a rock. It held the road snugly, its engine purring like a contented cat.

Daniel watched the hedges flying past, and the continuous succession of telegraph posts which seemed to melt into each other. In spite of the speed at which they were travelling, he felt no uneasiness. It was apparent that Jubal Straust was an excellent driver.

Within an hour they were less than five miles from Leighton Buzzard. Jubal glanced at his watch and turned a triumphant smile towards the dapper little police surgeon.

"Five o'clock," he declared. "And I am still alive!"

His eyes travelled from one side of the road to the other, then straight ahead, looking for the least threat of danger. The road was deserted as far as the eye could see. It appeared that Jubal Straust had escaped the fate which had menaced him!

Letting the speed of the car drop to a mere forty miles an hour, Jubal put one hand in his waistcoat pocket and produced the vial of indigestion tablets. He shook one of them out on his palm and conveyed it to his mouth.

As he did so, his face was twisted with a spasm of pain, and the vial dropped from his fingers, scattering the tablets over the floor of the car. His body writhed in awful agony. With a groan he twisted sideways on the seat, the steering wheel jerked out of his unresisting fingers, and the car swerved across the road and skidded into a telegraph pole.

Something hit Doctor Britling's head with terrific force, then everything went black.

Doctor Britling Arrives at the Mansion

THE JADE CLOCK on the mantelpiece of the billiard room chimed five times, and the short, burly man who was in the act of aiming for a simple cannon, miscued and sent the spot ball ricocheting from cushion to cushion. The light which flooded the green table from three powerful shaded bulbs revealed his face, grey in complexion and twitching with anxiety. A round face, heavily fleshed, with the full cheeks of a baby—and the unpleasant little eyes of a rat. Although he appeared to be no more than forty, he was completely bald except for a fringe of sandy-coloured hair above his ears and at the base of his skull. He uttered an oath as he turned from the table and flashed a resentful glance at the chiming clock.

"Nerves, my dear Annerley," drawled the other player, detaching himself from the shadows which fringed the lighted table.

His head and shoulders came into the oblong splash of light as he carefully sighted a difficult in-off-the-red along his polished cue. He was apparently about the same age as his opponent, but in appearance presented a striking contrast. He had a long, lean face, pale in complexion, topped with dark hair brushed straight back from the forehead and streaked with silver at the temples. Beneath his high forehead gleamed two large dark eyes, utterly inscrutable in expression.

There was a faint click as ivory met ivory and the plain ball ran smoothly to a pocket and dropped in. The red ball rolled slowly to within a few inches of the spot ball, leaving position for a series of cannons of which the player proceeded to take full advantage.

"It's five o'clock," said Annerley huskily.

His opponent took careful aim for his next stroke before

replying. "Is it?" he murmured indifferently, as the red ball snapped into a pocket.

Annerley favoured him with a resentful look, then crossed the room to a table by the closely curtained-windows, on which stood a decanter of brandy, a soda-syphon and two glasses. His opponent looked up sharply at the sound of liquid gurgling into a tall glass.

"I shouldn't have any more if I were you."

Annerley's face gleamed white in the shadow. "Good God, Levison, I'd go mad if I didn't," he declared shakily. His head went back and three fingers of undiluted brandy trickled down his throat.

Gideon Levison shrugged his shoulders and dropped his eyes to the green cloth. Annerley poured himself another drink and came back to the brightly lighted table with a glass of amber liquid in his hand.

"Jubal should be back soon," he said, his voice struggling for calmness.

"If he's coming back," said Levison suavely, his dark eyes carefully studying the difficult shot he was about to attempt.

Mark Annerley's hand shook and a drop of brandy splashed on the green cloth. "You—you don't think he—he's—dead—already?"

"The warning he received last night said five o'clock," Gideon reminded him calmly.

"But...but..." Annerley's voice trailed away to a whisper, and his eyes flickered to the white face of the clock, which registered four minutes past five.

Gideon Levison straightened up and looked contemptuously at the other man across the bright expanse of green. "Did you ever know Marckheim to say a thing he didn't mean?"

"No—o—o."

"Then you can be certain that at five o'clock he made an attempt at least to kill Jubal. Knowing both Marckheim and Jubal as I do, I should be prepared to bet that the attempt was successful. It would not be a difficult matter to kill Jubal. He has such an exaggerated opinion of his own cleverness that he would be easily trapped by the simple, the obvious. If Markheim has kept his word, I shall expect to learn that he killed Jubal by some staggeringly simple method that our clever young friend hadn't for a moment expected."

Annerley drained off the brandy, and his trembling fingers reached out to put the glass on the mantelpiece. It slipped out of his hand, and fell with a crash to the fireplace. He jumped nervously at the sound.

Gideon Levison chuckled. "Why do you suppose Marckheim chose Jubal as his first victim? —Because he knew he could kill him. He even named a definite hour, to show how simple it was. The idea, of course, was to put the wind up the rest of us. He has evidently succeeded as far as you are concerned."

As he bent over the table again there was a twinkle of malicious amusement in his eyes. "No one is so easy to kill, my dear Annerley," he purred, "as the man who is already frightened to death!"

The other moistened his dry lips nervously. "Gideon, you can't really believe that Marckheim means to go through with this—this wholesale murder," he whispered huskily. "He—can't, I tell you; he can't! Why, he'll hang if he does!"

"Do you suppose that will worry him?" retorted Levison. "Revenge is sweet, and he'll go for it, no matter what the consequences may be. I said when the first warnings came that he'd do his best to kill us to the last man. I still believe that. I don't expect that many of us will be alive a week from today."

He laughed at the frightened expression on Annerley's face. "Cheer up, Mark," he scoffed. "You'll be the last to die."

"You really think so?" muttered Annerley hopefully. "Why?"

Levison took careful aim at the red pot before replying. "Because you're in a blue funk, he murmured mockingly. "He'll leave you to the last to enjoy you're terrified squirming as the rest of us die and your turn comes nearer!"

Annerley snarled a retort through his clenched teeth. The other laughed lightly, and stooped to play a thin cannon.

For a few minutes there was no sound in the room but the clicking of ivories as Levison added points to his break, amassing a respectable score. Annerley leaned against the mantelpiece with a scowl on his heavy-jowled face.

Suddenly the door was thrown open and a large man hurried into the room. Annerley straightened up abruptly, with a startled exclamation. The newcomer laughed harshly.

"Got the wind up?" he demanded scornfully.

Striding across the room, he threw back the heavy curtains which masked the French windows, admitting a flood of sunshine which made the table lights look feeble by comparison, then he turned to the billiard players.

Well over fifty, he was almost a giant. His shoulders were massive, his chest was deep, but soft living had added to his huge body with rolls of loose flesh. An unruly shock of iron-grey hair tipped his head which might have been roughhewn from a block of granite. The features were large, and beneath the large blunt nose was a thick moustache. The wide jaw was covered by a spade shaped beard, which reached beyond his collar. Face, neck and hands were burned by the sun to the colour of bronze. He wore a double-breasted suit which hung loosely on his tremendous frame.

"A message has just come over the phone," he said in a deep harsh voice. "From this Doctor Britling whom Jubal went to fetch. The Hispano is smashed up six miles from here and Jubal is dead." His heavily-lidded eyes turned from one to the other of his companions. "Murdered," he added expressively.

Mark Annerley's jaw dropped and his eyes bulged with fear; his complexion, naturally sallow became positively green in hue; his thick lips parted and twitched at the corners. "Murdered! My God! This is awful!" he screamed.

Levison caught his shoulders and shook him roughly. "Shut up!" he rasped. "Do you want the old man to hear?"

Like a pricked balloon, Annerley collapsed limply into a chair. "What does it matter if he does hear?" he giggled hysterically. "Do you suppose Israel Straust is going to waste any tears over the death of his son? That old rattlesnake? It will be his own turn soon, in any case!"

"Where is Doctor Britling, Quail?" asked Levison calmly.

"At the local police station," replied Hubert Quail with a frown. "He's coming up here now with the Sergeant in charge."

"That's awkward."

"Hm, yes," agreed Quail. "Police interference means publicity, and we can't afford publicity."

Levison walked to the window and looked out across the cool green lawn that surrounded the magnificent country house of Israel Straust, across the gay riot of colour formed by the flower beds, to the wide rim of the sky which today seemed an inverted plate of bright blue. His attention seemed to be concentrated on a flight of birds which skimmed across the horizon.

The others eyed his tall, slim, figure hopefully. Either of them would have admitted that Levison's brain was the superior of his own. They were prepared to leave to him the handling of the present predicament.

"Send someone to fetch Broadribb," he said, turning from the window. "He may as well do some work in return for his heavy fees as the old man's personal medical attendant. He lives in a cottage a few hundred yards away. He's got to tell this police sergeant that Israel is too ill to see him."

"Will he do that?" queried Hubert Quail doubtfully.

"What's he paid for?" snapped Levison. "Of course, he'll do it. I'll see the police sergeant. If I can't pull the wool over his eyes, he ought to be commissioner of Scotland Yard. I wonder what Jubal told this Doctor Britling—more than was wise I'll bet a thousand. Whatever Britling knows he'll have told the police of course. He's more than half a policeman himself."

"You, my dear Gideon, are the most accomplished liar in the world," growled Quail. "If you can't explain away whatever the policeman suspects no one else can."

"Quite," said Levison modestly.

Hubert Quail pressed a bell-button and instructed the footman who came in response to go for Doctor Broadribb. Within a few minutes the obliging doctor arrived in his two-seater, and was given his instructions by Gideon Levison. He objected at first to deceiving the police, but yielded at last to Levison's tight-lipped insistence. He was sent to another room to await the time when his services would be required.

Levison went to break the news of his son's death to the aged financier Levi Straust. How the old man took the news will never be known, for Levison was silent afterwards on the subject—but since a footman who entered his master's study an hour later to remind him to dress for dinner found him deeply engrossed in a game of patience, it cannot be assumed that it had affected him very deeply.

Returning to the billiard room, Levison opened the French windows and strolled out to the brick terrace which surrounded the house, followed by Quail and Annerley. They made an incongruous trio as they paced up and down; Levison, tall and slender, conservatively garbed in a well-cut dark blue suit and immaculate white linen shirt; Quail, tremendous in girth, in baggy trousers and a shabby jacket; Annerley, short and podgy, loudly dressed in a close-fitting grey checked suit and socks, with a shirt and tie that were costly poems in coloured silks.

They had not been walking long when a small car came up the drive and drew up a few feet away from them. There were three men in it; a uniformed police sergeant; a constable, also in uniform, who sat at the steering wheel; and Doctor Britling, whose thin face was decorated by a strip of sticking plaster, and who clutched in one hand a small kitbag and in the other, his rolled umbrella. Doctor Britling and the senior police officer climbed out of the car and walked towards the three men who awaited them.

Levison came forward to meet them. "Doctor Britling," he said in his most engaging manner. "I have heard of you, although I haven't previously enjoyed the privilege of your acquaintance. Allow me to introduce myself, I am Gideon Levison. I regret that our first meeting should be in such tragic circumstances. This is Mr. Quail, to whom you spoke on the phone, and this is Mr. Annerley."

Daniel acknowledged the introductions with a series of curt nods. His shrewd grey eyes rested appraisingly on each of them in turn. "This is Sergeant Deakin of the local police," he said drily.

"I am pleased to meet you, sergeant," said Levison pleasantly. "Won't you please come this way—it will save time."

He led the way through the French windows into the billiard room, followed by the dapper little police surgeon, and the stolid looking sergeant; Quail and Annerley brought up the rear.

"How did the—er—tragedy occur?" Levison asked. "Quail said a smash—did the car skid or something of the sort?"

Daniel shook his head. His eyes flickered from Levison to Quail, and from Quail to Annerley, with the darting motion of goldfish in a glass bowl. "The accident was the result, not the cause, of the death," he replied. "Mr. Straust was poisoned. Just before he died, he swallowed a tablet which must have contained the poison. He had previously informed me that he was required by his doctor to take one every hour. I can only assume that a poisoned tablet was substituted for one of the indigestion tablets. The others are perfectly harmless."

"One every hour!" gulped Annerley hysterically. "Don't you see, that was why the hour of his death could be foretold so accurately! It was easy to arrange the tablet in the vial so that Jubal swallowed the poisoned one at five o'clock! And Jubal was too much of a hypochondriac to forget to take them exactly on the hour."

"Simple," murmured Levison. "How beautifully simple!"

Annerley seized the decanter and glass in shaking hands and poured himself a liberal portion, spilling more brandy on the carpet than went in the glass. He tossed it off, trembling in every limb. "My God!" he cried. "He'll kill us all without mercy, just like—like flies!"

Daniel went forward and calmly took the decanter and glass from his trembling fingers. "From hysteria to insanity is a short step, Mr. Annerley," he said. "I should advise you to pull yourself together. Don't have anything more to drink. It would be as well for you to go and lie down. I think I have a little something in my bag which will calm your nerves."

"No!" exclaimed Annerley wildly. "No! I won't take any medicine. My God! Jubal died that way!"

Levison opened the door and signalled with his eyebrows to Police Sergeant Deakin. "My friend is upset, sergeant," he said quietly. "Perhaps it will be better if I interview you elsewhere. Please come this way. As his medical attendant, Doctor Broadribb, will tell you, Mr. Israel Straust is not well enough to see you, but I shall be only too pleased to give you any information in my power."

It was neatly done. By sheer personal magnetism he drew the reluctant police officer out of the room, and closed the door behind him. Hubert Quail began to breathe more freely. Levison was the most accomplished liar in the country!

Doctor Britling Meets the Group

"Claret, sir?" The portly butler held the beautiful old claret jug at an angle above one of the imposing row of glasses that stood at Doctor Britling's elbow.

Daniel shook his head. He had enjoyed a glass of excellent sherry with the soup, and he intended to allow himself one glass of port later, but the succession of wines that accompanied the various courses, admirable though they were, did not appeal to him on this particular evening. He wanted a clear head for the discussion which must inevitably follow on the heels of dinner.

His shrewd grey eyes rested upon each of the faces that were grouped around the table, thrown in sharp relief by the splash of light from the alabaster bowl above, which illuminated the table and left the rest of the room discreetly shadowed.

At the top of the table sat the host, Israel Straust, a very old man with an emaciated frame that was bent like a question mark, skinny arms and legs, and long withered fingers, like the bunched talons of a bird of prey. His face was shrunken and shrivelled and his mouth was no more than a thin slit in his face. The skin about his eyes was pouched and wrinkled. A long white beard tapered from his chin to the diamond that gleamed in his shirt front, and his narrow cranium was completely bald. Israel Straust crouched over his plate like a huge spider, his sharp eyes darting restlessly about him as he gluttonously devoured each of the courses that were set before him.

Seated to the right of the old man was Cora Annerley, a hard-faced, glittering blonde with hair the colour of a new penny, and greenish eyes. A rope of magnificent pearls gleamed at her throat, and her fingers wore a small fortune in precious stones.

Hubert Quail, his massive frame overflowing the chair in

which he sat, was on Mrs. Annerley's right, but throughout the entire meal he had not addressed a single word to her. Disdaining the epicurean courses which followed one another, he ate a huge steak, three-fourths of a foot long and over an inch thick, heaped high with mushrooms and fried potatoes, and washed down with Pilsner lager, of which he drank prodigious quantities.

Doctor Britling sat next to Quail.

Across the table, on the host's left, sat Gideon Levison, his dark eyes glowing with cynical amusement as they watched Doctor Britling's appraising glances at each of his fellow diners. Levison ate a little of each course and drank sparingly of each of the wines offered him.

Beside Levison sat a young girl, the niece of Hubert Quail. Straight and slender as a boy, she had a boy's natural grace and carriage. She was eighteen, but her simple white frock, cut modestly high at the neck, and fitted with sleeves to the elbow, and the long plait of brown hair which dangled down her back made her seem younger. She was distinctly pretty. Her crisp curls made a frame for her face, which was creamy in complexion, with lips like ripe cherries, a short straight nose, and a dimpled chin. Her eyes were hazel in colour and throughout the meal were focussed demurely on her plate except for an occasional timid glance at her uncle or at Doctor Britling.

On Mary Quail's left sat Mark Annerley, whose composure if not his courage had been restored since his hysterical outburst in the billiard-room. There was a peculiar glitter in his piggy eyes which Daniel did not care to see; it suggested to the police surgeon that cocaine had probably been responsible for the return of Annerley's self-control.

The atmosphere in that large room of mellow walnut and rich draperies was as strained as it must have been when the Borgias wined their enemies. Death was an inevitable guest at the feast; they could almost feel his chill breath on their cheeks. There was a tension in the air that even their host's fine old wines could not dispel.

The conversation had dwindled to nothing.

Cora Annerley shivered suddenly as though her white shoulders had been touched by icy fingers. "This is like a funeral!" she declared. "We're about as lively as corpses! Why doesn't someone say something? Uncle Izzy," she turned to the aged man at the top of the table, "do be polite for once. Tell me that you like my dress."

The old man's hand, holding a fork on which a portion of grouse was impaled, paused on the way to his mouth. He turned his bowed head and peered at her from beneath heavy eyelids. "I am no judge of these matters," he said, his eyes slowly travelling from her shoulders to her waist. "It would be well enough, I suppose, but for the artificial flowers."

He turned his attention to the fork, which continued its journey to his mouth. Cora Annerley's eyes flamed with anger.

"After all," said her husband placatingly, "this is hardly an occasion for merriment with Jubal—" He hesitated, and did not finish the sentence.

Mary Quail looked at her uncle timidly. "Mrs. Levine told me that poor Jubal is dead," she ventured. "It seems so awful—he was alive and well at luncheon. How did it happen?"

Before Quail could reply, Gideon Levison patted her hand gently. "Jubal died in a motor accident," he told her. "You know he has had many narrow shaves before. I've warned him repeatedly that he was asking for trouble. He always drove at an outrageous speed. Don't be distressed about him, child. Death is not so very terrible. Death is merely the last blind corner in the road of life."

In a little while Cora Annerley and the girl retired to the

drawing room. Gideon Levison rose and held the door open for them, then returned to the table, taking the chair that Mrs. Annerley had vacated. Mark Annerley moved into the chair to the left of Israel Straust, so that the four financiers were bunched together a little apart from Doctor Britling. The butler placed a decanter of Napoleon brandy, a decanter of rare old port, a box of Coronas and a heaped silver platter of nuts upon the table and withdrew, leaving them alone. Annerley glanced awkwardly at his three associates, and then at Daniel. It was evident that the time had come when Daniel was to be told—as much as the financiers wished him to know.

As a preliminary, cigars were lit and five glasses filled with brandy. Daniel was pleased, when he sampled the mellowness of the liquor, that he had changed his mind about allowing himself port only. It was a brandy such as few are privileged to taste once in a lifetime.

"Doctor Britling," said Israel Straust in his thin, reedy voice. "This afternoon my son called upon you in London to enlist your aid on our behalf."

Daniel inclined his head gravely.

"What did he tell you?" The old man's eyes narrowed as he waited for a reply.

"He told me that all of you had received threats against your lives. Threats that you were inclined to regard seriously."

"Nothing more than that?"

"Nothing. I asked him the name of the man who had threatened you, but he declined to say, except in the presence of his colleagues."

Gideon Levison leaned forward, and a quick twist of his lips rolled his cigar to the corner of his mouth. "He didn't know!" he snapped. "We have no clue to the identity of the letters. All we know is that we have each received a warning, and that Jubal received a second one, which heralded his death. There are many cranks who send letters of that sort to prominent financiers; men who imagine that they have been wronged; men who have been unfortunate in speculation."

"That," said Daniel suavely, "is what you told the police. Sergeant Deakin believed it. I don't." His shrewd grey eyes travelled round the half-circle of mask-like faces that were turned towards him.

"Mr. Jubal Straust was in a state of extreme nervousness this afternoon," he murmured slowly. "Mr. Annerley, if I may say so, was at the borders of hysteria a few hours ago. You, Mr. Levison and you, Mr. Quail, are made of sterner stuff, but from the significant bulge on Mr. Quail's hip, and the wariness with which Mr. Levison moves in the dark, it is obvious that you are both on your guard against something. Mr. Straust has a habit of glancing over his shoulder at the shadows that lurk in his own dining room. All four of you look up sharply when the door opens. Why? Would the threats of an unbalanced crank, a man unknown to you, produce that effect on four men of your acknowledged ruthlessness? I think not. Obviously, you are well aware of your enemy's identity—and know enough about him to take his threats seriously."

Israel Straust chuckled grimly and pointed a gnarled finger at Levison. "You aren't clever enough by half this time, Gideon," he cackled maliciously. "Lies won't pass with this smart little doctor. What do you say? Shall we tell him the truth?"

A smile softened the hard lines of Levison's long thin face. "By all means," he agreed.

Hubert Quail helped himself to a handful of walnuts and cracked one between his thick fingers. "Why not?" he said. "We can't expect him to be of much help if we don't."

"Please yourself," mumbled Annerley pouring himself another glass of brandy.

Straust sipped appreciatively from his own glass. "It is an ugly story," he said, with a faraway expression is his rheumy eyes. "A story of friendship betrayed, of the depths to which the desire for gold will lead men, of deliberate treachery. Not at all a pretty story."

Mark Annerley squirmed in his chair and his face went white. "Draw it mild," he said roughly. "You were in it too."

"We were all in it then," said Israel Straust wearily. "And we are all in it now. All but Jubal. Jubal has paid—as we shall inevitably pay."

Cora Annerley Has a Surprise

THERE WAS A pregnant, almost audible silence. Straust's eyes looked at Doctor Britling through the haze of steel-grey cigar smoke that overhung the table, and the bitter wisdom of a troubled face was mirrored in their depths. There was an odd, pathetic dignity about this old man, whose grip on life was so enfeebled, whose body was little more than a bundle of bones.

"It was fitting that my son Jubal should be the first to die," he said. "For it was his brain that first conceived the plan of making a scapegoat of Arthur Marckheim. Twelve years ago, all six of us were partners in the Eldorado Investment Trust. Arthur Marckheim was the brains of the partnership; he was a financial wizard, that man. The rest of us—even Gideon—were babies beside him. But reckless! The risks he took would have turned your hair white. Somehow, he managed to steer clear of the law and we all made money. But what good are one hundred per cent profits if the risks are also one hundred percent? One day the inevitable happened. Gideon heard a whisper that the affairs of the company were to be investigated at the instigation of the Public Prosecutor.

"He called a meeting at which Quail, Annerley, Jubal, Gideon, himself, and humble old Israel Straust were present. Marckheim was not there. He was in Germany on business. Well, the position was serious. As it happened, an investigation of one of our flotations would have resulted in terms of penal servitude for all of us. It was Jubal who saw the way out.

"With the acute business acumen we all possessed it might have been possible for us to cover up our traces, but the law must have its sacrifice. Someone must be the scapegoat. And that scapegoat? Who but Marckheim who was so conveniently out of the way?

"Marckheim was our friend. We used to pat him on the back and call him a good fellow. 'Good old Marcky'. We used to drink with him, play cards with him, watch the Derby from his coach, like the good friends we were."

Annerley's face was twitching nervously; Gideon Levison was examining his fingernails calmly; Quail leaned forward with a savage scowl. "There's no need to go into all that," he growled.

"What need indeed?" agreed the old man drily. "It is an old story. Besides, what is friendship? Its commercial value is nil. Will a banker accept it as security? Will a pawnbroker take it in pledge? We followed the rule of the wolf pack. When the leader of the wolf pack stumbles, he is torn to pieces by his followers before he can rise.

"We were cunning enough to whitewash ourselves at the expense of Marckheim. In addition, we sold short the stocks in which the Eldorado Investment Company was interested. When Marckheim returned from the continent he was arrested and the company crashed. Our manipulation of the stocks enabled us to divide half a million pounds.

"You may remember the case, Doctor Britling. We went into the witness box, one after another, and testified that Marckheim had run the company to suit himself, and that we were innocent of any trickery which had been accomplished. Skilfully doctored documents bore us out. Marckheim stood in the dock, his face expressionless, and watched us with eyes as cold as death.

"The judge commiserated with me—I was even then an old man—for having been dragged by an unscrupulous partner into a degrading scandal. There were those, of course, who whispered that all was not as it seemed. But we had done the thing well. Marckheim was sent to prison for ten years.

"After the trial we separated. It was not to be expected that we could trust each other. I would not have trusted my own son, and he would not have trusted me. We knew each other, you see, for what we were. We went our several ways. Jubal opened an office in Throgmorton Street, and practised the sharp tricks he had learned from Marckheim, only more cunningly, with one eye on the law. Hubert returned to diamond broking, the business of his younger days. Gideon became a respectable banker. Mark bought theatres. And I? My old nose continued to smell out money as it has done for eighty years. I can smell money as the nasal organ of a vulture smells blood."

Israel Straust cackled, and his eyes swept the pale faces of his associates with grim glee. They came to rest on the podgy face of Mark Annerley, with an expression of malevolent amusement.

"Marckheim had a wife, a beautiful young woman with whom he was madly in love." He continued watching Annerley's face narrowly. "On her, he lavished money—cars, clothes, furs, jewels—whatever she wanted was hers for the asking. Her name—was Cora."

Annerley sprang to his feet upsetting his glass and overturning his chair in his fury. "Damn you—you old swine," he shouted. "Keep Cora out of this!"

Straust met the other's furious glare with calm, deliberate eyes. "How is it possible not to mention her?" he asked quietly. "Was she not also one of Arthur Marckheim's faithless 'friends'?"

Gideon Levison's voice cut the air like the lash of a whip. "Sit down, Annerley!"

For a moment Annerley waivered on his feet, then he collapsed into his chair and buried his head in his hands. The maudlin sobs of a drunken man who is sorry for himself shook his fleshy body.

"There's no need to pile on the agony, Israel," said Levison curtly. "We are none of us proud of what we did."

"I least of all," replied the old man soberly. "To tell it, then, in the fewest words, Cora Marckheim became Cora Annerley. That is the reason she too received one of these papers."

He drew a folded slip of paper from his pocket and flattened it on the table. It was identical with the paper which Jubal Straust had shown to Doctor Britling in the latter's Orchard Street flat that afternoon; two crosses one above the other and a crude representation of a skull and crossbones were drawn upon it.

"The reminder that we double-crossed him," said Israel Straust quietly. "And that the penalty is death!" He looked at Doctor Britling with a wry smile. "Almost I think we deserve to die," he remarked.

"Almost I am inclined to agree," said Daniel sternly.

"And yet, we look to you to help us to avert that fate," the old man murmured.

"Death," said Daniel coldly, "is not for one man to mete out to another. For that reason I will help you."

Israel Straust nodded calmly. "When Marckheim went to prison," he proceeded, "he sent each of us a little present. I still have mine."

Fumbling in a pocket he produced a small worn leather bag, unfastened the leather string which tied it at the neck, and turned the bag upside down. A stream of threepenny bits tinkled onto the plate glass table top and rolled across it, some of them dropping to the carpet.

"Thirty pieces of silver!" said the old man. "An odd gift!"

Hubert Quail put out a large hair-covered hand and swept the rest of the coins to the floor. Drawing the decanter towards him, he half-filled a tumbler with neat brandy and drank it at a gulp. Daniel noticed that the backs of his hands were crossed with scratches which appeared to have been inflicted by the claws of a cat.

"Two years ago, Marckheim came out of prison," Israel

Straust continued smoothly. "Jubal and Gideon met him, with certified cheques from each of us in their possession, to the total of fifty thousand pounds. That was our peace offering to Arthur Marckheim. He tore those cheques into shreds and strewed the gutter with them. He said: 'Tell the old fox and the little fat pig and the big bear and my dear wife that I will exact payment when and how I choose.'" The old man cackled. "I wondered how he would have described Jubal and Gideon if they had not been there to receive the message in person? Gideon, a snake, certainly. And Jubal, a jackal, I think. We put detectives on his trail, to keep us in touch with his movements, but within twenty-four hours he had eluded them, and we have heard nothing of him since, until the coming of the warning notes. We have continually advertised for him without success. We are prepared to pay him a quarter of a million pounds in settlement of our debt. But Marckheim doesn't want money. He will exact payment in coin of his own minting."

At that moment a startling interruption occurred. The door was suddenly thrown back upon its hinges and Cora Annerley stumbled into the room. Her face was white and haggard with fear. Her eyes stared wildly at the five men.

"My God!" she screamed hysterically. "He's in the house!" Staggering forward breathlessly, she shook her husband's shoulder roughly. "You drunken beast, why can't you do something?"

She whirled and looked appealing at Levison. "Gideon...for the love of God! ...I'm frightened!"

"Pull yourself together Cora," exclaimed Levison sharply. "Panic will only make matters worse. What is it?"

The women held out a ring in trembling fingers. "Arthur gave me this...years and years ago...he picked it up in Venice...a replica of the poison ring of Cesare Borgia...there's...there's a...a secret compartment in it...meant—Oh, God! —meant for holding poison. There's never been anything in it as long as I've had it…a day or two ago it was empty…I looked in it just now…and…"

She touched a minute spring in the gold circlet of the ring and the jewel fell back in its setting. Out on the table dropped a small white pellet.

Doctor Britling picked it up and held it to his nostrils, then tasted it gingerly with the tip of his tongue.

"Prussic acid," he said grimly.

A Game of Poker

THE GROUNDS SURROUNDING the country mansion of Israel Straust were shrouded in darkness, relieved here and there by slanting oblong splashes of light that stained the grass from the windows. The moonbeams that filtered through the tall trees that stood like sentinels along the high garden wall, touched the shrubs and bushes with the silver fingers of enchantment but heightened the gloom of the long shadows that fell behind them. The gaunt skyline of high gables and peaked roof made an ugly silhouette in the moonlight. Two glowing red circles moved at uneven heights through the darkness, beneath them, twin patches of white gleamed faintly.

A husky voice spoke suddenly: "Who goes there?"

There was a low sibilant laugh. "You, Mr. Levison?" said the husky voice. "O.K., sir."

The tall thin figure of Gideon Levison and the short thin figure of Doctor Daniel Britling moved on over the velvet turf, leaving in their wake the tantalising fragrance of cigar smoke.

"You see," said Levison, "it is impossible for anyone to move unchallenged about the grounds."

"Not, at least, if they smoke cigars, and wear dinner clothes," agreed Doctor Britling dryly.

Levison chuckled. "You mean that the red glow of hot ash and the white gleam of starched shirt front are easily detected? Ah, but even if one dressed in black and moved with the furtive stealth of a mouse, it would be difficult to make one's way undiscovered through the garden. The wall, my dear Doctor, is ten feet high and unobtrusively wired along the top to an alarm bell. We employ twelve muscular sentries—all ex-policemen or ex-pugilists—to patrol the grounds. Six of them are on duty at the present moment; they will be relieved at dawn by the others."

"You have been commendably thorough," murmured Daniel.

"That is not all," replied Levison. "For your benefit let me stage a little demonstration, Doctor."

From his pocket he withdrew a small silver whistle which he placed to his lips. A single blast blew and something happened that was like the transformation scene in a pantomime. Where there had been darkness, now all was light. The shadows fled as powerful searchlights from the roof stabbed the darkness with broad blades of light. All over the garden a dazzling radiance was born. Every tree, every shrub, each blade of grass was revealed for what it was. It would have been impossible for anything larger than a mouse to have concealed itself from that searching glare. Burly men were revealed with automatics in their hands. There was a great rushing of wings as a flock of birds rose from the trees.

Another blast of the whistle and Daniel found himself blinking in the darkness again.

"Rather neat, don't you think?" suggested Levison.

"Hard on the eyes," Daniel replied. "I can hardly see." The glowing end of the cigar a few inches from his nose seemed painfully brilliant compared with the sudden blanket of darkness.

"Annerley contrived it all," Levison remarked. "He is terrified of the dark. "When he walks in the garden at night, he whistle-blows every few minutes."

"And yet," said Daniel dryly, "the man he fears is able to penetrate to the house at will."

"It would appear so," agreed Levison thoughtfully. "The second warning that Jubal found on his bed last night, the poisonous pellet that Cora found in her ring half an hour ago— they give one a damned uncomfortable feeling. And yet how can Marckheim possibly gain entrance to the house?"

"He probably doesn't," replied Daniel. "I should think he is working through a confederate."

Levison's sharp profile was outlined for a moment as they strolled past a lighted window, and his expression was thoughtful.

"That seems likely," he admitted. "But who can that confederate be? Apart from ourselves, there is no one about the place except Annerley's secretary, the domestic staff, and the twelve sentries. The latter are picked men whose references are unimpeachable. As for the domestic staff, all of them have been with Israel for years."

He described the servants individually, mentioning the length of service in each case. Harcourt the butler, solemn faced and portly, dignified with the burden of sixty-odd years, who had been in the employment of Israel Straust since before the war; Mrs. Levine, the housekeeper, withered, frail, and old, with nine years of service; her grandson, Sidney Levine, a crippled youth who did odd jobs about the house and garden, and secretarial work for his employer; Jules, the Swiss chef, who seldom stirred out of his kitchen, and who had cooked for Straust for fourteen years; Smithers, the footman, who had been born in the neighbourhood, and had grown up from boyhood in the financier's service; Moxon, the grey-haired gardener, who cared for nothing but his roses and the fine old lawn; the six young women who completed the domestic staff, and who had none of them been in the house for less than three years. Since Arthur Marckheim's release from prison no new domestics had been engaged.

"That leaves only Adrian Carver, Annerley's secretary, to be accounted for," concluded Levison. "A pleasant rather easy-going youth of about twenty-three. We've had him thoroughly investigated, and find that he's quite all right."

He waved his slender, well-kept hands in an expressive gesture. "That is the layout, Doctor," he said. "As you can see for yourself, it seems impossible for Marckheim to get into the house and equally out of the question for him to have a confederate within. The fact remains that he has found a way to break through our defences. Jubal died miles from here, but the poisoned tablet that killed him must have been placed among the others while he was in this house. Perhaps the next to die will be killed in the house itself."

They paused outside two lighted uncurtained French windows which opened into the library. Within they could see Israel Straust playing patience with cards laid out on a small table in the centre of the room, Hubert Quail examining a row of books without much interest, and Mark Annerley, with a long glass of amber liquid in his hand, hunched up in a Sheraton chair beside the fire.

"The curtains are left apart so that in passing the guards can glance in and see that everything is in order," commented Levison. "Personally, I haven't much faith in the efficiency of such measures. Marckheim is the cleverest man I have ever known. All the ex-policemen in the world won't circumvent him. For my part, I wish he'd strike and get it over. This isn't the first time I've matched my wits with death. I got my start in South Africa, in one of the toughest neighbourhoods in the world. I've killed more than one man in self-defence. Marckheim won't find me an easy victim. If he makes a slip he is likely to taste death himself."

This was said in a calm, conversational tone, as though Levison was commenting on the weather. He turned a handle and pushed the French windows open. "Let's go inside," he said.

Mark Annerley whirled round in his chair as they entered,

a flicker of fear dawning in his eyes, and dying out slowly as he recognised them. Quail barely spared them a glance from the book he was casually scanning. Israel Straust did not look up from his complicated game of patience.

"Cora's got the wind up about the poison she found in her ring," said Annerley gloomily.

"Cora's a damned fool," growled Quail. "The time to get the wind up is when Marckheim slips poison into her food."

"I don't think he intends to do that," said Doctor Britling quietly. "If I guess correctly, he will make no direct attack on Mrs. Annerley. He will simply keep her supplied with the means to commit suicide, and leave it to suspense and remorse to do the rest."

"Suspense, possibly," grunted Quail. "But remorse!—not likely! Cora has about as much conscience as a snake has hips."

Privately Daniel was inclined to agree. An observer less shrewd than he would have come to the conclusion that Cora Annerley was as hard as nails. Fear might shake her nerve, but it was difficult to image her suffering from the pangs of remorse.

At that moment, the door opened and Mrs. Annerley came into the room. She had repaired the ravages that hysteria had wrought on her make-up, and looked completely self-possessed, except for a vague uneasiness in her greenish eyes.

"I can't bear to sit up in my room alone," she explained. "So I came down to join you. Can't we do something to liven us up a little?"

"Poker?" suggested Levison.

"All right for you," growled Annerley. "You and Izzy always win. I lost three thousand to the pair of you last night."

"You'll never win if you grin like a Cheshire cat when you're sitting on a decent hand," retorted Levison. "Stay out if you like. What about you, Cora?"

"Anything," said Mrs. Annerley viciously, "is better than mooning about like a lot of stuffed owls."

"Count me in," said Hubert Quail.

Israel Straust gathered up his patience cards and Levison grouped chairs about the table. Annerley sat down in one of them with a surly grunt.

"You'll play, Doctor?" invited Levison.

Daniel shook his head. "If you don't mind, I'll watch. Your stakes are a little beyond my means."

It was interesting to watch the faces of the players. Gideon Levison and Israel Straust were evenly matched. Their faces, regardless of the strength of their hands, were as expressionless as wax dolls. Hubert Quail was less capable of controlling his facial muscles, but his shrewd ability to value his hand kept his losses to a minimum. Cora Annerley was capable of bluffing— and winning—with a pair of deuces, but was quite likely to get cold feet and throw in with a full house in her hand.

Mark Annerley lost steadily. His face might as well have been a mirror so faithfully did it reflect the value of his cards. As his pile of white, red and blue chips dwindled, his expression became ferociously sullen.

"There's no luck in these cards," he growled. "Let's have a new deck."

He rang a bell and instructed the butler who answered it to bring a fresh pack. When the new cards came he tore the outer covering off them and passed them to Quail, whose turn it was to deal.

The first hand dealt with the new pack brought him no better luck than before. It became evident that this hand was to be a duel between Israel Straust and Gideon Levison. The others dropped out as the betting mounted rapidly.

The two men, young and old, were seated opposite each

other and the light fell directly on their pale, impassive faces. Levison's five cards lay face downwards on the table in front of him, so that not even the players who had dropped out were able to obtain the merest glimpse of them. Without a flicker of an eyelash Levison pushed chips to the value of a thousand pounds into the pot. This was the largest bet of the evening, but no one looked surprised.

"Raise you five hundred," murmured Straust, in his thin, high voice, a skinny claw supplying the necessary chips.

"And five hundred," smiled Levison.

Straust calmly swept another pile of chips into the pot. "Five hundred more, my dear Gideon."

Levison unconcernedly met the other's bet and quietly counted out still further chips. "Raise you a thousand."

The betting went on until there was over thirteen thousand pounds in the pool, over half of it in pencilled I.O.U's. Israel Straust squinted sideways at his opponent, who had just made a thousand pound raise. His rheumy old eyes had a thoughtful expression. "I'll see you," he said, scrawling an I.O.U for the requisite amount.

Annerley uttered a course laugh. "Frightened you has he?" he gibed.

"The wise old fox," said the aged Straust gravely, "is wary of the trap."

One by one, Levison slowly turned over four of his five cards. Three aces and the joker—which counted as a fourth ace!

"You win, my dear Gideon," said Straust calmly. "Remind me to give you a cheque. I doubt if I have sufficient ready money in the house."

"What was the fifth card?" asked Annerley leaning forward to turn it over.

Levison's slim fingers closed over the card. "The fifth card," he said quietly, but with an ominous glitter in his eyes, "is none of your concern."

He gathered up the cards, and putting them with the rest of the pack, proceeded to shuffle calmly. They were cut, and he dealt them with sure fingers.

Hubert Quail gathered up his hand, holding the cards flat together, and spread them out slowly. As he did so, his bronzed complexion deepened to an angry red. The veins on his wide brow swelled ominously. An oath grated through his clenched teeth. He tried to speak but only an incoherent stuttering made itself heard.

Cora Annerley, who was sitting next to him, looked over his shoulder at the cards. Her eyes widened with horror. Quail slammed the cards face upwards on the table.

The others stared at them in silence.

The king of spades, the king of hearts, the seven of diamonds, the two of hearts—and a card such as never was in any pack since playing cards were invented. A card on which was drawn two crosses, one above the other, and a crude representation of a skull and cross bones!

The man who had received it glared at the others. "Is this a joke?" he snarled.

"It—it was a fresh pack," stammered Annerley. "No one could have tampered with it. It—It's uncanny!"

"Don't be absurd!" snapped Levison. "There's an obvious explanation. The covering of the pack could easily have been steamed open, that—that thing substituted, and the covering resealed again. There's always a plain-faced card included with every deck. It would be a simple matter to draw that childish trademark on it."

Mark and Cora Annerley moved away from Quail uneasily,

as though he were a leper. The man who had received the death card sat alone.

His thick lips twisted into an ugly grin. "So," he hissed. "I am to be the next to die!"

2

An hour later, when Levison and Doctor Britling were smoking a last cigar on the terrace, Levison turned to the dapper little police surgeon, an odd smile wreathing his lips.

"The fifth card, which Annerley was so anxious to see, when my four aces beat Israel's full house…" he murmured.

"Yes?"

"That fifth card," said Levison calmly, "was the one which was dealt to Quail the following hand. The one Marckheim faked as a warning to one of us. I realised in a flash as I picked it up that Marckheim could have no means of deciding beforehand who was to receive it, so I kept quiet and put it back in the pack to give one of the others a chance. Poor Quail! I'm afraid his own behaviour, and the conduct of the Annerleys, will make it obvious to the person who is watching for such signs exactly which of us is marked for death!"

Daniel could only stare in silence at the man who could calmly bet in thousands with the death card in his hand!

Exit Hubert Quail

THE MORNING SUN looked in at the French windows of the breakfast-room, which were invitingly ajar. It warmed the bright yellow walls and gleamed upon the polished surfaces of the furniture. Its reflection in the mirror above the mantelpiece brightened a patch of the ceiling, and its rays danced and played upon the shining silverware with which the breakfast table was laid.

Outside, the rich green of turf three hundred years old stretched smoothly to the rose-garden which was gay with vivid colour. A row of sprinklers arranged upon the lawn threw up fountains of fine spray to make a riot of colour in the rays of the sun. A bird, high in a tree, was pouring out his joyous soul to a beautiful world. Butterflies fluttered from flower to flower, beauty flirting with beauty for a brief season. The droning, pulsating rhythm of honey bees made the air drowsy, as the exquisite flower scents made it sweet.

At a long table near the French windows two men faced each other over the elaborate paraphernalia of breakfast. The elder, a weary-faced man of about forty, who ate with a grim, silent purposefulness, had a morning paper propped against the marmalade dish in front of him. His eyes stared at it while his hand guided the food unerringly to his mouth. He was stout, red-faced, and the receding tide of his hair had left a smooth sweep of polished scalp between his eyebrows and the back of his head.

The younger, Adrian Carver, divided his attention between unfruitful attempts to read the back page of his companion's paper, and the food before him. His slender face had an intelligent expression, contributed to by his large dark eyes, but weakness was expressed in his full lips and slightly receding chin.

At last, with a little sigh of contentment, Adrian pushed back his plate and lit a cigarette. "Anything in the paper this morning?" he asked.

His vis-à-vis, one Albert Moody, captain of the guard which patrolled the house, favoured him with a sour glance.

"Why don't you look at your own paper and find out?" he grunted through a mouthful of devilled kidney.

"There's a run on the papers this morning," replied Adrian cheerfully. "Everyone wants to see what they have to say about Jubal."

"Mr. Straust, junior, to the likes of me and you," retorted Moody, drawing his knife through the exact centre of a fried egg and manoeuvring half of the egg into his mouth.

A burly man appeared on the terrace outside the French windows and saluted Mr. Moody.

"Mr. Quail alright?" asked Moody gloomily.

"I've been knockin' at his door at 'alf hour intervals since eight o'clock," replied the other. "'Is langwidge the first time was a treat. 'E don't appear to 'old with early rousing."

"Orders is orders," said Moody. "Ain't up yet, is he?"

"Nor likely to be, neither, from the things he says between swears."

"If he swears, he's O.K.," said Moody saliently. "But when he's silent, you let me know on the hop."

The other, an ex-prize-fighter, saluted clumsily and withdrew.

"Why this tender solicitude for the well-being of Brother Quail?" asked Adrian curiously.

"All I know is my orders," replied Moody. "Which are to keep in regular touch with the gentleman."

Adrian glanced at the clock, which registered half-past ten. "Rather late for a man of your importance to be breakfasting, isn't it?" he murmured reprovingly.

Mr. Moody gave him a cold stare. "I've been up and about since four this morning," he growled. "More than some people can say for themselves. Mrs. Levine was kind enough to invite me in for a bite. A man can't go forever on an empty stummick."

"Quite," agreed Adrian.

There was an awkward pause. Mr. Moody turned his disapproving glance back to his paper; Adrian drew on his cigarette and exhaled a cloud of steel-grey smoke with indolent satisfaction. Owing to the agitation of his employer, Mark Annerley, he had no pressing duties to perform, and a lazy life entirely suited him.

Mr. Moody rounded up the last crumbs of kidney and drops of gravy from his plate with a segment of bread, and inserted the savoury tidbit into his mouth.

"This Doctor Britling," said Adrian, "what's he doing here?"

"Makin' hisself a blanketty nuisance," replied Moody judicially. "Since seven o'clock he's been nosing about, prying into everything, and questioning the domestic help. I heard him askin' one of the maids who washed the pots and pans. A ruddy sensible question to ask, I must say! Amatoors," he added crumbily. "Amatoors are always like that."

"Doctor Britling isn't an amateur," retorted Adrian. "He's one of the greatest criminologists in the country. If he asked who cleans the pots, you can bet he had a reason for wanting to know. Lord, I'd like to be him! I've always wanted to investigate a murder."

His eyes became brighter, and his lips parted; a flush mantled his cheeks. Adrian Carver was a young man with a highly-developed enthusiasm for adventure, for romance, for anything but work.

"Huh!" exclaimed Mr. Moody phlegmatically.

Adrian looked at him with an expression of distaste. "You have no soul," he remarked scornfully.

Mr. Moody was not perturbed by that lack. "D'you mind removing your elbow?" he requested. "I can't get at the butter."

Adrian removed his elbows from the table and dug his hands deeply into his pockets.

A Pomeranian dog pattered through the open door into the room. It sniffed at Adrian's ankles. He reached down absently and patted its head. Suddenly he felt its little body stiffening. Looking up, he saw that a kitten had come in through the French windows. A tiny orange kitten, which belonged, he remembered, to Mary Quail.

The dog bounded forward, yapping furiously, and the kitten squirmed away with its back arched. It put up a paw with claws extended, and, as the dog shot forward, struck it a sharp blow on the nose. Then it turned and streaked out the way it had come, the dog barking madly in hot pursuit.

A slim girlish form appeared in the doorway. Brown stockinged legs flashed, and a pigtail streamed as Mary Quail disappeared through the French windows after the kitten and the dog.

"Pretty kid," murmured Adrian reflectively.

"Too skinny," responded Mr. Moody. "I like 'em with a little fore and aft. These hipless ones don't fill the eye as a woman ought."

Cora Annerley hurried into the breakfast room with light of battle in her eyes. "Seen my Dodo?" she demanded. "I heard him barking."

"Gone out there," replied Mr. Moody, with a jerk of his thumb. "After a cat."

"That confounded kitten!" she fumed. "I'll tell her uncle and he'll make her get rid of it." She ran into the garden, crying: "Dodo! Dodo!"

"Women!" said Mr. Moody, expressively, picking his teeth with a sharpened matchstick.

Adrian lit another cigarette lazily. "We return to the query," he murmured. "Is there anything in the paper this morning? Anything about the late lamented Jubal?"

"Read it yourself," said Mr. Moody handing him the paper and jabbing at a particular column on the front page with a stubby forefinger.

Adrian spread the paper on his knees and read the following paragraph:

TRAGIC END OF FAMOUS FINANCIER
MR. JUBAL STRAUST KILLED IN MOTOR SMASH

The *Morning World* learns that Jubal Straust, the well-known stockbroker, and only son of Israel Straust, of Grey Towers near Leighton Buzzard, was fatally injured yesterday afternoon in a motor accident while driving to his father's home. William Giddings, at one time known in boxing circles as The Hoxton Butcher, was in the car at the time, and was removed to the local infirmary in an unconscious condition, suffering from severe head injuries. Another occupant of the car, whose identity has not been revealed, escaped with a severe shaking and was able to continue his journey to Grey Towers. According to the police statement, the accident was caused through a skid while the car was travelling at great speed. The chassis was badly bent and the coachwork extensively damaged. (Pictures on back page.)

An obituary notice of the dead man, which would have made enthralling reading to a student of fiction, was added. Adrian glanced over it casually and looked up.

"I can see Levison's hand in this," he stated. "I know now what he was speaking to that policeman about for an hour yesterday evening. He was persuading him to give out this account of Jubal's death—and he succeeded."

"I suppose the reporters are here in force," he added.

"If they are," said Moody grimly, "they won't none of them get in. I've got my orders about that! The district police inspector called this morning and saw Mr. Levison. Had a very friendly chat they did."

"They would," agreed Adrian. "Trust the wily Gideon."

His expression became thoughtful. "If a chap only had some money, what a killing he could make! Before the day's over, the bottom will fall out of every stock in which Jubal Straust was interested. The news that it was murder is bound to leak out, even if the police think it policy to hush it up for the present, and then—Jove!—won't there be some fun! A man who could sell Inca Copper and S.N.T. Tin for all he was worth before the news breaks would clean up a fortune!"

Adrian heard a faint movement and looked up to see Gideon Levison, his eyes shining curiously, standing at his side. A slow smile twisted the corner of Levison's thin lips.

"I don't know whether you have any money, Moody," he said softly. "If you have, I should advise you to keep it in the Post Office Savings Bank."

"I do, sir," Moody assured him respectfully.

"You are very wise," Levison's expressionless dark eyes looked down at Adrian's pale face. "And you, Carver, are a very stupid young man. A Stock Exchange seat is worth a fortune because of the thousands of woolly lambs who think they can devour the sly wolves. It is obvious that your brain—and your tongue—are not suited to this environment. I must speak to Mr. Annerley about you."

As he turned quietly away, Mary Quail came through the French windows with the orange kitten in her arms. She was wearing a short blue serge skirt, and a tight-fitting dark red pullover, which revealed her lithe young figure to advantage.

Levison smiled at her affectionately.

"Your kitten has been in trouble again, child? Be careful or your uncle will hear that you still have it, and then Binkie's life won't be worth much, I'm afraid."

He stroked the furry little animal gently.

"Mrs. Levine offered to look after Binkie for me," said the girl contritely. "He must have escaped while she was busy elsewhere."

At that moment Mrs. Levine entered the room. She was a little old woman, on whose face patience was indelibly written; her snowy hair and withered cheeks gave her the appearance of great age. A pair of steel-rimmed spectacles of old-fashioned design were perched precariously on her nose, and two mild eyes peered anxiously through thick lenses at the girl.

"I'm very sorry, Miss," she said. "The naughty little thing escaped when my back was turned. I do hope he hasn't been in mischief."

"Nothing very serious, Mrs. Levine," Levison assured her. "But keep a closer watch on him in future or Miss Quail is likely to lose him."

Running footsteps clattered on the staircase outside, and the door was thrown violently back upon its hinges. The burly man who had previously reported to Moody burst into the room in voluble haste.

"Mr. Quail," he gasped. "'E don't answer. I've knocked and knocked and there ain't the faintest stirring in the room."

Without a word Levison dashed out of the room and took the stairs two at a time, followed hurriedly by Mr. Moody, Adrian, and the man who had given the alarm.

Levison halted at the door on the first floor, and knocked imperatively.

"Quail! Quail!"

There was no reply. He shouted again, and renewed his assault on the door. He hammered upon the panels and shook the door handle vigorously until the noise echoed down the corridor.

"Quail! Quail!"

A little group of people collected on the landing: Mark Annerley, who was looking apprehensive; Mary Quail, who had become very white; Adrian Carver, and two hired bodyguards. Levison looked over his shoulder at them.

"Give me a hand," he rapped out sharply. "We've got to get this door open."

Moody and his assistant put their shoulders to the door and heaved. With a crash of splintering wood it fell back and hung drunkenly on one hinge.

There was sudden silence. The shuffling of feet ceased. Even their very breath seemed to die away when they saw Hubert Quail kneeling awkwardly on the floor beside the bed, his limp hands seeming to clutch at the bedclothes, his eyes staring with a look of awful intensity.

Mark Annerley began to stammer something incoherent in a shaking voice.

"Uncle!" cried Mary Quail. "Uncle!"

Adrian took her arm gently and led her out of the room. With a little cry, she swayed towards him. He put his arms about her and let her sob on his shoulder.

Doctor Britling pushed his way through the little group of people who were clustered about the door. He asked no questions but went forward and touched Quail's shoulder. At the touch, the kneeling man fell sideways and sprawled full length upon the carpet. There was a poignant breathless silence as Doctor

Britling knelt down and felt the prostrate man's heart. The others were waiting with hushed expectancy for his verdict.

He rose to his feet again slowly. His eyes travelled round the ring of scared white faces. "He's dead," he said simply.

Outside in the garden, Cora Annerley was calling to her Pomeranian dog:

"Dodo! Dodo! Bad little dog, where are you? Come, Dodo! Come, Dodo!"

How Quail Met His End

To mark Annerley it seemed a most amazing thing that a bird perched in the branches of some tree should continue to warble a carefree song; that the faint breeze should tantalise his nostrils with the perfume of summer flowers; that sunbeams should play like wayward children in the room where Hubert Quail lay dead.

Did death, then, mean no more than that? No more than the fluttering of a leaf from a tree in autumn? Did the sombre wings of the dark angel cast no faintest shadow on the fairness of a summer morning? It was terrible, it was unjust that man, the ruler of the earth, should pass to clay mocked by the undisturbed serenity of nature.

Yesterday the sun had shone upon the still corpse of Jubal Straust; today it shone upon the crumpled body of Hubert Quail. Would—it was a thought that made him shiver—would the sun still shine when his own body lay cold in death?

Where was God that such things could happen? Why did not the heavens darken and a thunderbolt smash across the sky to destroy the man whose hands were stained with the blood of Straust and Quail—the man who had threatened to kill Annerley himself. Where was God?

"God!" repeated Levison scornfully, his cold eyes quelling at a glance Annerley's hysterical outburst. "What have you done in the forty years of your life that He should come at your call, because you are afraid of the dark?"

"No…" Annerley shook his head. "It isn't the dark that frightens me. It's the light. The callous sun that shines unmoved by death…"

He thought that he was speaking the words aloud, but he was only mumbling them over and over in the recesses of his mind.

As though it was an unreal picture, flickering on a silver screen, he saw Quail's body lifted to the bed by Levison and the two hired guards. The guards were powerful men, and Levison was strong, but they strained at the task. Death had robbed Hubert Quail of everything but his huge garment of flesh.

At a nod from Levison, the guards left the room closing the door behind them, and Levison, Annerley, and Doctor Britling, were left alone with the dead man.

Doctor Britling bent over the body, which was clothed in blue silk pyjamas, open almost to the waist, exposing a bronze neck and a chest covered with a thatch of matted hair. The limbs were neatly arranged and the head was supported by a pillow. There was something about the eyes that made the police surgeon shiver. With meticulous care, Daniel examined the dead man. For a long time, he looked at the huge hairy hands, crisscrossed by a score of long scratches.

"Mary's kitten did that yesterday," remarked Levison. "Quail's peculiarity was that he was terrified of cats. He was mauled by a leopard in South Africa and has never since been able to bear the presence of felines of any description. The little animal got into his room somehow, and Quail almost went mad. He tried to strangle it and got those scratches in the attempt. Fortunately for Mary's sake I managed to intervene just in time."

Daniel nodded and went on with his examination.

In due course he turned his attention to the scene of the crime. On the floor beside the bed he found a crumpled newspaper and the remains of a cigarette which had burnt itself to ash on the carpet. A rug beneath the open window lay in an untidy heap as though someone had slipped on it and kicked it aside. The dust on the window ledge has been disturbed by something soft which had rubbed against it, and there were one or two minute scratches on the paintwork of the frame.

Daniel moved about the room, inspecting the furniture, and the dead man's effects. Not a corner escaped him. He opened drawers, cupboards, and suitcases, turning over and carefully examining even the smallest and most innocent-looking articles.

Finally, he went down on his hands and knees and crawled about the floor. He peered under every bulky article of furniture, using an electric torch to pierce the gloom, and covered his hands and the knees of his trousers with dust to no purpose. Nothing more important than spent matches, a collar-stud, and large quantities of dust and fluff rewarded his efforts.

He rose to his feet, dusted the knees of his trousers with a large white linen handkerchief, and turned to find the wild eyes of Mark Annerley staring at him.

"How did he die?" whispered Annerley.

"I don't know," replied Doctor Britling gravely.

"You—don't—know!" There was a shudder in each word.

"Oh, he was poisoned, obviously, but how it was administered, or which of many poisons was used, I haven't the slightest idea."

Doctor Britling paced the room with long strides, his head tilted at an angle towards the carpeted floor.

"He died about half an hour ago. At the time he was in bed reading his newspaper and smoking a cigarette. The door was locked but the window was open…"

Going to the window Daniel looked out. The bedroom was at the rear of the house and overlooked the garden. It was good twenty feet from the window to the smooth turf below, and the walls were in good condition. Nowhere did the surface offer a foothold. Directly below were the windows of the breakfast-room.

"No living man could have climbed that wall without being seen," he ruminated. "And besides, Quail was a big man; he would have struggled…There are no signs of a struggle."

He glanced upward with a frown. Directly above was another window which presumably belonged to a second-floor bedroom, and above that the guttering of the roof projected. He could see that it would not be difficult for an active man to swarm down a rope from the window above, or the roof, to the dead man's bedroom. But again there was the objection that he would certainly have been seen—while Daniel stood at the window, three different guards passed and looked up—and that Quail would have put up a terrific fight for his life in an intruder had entered the room.

"Have you any idea whether the poison was administered internally or otherwise," Levison asked quietly.

"Oh, externally," replied Daniel promptly. "An internal poison which acted so quickly as this one would leave traces in the condition of the mouth and throat. There are none. I should say that it was applied through a puncture in the skin."

"I see...but how the dickens could anyone climb down a rope from above, enter this room—Quail was awake at the time—and inject poison into the veins of a huge man like that, without a struggle? Except for that rug beneath the window the room is perfectly tidy. Why, Quail would have strangled him!"

"It doesn't sound very feasible," Daniel admitted.

"I tell you, it couldn't be done," declared Annerley flatly.

Levison's eyes wandered to the trees that shaded the lawn a few yards away.

"In Central Africa the pygmies used darts tipped with poison, which they fire from blowpipes," he said thoughtfully. "From a high branch in one of those trees one could see into the room..."

"And one would be bound to be seen by one of the guards," retorted Doctor Britling drily. "Besides, in that case, what became of the dart? It isn't lodged in the body, and I've gone over every corner of the room without finding anything of the sort."

"It—it's uncanny," muttered Annerley.

Drawing a cigar-case from his pocket, Daniel extended it towards Levison and Annerley, who silently shook their heads. He selected a cigar, pierced the end cautiously, and lit it with precious care. He was as calm and unruffled in manner and appearance, as he drew on the long brown cylinder and exhaled a cloud of fragrant smoke, as though the man on the bed were only sleeping, instead of dead—murdered! Daniel had seen too many dead men to have many qualms about death.

"Who has the room above?" he asked.

"I—I—I have," stammered Annerley.

"When were you in it last?"

"A—about eight o'clock this morning."

"H'm." Doctor Britling's grey eyes narrowed. "Do you happen to know whether anyone was in the room about half an hour ago?" he asked Levison.

"Young Carver was there, and Moody, the chief of our—er—private police force," answered Levison promptly. "Breakfasting."

"Were they sitting within view of the windows?"

"Yes, directly opposite. Carver was facing the windows."

Doctor Britling nodded. "I should like a word with Mr. Carver."

"Good God!" exclaimed Annerley. "You don't think he—"

"I don't think anything. I am merely casting about for a starting point."

They left the room and Levison locked the door and put the key in his pocket. "Don't bother to come downstairs with us," he said to Annerley calmly. "I should go and lie down if I were you—not too near an open window!"

Doctor Britling and Levison went downstairs, leaving Annerley staring after them with a dumbfounded expression in his unpleasant little eyes. On the ground floor they met the butler, who was despatched to find Adrian Carver and send him to the breakfast-room at once.

In the breakfast-room, Doctor Britling seated himself by the open windows where he had a view of the garden. He looked out at the sun-drenched lawns, and the flowerbeds, like pools of colour, and wondered, as Annerley had done, that man's dark deeds do not sully the beauty of nature.

There was a knock at the door and Adrian Carver came into the room. His large dark eyes were shining with excitement, and his lips were parted, revealing his strong white teeth.

He shot a quick glance at Levison, whose face was grim, but curiosity was bubbling up in him, and it had to find an outlet.

"I say!" he breathed. "Is it really murder?"

"Why should you think so?" rasped Levison.

"Well!" the young man threw his arms wide in an embracing gesture. "Isn't it obvious to the merest intelligence?"

"I think I have said before that your intelligence—and your tongue—are not suited to this environment," said Levison grimly. "I do not think you will be with us long."

Adrian dropped into a chair coolly, and hitched up the knees of his trousers with admirable sangfroid. "I see. I'm to be sacked. Then I've nothing more to worry about."

"I understand that you were in this room half an hour ago, Mr. Carver," said Doctor Britling quietly, with an amused twinkle in his eyes. "Is that so?"

"So, it is murder!" exclaimed Adrian shrewdly. "Murder and I'm on the spot! This is luck!"

"Answer my question please."

"Yes, I was in the room at that time. So was Moody. You'll like Moody, Doctor—a blunt, straightforward chap."

"Never mind Moody. I want to know if you saw anyone in the garden about that time."

The young man shook his head. "Not a soul, except the strong-arm men, who were looking beneath rose bushes and cross-examining caterpillars; unless you mean people who went into the garden from this room. Both Mary Quail and Mrs. Annerley did that."

"Oh?"

"Yes. As a matter of fact—May I smoke? Thanks! —as a matter of fact, there was a bit of a scrap this morning between Mary Quail's kitten and Mrs. Annerley's pom. The dog was in here—I was stroking him—when the kitten strolled in from the garden. There was the usual rumpus and the pair of them bolted, hell for leather, out of the window, the dog after the cat. Miss Quail heard the commotion and ran through the room after her kitten. Mrs. Annerley followed suit a moment later, in the interests of her bally dog."

"I see. Apart from this cat-and-dog affair, you saw and heard nothing that was in any way suspicious?"

"Nothing. Oh, wait a moment! Now I come to think of it, just before the kitten appeared, I heard a faint 'plop'. It sounded like—well like a wet rag being dropped on the ground outside."

"A faint 'plop'?"

"Exactly. It was then that I felt the dog stiffen."

"Could the noise have possibly been made by the explosion of an air-pistol?" Daniel suggested. Adrian Carver wrinkled his forehead.

"It might have been," he said doubtfully. "I wouldn't swear to it."

But an air-pistol, as Daniel reflected ruefully would have left a slug or dart as obvious evidence of its use, in the body, or lying about the room!

The door opened, and Mrs. Annerley came into the room. Beneath her make-up she was deathly pale, and her face was haggard. Her pallor was accentuated by a tight-fitting frock of green crepe-de-chine.

"I'm looking for my dog," she said with a wan smile. "The naughty little thing is hiding in the garden."

Daniel rose and held the windows wider to let her pass through. After a brief pause, with a shrewd glance at Levison, he followed her into the garden. They walked across the crisp turf, Mrs. Annerley crying: "Dodo!" in a high soprano; Daniel peering under bushes and shrubs.

Near the end of the garden, the police surgeon stooped and dragged something from beneath a bush.

His face was grim as he bent over his find. It was the body of a Pomeranian dog!

A Dangerous Kitten

Doctor britling threw away the chewed stump of his cigar, and lit another. He paced up and down the break-fast-room, exhaling clouds of smoke that trailed in his wake. His eyes were almost shut, and his face was quite expressionless, but behind his smooth brow a shrewd brain was fitting together the jigsaw puzzle of the murder of Hubert Quail.

Adrian Carver, at the police surgeon's request, had taken the hysterical Cora Annerley to her own room. The lifeless body of her pet lay upon the table; Levison was bending over it. He was touching the inert animal with a slender forefinger, trying to read from it the riddle of its death.

"Man and dog were killed by the same agency," said Daniel quietly. "The symptoms in each case are identical."

"What killed him?" asked Levison, raising his head.

"A scratch on the nose," replied Daniel.

Levison stared at him incredulously. "For heaven's sake man, don't jest."

"On the contrary, I'm telling you the gospel truth."

Crossing the room to the fireplace, Daniel touched a bell button let into the wall. He continued to walk up and down until the agitated face of Harcourt, the butler, appeared in the doorway.

"Ask Miss Quail to come here, please," he said. "And request her to bring her kitten. Preferably in a basket."

The aged servitor's eyes were staring nervously at the stiff, hairy bundle that lay on the table; it was not until Daniel repeated his instructions that Harcourt bowed slightly and withdrew.

Daniel went to the window and called in Moody, who was

hovering about outside. "Take that to the garage and stow it away out of sight," he said, nodding towards the dead dog.

Moody raised his eyebrows slightly, but took the corpse by its four legs and carried it out of the room.

Daniel glanced at Levison to find the man eyeing him curiously.

"You've got something up your sleeve!" declared Levison.

"I'm beginning to see light," replied Daniel.

The other looked uncomfortable.

"Look here," he said, betraying awkwardness for the first time since Daniel had known him. "Is it absolutely necessary to bring Mary into this? She's just a kid, Britling."

"Absolutely necessary," replied Britling flatly.

They were interrupted by the timid entrance of Mary Quail. The girl was carrying a closed basket in which something rustled. She placed it on a table and turned to face the dapper little police surgeon.

"You sent for me to bring Binkie," she said tremulously.

"Yes, won't you please sit down?" said Daniel, with a reassuring smile.

Mary perched herself gingerly on the extreme edge of a chair. Her hazel eyes were rimmed with red, and her cheeks were unnaturally flushed.

"You've been crying?" asked Daniel gently.

She looked up at him with a touching little smile. "Yes. I couldn't help it. It was so terrible for Uncle to die like that."

"You loved him?"

Her eyes clouded, but she looked at Daniel frankly.

"No, I didn't love him," she admitted. "I think at times I—I almost hated him. He could be so cruel—oh, terribly cruel. Is it wrong for me to say so, now that he's dead? But it's the truth, and one must tell the truth, mustn't one?"

There was something brave and pathetic about her earnest striving to be fair to her uncle, and yet true to herself. Her dark brows came down in a straight line over her puzzled eyes.

Levison uttered an impatient exclamation, but was silenced by a peremptory wave of Doctor Britling's hand.

"Of course, you must tell the truth," Daniel agreed soberly. "Now that your uncle is dead the truth cannot hurt him."

He put his hand on the closed basket. "Your kitten is inside?" he asked.

Mary nodded, and her face lit up for a moment. In some ways she was much younger than her years.

"Yes. I call him 'Binkie'. He's a darling. The first real orange kitten I've ever seen. Sydney Levine gave him to me."

"Did your uncle know you had it? He didn't like cats, did he?"

Mary's pretty face drooped. "No, he hated them like poison. Only yesterday, one of the maids let him out of my room by mistake and somehow, he got into Uncle's room. Uncle was furious. He tried to strangle the poor little thing but Uncle Gideon stopped him. After that, it would have been too dangerous to keep him in my room. Mrs Levine offered to look after him for me. Uncle thought I'd got rid of him—I'm—I'm afraid I lied to him that I had."

"I see." Daniel stood up and beamed down upon the girl. "Well, Miss Quail, that's all for the present. I'd like you to leave your kitten with me; I promise that no harm will come to him."

Mary thanked him and left the room. Daniel looked after her slender, graceful form until the door closed behind her and hid her from his view.

"A charming child," he murmured.

He turned away and picked up the tablecloth, which, in the excitement that had ensured since Adrian Carver's belated breakfast, had been left on the sideboard.

"May I ask why you want the kitten?" asked Levison, opening the basket.

Doctor Britling spun round hastily. "For God's sake don't touch it!" he cried.

Levison dropped the lid hastily. "What the dickens..."

Daniel opened the basket gingerly and swathed the kitten carefully in the tablecloth until only its head showed. He wrapped the cloth round and round until the kitten, mewing in protest, was wrapped like a mummy. Lifting it out of the basket, he placed it on its back on the table.

"Lend me a hand, will you?" he requested over his shoulder. "I want you to hold the little animal firmly on his back."

In grim silence, Levison complied. Exercising extreme caution, Daniel withdrew one of the kitten's paws from the voluminous wrapping, and, holding it warily, pressed the central pad to extend the claws. For a long moment he examined the claws intently. When he looked up his face wore a satisfied expression.

"Allow me to introduce you to 'Binkie'," he said quietly. "The murderer of Hubert Quail!"

With Gloved Hands

T HE MURDERER OF Hubert Quail!" Gideon Levison stared from the kitten, swaddled in layers of cloth, to the smartly dressed little police surgeon. His dark eyes wore a startled, incredulous expression.

"A kitten killed Quail," he murmured in an awed tone. "But—but—why, it seems ridiculous."

"Nevertheless, it is true," said Daniel steadily. "His claws are tipped with a gummy substance, probably a combination based upon one of the curare group of poisons."

Levison mentally digested the information. "Then killing Quail was only chance? The kitten might have killed any of us." He shook his head definitely. "No, that's not like Marckheim. He'd never do anything so haphazard as that."

"There was no element of chance in it," responded Daniel gravely. "Quail was the kitten's intended victim. How otherwise could it have found its way into his bedroom, since the door was locked on the inside? The kitten was manoeuvred into the room. The whole thing was planned rather ingeniously. I am beginning to share your respect for the mental powers of Arthur Marckheim. He would make a fascinating psychological study."

Picking up Binkie, he replaced him in the basket. "Do you know where there is a fishing rod in the house?" he asked.

"Yes, Annerley has one. He's rather a keen fisherman."

"I'd like to borrow it for a few minutes."

"I daresay it's up in his room; we're all camping out in our bedrooms, more or less, these days."

"The other clues to the riddle are upstairs, between Quail's bedroom and the roof," said Daniel, picking up the kitten's basket. "I suggest we go upstairs and investigate. The kitten was lowered to Quail's window either from the bedroom above—Annerley's room—or the roof."

They went upstairs. Daniel carried the basket containing the kitten. As they went, a door below the stairs opened, and the white cap of Jules, the Swiss chef, appeared in the aperture; as they passed the drawing-room the butler, the footman, and a parlour maid ceased a heated discussion they had been holding and made awkward pretence of attending to pressing duties. Through the half-open door, Levison and Doctor Britling were aware of three pairs of eyes staring at them in horrible fascination. Death had thrown about them his mantle of morbid enchantment. They were part of the macabre drama that was being enacted before the startled eyes of the servants, and only one player in the drama had greater importance in the eyes of the audience than they—and that was the murderer. The murderer, who might even now be walking about the house, free from suspicion, perhaps mingling with the servants themselves, sharing with grisly glee in the flood of gossip that death had unleashed.

On the first floor landing they found Adrian Carver, who was cautiously trying the handle of the door behind which lay the dead body of Hubert Quail. In response to Levison's fury he smiled charmingly and withdrew.

"A most persistent young man," commented Daniel.

Levison made no reply, but there was an ugly glitter in his dark eyes.

Annerley was in bedroom, looking out of the window. He wheeled with a startled exclamation as they came into the room without the formality of knocking.

"That secretary of yours," snapped Levison, cutting short his angry flow of remonstrance. "Get rid of him. He's altogether too nosy. Write him a cheque and pack him off at once."

With a sullen shrug of his shoulders, Annerley slouched

towards the door. With his hand on the door knob, he paused and looked back. "What are you two going to do in here?" he demanded.

"We're going to make an effort to save your hide," retorted Levison.

The other's fists clenched, but he left the room in silence, slamming the door behind him.

Levison went to the window and examined the ledge carefully. He bent down and looked closely at some marks upon the wooden frame.

"Finger marks!" he exclaimed. "Made—confound it—by a gloved hand."

"Did you expect anything else from the wily Mr. Marckheim?" said Daniel. "Criminals—even the amateurs—know far too much nowadays."

He had put down the basket and was fitting together the component parts of a fishing rod which he had discovered in a corner enclosed in a brown limp leather case. He fitted the rod together and attached the reel. In a pocket in the case was a leather wallet containing hooks and flies. He fasted one of the hooks to the catgut line.

Reaching into the basket he produced the kitten and carried it to the window, still safely wrapped in the tablecloth. About the kitten's neck was a bright blue leather collar with a silver ring and nameplate attached to it. Making sure that the collar was securely fastened, he slipped the fishing-hook through the ring and manipulated the kitten through the open window, whisking off the cloth, as the little animal slowly spun downwards at the end of the line.

Playing out the line slowly, he lowered it until it was on a level with the window ledge below. A skilled manipulation soon inveigled the helpless little ball of fur to the window ledge. He dipped the rod to disengage the hook, then struck the kitten one or two sharp blows with the end of the rod. With a plaintive mew, the kitten dropped into the bedroom of Hubert Quail.

Levison drew a deep breath. "So that was how it was done!" he exclaimed huskily. "How infernally cunning!"

Daniel reeled in the line and began to take the rod to pieces again. "You can imagine Quail, who hated cats, suddenly becoming aware of the kitten's presence in the room," he remarked. "Rising in a fury, catching it, and probably trying to wring its neck. It scratched him, and escaping, leapt through the window to the garden below. The sound of its landing must have been the faint 'plop' that Carver heard before it appeared at the French windows."

"Talking of Carver," said Levison grimly, "Look!"

Following with his eyes the direction of Levison's pointing finger, Doctor Britling saw Adrian Carver walking down the drive between Moody and another burly man, who escorted him to the gates. As the gates were opened for the young man, he looked back, and, seeing the faces at the window, blew a mocking kiss. Suitcase in hand, he passed through the gates, and they clanged to behind him.

"I'm sorry," said Daniel simply. "I liked that young man."

"So did I," replied Levison surprisingly. "But it was impossible for him to remain. I only hope he won't open his mouth too widely to the reporters. There's quite a little gathering of them hanging about the gates, like a lot of carrion crows. One of them tried to climb the wall; he won't recover in a hurry from the crack on the head he received from one of the guards."

"What about the local police?" asked Daniel.

Levison laughed. "They're making solemn arrangements for an inquest on Jubal," he replied. "And following a lead I gave them which will take their best man to London for a few hours.

I haven't appraised them yet of Quail's death. There'll be trouble about the delay, but I'm not worried about that. When I do tell them, the place will be swarming with flat-footed, large-bellied constables and inspectors and what not. There's time enough for that after we've gone over the ground ourselves."

They went downstairs to secure the kitten, Daniel carrying the tablecloth in which it had been wrapped and its basket. As they entered the room where the murdered man lay, the kitten scurried across the floor and dived under the bed, flattening itself against the wall. Daniel closed the windows and the door and was about to go down on his hands and knees to reach under the bed when Levison pushed him back.

"This is my job," he said quietly.

He poked about under the bed with a walking stick, which had belonged to the dead man, and forced the kitten out into the open. It sprang to a chair and leapt from there to a chest of drawers, knocking over a bottle of hair-oil in its retreat, with arched back, to the wall.

Daniel approached gingerly with the tablecloth in his hands, but the kitten evaded him and jumped to the bed. For a moment it sprawled there, clawing at the sheet which covered the man it had innocently killed, then it scampered down his draped legs and launched itself to the floor. Another chair was a stepping stone to the mantelpiece; from which its flying body swept an onyx clock which smashed to the hearth. It crouched on the precarious perch the mantelpiece afforded, its yellow eyes gleaming wickedly, its tail swishing with anger.

Its extended claws contained enough death to exterminate the entire household!

Gripping the walking stick by the ferruled end, Levison approached the mantelpiece cautiously and hooked the handle about the kitten's neck. With a sudden jerk, he catapulted it to the floor. Pouncing quickly, he gripped Binkie by the scruff of the neck before the kitten could put up a claw to protect itself. Swish! The cloth went about it, and plop! It was dropped into the basket and the lid was slammed down and securely fastened.

"What are we going to do with the little brute?" asked Levison hoarsely.

"Keep it for Scotland Yard," replied Daniel.

"They're welcome to it!" grunted Levison, mopping his brow.

A Letter to Eunice

DOCTOR DANIEL BRITLING sat at a writing-table placed beneath the bow window of his bedroom at Grey Towers, and his eyes searched the horizon for inspiration, while his white teeth chewed upon the end of his fountain pen. He was about to write a letter to his sister, and he knew that no matter how much he told her she would want to know more. That made it difficult, for there were many things he had no intention of telling her, and it was necessary to achieve the appearance, at least, of frankness.

He made several abortive starts before the letter began to take shape.

My dear Eunice:

Chief Inspector Howells, of Scotland Yard, has arrived here and is in charge of affairs, so I have retired to my room in a fit of the sulks, and am taking the opportunity of writing a belated letter to you. Howells, I may mention, was distinctly taken aback at encountering me here. I have told you about him often—a large, truculent fellow, who regards me with jaundiced eyes. If you remember, I nobbled the murderer in the Hawk Club case right under his nose when he was almost ready to put the wrong man in the dock. Since then, he's been curt to the point of rudeness on every occasion when we've been associated, and watches me like a hawk while I'm examining the body, if there is one. I believe he'd like me to conduct my examination at a distance of twenty feet lest the dead lips whisper to me the identity of the murderer before he's had the opportunity of hanging the wrong man.

At all events he's here in force with a corps of cameramen, fingerprint experts and whatnot. The proceedings started with a dickens-of-a-row between Howells and the local chief constable on one side and Gideon Levison (the banker) on the other, about the delay in notifying the police about the murder of Hubert Quail (yes another of the six has died; his body was discovered in his room about eleven o'clock this morning, and the police weren't informed until this afternoon; I expect you'll have read all about it in the papers by the time you receive this). Levison won the argument hands down. He would—he's the coolest card I've ever met. Hard and utterly callous in many respects, but a man to the core. Howells would have liked to make this house his headquarters in the neighbourhood, but Levison told him point-blank that there were no vacant bedrooms (there are at least seven) and that if he wanted to stop for the night, he'd have to sleep on two chairs. So, Howells is putting up at the local pub. From now on, I understand, a uniformed constable will be stationed at the garden gate and in the hall of the house. Much good they are likely to be! We—I say we because, since the arrival of Howells, I have begun to identify myself with Levison—we are to be permitted to retain the twelve pugilists who patrol the grounds of the house, but they are not on any account to be provided with firearms. Levison seemed shocked at the very idea, and he suavely assured Howells that of course they wouldn't be. (Each of them has at least one huge automatic!)

Quail, the second victim, was killed by the poisoned claws of a kitten which was lowered to his bedroom window on the end of a fishing line. I had worked that out before Howells arrived on the scene, but he wasn't at all grateful to me for having saved him work and brain fog. He muttered something, not at all beneath his breath, about interfering busybodies! I became very much upon my dignity, and withdrew, not angry, but very, very hurt. You would have enjoyed the scene!

That man, Eunice, can go down on his bended knees to me—and will do, if any of the others die—and I won't help him a scrap. I only hope Marckheim devises some particularly unpleasant surprise for him! There's nothing I'd like better than performing an autopsy on his fat carcas. It may be a horrid nasty temper, but that's the way I feel.

On re-reading the previous paragraph, I realise you don't know who Marckheim is. I mean Arthur Marckheim who you will remember went to prison twelve years ago in connection with the Eldorado Investment Company swindle. It appears that he was made the scapegoat by his associates in that affair, who were, of course, the men who have called me in to help them. Marckheim is now out of prison and revenging himself on his faithless partners. No matter how much one may deprecate his methods, one can hardly blame him.

Eunice, I've become discouraged. Jubal Straust, who first invited me to investigate this case, died at my side a couple of hours later; within sixteen hours of my arrival in the house the murderer had claimed his second victim. My presence was utterly useless to them. What good am I to these condemned men if I can only discover how they died after they are dead, and cannot save them? I am beginning to fear that the three men and one woman who remain will inevitably go the same way, and I feel acutely my absolute incapacity to prevent it. Marckheim is a remarkably clever man, and I have never laid claim to cleverness. Such success in criminology as I have enjoyed has been gained pure and simply by keeping an open mind and by nosing into every conceivable corner.

The two who have died have not affected me very deeply, and I shall shed no tears over the passing of Mark Annerley, but I am afraid that I will feel it very deeply if Levison dies. I have conceived a great liking for him. Courage like his is a very wonderful quality and compensates in my opinion for his many bad ones.

Old Israel Straust, the owner of the wonderful old mansion in which this drama is being enacted, is an extraordinary character. As I write, I can see him through the window pottering about in the garden. He loves flowers—odd, isn't it, since the death of his only son left him unmoved? He looks like an old and withered crow, with his long black coat flapping about him like wings and his head bent inwards, his shoulder bowed as though a heavy load were pressing up his neck. He wears an ancient black felt hat, the brim of which, soaked by many rains, droops about his ears. He goes for a drive in his 'Rolls Royce' every afternoon, driven by Sydney Levine, the crippled grandson of his housekeeper, and all that one can see of him, huddled alone in the wide rear seat, is a rusty black hat, voluminous black cloak, long white beard. and huge nose. I cannot believe that Marckheim will kill him; his grip on life, in any case, is feeble.

They do us very well here. My bedroom is large and airy, with walls panelled in black oak that must have cost a small fortune. The furniture is Jacobean, genuine antique, every bit of it and—luxury and luxuries! —I have a private bathroom with walls of sea-green tile and a long deep tub; the floor is carpeted with pale-green rubber. There is a profusion of soaps and bath salts and a huge mound of thick, fleecy towels. What it is to be a millionaire! Last night, I lay and soaked in warm water for over an hour, revelling in the embracing heat. This environment would soon make me a hedonist!

This will amuse you, I know, and interest you more than anything I have already written; in spite of the lavish surroundings and the high polish that is apparent on all the furniture, there is dust and fluff under the beds and everywhere else where it is not noticeable! Israel Straust, of course, has no women folk of his own, and his housekeeper, Mrs. Levine, is a woman of advanced years. Apparently, she is not particular as long as dirt does not obtrude itself! The maids, I should imagine, have an easy time of it. How you would love to take them in hand for a week! I can picture them running about like frightened hens, while you make the dust fly with a whisk-broom!

Daniel put down his pen and read what he had written. He deleted a word here and there and added a sentence or two. It would be best, he decided, not to say anything about when he might be expected home. Eunice would say quite sufficient about that when she wrote in reply! And besides, it was impossible to fix a definite date. Whatever happened, he was determined to stay and see this affair out to the end.

Picking up the pen he wrote the last lines:

You will understand, of course, that this letter is for your eyes alone.

Your affectionate brother,

DANIEL

He put the letter in an envelope, sealed it, and addressed it to Miss Britling. For a little while he sat at the window watching the scarecrow figure of Israel Straust as it moved with slow uncertain steps through the garden. He saw Mary Quail, her dress a flutter of white, come running down a path and offer her arm to the old man. They walked on together, presenting an odd picture that was somehow touching.

Glancing at his watch, Daniel realised that it would soon be time for dinner. He went into the bathroom which led from his bedroom and started a flow of warm water running into the tub.

The footman, who had laid out his clothes the previous evening, had not appeared, probably because of the disruption in the household arrangements caused by the arrival of the Scotland Yard officials, so Daniel performed that office for himself. It was while he was thus engaged that his eyes fell on a square white envelope that lay on the carpeted floor near the door of his room. He stood looking at it for a moment, with a dress-shirt in his hand. He was prepared to swear that it had not been there when he sat down to write his letter to Eustice—and he had heard no faintest rustling while had been writing.

With a philosophic shrug of the shoulders, he stooped and picked it up. He tore it open, extracted a single sheet of notepaper, and read the few lines that were typed in the centre of the page:

> What a clever little man you are, Doctor Britling! It did not take you long to discover how Quail died. I doubt whether the estimable Chief Inspector from Scotland Yard, who is now blundering about the house, would ever have solved the riddle for himself. It is a pity that the world must be deprived of your shrewd brain, but you took your life in your hands when you ignored my previous warning. I am afraid I must send you to join Jubal Straust and Hubert Quail.

Daniel read the letter with steady eyes, then placed it upon the mantelpiece. His face was expressionless as he started to undress, but his eyes were very thoughtful. He knew only too well that Marckheim's bite was worse than his bark! But there was no cowardice in the little police surgeon's composition.

A few minutes later, a faintly discordant noise betrayed the fact that Doctor Britling could still summon sufficient spirit to sing in his bath!

Dr. Britling's Peril

"COCKTAIL?" SUGGESTED Gideon Levison.

"I think I am entitled to one on this occasion," replied Doctor Britling drily.

Levison looked at him with one eyebrow cocked. "Something in the wind?"

"Only the trifling matter of my imminent decease," said Daniel drily.

This rather startling remark did not disturb in any way the perfect composure of Gideon Levison. He continued to manipulate the cocktail shaker in expert fashion, although he turned his sleek head in Daniel's direction and favoured him with an enquiring glance.

The hour was a quarter to eight, and they were in the library awaiting the announcement that dinner was served. Mark Annerley was the only other occupant of the room, but he had consumed so much alcoholic stimulant in the course of the day that he was there in the flesh only. He was now engaged in sleeping off the effects of his dissipation in the depths of a comfortable armchair from which every now and again came a fitful grunting and sighing, somewhat akin to the sounds a sleeping dog utters when he is a prey to exciting dreams, but with an undernote of fear running through it.

Levison filled two glasses with pale green liquid and handed one to Daniel, who sipped it appreciatively.

"Alright?"

"Excellent, thanks."

"Good!" Levison sampled his own. "H'm, not bad. Tell me, what exactly did you mean by the remark you made?"

Daniel handed him the letter he had found on the floor of

his bedroom. Levison read it with raised eyebrows. When he looked up there was a worried look in his eyes which Daniel had not seen there before.

"Doctor," he said gravely, "I should clear out, if I were you."

"Don't talk rot!" retorted Daniel brusquely. "If you were me, you'd stay. You know you would."

A faint smile flickered across the others lean face. "Perhaps I should. But that doesn't alter the fact that you're in danger— terrible danger." He reclined against the table, and swung one black-clad leg. "Something tells me that we're fighting the inevitable," he remarked, calmly. "Frankly, I don't think you or anyone else can help us. I hate to think of you risking your life to no purpose. I wish you'd go."

Daniel met his gaze squarely. "I intend to stay."

Levison tapped the letter with a long slim finger, and his dark eyes looked straight into Daniel's grey ones. "I shouldn't underestimate this warning."

Daniel met the gaze squarely. "I'm estimating it at its face value," he replied simply.

There was a pause while they exchanged understanding smiles.

"Will you shake hands?" Doctor Britling took the proffered hand and shook it warmly. "You're an obstinate little devil," said the financier lightly. "Another cocktail?"

"Thanks, I will."

As they sipped their cocktails, Levison produced a square white envelope which was the fellow of the one which had encased the warning message Doctor Britling had received, extracted a single sheet of notepaper, and handed it to his companion without comment. The words: "You are the third," typewritten in the centre of the sheet, was the brutally brief inscription.

"He's going to be busy with two murders to arrange," said Levison drily, watching Daniel's face.

"You'll be on your guard every minute," Daniel almost pleaded.

The other's face set in grim, hard lines. "Yes. This time his task won't be easy." Leaning backwards across the table, he picked up an evening newspaper and spread it flat, pointing to a line of large type which was spread across the entire width of the page, reinforced by several minor headings and two columns of print:

FIVE FINANCIERS MARKED FOR DEATH!
TWO ALREADY MURDERED IN COLD BLOOD
DRASTIC REVENGE PLOT ALLEGED

"The work of Chief Inspector Howells," said Levison grimly. "I had to tell him the whole story, and the fathead gabbled it to the reporters. For that he dines tonight at the village pub—or not at all!"

"It had to come out sooner or later," Daniel pointed out.

"Naturally, but I've held it up this far for a damned good reason." Levison indicated a paragraph set in larger type:

PANIC OF STOCK EXCHANGE
TWELVE STOCKS BLACKLISTED

As the result of frenzied dealing in the shares of companies in which the five financiers, two dead, and three alleged to be doomed, were interested, the value of the stocks hurriedly unloaded dropped to a matter of shillings from a previous value of pounds. Trading in these stocks has been temporarily suspended. The companies affected are...

"Fortunately, I've come well out of it," he remarked quietly. "Yesterday afternoon when I heard about the death of Jubal I 'phoned my agents to sell these stocks short and continue to sell until further orders. Today, when the panic broke, I bought back all I had contracted to deliver at a fraction of the price for which I sold. I've made, at a conservative estimate, a million pounds on the deal."

Daniel eyed him curiously. "You had the nerve to conduct a gigantic operation like that while your very life was in danger?"

The other laughed bitterly. "It's in the blood to take advantage of opportunity, no matter in what manner she knocks. Mark, on the other hand, could think of nothing but his skin. He isn't sober enough to realise it yet, but I should imagine he's wiped out."

"What—" Daniel repressed the question he was about to ask, but Levison was shrewd enough to guess its import.

"You were going to ask what use a million pounds will be to me if I die tonight?"

"Something like that," Daniel admitted reluctantly.

"Put like that, the struggle for money is futile," Levison murmured reflectively. "I couldn't take it with me. I might leave it to charity—a Fund for the Relief of Distressed Clericals!" He laughed at that. "Yes, that's an idea! Ministers are the greatest suckers in the world. I'd like to feel they were getting back a little of what I've taken from them."

Dinner was a subdued affair. Only five were present out of the seven who had dined together the previous evening. Hubert Quail had been removed from the need for earthly sustenance. His niece was dining alone in her room. The conversation was disjointed and desultory, and no one, apparently, had much of an appetite.

Halfway through the meal, Cora Annerley, whose face was

thick with make-up to hide the ghastly pallor beneath, leaned across the table and laid two white pellets in front of Daniel.

"I found one of them in my ring this morning," she said hoarsely. "And the other in the same place while I dressing for dinner. I had locked the ring away in my jewel-case and there was no sign that the lock had been forced, but there they were. They—they almost seemed to mock me...death in my ring, every time I look there. I'm beginning to be afraid."

Daniel put the pellets of poison in his waistcoat pocket.

"They can do you no harm—in your ring," he reminded her.

Mrs. Annerley looked away sharply, as though she were afraid that her eyes would betray the struggle that was going on in her mind.

Old Israel Straust cackled with malignant laughter.

As Levison and Doctor Britling were leaving the dining room together, they encountered Chief Inspector Howells, who was about to leave the house. Ignoring Doctor Britling, he addressed Levison with an unpleasant light in his eyes.

"I'm returning to the Yard for a consultation with the Chief Commissioner," he said brusquely. "I'm taking with me the fingerprints of every person in the house or grounds with the exception of yourself Mr. Straust, Mr. Annerley, and" —he turned heavy eyes on Daniel— "Doctor Britling, here. If Arthur Marckheim is in the house disguised, or if any persons known to the police are employed among the domestic staff, I'll know about it in a few hours, and will communicate with the local police, who will know what steps to take. I'm leaving a plainclothes detective and two constables in charge, and I'll be back in the village myself before dawn." He coughed aggressively. "It will be necessary, of course, for me to place the facts of your obstruction of the police before my superiors. Doubtless you will hear further of the matter in due course."

"I shall be delighted," replied Levison suavely. "Excuse me, will you? I need a little fresh air." To Daniel he added, "Going for a stroll, Doctor. Care to come?"

"No thanks," replied Doctor Britling. "I've something I want to do in my room."

His eyes added the unspoken warning to be careful.

Levison patted his shoulder lightly. Running down the steps of the house, he strode across the lawn towards an obscure garden gate where he was unlikely to encounter any reporters.

Chief Inspector Howells glared after him in silence for a moment, then beckoned to one of his subordinates who was waiting in the hall with a closed basket (which Daniel instantly recognised) in his hands.

"We've got a journey in front of us, my lad," he growled. "Let's get a move on."

Doctor Britling turned away. As he mounted the stairs to his room, he heard a sudden shout from behind and the orange kitten sprinted past him. The detective who had been carrying it had fumbled with the catch of the basket to make sure it was secure; the lid had popped open, and the kitten, grasping an opportunity, had squirmed out. White-faced with alarm, the detective hurried up the stairs on Daniel's heels. As they reached the first-floor landing, they saw the kitten scampering along the corridor.

It scuttled through the door of Doctor Britling's room, which was slightly ajar. The door opened wider, and there was a faint tinkle of broken glass. Daniel grasped the arm of the detective, who had been about to follow the kitten into the room, and drew him back to the head of the stairs.

"If I'm not mistaken, the kitten has run into a trap which was meant for me," he said grimly. "Don't you make the same mistake!"

He waited a little while, then pushed the door of his bedroom wider gingerly and switched on the light. On the floor just inside the room lay the limp body of the orange kitten and the broken pieces of a glass bomb about the size of a cricket ball, which had been suspended over the door.

A faint odour of peach-blossom hung on the air…

"Cyanide gas," commented Doctor Britling. "One good sniff and I'd have been a goner," he added inelegantly.

The Return of Adrian Carver

THE EVENING PASSED slowly as Doctor Britling waited for Levison to return. Nine o'clock…ten…eleven…the laggard hands crept sluggishly over the face of the clock, but still there was no sign of the tall, erect figure for which he waited.

Daniel sat in the library with his head sunk on his breast and a chewed stump of cigar between his teeth, listening to the monotonous tick…tick…tick as the seconds slipped away into space. Israel Straust was crouched over the inevitable game of patience before the dancing flames of the fire. Mark Annerley was mercifully sunk in slumber his open mouth emitting shuddering snores. His wife was reading a book, but very now and again her eyes wandered from the printed page to stare unseeingly into the curling smoke and flame in the grate.

At ten the sky darkened. A gust of wind swept the rustling branches of the heavy oaks that surrounded the house, and the windows were spattered with raindrops. A blinding flash rent the lowering sky, followed by a rumble of thunder, like cannonballs rolling down the golden stairs of Heaven. Then the storm broke with demonical fury. A tempestuous wind raged about the house, shrieking down the tall chimneys like a lost soul suffering the torments of the damned. A flood of rain drenched the turf and pattered on the brick terrace that fringed the house.

Annerley shivered and sat up, blinking owlishly in the light. He listened to the furious raging of the storm and the mounting clamour of the thunder with a startled expression.

Straust looked up from his cards with an evil, mocking laugh. "Did you think that the Devil had come for you?" he purred. "Or are you wishing he had? Of the two, I think you fear Marky most."

"Damn you!" shouted Annerley, jerking up in his chair, his face suffused with red. "Don't use that name! I can't stand the sound of it!"

The old man's eyes glittered malignantly. "Marky," he repeated, his curling lips revealing the blackened stumps of his teeth. "We used to pat him on the back and call him that. Good old Marky! That was in the days before—"

Cora Annerley shot him a glance full of venom. "What are you trying to do?" she demanded huskily. "Wrack our nerves to shreds!"

Daniel started at that. His head came up slowly, and he stared at his host with a peculiar light in his eyes. An amazing idea had been born in his brain. Supposing—but no, the thought was too fantastic, too bizarre, to be harboured for a moment. And yet, wasn't everything that had happened in this house fantastic, bizarre?

That shrunken mockery of a man, with the long nose the tapering, stringy beard, the bent form, would be easy to impersonate, just as the caricature is easiest to draw…He was so distinctive, his appearance was so unmistakeable, that a skilful actor could make himself up as an exact double. What was it that Daniel had written to his sister only a few hours ago? —"All that one can see of him, huddled alone in the wide rear seat, is a rusty black hat, voluminous black cloak, long white beard, and huge nose…" Who familiar with the aged financier, and seeing such a figure, would doubt that it was Israel Straust?

Supposing (unreal though it appeared) that Marckheim had made the old man his first victim, concealed his body, and assumed his identity…sent the sinister warnings to the others and gathered them together at Grey Towers, where he would be able to deal out death to each in turn, disguised perfectly as one of themselves.

It would be exactly the master stroke of diabolic cunning that would appeal to the twisted brain of Arthur Marckheim. To kill them, one by one, unsuspected by his victims or by the police; to watch, with fiendish eyes, their antics as the shadow of death enfolded them...

And yet, seeing that palsied, trembling hand, that rheumy eye, that faintly nodding head, how could one doubt that senility inhabited the withered shell that huddled over the cards, touching this one with a skinny talon, moving that one to another position in the intricate pattern?

But the thought would not be stilled that Marckheim might be sitting there, chuckling at his own supreme cunning, at the subtlety of his revenge.

While Daniel pondered the matter, the telephone rang.

Annerley looked up dully, but made no move to answer it, so Daniel rose and picked up the receiver. "Hello?"

The voice of Chief Inspector Howells came to him from the other end of the wire. "Am I speaking to Mr. Levison?"

"No. This is Doctor Britling. Mr. Levison hasn't yet returned from his stroll."

A harsher note was evident in the other's voice when he spoke again. "I'm just leaving the Yard to return to your neighbourhood, but I thought I'd better ring up Levison to tell him that we've checked the fingerprints of the servants and are satisfied that Arthur Marckheim is not in the house."

Daniel's eyes flickered to the bowed figure inclined over the cards. "I wonder," he said, and hung up.

With another glance at the object of his suspicion, he strolled across the room and opened the French windows. The storm which had ranged for an hour was abating; the subdued whine of the dying wind sounded like a funeral dirge. As he closed the windows behind him, a fitful spasm of rain spattered his dinner-clothes and dimmed the lustre of his patent leather pumps, as though a giant, weary of his game, were tossing abroad his last handfuls of water. The clock in the room behind him mournfully chimed half-past eleven.

Lighting a fresh cigar, he sauntered across the soggy lawn, his uneasiness concerning Levison returning. As he passed a bush, drenched leaves brushed icily against his cheek and dripped a cold globule of water down his neck. A light flashed in his face, but was hurriedly put out as the vigilant Mr. Moody recognised him.

"Hell of a night, sir," muttered Mr. Moody.

Suddenly the strident clamour of the alarm bell shattered the silence. There was a hoarse shout and electric torches flashed upon the wall that surrounded the garden. For a moment, the figure of a man was silhouetted astride the wall, then it fell sideways and disappeared out of sight.

The gloom was pierced by the intersecting rays of many pocket torches and burly figures could be seen running awkwardly about and shouting hoarsely. Then the garden was drenched in light.

Daniel stumbled as the sudden brilliance dazzled his eyes, and he staggered with outstretched arms into the hands of a large man who gripped him tightly. It was Mr. Moody, who was volubly apologetic when he realised upon whom his thick fingers had closed.

The police surgeon retreated to the terrace, and, his eyes becoming accustomed to the bright light, looked searchingly across the cropped turf to the high wall where the garden ended. On that side of the house, at least, there was no sign of an intruder. He stood there for some minutes watching for further developments.

He started as a fingertip touched the back of his neck, and

whirled to find a slim, white-clad figure standing in the gloom just inside the French windows of the dining room.

"Sssh!" The whisper reassured him. "It's me, Mary Quail. He's in my room."

"He!" Daniel was startled. "You can't mean the man who has just broken in?"

"It's Adrian—I mean, Mr. Carver. He asked me to fetch you."

In astonished silence, Daniel followed her thorough the dim room and up the deserted stairs. As they reached the second-floor landing, the pounding of heavy feet below apprised them that the house was being searched.

Mary opened the door of her room and let him in. Adrian Carver was standing by the window watching the commotion in the garden through a gap in the drawn curtains, his cheeks flushed with excitement.

"What a lark!" he breathed. "I knew I could beat their wonderful system!"

"You're a damned young fool!" snapped Daniel angrily. "What's the meaning of this?"

The young man looked crestfallen. "It was such wonderful luck," he grumbled, "being in a house where staggering things were happening. Murder! Gosh! I've always longed to be on the inside of a really clever murder! When Levison had me thrown out, I swore to myself that I wouldn't stay out. So I've come back—and here I am!"

"I met him on the stairs," supplemented Mary.

Adrian flashed her an admiring glance. "She's been wonderful!" he said warmly. "She knew there'd be a dickens of a row if I were caught, so she hid me in here and went for you. We both thought you'd sympathise."

"Oh," Doctor Britling's eyebrows rose grimly. "And what did you expect to gain by this—this absurd piece of dare-devilry?"

"Why, why, I thought I might work undercover; perhaps discover the murderer…"

Daniel uttered a short dry laugh, which was utterly devoid of humour. "Didn't you realise, that even if you escaped capture by the guards, such a project as you intended would lead you into appalling danger, for which you are utterly unprepared; that the man you so boldly planned to unmask might add you to his victims; that—"

He broke off sharply as he realised Adrian's eyes were glistening with enthusiasm.

"Yes, I realised all that," the youth agreed eagerly. "That's the fun of the thing…"

"Fun!" Doctor Britling spat out the word. "Fun! You must be mad!"

He tossed his sodden cigar stump into the empty fireplace. "How did you manage to escape the guards?" he asked.

A rippling laugh gurgled from Adrian's throat. "That was easy! I had it all worked out in advance. Directly I climbed the wall the alarm bell rang, as you know, and someone flashed a light in my face. I dropped into the garden. The guards were running about, flashing their lights everywhere—you know how ex-pugilists run, with awkward lumbering strides—so I ran about that way myself, flashing my light about and shouting in a gruff voice, working nearer the house all the time. It was a perfect disguise; none of them suspected me—they didn't expect an intruder to run about in the dark with them, helping them look for himself! When the boasted lighting system was turned on this is the joke of it all! The light was so bright that no one could see a thing. I'd counted on that, of course. I sprinted softly for the house and met Mary—Miss Quail, on the stairs."

The noise of pounding feet was drawing nearer; with every passing moment the search was becoming hotter.

"So…murmured Daniel. "That was how it was done…H'm, quite ingenious of you."

"I thought so," said Adrian modestly. "You won't give me away, will you?" he added.

Doctor Britling hesitated. Mary Quail put a hand on his arm and looked at him appealingly. "Oh, you won't do that? Please, please say you won't?"

"The guards will be here directly," Daniel pointed out.

"They won't look in here," Mary whispered. "If—if you tell them the room is empty."

With a chuckle, Daniel pinched her smooth cheek. "Minx!" he said. "I ought to hand you over," he added, looking sternly at Adrian, "but Moody might be inclined to visit his ire on you for hoaxing him so neatly."

He went out of the room and closed the door. The girl and the youth, crouching close to the panels, heard him answering a question put by a gruff voice, then the searchers passed on.

In a few minutes Doctor Britling returned. "They've gone downstairs again," he said.

The warm lips of Mary Quail brushed his cheek. "You're a dear," she whispered.

Daniel nodded to Adrian. "When the coast is clear I'll smuggle you down to my room. You can spend the night on the bathroom floor. I think there are sufficient towels to make you a reasonably comfortable mattress.

"You utter idiot!" he added.

Levison the Next Victim

L EVISON WALKED MILES through the gathering dusk without noticing, or caring, where his feet carried him. At length he came to a country inn, and went into the parlour to rest.

The place was filled with the wholesome smell of honest beer, and the low rafters were wreathed with curling blue smoke; the atmosphere was hazy with it. Through the haze he saw half a dozen cheerful red faces, half a dozen large red hands holding pint mugs; half a dozen pipes glowing in as many mouths. The landlord, a smiling man, comfortably padded with flesh about the waist, beamed welcome from behind the chipped oak bar. Although Levison was in dinner clothes, there was no curiosity in the frank eyes of the men who sat on rough wooden benches round the low room, only a friendliness that warmed his heart. One or two of them greeted him quietly; an old man murmured that it was 'blowin' up for a wild night.

A wild night! Only Levison knew what the night was likely to be for him. It might be his last on earth.

He spent the evening pleasantly, drinking beer out of a pint mug and chatting with farm labourers who did not know that he was a great man in the city, reputed to be a millionaire, and who would not have cared if they had known.

They talked of politics, of the weather, of the state of the crops, even of the B.B.C. programmes, listening attentively when Levison spoke, and volunteering their own views without diffidence. Here, in the friendly atmosphere of a country inn, one man was as good as another. The talk drifted to the five financiers whose fate had occupied so much space in the evening papers. Opinions differed as to the justice of Marckheim's revenge.

"'Tis a turrible thing to kill in cold blood," observed an old man gravely.

"They behaved like dogs," demurred another. "'Tis rightful they should die like dogs. Don't 'ee agree, sir?"

"I do," said Levison soberly.

But Levison did not intend to die.

The rain came on just before closing time. The landlord lent him a raincoat, soiled by years of hard wear and cut to fit a shorter more spacious figure than that of Gideon Levison, but he accepted it gratefully and went out into the storm, the wind whipping its white frock against his legs.

For two hours he walked, chewing more than he smoked of innumerable cigars. And while he walked, unconscious of his drenched garments and mud-stained trousers, his brain was wondering the urgent question of its own personal safety. Levison harboured no illusions. He knew that Marckheim would kill cold-bloodedly, without scruples, without mercy. But Levison was not an easy man to kill. More than one potential killer had found that out!

A dozen scars on his lean body testified to the attempts on his life that had been made in the bad old days in South Africa, by men who believed (not without reason) that he had wronged them. Not one, but many men had sworn to kill him, but Levison lived to walk the world with that springing stride of his, while some who had sworn to kill him were themselves food for the worms.

Levison had brains. Levison had courage. Levison had no conscience. He was the perfect killer, cold, shrewd, and callous. And now a killer as cold-blooded as himself was waiting, watching, spying, for an opportunity to do unto Levison what Levison had done to others. But Levison was not afraid. Fear had no place in his composition. He was all steel muscle and elastic sinew, controlled by sharp brains, made formidable by iron nerves.

Fear! Yes, he knew what it meant, he had seen it in the wide eyes of men as a bullet snapped toward them to gouge its way through flesh and bone. He had seen it reduce men of iron to men of jelly. But nothing had ever stirred fear in Levison himself.

Danger made his brains like ice and his hands sure. Death would not find him an easy captive.

He had cheated Death before, only to console the dark angel with another victim. This might be one more time when the man who came to kill would remain to gasp out his life in a pool of his own blood.

It was almost one o'clock when he returned to Grey Towers. His sharp eyes darted to the right and left of him as he approached the dim gateway by which he must enter the garden. No blacked mass loomed among the drooping shadows. The hour of encounter was yet to come. A burly guard admitted him, and he walked swiftly across the spongy turf and entered the house. In the hall his eyes detected the ponderous outline of a large man in a sturdy chair; silver buttons gleamed in the gloom of a far corner. The chair creaked as the uniformed policeman moved to obtain a closer view of the newcomer. Levison paused for a moment where the shaded light of the hall chandelier threw his profile into sharp relief.

"Good night, officer," he said pleasantly.

"Good night, sir," replied a gruff voice.

Levison smiled faintly as he walked softly up the stairs. The timidest spinster in London would sleep untroubled by fear with a policeman's comforting bulk in her hall, but he who was the reverse of timid, he who had never known fear, drew no comfort from the constable's presence. The arm of the law was too puny a thing to protect him from the man who sought his life. Levison must depend on his own brain and muscle, on his own iron nerve.

The old house was badly illuminated in the corridors and on the stairs. The stairs were a dissolving mass of light and shadow as Levison groped his way up. His eyes, staring steadily into the gloom, were on the alert for the slightest movement; his ears listened keenly for the faintest sound. His right foot tested each step before he rested the weight of his body on it. There was no telling when or in what manner Death might strike.

When he was almost at the top, a white face peered over the banisters. Levison tensed himself, but a low whisper reassured him. It was Doctor Britling, who had been waiting in silence for his return.

"Thank God you're back!" Daniel murmured. "I've been on pins and needles."

"You're a decent little chap," muttered Levison. "But don't worry about me. I can look after number one! For heaven's sake look after yourself!"

With a softly spoken 'goodnight,' Daniel disappeared into his room.

Levison turned the handle of his bedroom door and pushed the door slightly ajar. Cautiously, his fingers slipped through the narrow aperture and found the electric light switch, flooding the room with light before he stepped inside and closed the door behind him. The room was apparently empty, and there was nowhere for an intruder to hide except inside the clothes closet, or beneath the bed.

Levison chuckled grimly as he thrust a walking-stick under the bed and jabbed it about as any timid spinster might. But he was taking no chances. He opened the door of the closet and flattened the clothes that hung in it against the wall before he was satisfied that he was alone in the room.

He locked the bedroom door and as an afterthought, shot the stout bolt with which it was equipped. No door secured only by a lock would keep out the man who was in Levison's thoughts. When he was clad skimpily in pyjamas, he went to the window, which was open a foot at the top, and shut it. As he hastened the catch he made a wry face, for he was a lover of fresh air. But Death had come to Hubert Quail through an open window, and Levison did not intend that Death should come that way.

Queer that his mind should harp on the subject of Death. The fingers of one hand would not have sufficed to enumerate the times the shadow of Death's dark wings had passed over his head leaving him unscathed, and he had never felt like this before. Somehow, this was different; his thoughts ran in a circle, the centre of which was the menace against which he must be ever on guard.

Even in bed he did not feel quite comfortable. He rose at last and attached a large ornamental vase to the catch of the window by a length of cord. He adjusted it so that the vase must smash on the floor if an attempt was made to raise the window. This device he duplicated on the window of the bathroom adjoining his room.

He turned on the reading lamp above his bed and switched out the light in the centre of the ceiling before slipping between the sheets again. He would read for a while before going to sleep, he decided. Reading would soothe his mind and banish the problem that threatened to keep him awake. His nerves were perfectly steady, but there was that insistent voice in his brain which kept on saying:

"Levison, beware!"

It had never nagged him like this before, but then, he had regarded as fools the men who had made previous attempts on his life. The man of whom that nagging voice warned him was no fool. He had brains as cunning and nerves as cool as those of Levison himself. He had killed Hubert Quail by a fiendishly clever method. He had sworn to kill Levison…

"Levison, beware!"

He found himself unable to concentrate on his book. The printed lines melted into a meaningless blur before his eyes. Was it humanly possible, he wondered, to kill a man who was alone in a room, the door of which was locked and bolted, the windows of which were shut and securely fastened? If so, how could it be done? If human ingenuity could devise a method, surely Levison himself could solve it—and foil it!

He revolved the puzzle in his mind. No, it couldn't be done. To kill a man in the present circumstances was to work him up to such a pitch, by playing on his nerves, piling on the uncertainty. That could be done; but not in Levison's case. Levison was not the type to commit suicide. Levison had never known fear.

"Levison, beware!"

It was auto-suggestion, of course, that little voice in his brain that kept on reminding him that this killer was not like other killers, that this killer was to be respected; to be guarded against, to be anticipated, to be—he had almost admitted—feared. But fear had no part in Levison's composition.

Ignoring the whispers that distracted his mind, he concentrated on his book. Page after page was thumbed over as he became absorbed as the story unfolded.

Then the light went out! With startling suddenness the room was plunged in darkness.

Levison sat up, propped upon an elbow, and pushed the book away from him. His brain was as cool as ice, and his eyes unflinchingly probed the darkness that hedged him in. His ears were on the alert for the faintest sound that might disturb the pregnant silence. But nothing happened. The room was as still as it had been before the light went out.

His own breathing began to sound loudly in Levison's ears. The room seemed to be filled with the sound of the beating of his heart, magnified by the tension of his nerves to the loudness of sledgehammer blows.

"Levison, beware!"

The whispering voice was louder now as though the danger had come nearer.

This wouldn't do. He must have perfect control of himself to meet and avert whatever threatened.

His keen ears detected a faint slithering noise, followed by a subdued rustling. Such a sound as might have been made by a snake writhing on its belly through dead leaves. But this was the country mansion of Israel Straust. Here there were no snakes, and no—ridiculous thought!—no dead leaves!

The slithering and rustling continued, and a new sound mingled with them, a faint whimpering that rose and fell fitfully like the moan of a dying wind. But the storm, he knew, had died an hour ago. No breath of wind stirred anywhere.

Odd how chilly it was becoming in the room, though it was summer and the window was securely fastened. It was cold, and at the same time stuffy. Levison felt his flesh rising in little pimples, and his lungs were bursting for breath. His head seemed to be swollen to the size of a pumpkin.

"Levison, beware!"

Pitter, patter...pitter, patter... A new sound jarred the silence, a sound like dried peas rattling on the taut skin of a drum.

Levison threw back the bedclothes and his trembling feet slipped to the floor. The danger he could not fathom was breaking his iron nerve. His heart was pounding wildly; his breath was coming in choking gasps; his scalp prickled, as though with the touch of icy fingers; his forehead was bathed in cold perspiration.

He tiptoed towards the chest of drawers where he kept his automatic. His foot touched something smooth and cold and a nerve-shattering noise sounded. With an inarticulate cry, he dodged and there was another loud bang.

Throwing caution to the winds he plunged to the chest of drawers and pulled the handle of the drawer which contained his weapon. He wouldn't die tamely, like a sheep beneath the butcher's knife; if I die, he must. He'd have company into the Valley of the Shadow!

The drawer was stiff, and he tugged at it, his fingers itching for the comforting feel of the smooth handle of his automatic.

A flash of flame stabbed the darkness. The room was filled with an echoing report and the acrid odour of powder fumes. Without a word or cry, the body of Gideon Levison thudded to the floor.

Marckheim had won, after all.

A Desperate Case

DOCTOR BRITLING AWOKE and sat up in bed. The faint rustling sound that had roused him was still audible, and with it was mingled a laboured breathing. It seemed to be coming from the direction of the door. He put out a steady hand and switched on the light above his bed.

By the door, his dark eyes blinking in the light, stood Adrian Carver, dressed in a soiled trench-coat and a pair of Doctor Britling's pyjamas, the latter revealing almost twelve inches of hairy leg. His hand was fumbling with the key in the lock of the door.

Daniel slid his legs out of bed and stood up. "Walking in your sleep?" he asked dryly.

"I thought I heard someone moving in the room next door," whispered Adrian.

"That's the room Quail had. It was locked and sealed by Chief Inspector Howells. You must have been mistaken." The little police surgeon eyed the young man suspiciously. "I wonder if I made a mistake in hiding you from the guards?" he murmured speculatively.

"Good Lord, you surely don't think—"

At that moment the room was plunged in darkness.

There was brief spell of ominous silence, broken only by the sharp breathing of the men.

"Carver," said Daniel quietly.

"Yes, sir?" There was quiver in the young man's voice, a quiver of excitement rather than fear.

"There's an electric torch on the dressing table. Get it."

"Yes, sir."

Adrian groped his way across the room and fumbled for the

torch. He found it, and played a beam of light upon the door. Daniel stepped into the circle of light and listened with his ear close to one of the door panels.

There was a tense moment of suspense, then a shot rang out...

Doctor Britling twisted the key in the lock, threw the door wide open, and darted into the darkened corridor with Adrian at his heels. The light wobbled drunkenly in the young man's hands as he ran. Suddenly it was knocked from his fingers and clattered on the floor of the corridor, becoming extinguished as it rolled to the wall. Someone rushed past Adrian and went running down the stairs.

From a room along the corridor came the shrill screams of a terrified woman.

Adrian was about to follow the figure that had disappeared into the pitch-black cavern of the stairs, but Daniel plucked at his sleeve. "Find the torch!" the little man hissed.

The youth went down on his hands and knees and pawed along the carpeted floor until his fingers came in contact with the smooth metal cylinder. Fortunately, it had suffered no harm from its fall. He shone it on the door of the room that had been Hubert Quail's. The keyhole was covered by an unbroken circle of red.

"The seal's intact," said Daniel. "We'll try the next room, Levison's room."

As suddenly as they had gone out, the lights came on again. Doors all over the house were opening and startled voices were shouting questions; the tramping of heavy feet sounded on the stairs.

Daniel hammered at the door of Levison's room. There was no answer but the echo of his own pounding fist. He tried the handle but the door was locked.

The corridor was filled now with scantily clad forms. A ring of white faces crowded upon Daniel as he turned from the door. Cora Annerley, her eyes staring with horror; her husband, his fleshy face pasty and quivering; Mary Quail, with one hand clasped to her throat; one or two frightened servants, among them Sydney Levine, a crippled youth, whose deformed body presented a remarkable contrast to his face which had an almost angelic beauty—his left shoulder was drawn up almost to his neck, making his head sit askew, and under his left armpit was tucked a crutch which did the work of his apparently withered left leg; three or four burly men, among them the inevitable Mr. Moody, and a uniformed policeman.

They were crowding upon Daniel, asking him questions, panting hysterical remarks. He signalled to Moody, who shouldered his way past the others. "Clear everyone out of the corridor," he said briskly, "excepting Mr. Carver. Send them to their rooms and tell them to stay there."

In a few moments, the corridor was empty save for Daniel, Adrian, the policeman, a plainclothes detective who had just appeared, and Mr. Moody.

"Now," said Daniel grimly. "We'll break down that door!"

The plainclothes man shuffled his feet uncomfortably. "We'd better phone the Chief Inspector first," he ventured gruffly. "He'll be back at the *Duke's Head* by now. Orders were that if anything happened during the night he was to be summoned before any steps were taken."

"Never mind the Chief Inspector!" retorted Daniel, white with fury. "Do as I say!"

The little man bristled with the ferocity of a wild cat. Before his fierce eyes the detective wilted. Broad shoulders were applied to the door, and a mighty heave wrenched it bodily from its hinges.

A shocking sight met their eyes as they crowded into the

room. The body of Gideon Levison lay on its back on the floor, the head propped sideways against the wall, the legs and arms sprawled limply like the limbs of an effigy of straw. Blood oozed from a blackened hole in the right temple.

About the floor lay a number of inflated toy balloons which bobbed up and down in the draught from the open door, and two flattened pieces of coloured rubber which had once been similar balloons.

With a shuddering sigh, Doctor Britling knelt beside the limp body and took the dangling wrist between his lean fingers for a period that seemed endless to the men standing awkwardly in the doorway. He crouched upon the floor and when he rose tears brimmed in his grey eyes.

He motioned to Moody. "Get your men and fetch up the long table from the breakfast-room—" His voice was no more than a hoarse whisper. "—put it in my room."

Moody hastened to obey.

Doctor Britling turned to the detective and the uniformed constable. "You two carry him into my room," he said. "For God's sake be gentle with him."

This time he was obeyed without question. As they carried the body out of the room, Doctor Britling followed with Adrian at his heels. "Fetch a bowl of boiling water," he threw over his shoulder at the young man.

The body of Gideon Levison was placed on a sheet upon the long table which Moody and his men arranged in the centre of Doctor Britling's bedroom. Beside it, on a smaller table, lay a steaming basin of water. Doctor Britling unceremoniously ushered everyone but Adrian Carver out of the room. He turned the key in the lock, and flashed a swift appraising glance at the young man.

"Afraid of blood?"

Adrian's face was as white as the sheet on which the body lay, but he bravely answered: "No, sir."

"Very well." Daniel detached the portable lamp clamped to the back board of his bed, lit it, and handed it to his companion. "Hold that."

A pair of scissors glistened in his hand. Snip...snip...snip, they clipped away at Levison's lank black hair.

Doctor Britling went into the bathroom and returned in a few moments with a shaving brush foaming with lather and a shining razor. The brush covered the uneven stubble with white froth and with swift sure strokes, Daniel completely shaved Levison's scalp.

He opened a small black bag which had been part of his luggage when he arrived at Grey Towers and produced a case of shining instruments; bandages, gauze and lint. Tearing up some strips of white muslin, he manipulated them with a short length of wire into a makeshift anaesthetic mask. This he clapped over the nostrils and mouth of the man who lay motionless on the table.

"Turn your eyes away," he said gently. "But keep the light steady."

Adrian looked away, struggling to stifle an attack of nausea which threatened to overcome him.

The circle of brilliant light was focussed on the head, and the thin blade that shimmered in Doctor Britling's long fingers.

Adrian was beginning to waver slightly on his feet when Doctor Britling uttered a satisfied exclamation. Adrian looked round, the light wobbled for a second, and he looked away quickly.

"Bear up, my boy," murmured Daniel gently. "It won't be long now."

By a supreme effort, Adrian managed to hold himself erect until Levison's head was swathed in bandages.

"It's all over," said Daniel at last.

The lamp slipped from Adrian's nerveless fingers and crashed upon the floor. The walls of the room seemed to spin round him, and everything went black as he lost consciousness.

He regained his senses to find himself lying on the bed with Daniel bending over him and the pungent taste of brandy in his mouth. For a moment he blinked up at the face that beamed down at him, then he sat up weakly.

"Sorry to have been such an ass," he muttered thickly.

"Now you're talking like an ass," retorted Daniel cheerfully. "You did splendidly, my boy. I would have spared you the ordeal, but I was afraid the others would fail me at the crucial moment. I know these red-faced men who are so easily upset."

A faint smile wreathed Adrian's lips.

The door was shivering with the blows of a fist that pounded on it violently. "Open the door!" clamoured the angry voice of Chief Inspector Howells.

"Go to H—!" replied Doctor Britling.

"I'll give you ten seconds to open it, Britling—then I'll break it down!"

With a grim expression on his thin face, and a wicked-looking scalpel in his hand, Doctor Britling unlocked the door. It was thrust violently open, and Howells, his face contorted with fury, burst into the room. Daniel calmly locked the door again and put the key in his pocket.

"Look here," shouted Howells, "you've absolutely no right to tamper with the body—"

Daniel waved the shining scalpel before his astounded eyes. "The blade of this is considerably sharper than a razor," he said quietly. "If you utter one word before I give you permission, I'll—" The steady eyes of the quiet little man quelled the spluttering detective.

"Levison has about one chance in a hundred of living," Daniel continued. "He would have had no chance whatever if I hadn't operated at once. He won't have one chance in a million if his enemy learns that he isn't dead. That's where you come in. You're going to behave as though the attempt on his life had succeeded. That's what you're going to tell your subordinates, the people in this house, everybody. You're even going to announce it to the press. For a start you'll phone the Yard to that effect—you can write the truth to the commissioner later. In the morning you'll phone the local police and tell them to send a conveyance for Levison's body. Speak loudly so everyone can hear you—you're good at that. Levison is dead—get that into your thick skull and act accordingly!"

An Investigation

ALTHOUGH HE HEARTILY disliked Doctor Britling, Chief Inspector Howells was not a fool. In his own plodding way, he was quite a shrewd man. He was sufficiently shrewd to realise that the brain of the man he disliked was superior to his own. He accepted therefore Doctor Britling's edicts. He did not relish being threatened with a sharp blade held perilously near the tip of his nose, but he made allowances for the emotional stress under which Daniel was labouring. He said, therefore: "Put that confounded thing away and let's thresh out the matter like sensible men."

Daniel let the scalpel fall with a clatter among the other instruments. "I'm sorry. I was carried away for a moment."

"That's alright," said Howells, awkwardly. "We all go off the rails at times, and, well, I was a bit hasty. Now, just what is it you want me to do?"

Doctor Britling repeated his previous remarks, this time with less emphasis.

The Chief Inspector nodded: "I agree with you. The obvious thing to do is to let it be thought that the attempt on Levison's life succeeded."

So it was that a few moments later a dark figure crouched behind the door that led to the kitchen 'heard' Howells in the hall telephoning Scotland Yard. The Chief Inspector was not aware of the listener's presence, but he spoke loudly so that anyone who cared might hear. He had already dispatched a subordinate by motorcar to Scotland Yard with a true account of the night's dreadful happening.

"Is that Sir Basil Mumford? This is Chief Inspector Howells speaking from Grey Towers, near Leighton Buzzard. There has been a new development in the case, Sir Basil. Mr. Gideon Levison has been shot...Yes, he's dead...The body was discovered half an hour ago in the bedroom he occupied here. Doctor Britling operated at once, but it was wasted effort. The bullet had penetrated his brain...No, I haven't had time to investigate yet, but it's a mystery to me how the murder could have been accomplished. As I understand it, the door was locked and bolted and the windows securely fastened. A booby trap arrangement was fitted to the catch of the windows in the bedroom and the adjoining bathroom, apparently by the dead man himself, which should have made it impossible for either of the windows to have been raised without the alarm being given. Suicide?—out of the question, Sir Basil...No, there's no sign of a weapon about the room I am told...Yes, I'm going up now to join Doctor Britling in a thorough investigation...Yes, Sir Basil, I'll do my best to work with him, but you know what an annoying little devil he is. Always wants to keep everything up his sleeve until he's got the solution... Yes, I realise that. I'll do my best...Yes, sir, I'll report by 'phone in the morning. Very well, Sir Basil. Goodnight, sir."

The Chief Inspector replaced the receiver and went upstairs, smiling ruefully to himself. The Old Man wanted him to work with Britling, did he? Well, that suited Howells. He wouldn't let the little devil out of his sight for a moment if he could help it, until the case was cleared up. There would be no stealing a march from him from now on...

Daniel had already stolen a march to the extent of having entered the room in which the attempt on Levison had been made. Howells found him sitting on the bed holding the crumpled skins of the two punctured balloons and looking with speculative eyes at the other coloured globes that bobbed about the floor. Howells had not previously entered the room, and he knew nothing of the odd playthings that littered it.

"Balloons," said the astonished Scotland Yard Official, raising his eyebrows.

"Balloons," agreed Daniel calmly.

Howells stooped and picked one up; held it to the light; pinched its smooth sides; trying to read the riddle of its presence in the room. "Doesn't look in any way out of the ordinary," he ventured cautiously.

"It isn't," responded Daniel. "Similar balloons may be purchased for a penny in any toyshop."

"Then what the dickens—"

"That's what I'd like to know."

"It's a puzzle how they could have been introduced into the room with the door and windows locked," the detective muttered, moving restlessly about the room, examining the shattered door and the makeshift burglar alarm on the window.

"Unless Levison brought them in himself," supplemented Daniel. "Which isn't likely."

"Coloured balloons…a locked and bolted door…snugly fastened windows…no way for an intruder to get in…no gun lying about…and a man shot in the head," snapped Howells irritably. "It's fantastic."

"Marckheim," said Daniel, "should bequeath his brain to the British Medical Association. It would make a fascinating study. Or perhaps it would be better to keep him alive in some asylum, so that alienists from all over the world could experiment with him."

"Marckheim," repeated Howells, in a tone of exasperation. "Always Marckheim! I tell you it's impossible for him to be in the house!"

"And I tell you that he is in it!" Daniel rose with the inflated balloons in his hand and walked to the corner where Levison's crumpled body had been found. He looked appraisingly at the spot, shaking his head gently, then raised his eyes to the gaping hole high in the plaster of the wall in which the bullet that had sped through Levison's right temple had imbedded itself.

He stroked his chin—and left a smudge of black on his grey beard.

"Your fingers are dirty," said Howells mechanically.

Daniel glanced at them and then at the crumpled pieces of coloured rubber in his hand. With a speculative light in his eyes, he picked up one of the inflated balloons and stroked his palm across its smooth surface. His hand came away streaked with black.

"Soot!" he exclaimed, a gleam of interest dawning in his eyes. Fumbling in his pocket he produced his electric torch and, kneeling beside the hearth, directed a ray of light up the chimney. For a moment he peered searchingly upwards, then he leaned sideways and thrust his arm into the yawning cavity. It reappeared, grasping a string on which was threaded a number of thin wooden discs and, between each disc, were slips of parchment paper. He shook the string and it emitted a faint sound like—he searched his mind for an analogy—like something crawling through dead leaves.

"There is a hole in the inside wall of the chimney, where a few of the bricks have been removed," he said. "This is how the balloons entered the room."

"You can't shoot a man through a hole in the inside wall of the chimney," declared Howells.

Doctor Britling shook his head. "No," he admitted, "you can't."

The Chief Inspector stared at the peculiar contrivance in Daniel's hand. "What on earth is that meant for?"

"As a theatrical property man would express it," replied Daniel, "—sound effects."

He strode to the doorway and went into the corridor, followed by Howells. They halted at the door of the next room—the room in which Quail had died—and Daniel tried the handle. The door swung open at his touch.

"Why—why, I locked it before I left for Scotland Yard this evening," gasped Howells. "I plastered the lock with sealing-wax, and stamped it with my ring." He bent down. "And the seal's unbroken!"

Daniel's fingers fumbled with the 'seal'—and ripped it off! He held it up. "A skilful imitation, painted on gummed paper," he said drily.

In the wall of the chimney, they found the other side of the hole through which the balloons had been dropped into Levison's room, and, lying on the hearth a hollow wooden cylinder covered at each end with sheepskin. Daniel shook it and they heard a peculiar pattering noise.

"Ingenious," murmured Daniel. "Very. Adrian was right in thinking that he heard someone moving about in this room. It was Marckheim—or a confederate. He brushed past us in the dark when the shot that wounded Levison gave the alarm, and was forced to leave this little toy behind."

"What's it all about?" demanded the Chief Inspector. He was becoming annoyed with Daniel. The little devil was repeating his trick of keeping everything up his sleeve until all the strings were in his fingers.

"Let's go back into the other room and I'll show you."

In the other room he turned out the light.

The Chief Inspector's flesh prickled as he heard faint, unpleasant noises from the gloom where Daniel stood. He darted a glance over his shoulder at the comforting patch of light from the corridor which was framed in the doorway."I'm a fool, I know," he muttered, "but that noise gives me the creeps. There's something about it, well, uncanny, if you like."

Daniel turned on the light again, still jiggling the string and the hollow wooden cylinder. "And if you heard it in the pitch dark, with no idea what caused it, and knowing that an unscrupulous man had designs on your life—" he suggested.

"I'm afraid I'd get the wind up," grunted Howells.

"And then?"

"Oh, I'd break for the door, I suppose."

"Ah, but if the door was bolted?"

The Chief Inspector pulled a wry face. "I don't know. I'd be in a devil of a fix."

"If you had a revolver—"

"I'd go for it!" declared Howells with conviction.

"Levison had a revolver. He showed it to me yesterday. He kept it," —Daniel pointed— "in that drawer."

Howells strode across the room and tugged at the drawer Daniel had indicated.

"Look out, you fool!" Daniel lunged and thrust Howells aside as a report sounded, and a bullet whizzed across the room, burying itself with a thud in the wall.

The scared face of a policeman showed itself in the doorway.

"It's alright," Daniel assured him. "Go and keep the others away from here; tell them everything is alright."

Howells was mopping his forehead with a large handkerchief. "I never want a clearer view of death than that!" he gasped.

"Hold your ears," snapped Daniel. Standing to one side, he tugged at the drawer, and a report sounded; another bullet bit into the gaping hole in the wall, and the drawer jerked violently almost wrenching itself from his grasp. Holding the handle with all his might, he propped it open with a book placed on edge.

Inside was Levison's revolver, its butt fastened with a hinge to the base of the drawer; a spring drew the muzzle upwards as the drawer was opened; another spring pulled the trigger when the mouth of the weapon was pointing at a certain angle.

On further inspection, they found a third spring fastened to the underside of the drawer and the frame of the chest, which had tugged the drawer shut as Levison's limp fingers had released the handle…

"So, that was how it was done," remarked Daniel, softly. "Poor Levison! If only he had remained in bed, no harm could have come to him!"

Revolt!

THREE O'CLOCK IN the morning...

Within the thick stone wall of Grey Towers, fear lurked like a wraith. It was as though a winding sheet wrapped and enfolded the house and its occupants. Eyes held furtive terror; voices whispered fearfully, and died in the middle of speech; heads peered nervously over crouched shoulders as though the shadows teemed with unmentionable horrors.

Even the men who paced the garden, employed as protectors of those within the house, walked in pairs and their lights, like the swords of uneasy soldiers, stabbed often into the bushes that loomed up through the dripping mist...

A tall square figure paused at the open door of the house and walked a pace or two into the garden. As a match flared in his cupped hands, he was bathed in the light of several torches.

Chief Inspector Howells laughed harshly and strolled back into the house, his pipe glowing between his tight lips. He stretched himself with a yawn as he wandered into the library that led from the panelled hall.

A single pedestal lamp lit the centre of the room; bending over the table upon which the circle of light fell sat a crooked misshapen figure. Black, malignant eyes leered up at Howells and stumps of teeth were revealed as thin lips twisted into an enigmatic smile. A skinny claw moved a card from one part of the table to another, while the eyes of Israel Straust peered unblinkingly at the Chief Inspector. The old man said nothing; he only looked, with an odd penetrating gaze which brought an uncomfortable chill to the Scotland Yard official's spine.

Howells opened his mouth to say something, but the words were stillborn in his brain, killed by that disconcerting stare. It was as though Straust was trying to shake his nerve. Well—the detective's jaw hardened—two could play at that game. He backed away until his legs came in contact with the seat of a chair and he dropped into it almost with a sigh of relief. He was tired—Lord! How tired!—and a short rest would do him good.

It was beyond him to remove his eyes from the old man whose thin fingers were shuffling the worn pack of cards; whose withered body was clad in a nightgown and an ancient green robe. The eyes of Israel Straust had dropped to the table again, looking at the white faces of the cards he shuffled and dealt monotonously.

The clock on the mantelpiece ticked away the seconds...

Adrian Carver paced the floor of Doctor Britling's bedroom, smoking innumerable cigarettes. Try as he might, he could not keep his eyes from wandering in morbid fascination to the bed where Doctor Britling was bending over a motionless form. He reached the window and looked out into the night at the watery moon that travelled over the sullen sky. The cigarette flipped from his fingers to fly, with a trail of red sparks in its wake, into the gloom below.

"Look here," he said. "I'm worried about Mary. Where is she?"

"In her room, I should think," replied Doctor Britling, without raising his head. A hypodermic syringe glistened in his hand as he injected morphine into Levison's arm.

"Poor kid," exclaimed Adrian. "She'll be scared to death."

Daniel did not reply.

The young man walked to the door and paused with his fingers on the handle. "I'm going to see if she's all right."

"Do as you please," said Daniel. "I've explained your presence to Howells and he's given instructions that you're to be allowed the run of the place, although technically you're under arrest. I shouldn't make any attempt to leave the grounds though, if I were you."

"I shan't," said Adrian. "Thanks," he added gratefully. The door closed behind him.

Daniel turned with a sigh from the recumbent figure on the bed and replaced the hypodermic syringe in its case. He crossed the room and went into the bathroom, closing the door behind him. He tried the hot water tap speculatively, and a weary smile flitted over his worn features as a steaming flow resulted.

A few minutes later he was lying in the porcelain tub, wrapped in gratifying warmth. For hours he lay like that, his toes creeping up every now and then to twine around the tap marked 'hot' to admit more steaming water.

Adrian and Mary Quail stood beneath a spreading old oak in the garden. The girl looked over her shoulder with a shiver at the gloomy outline of Grey Towers, and moved a little closer to the boy. "There's—there's something—sinister—about that house," she whispered. "Something uncanny. Oh! Adrian, it's been dreadful, sitting alone in my room wondering what new horror would happen next. I thought I should go mad."

She brushed a shaking hand across her pale forehead. "They were alive such a little while ago; Uncle, and Gideon, and Jubal. That's what makes it so terrible, so appalling; that within a few short hours all of them should die." The word 'die' came with a shudder from her lips.

"Death isn't so very terrible," murmured Adrian soothingly.

"Why! That's what Uncle Gideon said! He said that—that Death was only the last blind corner on the road to life."

"You're cold," said Adrian feeling her small hands.

"I feel that I'll never be warm again."

"Shall we go in?"

She drew him back. "No! Please let's stay out here. The air in there stifles me. Oh!"—she reached out her thin arms to the dark sky. "Oh! Will the morning never come?"

Hunched in a chair in his wife's bedroom, Mark Annerley tried to shut his ears to the song she was crooning. A song without words, almost without tune, with an eerie note to it; an undertone of dull despair.

Cora had gone mad, he decided. That was why she was dressed, in the early hours of the morning, in the shimmering evening frock she had brought from Paris a few weeks ago and had not previously worn; that was why she was sitting at her dressing table smearing cold cream upon her face; that was why she was crooning the infernal song that gave him the creeps. She was mad. Stark, staring mad!

With a fleecy towel, Cora wiped away cold cream, powder and rouge; as she stared at her reflection in the mirror, peals of horrible laughter came from her lips, an uncanny sound that brought Annerley trembling to his feet.

"What's the joke," he snarled.

"Joke?" She rocked with laughter. "Joke? Isn't life itself only a horrible joke?"

She turned a twitching face toward her husband and for the first time he saw her as she was, stripped of her mask of cosmetics; wrinkled, haggard and desiccated, with dead eyes sunk in dark hollows.

"What a fool I've been," he cried bitterly. "What a fool! I should never have taken you when Marckheim went to prison. He might have forgiven the—the other—but that, never. He'll kill me, do you hear?—kill me! And it will be all your fault. You, yours, you—" He unleashed a torrent of abuse at her to which she listened with a cold, meaningless smile.

"If only he would strike quickly," he groaned. "It isn't death— it's the waiting, the awful waiting to die!"

Cora rose and held her hand under his eyes, with something white shining in the palm; a little white pellet, half the size of a pea… "You want to die? Here is death. Death certain and swift. Take it, cheat him! Cheat Marcky and have the last laugh!"

With an oath he struck down her hand and the white pellet rolled over the floor. For a moment he stood glaring at Cora, who quietly re-seated herself before the mirror and began to make up her face with great care, as though in preparation for the Opera; then he stumbled frantically from the room.

Down the stairs he reeled drunkenly, to sway for a moment at the door of the library. Howells and old Israel Straust were there, and one grimly watching the other from the shadows. Annerley turned away. He couldn't bear to sit and watch the old crow flipping over his cards. He went into the breakfast room, switched on all the lights, and dropped heavily into a chair beside the empty grate.

His fingers were nervously tying themselves in knots and his lips were moving soundlessly. In a few minutes a drowsy lethargy overcame his fears and he fell fast asleep.

The housekeeper's room was a cosy place with shaded lights and a warm fire. Easy chairs, shabby but comfortable, were placed on either side of the hearth. In one sat Harcourt the butler, his heavy face almost as white as his sparse hair, his trembling hands stretched out to the roaring flames; in the other, Mrs. Levine, with the sewing that always occupied her leisure moments on her lap.

"Thank God for a fire, Mrs. Levine," said Harcourt, hoarsely. "This has been a night to chill the very marrows!"

"That's the solemn truth, Mr. Harcourt." The housekeeper's spectacled eyes glanced nervously over her shoulder. "I've never been so frightened in all my life."

"Little did I think, when I took service with Mr. Straust, that one day I'd be shivering in my shoes at this ungodly house," gulped the butler. "As I daresay I've told you many a time, Mrs.

Levine, I've always served the most respectable families. I was twelve years with the Duchess of Bolton—there was a lady for you; you knew what to expect from her. There was never an untoward happening in her house in all the years of my service. It was the money that tempted me into this house, Mrs. Levine. I confess it to my shame. I left the dear old Duchess because Mr. Straust offered me more money than I was receiving. But money don't pay for shattered nerves. I'm an old man and I can't stand these upsets and goings-on."

He leaned forward and waved an ominous finger beneath the housekeeper's nose. "Besides," he muttered darkly, "the Guv'nors too queer in his ways for my liking. It's my considered opinion, Mrs. Levine, that he isn't right in the head."

"Where could you find a master who would treat you better?" Mrs. Levine demurred. "Crazy he may be, but such a fine, generous old man as he is! Who else would have allowed me to keep my Sydney by me?"

The butler turned to the deformed youth who sat between them, the firelight dancing on his sad, beautiful features.

"Play us something, Sydney," he urged. "Something," his thin voice quavered— "something to drive away the bogies."

The cripple placed his crutch along the top of the piano that stood in a corner and his long fingers strayed carelessly over the keys.

Although the sitting room allotted to the lower servants was brilliantly lit, the occupants were huddled together by the fireplace. All the bells in the house might have rung simultaneously for hours, and not one of them would have stirred to answer.

"Firs' thing in the morning," a husky voice was whispering, "I'm going to pack an' clear out. I won't stay, not for a million pounds, I won't. I'd never dare to close an eye in this house again!"

Six trembling voices expressed agreement; seven pairs of wide eyes peered furtively over hunched shoulders…

The snores of the Swiss chef punctuated the silence of his darkened bedroom…

Burly men walked the garden flashing lights into the innocent depths of rosebushes.

Removal of Levison

A LARGE BLACK MOTOR van drove through the gates of Grey Towers and up to the house; reversed across the driveway, and back up to the front door. Some of those who watched it shivered, for it was the conveyance that yesterday had taken the lifeless body of Hubert Quail to the morgue. Today it had called for the body of Gideon Levison.

The driver, a sallow young man with a Woodbine drooping between his lips, hopped out and unlocked the wide rear doors. His mate, short and bowlegged, with a Woodbine stowed behind his red ear, climbed out of the interior of the van, pulling behind him the wooden frame of a stretcher. Carrying the doubled-up contrivance between them, they swaggered into the house.

A policeman who had been walking up and down in front of the house strolled across and looked in at the rear doors of the van. He did this casually, as though inspired only by careless curiosity, and it was not particularly noticeable that he held the doors within a foot or so of each other, in each of his large hands, his body completely filling the aperture. Certainly, no one could possibly have heard the whispered exchanges that ensued between him and the young doctor who was sitting at the extreme rear of the interior.

In a few minutes the driver appeared again, following his snub nose, which was in imminent danger through the perilous angle of his cigarette. His arms were stiff by his sides, clutching the two handles at the head of the stretcher; his mate rolled a little with the weight of the rear handles. Between them lay a motionless form covered with a long white sheet.

"Stand away from them doors," growled the driver.

The policeman stood back, throwing the doors open; the

stretcher went in with a clatter; the doors were slammed to. Inside the young doctor was bending anxiously over his patient, but the doors hid that... The driver swaggered to the front of the van, put one hand on the right mudguard and grasped the starting handle firmly with the other, rolled his Woodbine with a twist of his lips to the extreme corner of his mouth, and pulled upwards sharply.

The van began to shiver and shake, and the driver climbed into his seat. He made a mock polite gesture to the policeman.

"Toodle-oo, ol' cock! Gimme a ring when you want me again—on'y too pleased to oblige!"

The van went down the drive, the sinister black van that was used to convey 'stiff 'uns' but it was carrying the body of Gideon Levison not to a cold slab in the morgue, but to the local hospital where a private ward and a world-famous specialist were awaiting him!

Doctor Britling had watched the proceedings from the window of his bedroom. Now he went downstairs slowly, and entered the breakfast room. The room was empty, and the long table on which he had operated on Levison in the early hours of the morning, now restored to its proper use, gleamed with an array of silver and china. A pile of newspapers lay at one end of the table.

Daniel found a *Morning World* and glanced through it listlessly. At a touch on his arm, he looked up to find Harcourt, the butler, standing at his side.

"A letter for you, sir."

"Thanks." Daniel glanced at the white envelope and recognised the prim, angular calligraphy of his sister. Evidently they had each been taken with the same inspiration yesterday; probably Eunice was now reading the letter he had written to her.

"Grilled herring, sir?" suggested Harcourt respectfully.

"No, thanks."

"Devilled kidneys?"

Doctor Britling shook his head. "Only coffee this morning, thanks. The thought of food revolts me."

Harcourt poured two streams of liquid, one of steaming coffee, the other of warm milk, into Daniel's cup. His white, wrinkled hands shook a little, and an amber splash stained the tablecloth. He replaced the coffeepot and milk jug on the table and covered them with a cosy, but made no move to leave Daniel's side.

"The—er—revulsion to food seems to be general this morning, sir," he murmured uncertainly. "One—er—one can hardly wonder at it…the—er—trying events of last night. I myself spent the early hours of the morning in an—an absolute twitter of apprehension. An absolute twitter, sir."

"There was no need for alarm on your part," said Daniel, sipping his coffee. "You were in no danger whatever."

Harcourt coughed behind his hand. "My stomach, if you'll excuse me mentioning it, sir," he said apologetically, "my stomach has been turning over and over all morning."

"Take a stiff dose of bicarbonate of soda," prescribed Doctor Britling. "And go and polish the silver."

The butler was startled. "The silver…er—yes, sir."

"The latter part of the prescription," added Daniel, "is most important. Polish all the silver in the house; two or three times, if there isn't enough to keep you busy all morning. All the bicarbonate of soda in the world won't settle your tummy until you do something to keep your mind off it."

"Yes, sir."

Doctor Britling slit open the envelope and extracted the six sheets of notepaper, covered on both sides with Eunice's minute handwriting, which it contained. He stifled a groan. If he was not mistaken, every line of the twelve closely-written pages would have a question to ask, or a rebuke to make. He read it in snatches, skipping over the more acrimonious passages. It had, of course, been written before his own letter reached her.

It was full of pious hopes that his bed-linen had been aired, that he was watching his chest, and that if he escaped pneumonia (the logical penalty for sleeping away from home) no direr fate (poison, or bullets? mused Daniel) would overtake him. The fool's errand which had taken him to Grey Towers was a matter for the police to attend to and he was only asking for trouble by meddling with it. At his age he might be expected to have more sense, though she doubted if he ever would even if he lived to be a hundred, which she didn't consider likely if he continued in his reckless behaviour.

Daniel's eyes roved wearily over the pages and came to rest, with raised eyebrows, on a passage of infinite importance:

Nephew Charles came to tea the day you left. He has grown a ridiculous little moustache which I told him very promptly to shave off at once—if his mother likes to encourage him in all sorts of lightmindedness, she needn't think I will— and was very full of his position with Simpkins, Somebody, and Thingmabob (I can never remember names), the firm of stockbrokers who took him into their office (as a glorified office boy, I believe) last January. You remember, Julia, ridiculous woman, wanted us to sell our securities and invest the money all over again through Charles, to help his standing with the firm.

From what Charles says I gather that the Stock Exchange is like a child's game only with sillier rules that any child would ever invent. You sell something you haven't got, and that makes the price go down and those who have it become frightened and sell it as well and you buy it for less than you sold it for and deliver it (although you never seem to see it) and the person who bought it from you, who, by this time doesn't want it. Charles says that's called 'selling short,' and apparently it usually starts a panic. I am not surprised. I used to think 'Up Jenkins' and 'Who's Got the Button' were stupid games, but they are positively intelligent compared to the games the financiers play. It seems ideally suited to young men of Charles's slight mental attributes.

Part of the game, Charles explained, was to know what the important men were going to do, and do the same. He said that last winter, when one wealthy financier was in bed for three days with a bad cold in the head rumours got about that he was dying, the price of his stocks dropped very low, and those that 'sold short' made fortunes. The financier shot himself, which is the gravest result of contracting a cold that I have heard of. It only goes to show that everyone should take the greatest possible care of the chest.

This morning, when I read in the paper about the death of Mr. Jubal Straust, who took you away yesterday, I realised at once that he had been murdered, although the paper said that it was an accident. That was one of the five financiers you went to help account for, and it seemed reasonable to presume that other attempts at murder, at least, would be made. If a cold in the head could make shares fall so alarmingly, surely, I reasoned, a murder, attempted or actual, would have even graver effects. I did my best to remember the names you told me, but all that I could recall was that one of them was Partridge, or something like that. I rang up Charles, and after some investigation, he asked if I was sure the name wasn't Quail. Well, of course, that was it, so I went round to see him with a cheque for our balance at the bank, less one pound, and my batch of War Savings Certificates—one of the funny rules of the game is that you need money to sell—and instructed him to sell short for me the stocks in which this Quail is interested.

Charles obviously thought I had taken leave of my senses, but my mind was made up, and he accepted the commission, although very unwillingly.

I haven't heard from him since, so I'm in something of a flutter to hear the result of my little venture.

I've just sent Hannah out to buy an evening paper from a boy who is shouting in the street something about a death drama in a country house. If another of your financiers has been murdered I do hope it's this Quail!—is that very bloodthirsty of me?

It is Quail! The evening paper is full of it...

Daniel ran his eyes down the pages. What the dickens had Eunice done? Bankrupted them? Made a fortune? He wished she'd come straight to the point and tell him. A postscript arrested his attention:

P.S. Charles has just phoned to say that the news reached the Stock Exchange long before it happened in the papers and there has been a panic. Isn't that wonderful? —just what I'd hoped for! I've made money, but he can't tell me how much until the morning...

A wry smile twisted Daniel's lip. So, Eustice, like Levison, in her own small way had taken part in the butchering of the bulls to make a roman holiday for the bears. Levison—and Eunice! Odd 'allies' he reflected. Human nature was a queer, twisted thing. Neither of them had hesitated to take advantage of another person's tragedy.

A paragraph in the body of the letter caught his eye.

Your murderer seems to have gone to a great deal of trouble to kill this Quail. It seems to me that he could have disposed of Quail and the unpleasant young man Straust and the others at the same time with considerably less bother. Obviously, he is able to move about the house at will. Why not, then, simply poison the food that was served to his enemies and wipe out all three at once? Or put poison in their morning tea? If he didn't want to risk the lives of innocent people who might also partake of the food? Surely that could easily have been accomplished?

Daniel stroked his short beard and a frown creased the corners of his eyes. There was a lot in what Eunice had written. It would have been easy to eliminate all six victims at once, with a minimum of risk and difficulty by poisoning the food they ate. Why had that not been done? Was it because the murderer was anxious that suspicion should not rest on those who had access to the kitchen? Was the murderer himself, after all, masquerading among the domestic staff? Or was it simply due to Marckheim's desire for a more spectacular form of revenge? There was food for thought in the problem.

A shadow fell upon the page, and he looked up to see Cora Annerley seating herself beside him. "Coffee?" he suggested, with a smile.

"Please," she replied tonelessly. She stretched out her hand, palm downwards, and dropped something on the table. "That's the seventh," she said.

Daniel frowned at the pellet of poison.

"No matter what cunning hiding place I've found for my ring," she said huskily, "when I've next examined it, there's always been one of these in it…"

"Then don't examine it," returned Daniel sharply. "Forget about it…"

"I can't." She took the pellet between her fingers. "If I were to drop it into this cup of coffee and drink it—"

The little police surgeon reached across, took the pellet from her, and put it in his pocket.

"You would die in a matter of seconds," he said.

"Would it be very painful?" Cora asked, watching his face.

"It would be very stupid."

She rose and went swiftly from the room. Daniel looked after her gloomily. It was only too apparent that Marckheim's cunning plan was succeeding; Cora was coming to the point where she would accept an emergency exit from life as a relief from the suspense which was breaking her nerve...

Still frowning, he lit his first cigar of the day and strolled through the French windows into the garden...

He wandered aimlessly across the turf and down a gravel path which led to the garage. Halfway between the garage and the house his foot kicked against something! He glanced down, then stooped and picked it up; held it in his palm.

It was a crude parody of a bird, about an inch and a half high, carved from wood, with feathers glued to it, and a hinge to its beak; an odd plaything to find in a garden where no child could have left it. He walked on, turning it over on his palm.

As he walked, he heard limping footsteps on the path behind him. He turned and saw Sydney Levine moving slowly toward him, his eyes searching the gravel carefully. Daniel waited until he approached...

"Lost something?" he suggested.

"Why, no sir," replied the youth, with a sad, sweet smile. "Not...this?"

The crippled looked with unfathomable dark eyes at the little wooden bird. "Dear me, no," he replied and passed on.

Daniel looked after him thoughtfully.

A Grim Chase

DOCTOR BRITLING STROLLED to the little gate that led from the garden to a quiet country lane; a gate seldom used; moss-grown along the lintel; with a stiff latch and squeaking hinges. A constable stood on duty at the gate, but his post was a sinecure. Here there were no reporters; no gaping crowds of sightseers; no amateur detectives clamouring for admission. Daniel opened the gate and walked a pace or two into the lane, which was rough and dusty underfoot, and lined on the other side with a hedge of wild rose. From the white blossoms that dotted the hedge a light summer wind carried a sweet, elusive scent.

Across the lane lay prim fields, like pocket handkerchiefs of many colours, green, golden and brown, spread in the sun to dry after the soaking of the previous night. As far as the eye could see they stretched, dipping toward the horizon; separated by hedges that knelt in huddled rows like quiescent sheep when evening comes. Deep in the hollow, gaunt old trees spread their stark, black arms heavenward like pagan worshippers praying to the sun that hung, like a golden platter, in the blue, cloudless sky. Across the sky a lonely swallow skimmed. Smoke curled drowsily from the tall chimneys of a rambling white house that nestled among the fields.

Daniel sighed and turned away.

As he entered the garden again Adrian came running up.

"I say," he cried, "I'm going to marry Mary Quail!"

"Don't be a damned young fool," Daniel retorted irritably.

Adrian's face fell and his cheeks reddened. "Dash it all, why shouldn't I?"

Doctor Britling tried hard to be patient. "Because, for one thing, you're both much too young; for another you have no visible means of support. You can't start married life without a job, my dear boy."

"I hadn't thought of that."

"I thought you hadn't," said Daniel dryly. "And yet you have the cheek to propose marriage to—"

"Oh, I haven't proposed yet," Adrian hastily assured him. "I've only just thought of it. You see, Mary's alone in the world, and a girl like that needs someone to look after her. I didn't see any reason why that someone shouldn't be me."

"And who is going to look after you?" asked Daniel softly.

"I beg your pardon?"

"Oh, nothing. But I shouldn't worry about Mary, if I were you. Her uncle was extremely wealthy and he had no one else to whom to leave his money. I should imagine she'll be amply provided for."

"Oh!" Adrian looked crestfallen.

"If you devoted yourself to hard work for the next fifty years," said Daniel sadly, "you wouldn't at the end of it have accomplished one tenth part of the money Mary is likely to inherit."

"Then I shan't worry about hard work!" declared Adrian fiercely. "I shall steal it, as Quail did."

"That takes brains," Daniel reminded him.

"Um."

"Exactly!" said Daniel.

His eyes were watching, with a perplexed frown, a large car that stood at the door of Grey Towers. At that moment a short fleshy man hurried down the steps and sprang to the driving seat. As the car moved away, Daniel started running over the cropped turf, but before he had reached the house the car had run through the gates into the road.

"Who was in that car?" Daniel gasped to Howells, who was standing in the hall.

"Mr. Annerley. He asked me to let him go off to London."

"You fool! You fool! And you let him go!"

"Well, he was scared to death about what might happen to him here, and I thought he'd be just as well out of the way."

"You thought! You thought!" stormed Daniel. "Damn it all, man, why do you suppose he was allowed to leave the house? Because Marckheim must have a plan for dealing with him outside! Otherwise, he'd have died before he put foot in his car!"

"There's a policeman with him to see him safely to London," grunted Howells uneasily. "He can't be much safer than that!"

"Blow your confounded policeman!" retorted Daniel inelegantly. "Here—get another confounded car! For the love of Heaven hurry, or we'll be too late. We've got to stop Annerley before whatever is in store for him is accomplished."

The little man fumed up and down the terrace in front of the house until a police automobile stood panting in the drive, then he jumped into the front seat beside the driver, and Howells and two constables piled in the back. As the car swung through the gates, excited reporters and cameramen scattered to waiting vehicles, followed, when they realised that something was in the wind, by such of the other sightseers as had come in motors. A procession of automobiles of every description followed the police car as it raced along the road.

Far ahead, his eyes glued to the winding white ribbon in front of him, Mark Annerley drove his powerful car like a man possessed. A whisper in his brain was repeating the words that Arthur Marckheim's voice had said to him in the cold, grey dawn:

"Within a few hours you will die...For you, Annerley, for every coward, death is a terrifying walk into darkness...You take that walk today!"

Today! And the house in which Death had reached out chilly fingers to grasp him lay only a few miles behind!

Faster! Faster! Flight was the only thing that could save him, headlong flight with the speed of forty horsepower carrying him out of reach of the man he feared.

The burly constable in the seat beside him squirmed uncomfortably as the spinning wheels bounced on the roadway; his face paled as a turning leapt at the car and was negotiated on two wheels.

"Take it easy!" he gasped. "For the love of God!"

Annerley replied with a burst of speed which eclipsed his previous efforts. A glance in his driving mirror told him that a car was following fast behind him. His foot drove the accelerator to the floorboards and the long car leapt like a mad thing. The speedometer needle crept higher…sixty-five…seventy…seventy-five, frantic, delirious miles an hour! The tyres screamed on the uneven surface of the road and threw up a shower of small stones that clattered on mudguards and coachwork.

"Today you die!"

Today…but Annerley was safe! Flight had saved him; flight had foiled the man who sought his life. Where was the poison that could reach him now, the bullet that could travel faster than his flying car? Death lay behind him, long miles behind him, miles clouded with the choking dust that hung in his wake. Life lay ahead, and Annerley hurried to woo it…

A fast train from London…a tall ship bound east from Southampton…a greyhound of the ocean that would put miles of rolling sea between him and Marckheim…

Faster! Faster! Let the flying wheels widen the gap between him and death!

For the first time in many days Annerley could breathe easily. He was safe. Nothing could touch him now.

Behind, the eyes of the men in the rocking police car stared at the cloud of dust that trailed in his rear.

"The crazy fool!" shouted Howells, above the roar of the pounding engine. "He'll kill himself, the lunatic!"

They hummed up a rise in the road and saw, skimming beneath them, the car they pursued. For moments it sped up the road, then, suddenly, it seemed to rise into the air. It swerved and hurtled sideways for an incredible distance, then slewed completely round and crashed through the hedge.

Daniel gripped the seat beneath him as the police car spurted down the dipping stretch of road. It pulled up with a grinding of brakes beside the wide gap in the hedge beyond which, by a full fifty feet, lay the tangled wreckage of Annerley's car. Orange tongues of flame already wreathed it, licking hungrily through clouds of black smoke.

The soil showed through two long scars the hurtling car had scored in the grassy field.

Two limp bodies lay like rag dolls some yards from the chaos of twisted metal and shattered glass.

Doctor Britling and Chief Inspector Howells ran side by side across the long grass. They knelt beside one of the ragged bundles and stared in silence at the bloodstained head.

There was no need for Daniel to touch Mark Annerley's limp wrist.

A man cannot live with three bullet wounds in his skull!

The Sinister Clock

DOCTOR BRITLING AND Chief Inspector Howells stared in perplexed silence into each other's eyes over the crumpled body of Mark Annerley.

The body with the three unbelievable bullet wounds in its head.

Behind them flames roared skyward from the mangled wreckage of Annerley's car, a two-thousand-pound bonfire, wreathed in columns of smoke. All about them lay minute particles of glass, splinters of wood, scraps of twisted metal. Across the grass on which they knelt was a broad smear of blood.

Howells was the first to find his voice. "This…is…uncanny! We saw his car…just before the crash…There was no sign of another car…no sign of any living thing on the road or in the fields that flanked it. Only Annerley and the man I sent to escort him to London were in the car…And yet, here is Annerley, shot in the head. Why, it's—I almost said—impossible!"

A peculiar light came into his eyes and he rose hurriedly and walked to the other limp body that lay a few feet away. He turned it over and looked down with a wry grimace at the white face, gashed and bleeding, of the policeman he had sent with Annerley. One of his arms and a leg were twisted beneath him in a grotesque attitude.

Howells looked away. "Then that isn't the solution," he muttered hoarsely. "I hoped it might be; I hoped that Marckheim—or an accomplice—had taken my man's place, in order to kill Annerley."

"The problem is deeper than that," replied Doctor Britling. "Marckheim was shrewd enough to kill him without committing suicide himself.

"Poor devil," whispered Howells huskily, looking down at the twisted form of the policeman. "I'm afraid he's dead. Take a look at him, will you?"

As Daniel rose to comply, Howells uttered a hoarse shout and threw himself upon the little police surgeon, carrying him bodily to the ground. They collapsed in a heap, and there was a roar behind them, an ear-splitting boom, as the petrol tank of the damaged car exploded and shot a tangle of metal and wood high into the air. Smouldering fragments showered to the earth all around them.

"Sorry," said Howells, helping Daniel to his feet. "I could see that coming off, and I hadn't time to give you a gentler warning."

Doctor Britling replied with a feeble grin, as he wiped out of his eyes the blood that trickled from a cut which had been made in his forehead by a splinter of glass into which Howell's large bulk had ground his face.

An excited crowd was gathering about the blazing wreckage. Enthusiastic volunteers were scooping up dirt and clods of grass with their fingers and throwing these futile handfuls into the flames. Two or three motorists were hurrying up with fire extinguishers. Press photographers were taking pictures of the smashed car from every conceivable angle, except from above, where the black clouds of smoke roiled. Cameramen from the principal newsreels were grinding frantically.

"For the love of Pete! Hold that a minute!" shouted one of them as a motorist aimed the nozzle of a fire extinguisher into the heart of the blaze. "What do you want to do . . .spoil the picture?"

A reporter, who had been thrown ten feet by the explosion of the petrol tank, was sitting on the running board of his car writing at furious speed a report for his driver to relay by the nearest telephone to the office of his newspaper. His face was black; his eyebrows and hair were scorched; his clothes were charred and tattered, but nothing mattered except that his story must reach his journal in time for the afternoon editions.

Doctor Britling knelt beside the inert body of the constable. "Dead," he said simply.

A gust of wrath shook the Chief Inspector's large frame. He beckoned grimly to one of his subordinates. "Stand guard over these bodies," he snapped, "and don't let anyone go near them."

Linking his arm in that of Doctor Britling, he drew the police surgeon out of earshot of the goggling crowd.

"Let's figure this out," he said urgently. "There must be a solution, and we've got to find it. The facts are simply these: Annerley was shot in the back of the head while he was driving his car at a speed of roughly seventy miles an hour. We were doing sixty-five, and couldn't catch him. No one was in the car with him but a policeman, whose record rules out the possibility that he fired the shots. Besides, with the first shot the car must have careered off the road and no one could fire two others and hit the target he was aiming at under such circumstances. The speed of the car would render it out of the question for anyone to take successful aim from the side of the road, even if the roadside and surrounding fields hadn't been deserted, as they were. There was no other car between Annerley's and the one in which we were following him. How, then, was he shot? Who fired, and from where?"

"The obvious answer is a mechanical contrivance," replied Doctor Britling promptly. "Marckheim seems to have a flare for such devices. He made his attempt on Levison with one, and there was more than a hint of mechanical ingenuity in the method whereby he killed Quail. Yes, something mechanical is the only possible solution; something timed to go off when Annerley's car was some distance from the house…"

"Timed? You mean something in the nature of a clock?" suggested Howells.

"A clock…" Daniel's eyes narrowed. "…I wonder…"

He drew from his pocket the little wooden bird, covered with tiny feathers, which he had found that morning on the gravel path leading from the house to the garage. He turned it over on the palm of his hand and examined it minutely.

The Chief Inspector peered over his shoulder. "What is it? Some sort of toy?"

Doctor Britling was too preoccupied with the thought that had dawned in his mind to realise that the other had spoken.

Chief Inspector Howells grunted.

But Daniel, unheeding, was pushing his way through the crowd that was assembled at the edge of the circle of scorched grass about the dying bonfire. He gripped the arm of one of the constables who was spraying the smouldering embers with the contents of a fire extinguisher.

"Concentrate on the rear of the car," he said. "I want the back rest of the rear seat saved if possible."

"There's not much of it to save, sir!"

The policeman was right; on closer inspection Daniel saw that the leather covering of the rear seat and the horse-hair stuffing which once had padded it were no more than a charred residue that crumpled at the touch. The floorboards were burned away, and the chassis, like the bare bones of some prehistoric monster, was lying at an angle in a welter of ash, blackened fragments of metal and leather, and churned up earth.

"Find a stick of some sort," said Daniel, "and poke about in there." He pointed to the litter in the rear of the car. "—let me see anything you find, no matter how unimportant it may appear to be."

The wreckage was now cool enough to explore, and the

constable started sifting the ashes with the aid of one of the crowd. In the first few minutes of investigation, he unearthed and important find—a small pearl-handled revolver, blackened and cracked with the heat to which it had been exposed.

Doctor Britling showed the revolver to Howells, who took it and broke open the cartridge chamber. It contained six empty shells.

"Three of the bullets lodged in Annerley's brain," remarked Daniel. "The others went wild."

Someone touched his arm and handed him a twisted strip of metal which had just been found, and a tiny wheel which was certainly not one of the component parts of a motorcar. Daniel spread out a newspaper on the ground, and laid upon it the little wooden bird, the revolver, the strip of metal, the small wheel, and some of the other objects which were passed to him in due course. Many of the saved articles he glanced at and discarded, but soon a little mound of metal parts, composed mainly of small wheels, was accumulated on the paper.

"That may once have been an ingenious contrivance," muttered Howells in some perplexity, "but it beats me how it could fire a revolver...and why the bird? Where did you get it? — certainly not about here, for I've watched you like a hawk ever since the accident. Come on, tell me, what has the bird got to do with the rest of this stuff?"

"A great deal," replied Daniel. "I found it, not here, as you remark, but on the path at Grey Towers which leads from the house to the garage. Almost, that little bird speaks for itself, although it has lost its voice. Think man, when it had a voice, what did it say?"

Howells pushed his hat forward and scratched the back of his head awkwardly.

"Well," he said emphatically, "I've never yet seen a little

wooden bird that said anything—and when I do, I'll put more water in my whisky!"

Daniel picked up the bird and moved its hinged beak up and down.

"When this little bird had a voice," he murmured softly, "it said: 'Cuckoo! Cuckoo! Cuckoo!'"

"By the Lord Harry!" exclaimed Howells. "A cuckoo-clock!"

"Exactly," agreed Daniel, drily. "A cuckoo-clock. Only this clock spoke with lead, and its voice spelled death. By some ingenious arrangement the device which operated the cuckoo was adapted to firing the revolver. The clock was concealed, of course, in the upholstery of the rear seat, with the muzzle of the revolver aimed at the driver's head. It was, if you remember, exactly ten o'clock when Annerley's car suddenly swerved off the road. The clock, you see, had just spoken…"

"Poor Annerley," he added. "No doubt he thought himself safe from his enemy. Marckheim wanted him to think that. The fiendish subtlety of his revenge lay in killing Annerley at the moment when he was beginning to crow inwardly at having escaped death!

A Telegram in Code

DOCTOR BRITLING SLOWLY ascended the front steps of Grey Towers. Held in his tightly-clenched fingers was the little wooden bird which had offered the first clue to the means whereby Mark Annerley had been killed. It was leading him now to certain theories regarding the identity of the killer. He had left Chief Inspector Howells to complete his investigation at the scene of the murder and had returned alone to test these theories.

He was almost sure that Sydney Levine, the cripple with the sad, beautiful face of a saint, was the murderer's accomplice. The problem was to discover in what disguise the murderer himself was masquerading. Somehow Daniel could not shut out of his mind his suspicion of Israel Straust...

As he entered the hall Cora Annerley came out of the library where she had been awaiting the return of the men who had followed her husband's car. Her green eyes asked a question— and answered it by looking at Daniel's face, on which the truth was plainly written.

"Then he's dead?" she said hoarsely.

Daniel nodded silently.

"How did it happen?" He told her, softening as much as he could, the brutality of Mark Annerley's passing.

Mrs. Annerley turned away and walked back to the library. "He would have been better to accept the escape I offered him last night," was all that she said.

Her back was turned toward Doctor Britling, so he could not see her expression as she said it.

The butler approached carrying a round silver tray on which lay a buff envelope. "A telegram for you, sir."

The police surgeon took the envelope and tore it open. The message enclosed was brief, but it conveyed much of importance. Below the address ran two typewritten lines:

Four thousand eight hundred and forty-two pounds. House-keepers are usually scrupulously tidy. Eunice.

The wording would probably have baffled anyone but Daniel, and even he did not realise for a moment exactly what it meant. When the full meaning of the words dawned upon his consciousness, he went into the breakfast room and sat down, his eyes staring unseeing through the wide French windows.

The first eight words, of course, referred to his sister's little speculation; they were intended to tell how much money she had acquired by it. But the rest of the telegram opened up a prospect which seemed too unreal to be possible.

He had said in his letter to her yesterday that although the visible surfaces of the furniture in the house were cleaned and polished, dust and dirt lurked in the places that did not normally meet the eye. He had suggested that Mrs. Levine, the housekeeper, was apparently not particular about the degree of thoroughness with which the maids did their work. The paragraph had been written in passing because he knew it was the very scrap of gossip that would interest his sister. And Eunice had instantly fastened upon the point of it, the point which Daniel had overlooked. 'Housekeepers are usually scrupulously tidy...' Did that mean something or was Mrs. Levine merely the exception that proved the rule?

Doctor Britling jumped to his feet, stuffing the telegram into his pocket and hurried out of the breakfast room. As he did so, he remembered that the fingerprints of Mrs. Levine had been taken, and that they were definitely not those of

Arthur Marckheim. Further, that she had been taken into the employment of Israel Straust seven years before Marckheim came out of prison. Daniel paused with a rueful expression on his keen, intelligent face. Fingerprints cannot lie. It was out of the question that Mrs. Levine should be Arthur Marckheim.

And yet…Eunice had given him a definite lead, which he had not noticed for himself; it was only fair to her that he should probe it to the bottom.

Harcourt was still in the hall fussing about aimlessly.

"Where is Mrs. Levine?" asked Daniel.

"In her room, sir," quavered Harcourt.

Doctor Britling went up to the first floor and through the green baize door that led to the servants' quarters. He knew his way about the rambling old house, for he had made a tour of inspection with Gideon Levison on the night he had arrived.

The mellow tones of an old piano came faintly along the corridor that lay behind the green baize door, coming as he soon discovered from the housekeeper's room. Daniel listened to the music for a moment before tapping gently on the door. A low, deep voice bade him enter.

He turned the handle and walked into the room.

In an armchair before the fire sat Mrs. Levine. A fleecy shawl covered her slender shoulders and there was a lace cap on her grey hair. She was knitting, and looked with a kindly expression in her mild eyes as Daniel came into the room.

At a piano in the far corner sat the cripple with the beautiful face, his long slender fingers straying carelessly over the keys yellow with age, producing a tintinnabulation of rippling melody. His crutch lay on top of the piano.

In the chair opposite to that which was occupied by the housekeeper, sat Mary Quail, leaning back in an attitude of graceful repose, her arms lying along the padded arms of the chair, her eyes closed as though the music had cast a spell upon her. The droop of her long eyelashes on her smooth cheek gave her an innocent, childlike appearance.

As Daniel stood uncertainly on the threshold, looking at the quiet homely scene, his half-formed suspicions were almost dispelled. It seemed ridiculous to suspect anyone so frail, so tranquil, as Mrs. Levine. And the crippled lad, whose face so resembled the visage of a sorrowing saint…it was absurd to suspect him!

And yet…

Mrs. Levine rose to her feet, and the crippled youth stood up also, supporting himself by resting one hand upon the piano; they were looking at Daniel, waiting to hear his errand. Suddenly he felt quite uncomfortable.

"Please sit down," he said to Mrs. Levine. Turning to Sydney, he added: "Won't you please continue playing? This is only an informal visit, if you will allow me that liberty."

The youth smiled and sat down again. His fingers moved over the keys, playing softly, sweetly, with the assured touch of an accomplished musician.

"I love to listen to Sydney's music," said the housekeeper proudly. "So does Miss Quail…she comes in often to enjoy an hour of his playing."

Daniel nodded and murmured something about the lad's exquisite touch. His eyes were travelling about the room, taking in every detail of the furnishings, which were, he noticed, typical of the taste of the lower middle class, and of a period a quarter of a century old; a period of heavily-fringed curtains and cumbersome furniture. The imagination of the Hebrew was absent. Apparently Mrs. Levine had made no changes in the appearance of the room since she inherited it from her predecessor.

The room was large, but the closely-curtained windows, and the many pictures which jostled each other on the wall gave it a crowded appearance. The portrait in crayons of a woman who had 'maiden aunt' written all over her thin, severe features (presumably belonging to a relation of the previous housekeeper, or that worthy herself); rubbed frames democratically with an engraving of Queen Alexandra; above their heads a huge photograph of Niagara Falls poured an unending torrent.

Against the wall stood three chairs with weak backs; a scrap of red ribbon tied to the middle rib of each was apparently intended to warn the unwary of their frail state.

The mantelpiece was cluttered with gimcrack ornaments. The pink china figures of a shepherd and shepherdess, each in charge of two bobby sheep, faced each other from the extreme ends and between them stood a clock which kept an erratic time of its own (and not infrequently no time at all); two vases of one size and two of another; a pair of brass candlesticks; seven china dogs of varying sizes and shade of repulsiveness, and a conch shell. It was all rather overpowering.

Daniel was about to withdraw when he noticed a picture on the wall beside the mantelpiece which seemed, somehow, to be out of place; it had not been hung, for one thing, in the close formation that distinguished the others. It suggested, in some way, that the enthusiastic muddler who decorated the room had not intended it to hang there at all. Walking forward, Doctor Britling tilted it upwards and was interested to see that the area of red wallpaper beneath was almost the shade of the inch or so of the sun-faded paper that surrounded it. Almost, but not quite, for there was a small oblong patch in the centre which had never been exposed to the sun; a patch where some object about seven inches high and four or five inches wide must have hung for many years!

"Pardon me," said Daniel, turning round. "But is it possible that a cuckoo-clock used to hang here?"

His eyes were closely watching the faces of the woman and her grandson but they detected no trace of emotion.

"Why yes," replied Mrs. Levine. "But it wouldn't keep time, so I had it thrown out a few days ago."

"I see." Doctor Britling replaced the picture and wavered towards the door.

When he was standing on the threshold it suddenly occurred to him to wonder why it was that Mary Quail reclined so motionlessly in her chair. The spell of the music did not account for it, since the music had paused when he first came into the room, and again when he had put his question about the cuckoo-clock. Mary had not stirred and her eyes had remained closed…

Doctor Britling crossed the room and touched the girl's wrist. She did not stir. He felt her pulse and was alarmed at the feebleness of its beat. His eyes narrowed as he noticed a tiny puncture on her arm just above the wrist…

Then things began to happen!

The cripple swung his crutch and it struck a vicious blow on Daniel's unprotected head. Daniel groaned and dropped to the floor. With incredible agility the housekeeper launched herself from her chair and her wrinkled hands fastened on his throat. Her lips parted and through her clenched teeth came a sound like the furious snarl of an angry beast. Her fingers squeezed until they seemed to be cutting deep into his flesh. Doctor Britling struggled and kicked, but the fingers only tightened like the iron jaws of a rat trap.

There was a roar in his ears and sparks of light seemed to stab his eyeballs.

Through the haze he saw the face of the person who was throttling him and it was grim and relentless!

Everything was blotted out by the yawning blackness that overwhelmed him…

Marckheim's Escape

M R. ALBERT MOODY stood in the doorway of Grey Towers and submitted the landscape to his critical inspection. His pale blue eyes stolidly contemplated the tiny white ruffles that flecked the azure blue of the sky; the dappled shadows on the cool green lawn; the red, yellow, and vivid purple masses of the flowerbeds that hedged the drive on either side; the flirting passage of a large butterfly with radiant wings. Nature, the wayward jade, was doing her utmost this morning to delight the soul of Mr. Moody.

Taking his pipe from his mouth, Mr. Moody spat appreciatively. A spider, in the act of scuttling from one crack in the brickwork of the terrace to another, was momentarily swept off its feet and submerged by this expression of approval of Nature's morning dress. It was up in a moment, however, and continued its journey warily. Again Mr. Moody removed his pipe from his mouth, and again he spat. The force of the volley flattened the spider, but with the elasticity of its kind it bobbed up again and retreated to its dugout between two bricks under the sustained fire of Mr. Moody, who scored four hits out of five spits. This highly satisfactory result provoked the faintest of complacent smiles on Mr. Moody's pink countenance.

He stood basking in the sun and looking about him for fresh worlds to conquer.

With no sound but the crunching of gravel beneath its wheels, a shining Rolls-Royce limousine glided along the path that led from the garage and pulled up opposite the front door. Sydney Levine was at the wheel; he climbed out slowly, limped into the house with the aid of his crutch, and went upstairs.

The critical light died out of Mr. Moody's eyes and was

replaced by a look of honest admiration. Mr. Moody had a proper reverence for Rolls-Royce cars. It was one thing to criticise the handiwork of nature, which cost nothing, and quite another thing to presume so far with a gleaming wonder which had cost two thousand pounds. Mr. Moody stood before this mechanical god in the spirit of worship which once brought the Children of Israel to their knees before the Golden Calf.

A touch on his arm roused him from his silent admiration and he turned to find Sydney Levine standing beside him. "Mr. Straust wants you to come up and help Miss Quail down to the car. She's feeling rather faint and he thinks a good drive will do her good." Mr. Moody moved with alacrity to obey.

Upstairs, Sydney ushered him into Mary Quail's bedroom where the girl was sitting on the bed with her hat and coat on. There was another person in the room, a person whom Mr. Moody instantly recognised; for was he not completely familiar with the bowed form, , the scraggy beard and the voluminous black cloak of his employer, Mr. Israel Straust?

Miss Quail seemed to be feeling very faint indeed. She was almost a dead weight as they helped her down the stairs, but Mr. Moody was quite surprised at the strength of the bent form that supported her on the other side. He wouldn't have suspected old Mr. Straust of such respectable muscles.

When the girl was comfortably accommodated on the rear seat—she kept her eyes closed, Mr. Moody noticed, as though the sun was too strong for them—the withered figure in the long black coat and drooping black hat climbed in beside her, with a smiling word of thanks for Mr. Moody's assistance.

"Only too pleased," stammered Mr. Moody, closing the door.

As Sydney Levine eased himself into the driving seat, with his crutch beside him, Mr. Moody heard a hoarse shout from above, and looking up saw the excited face of Adrian Carver at a small window on the first floor which Mr. Moody identified as the corner window of the housekeeper's room. The young man was gesticulating wildly and shouting something too loudly and excitedly to be altogether intelligible, something about 'stop' and 'that girl,' but with an aged millionaire beaming at him from the interior of a luxurious Rolls, Mr. Moody simply couldn't be bothered to listen.

After the car had purred away down the drive Mr. Moody looked up again, but Adrian had disappeared. He clicked his teeth disapprovingly. That young Carver needed taking down a peg or two. He had no respect for anyone, not even for the gilded halo of wealth. Bawling, and waving his arms like a lunatic, while a man was busy with an important person like Mr. Straust!

Adrian came pounding down the stairs and shook his fist under Mr. Moody's nose. "You blasted idiot!" he cried. "Do you know what you've done?"

"Done?" echoed the other in a tone of mild astonishment. "What do you mean, done?"

"You've only helped Marckheim to escape you thundering blockhead! And helped him to kidnap Miss Quail into the bargain. Oh, you fool! You utter fool!"

With that, Adrian dashed toward the gates. The big man hesitated for a moment, then lumbered after him.

A phlegmatic policeman with a large hand on Adrian's chest held the irate young man back. "Orders are orders," said the policeman, calmly. "You don't put a foot beyond that gate."

"You outrageous idiot!" stormed Adrian. "I tell you; Miss Quail's being kidnapped!"

Mr. Moody—a trifle pale—caught Adrian's arm and shook it. "What's all this about kidnappin'? What are you getting at?"

Adrian controlled himself with an effort, and took a deep

breath. "I was looking for Miss Quail," he panted. "Harcourt thought she might be in the housekeeper's room, so I went there… There was no one in the room except Doctor Britling, who was lying unconscious on the floor with a whacking great bruise on his throat…He was in a bad way, but he was able to tell me that Mary Quail had been there…That she had been drugged, damn it! Just then I looked out of the window and saw you, you confounded fathead, helping Marckheim and his confederate to abduct her!"

"But…but…but…" The solid earth seemed to shiver under Mr. Moody's feet. "But that was Mr. Straust!"

"It was Marckheim—in disguise!" Adrian almost bellowed. He jerked towards the gates, but the policeman held him back.

"Not so fast young man; not so fast," he growled. "It all sounds like a cock-and-bull story to me. I took a good look at the car as it passed and I'll take an oath it was Mr. Straust who was sitting beside the young lady. It won't do you know. You won't get past me that way. I've got my orders—"

"To blazes with orders!" retorted Adrian. "I tell you; Miss Quail is being taken away against her will. Are you going to calmly standby and let her abductors get clear away with her?"

A smug grin spread over the constable's large, red face. "P'raps Mr. Moody won't mind investigating the truth of your little tale," he replied knowingly. "It won't take a minute for him to go and see what's what."

Adrian stepped back, tearing himself free of the policeman's grasp. His eyes measured the distance to the gates, then travelled swiftly to the constable's broad chin. His right fist shot up and landed with perfect precision on the target he had chosen. The policeman swayed on his feet and into his eyes came an expression of dazed horror.

"Here!" cried Mr. Moody, aghast, "here!"

Adrian dodged his clumsy attack and tripped him up neatly. As the ponderous form of Mr. Moody sprawled upon the gravel, Adrian sprinted through the gates. There was only a handful of people gaping in the road and none of them made any effort to stop him, except a pink-faced young man, sitting at the roadside with his arm about a complacent girl, who struggled to free himself with a cry as Adrian grabbed the handlebars of a motorcycle which was parked near the gates.

"Hi!" he shouted vociferously. "Come orf that there!"

But by the time the pink-faced youth had disengaged his arm from the waist of his friend and struggled to his feet, Adrian and the motorcycle were rapidly disappearing in a cloud of dust along the road which the Rolls-Royce had taken.

His complexion rapidly deepening to purple, the amatory young man hurried up to the policeman and Mr. Moody (who had run into the road) with a look of anguish in his eyes.

"He's gone orf on my bike," he whined in an adenoidal voice. "Gone strite orf on it, 'e 'as!"

"Gawd!" whispered the policeman staring after the cloud of dust. "Now there won't half be a row!"

"You said it," was Mr. Moody's morose reply.

"Gone strite orf on it!" wailed the stricken youth.

Mr. Moody and the policeman withdrew within the gates to shelter from the voluble woe of the unfortunate owner and the scornful vituperative of his lady friend.

Mr. Moody followed the direction of the others startled gaze, and, to his horror, saw the white face of Doctor Britling framed in the open window…and looking more like the ghost of Doctor Britling than the dapper little police surgeon in the flesh…

Mr. Moody swore and spat. He started running at a lumbering gait toward the house.

DOCTOR BRITLING WAS sitting on the top step of the staircase where it joined the first floor landing when Mr. Moody found him. This was a far as Daniel had been able to stagger from the housekeeper's room. His head was resting on his hands and his face had a waxen pallor which contrasted oddly with purple bruise that encircled his throat.

"Wha—what on earth's happened?" gasped Mr. Moody.

"That," croaked Daniel weakly, "is what I'm trying to decide."

There was a fierce throbbing in his head, as though a score of boilermakers, armed with sledgehammers, were pounding on the wall of his skull. One spot was particularly tender. It felt as though it had been pillowed on a nest of wasps. That, Daniel realised was where the cripple—who wasn't a cripple!—had struck him with his crutch. That he told himself grimly, was a score he must settle with Mr. Saintly Face. There was also a score to be settled with the man—Marckheim, or an accomplice—who had passed as 'Mrs. Levine'.

For, or course, 'Mrs. Levine' was not a woman. Of that, Doctor Britling was positive. No woman of 'her' size could have possessed the powerful hands which had fastened on his throat. 'Mrs. Levine' was a man in disguise. Marckheim? Perhaps—but there was the objection that the fingerprints of the bogus housekeeper, which had been taken by a Scotland Yard expert, were not those of the ex-convict. And fingerprints could not lie! Or could they? Daniel was almost prepared to believe that Marckheim's ingenious brain could contrive even that.

The cripple was not a cripple. He had stood upright without support at the moment of striking at Daniel with his crutch. His head had straightened from the awkward angle at which it had previously ridden on his neck; his left shoulder which formerly had been drawn up under his jaw had squared with his right shoulder. 'Sydney Levine,' then, was nether crippled nor deformed.

Daniel raised his head with an effort. "Has anyone left the grounds within the last few minutes?" he asked painfully.

Mr. Moody began to feel increasingly uncomfortable. "Well… Old Mr. Straust—or it certainly looked like him—went out in his car a few minutes ago, with the young lady," he muttered, keeping his eyes on the stair carpet. "The young crippled chap was driving, as usual. Then…er…a few moments later Mr. Carver came tearing down with a—well, a lot of wild talk…"

"Which, of course, you were too intelligent to believe," remarked Daniel, in a dry tone that made the other wriggle. "Well, what happened? Where's Mr. Carver?"

"Gone off," said Mr. Moody, unconsciously echoing the pink-faced young man. "He—er—borrowed a motorbike and followed the Rolls."

"I'm glad someone's got a little initiative," declared Daniel. "There's a lot of the right stuff in that boy."

"Yes, sir," agreed Mr. Moody insincerely.

Doctor Britling struggled weakly to his feet and tenderly caressed his maltreated throat. "I suppose you'd better come with me," he said over his shoulder as he limped down the corridor towards the bedroom of Israel Straust.

Mr. Moody followed, with a sinking feeling in the pit of his stomach.

Without the formality of knocking, Daniel threw open the bedroom door and went in. The room was tenantless, but on the floor lay some crumpled articles of feminine wearing apparel which Daniel had last seen on the emaciated frame of 'Mrs. Levine'!

A faint sound led Daniel to a door in the wall, which he threw open. Beyond lay a large room with many wide windows, commanding an excellent view of the grounds about the house. It was the old man's bathroom, and such a bathroom as Daniel had never seen before. The walls were lined with bookcases filled with an amazing array of volumes. There was a huge stone fireplace in which, in spite of the warmth of the day, a wood fire burned brightly. The floor was covered entirely with a silver carpet, the pile of which was inches deep. The only sign of the use to which the room was dedicated was a long, wide, black marble bath which was sunk into the floor in the centre.

Mr. Moody uttered a strangled cry as he came through the door at Daniel's heels. Gagged and bound to a chair in the corner remote from the windows was the aged financier, Israel Straust! He was dressed solely in his ancient green dressing gown.

Daniel quickly produced a penknife, cut the rope that secured the old man to the chair, and massaged his limbs gently until the restored circulation enabled him to stand up.

"It was Marckheim…" whispered Straust feebly, when the gag was removed. "He came in here a little while ago, disguised as—as Mrs. Levine, and after some conversation about domestic affairs, struck me with something. I lost consciousness, and when I came to I was bound to the chair and Marckheim was removing his disguise and making himself up as my double…"

Doctor Britling turned sharply to the goggling Mr. Moody. "Go down to the gates and await the return of Chief Inspector Howells," he commanded. "When he appears, tell him I want to see him at once."

Mr. Moody confessed afterwards to a crony, over a congenial pint of beer, that he never knew how his legs—which had 'gone' at the knees—retained sufficient strength to carry him from the room.

When they were alone, Israel Straust put a withered hand on Doctor Britling's shoulder. "My friend," he said hoarsely, "I always knew that Arthur Marckheim would never kill me. Am I not too old and feeble to be worth the trouble? No, I knew he would find some subtler form of revenge for the old crow, Israel Straust. Some revenge that would shrivel the soul, instead of striking down the body…and he has found it. The perfect revenge. The most terrible punishment that he could have devised."

Suddenly Doctor Britling felt very sorry for Israel Straust. Never had he looked so old, so decrepit, so stricken as he did now.

"Before he went out of the room," said the old man shakily, "Marckheim came close to me and whispered a single word. That word was 'Echo'."

A spasm of pain contorted the withered features. "A very simple, almost an insignificant word, you will say—but it froze my very heart. My friend, for thirty years I have been a rich man. For thirty years I have steadily become richer. Three or four weeks ago my shareholdings were worth almost a million pounds. When we received the warning messages that Marckheim sent us, I sold as many of these shares as I could, for I knew that Marckheim did not threaten lightly, and if he succeeded in even a part of his revenge, those shares would become almost valueless. Even if I lived, I should be penniless. And poverty, my friend, is my nightmare. Money! Ah! To me money is life, light, warmth, power—everything that is to be desired. Have I not struggled for it all the years of my life? Have I not bled and suffered, even turned traitor for it? Money! Ah! That is the word that is written on my heart…

"I sold these shares, and the money I placed in a safe place— as I was pleased to imagine—so that no panic could destroy it, no thieves could steal it. Only one thing could procure access to it—and that was a little insignificant word. The word 'Echo'."

Daniel began to comprehend.

"The word, my friend, that Marckheim whispered to me. The word that shrivelled my soul. The word that told me my money was gone—that Marckheim had it. God alone knows how he discovered that word. I am an old man. Perhaps I have mumbled it in my sleep—it meant so much to me, you see. How he discovered it does not matter. All that matters is that he has taken my money, and left me, bereft of all that I cherished, a helpless, miserable old man. Ah! If he had only taken my life!" The rheumy old eyes brimmed with tears; the withered lips trembled; the claw-like hands twitched. The shrunken shell of the old man seemed to have caved in.

"Leave me please," begged Israel Straust.

There was nothing Daniel could say; nothing he could do, except leave the room in silence.

When he was alone, the old man shuffled to the black marble bath and turned on the hot water tap, then tottered across the room and opened a cupboard. His body twisted as though with unbearable pain, and from his thin lips came a faint moaning.

Old Izzy, the Pawnbroker, they had called him in Whitechapel forty years ago…Old Izzy, who lived (it was said), on a soup made of potato peelings and cabbage stalks…Old Izzy, whose life was one long penance, dedicated to the great God Gold…

And now Israel Straust was a poor man again…

His shaking hand drew a bottle from the cupboard, a bottle containing a drug to stimulate his heart, to make his blood flow more quickly in his veins…With a hypodermic syringe he injected a powerful dose into his arm.

Replacing the bottle, he untied the frayed silken cord about his waist and let the ancient green dressing gown slip from his meagre frame to the soft carpet. With something that glistened in his hand, he walked to the bath.

Carver Finds Marckheim

SIR BASIL MUMFORD paced the floor like a caged tiger, while his cigarette smouldered away unnoticed on a silver ashtray. His bushy eyebrows were drawn down over his sunken grey eyes; his square jaw had an ominous set to it; the closely-clipped moustache that fringed his upper lip seemed to bristle with fury. Sir Basil was in an ugly mood.

"I suppose you realise what the newspapers are saying about us?" he snapped. "I suppose you know the sort of damn-fool questions that are being asked in the House of Commons?"

Chief Inspector Howells coughed deprecatingly.

"Very unfair, sir," he mumbled. "We've done our best, sir."

The angry eyes of Sir Basil swept the walls of the library as though they were trying to destroy them with a single glance. It was a favourite trick of the Chief Commissioner to envelop even his inanimate surroundings in the aura of his wrath on the occasions (infrequent, it must be admitted) when he lost his temper.

"My dear Howells," he said icily, "we're supposed to be experts in the art of detecting, frustrating and apprehending criminals."

Doctor Britling, who was looking out of the window at the lengthening shadows which were creeping over the lawn with the sinking of the sun, sighed, and turned his head towards the others. "No man can claim to be an expert on an unknown species," he remarked, "and that's what Marckheim is. You have never before dealt with a criminal of this type."

The Chief Commissioner uttered an inarticulate sound expressive of contempt. "Nonsense!" he declared crushingly. "Marckheim! Why, the man's got you both hypnotised!"

Chief Inspector Howells looked wistfully at his irate superior who had motored down to Grey Towers when the late afternoon brought no success in the search for Marckheim, and then appealingly at Doctor Britling, into whose eyes came the light of battle.

"My dear Sir Basil," said Daniel suavely, "your attitude proves that you have completely failed to grasp what Chief Inspector Howells has been up against. In the first place through the deliberate evasions of Gideon Levison, the local police were kept in ignorance of the true state of affairs until after the murder of Hubert Quail; two murders had therefore been committed before Howells was put in charge of the case. In the second place, he had to deal with a man immeasurably cleverer than all three of us put together.

"Marckheim is none of your everyday murderers who dispose of their victims by stabbing or shooting them, or by putting arsenic or ground glass in their food. If he had been of that type, Howells would have nabbed him within a few hours of arriving in the house. No, Marckheim is an inspired fiend. Do you realise, for instance, that not even his victims had the slightest glimpse of him, even at the very moment of death? He worked completely under cover. Jubal Straust died in his car miles from here through eating a poisoned tablet which had been substituted for an indigestion remedy. Hubert Quail was killed by the poisoned claws of a kitten which was lowered from above to the window of his bedroom. Annerley was shot in the head by a revolver fired by the mechanism of a cuckoo-clock. Levison, who still lives, was wounded by his own revolver, ingeniously rigged up to fire when he opened the drawer in which he kept it. In every case, death has come from a totally unexpected source; every other source was closely guarded against.

"Of the four who are dead, one—poor old Israel Straust— died by his own hand. No attempt has been made on the life of Mrs. Annerley; and according to the hospital authorities, Levison has every chance of recovering. I admit the position is appalling but it might easily have been much worse. I think that Howells has done everything possible within—if he'll excuse me—within his limitations, and he doesn't deserve to have passed onto him the stupid tirades that have been launched by the Press and certain members of Parliament."

This latter pronouncement, delivered in a dry, dispassionate tone, was a bitter pill for Sir Basil to swallow, but he accepted it well. He held out his hand to his subordinate.

"Wash out all I've said," he remarked with a smile. "I was only letting off steam."

The Chief Inspector permitted himself the ghost of a smile for the first time within twenty-four hours.

"As I understand it, then, the position is this," said Sir Basil: "The car in which Marckheim escaped was found abandoned in a field near Aylesbury and no further trace of him has been discovered?"

"That's the position, sir," agreed Howells. "The surrounding neighbourhood has been scoured by the local police—I spent the entire afternoon participating in the search—but without success. Everything that can be done in that direction is being done, sir."

Daniel lit a fresh cigar and exhaled a cloud of fragrant smoke.

"Personally," he said, "I pin my hopes on young Carver."

The Scotland Yard officials looked at him doubtfully.

"Rather a scatter-brained youth, from all accounts," Sir Basil demurred.

"Adrian's a good boy," replied Daniel warmly. "It won't be easy to throw him off the scent. Either he's been added to the list of Marckheim's victims—which God forbid! —or he knows where Marckheim is hiding. In the latter case, he may be a captive. If he isn't, we'll hear from him in due course. Besides," the little police surgeon added softly, "he's in love with Mary Quail."

"The girl Marckheim had kidnapped?" said Sir Basil.

Doctor Britling nodded.

"I wonder why he abducted her?" murmured Sir Basil with a frown. "He has nothing against her, has he?"

"Perhaps she saw through his disguise as 'Mrs. Levine,'" suggested Howells. "A girl would sooner than a man. And possibly he means to use her as a hostage if we corner him."

"H'm." Sir Basil stroked his chin. "That's not unlikely."

At that moment the telephone bell in the hall shrilled a peremptory summons. With a glance at the others, Howells hurried out of the room to answer it.

They heard his voice raised in excitement. "Who? Yes, he's here…Who's speaking? Mr. Carver? That's good news!….Have you…Oh, all right, I'll fetch him."

The Chief Inspector's huge bulk appeared in the doorway. "It's Carver, Doctor Britling," he said, quite unnecessarily, "and he refuses to speak to anyone but you."

Daniel ran out to the hall followed by Sir Basil.

"Doctor Britling speaking…"

From the other end of the wire he heard Adrian's voice quivering with elation.

"I've tracked him down, Doc. I've tracked him down! He's led me a pretty dance, and I've smashed the motorbike to pieces, and my whole body is one mass of bruises—and—and—and I'm so hungry I could eat a cow—raw—but I hung on to him, and ran him to earth. His hideout is in South Kensington…an old house he's evidently had up his sleeve for a year or two…It isn't far from the tube station at Earl's Court…Meet me there as soon as you can…For God's sake bring a regiment; we'll need 'em! If I'm not on the spot when you arrive, I'll turn up directly—I'll be keeping an eye on the house…Hurry!" Adrian's voice became shrill with urgency. "Hurry! We've got to get Mary out of that devil's clutches!"

"I'll be with you in less than a couple of hours," responded Doctor Britling quietly.

He hung up the receiver and turned to the two men who stood expectantly behind him. "There's no time to talk now," he snapped. "A car—quickly! We're in a hurry!"

As a Flying Squad car hurtled them through the gathering dusk toward London, Doctor Britling repeated what Adrian had told him.

"If Marckheim's prepared that house for a hiding place," he concluded, "you can depend on it, breaking in won't be easy. We'd better be prepared for anything. Now, I suggest…"

He outlined his plan earnestly for some minutes, while the others listened attentively. When he had finished, Sir Basil nodded approval. The Chief Commissioner stopped the car at the next village and telephoned certain detailed instructions to Scotland Yard.

It was half past eight by Daniel's watch when the car pulled up outside the Earl's Court station of the Underground. Daniel jumped out and looked up and down the road pavement, but was unable to see anything of Adrian.

A hand plucked at his arm.

"Piper, guv'nor?" —whined a husky voice.

Daniel shook his head absently at the newsboy who stood in the gutter.

"Better have a paper, Doc," urged the youth in an entirely different tone.

Daniel's eyes flickered with astonishment. "Adrian!" he whispered, almost inaudibly.

"Walk to the corner of this street and take the first turning on the left," muttered the youth, his lips scarcely moving. "I'll meet you two streets down."

Daniel walked casually to the police car. Behind him he could hear the raucous whine Adrian had assumed, shouting: "Lite Speshul!"

"Wait here," he told the Scotland Yard officials in the car. "I'll be back directly."

A few streets away, at the corner of a road of old-fashioned three-storey houses, Adrian shuffled up beside him and offered a paper. Daniel accepted it and handed the youth a coin. With the coin between his teeth, Adrian fumbled in his ragged garments for change.

"I borrowed the outfit, papers and all, from a seedy chap who's probably blind drunk by now on what I gave him for them," he mumbled. "Don't show yourself, Doc, but peep round the corner and look at the fourth house on the left-hand side of the street. See that servant girl on the area steps, flirting with the postman?"

Daniel's eyes travelled in the indicated direction, and he nodded slightly.

"That's the house, and she's the look-out," whispered Adrian. "As a blind, she chats with errand boys and the like; otherwise it would look odd for her to be standing there so long. I tried to get off with her, but I wasn't good enough for her, I suppose. She's a pretty little bit of stuff, and she's making a hit with the postman, but—Doc—she's no girl! She's our old friend Sydney Levine!"

A Police Siege

About nine o'clock that night, a certain liveliness became evident in sleepy Silverthorne Road.

A stone's throw from the Earls Court station of the London Underground, Silverthorne Road can best be described as the sort of shabby-genteel residential street which is dying, and taking its time about the job. There was a symptomatic display of black boards in front of one or two of the houses inscribed in faded gilt lettering with the proclamation that bed and breakfast might be arranged for within. Each house in the street was exactly like its neighbour, even in the degree of stain and decay to which it had come through the ravages of time and neglect. They were all three storeys in height and built of brick disguised with stucco; iron railings surrounded each dingy area, and mounted with a short flight of chipped stone steps to the front door.

Usually, Silverthorne Road was frequented of an evening only by strolling cats and furtive stray dogs. Tonight, it was almost busy.

A ragged violinist was moving slowly along the gutter, scraping a bow across a battered fiddle to produce an atrocious mockery of music, with an anxious eye upon the windows as though, with misplaced optimism, he hoped to see a copper or two come pattering to the pavement; a loafer, in cap and muffler, came shambling down the street; a few yards behind him walked two dapper young men in soft felt hats and well-cut clothes, who paused at one of the 'bed and breakfast' boards as though the arrangement of such accommodation was the very mission which had brought them here; across the street a tall man climbed the steps of one of the houses and stood in the portico fumbling through his pockets, apparently for a latchkey; a removal van appeared at the corner and lumbered down the street...

A servant girl who had been lounging on the area steps of one of the houses stretched herself with a yawn and went indoors. As though her disappearance were a signal, the various pedestrians converged upon that particular house. The removal van backed across the street and came to rest with its rear wheels against the pavement; from it sprang a dozen shadowy figures.

Two policemen in uniform appeared at each end of the street and stood together in the middle of the road, apparently expecting traffic which would require quite a lot of controlling.

The large man who had appeared to be fumbling for a key was standing now on the steps and pounding lustily on the door of the house which was the centre of attraction. His violent knocking and ringing of the bell producing no result, he ran down the steps and joined two of the men who had arrived in the removal van.

"Nothing doing, Sir Basil," he reported.

"Are the men posted at the rear?" asked Sir Basil Mumford.

"Waiting for the signal, sir."

"Very well, Howells. Start the ball rolling."

Adrian Carver, still dressed in ragged attire, and even dirtier as to hands and face than ever, ran along the pavement and joined the trio. "I say!" he breathed, "What a lark!"

"It may be a bird of a different feather before very long!" retorted Doctor Britling grimly.

A shining police whistle appeared in Chief Inspector Howells's hand and he blew three blasts upon it. Almost at once the blasts were echoed shrilly from the rear of the house. Two men carrying axes ran up the steps and began to rain a shower of thudding blows upon the shivering front door. Down in the area there was a crash of broken glass. Then a plainclothes man who had smashed in a window bobbed a pink face up to the street level. "Shuttered with steel behind the curtains, sir!" he shouted.

Crowds began to collect like magic at both ends of the street, but they were kept in control by the uniformed constables whom Howells had thoughtfully provided.

In a few moments one of the men who were plying the axes looked ruefully at the blunted edge of his weapon. He ran down the steps and reported to Chief Inspector Howells that the door was evidently backed with sheet steel, or something of the sort.

This was a contingency that Doctor Britling had foreseen. Long cylinders were rolled out of the removal van and an acetylene blowtorch began to eat through wood and metal, throwing up a shower of sparks. Soon the charred twisted door was no longer a barrier. Men armed with revolvers poured into the house on the heels of Chief Inspector Howells. Odd-looking figures they were, with goblin heads and goggling eyes; one and all wearing gas masks!

This, too, had been one of Doctor Britling's inspirations, and it soon proved its soundness, for the lower part of the house was flooded with greyish vapour which would have spelled death to unprotected nostrils! It hung in a cloud some seven feet from the floor, seeming of too heavy a nature to rise higher.

Flashlights played through the room in the lower part of the house, but every corner was devoid of any human occupant. Policemen were surging now through the shattered rear door and the sound of trampling feet from the basement betrayed the fact that searchers were busy there. There was another door to be cut through by the acetylene blowtorch before the police could swarm up the staircase that lay beyond it, but the hissing blue flame made short work of that.

As Howells turned the light of his torch into the darkness

that shrouded the stairs, there was an orange flash above and an echoing report as a bullet clipped the light from his fingers. One of the men behind collapsed with a groan.

The Chief Inspector's revolver sent a hail of whining lead upwards, but only the thud...thud...thud of bullets lodging in the plastered wall resulted.

From the landing above floated a mocking laugh. "You'll never take me!" shouted a high-pitched voice. "Come after me—if you dare!"

There was a blinding flash, then a sheet of flame enveloped the landing, lighting the stairs with a dazzling brilliance. Hungry flames licked and danced on paraffin-soaked floorboards.

For a moment, Howells glimpsed a white face staring down from above, and he fired again, and plunged forward into the roaring blaze that was raging at the head of the stairs. His burly figure disappeared through the flames, but the men who tried to follow him were driven back by the terrific heat.

One of them ran out to the street. "The devil's set fire to the place!" he shouted. "Saint's alive, the whole street will burn to the ground in no time! There's dry rot in all these houses—they'll go up like match wood!"

Sir Basil whipped together the masked men who were tumbling out of the house. "You—" he instructed one, "send through a call for the fire brigade. You others give the alarm to the occupants of the other houses on this side of the street. Hurry!"

In an incredibly short time, the first floor of the house was a raging inferno. While the officers ran about warning the people in the neighbouring houses, Doctor Britling and Adrian Carver stood in the road looking upwards.

"Look!" cried the young man suddenly, his upturned face convulsed with horror.

At one of the windows a face had appeared, the face of a girl, white with terror. It vanished suddenly in a cloud of smoke.

"Mary!" shouted Adrian hoarsely. Running forward, he began to swarm up a drainpipe which hugged the wall of the house. As his slim form crept upwards, the glass of a window above his head shattered and fell outwards, and a burst of smoke and flame belched from the blackened frame.

For the first time in his life, Doctor Britling knew the emptiness in the pit of his stomach and the weak trembling in the legs which are symptoms of fear, cold and terrible. Fear, not for himself, but for the youth who was creeping slowly up the slender drainpipe that clung to the face of the burning house—and for the girl who had disappeared in a cloud of smoke from a window two storeys high.

It seemed inevitable that even if Adrian gained the smoke-filled room which was his goal it would only be to die in the flames with the girl he loved. The life of the building in which the flames roared could be measured in minutes only. Already the four yawning black mouths which marked the blazing rooms of the first floor were shooting out ragged tongues to lick and destroy the crumbling walls.

Adrian was clinging to the drainpipe between two of these belching mouths. The heat was terrific, but his twisted white face was turned upwards, and his scorched hands pulled him higher…higher…

His clothes were smouldering and one of the red tongues licked at his head with a sickening smell of singeing hair. Smoke filled his eyes, his nostrils, his mouth; there was a roar and hum in his ears. Only his will triumphed over his tortured body and forced it to creep upwards, inch by inch.

Above his head the pipe leant slowly outwards from the top, as though it were writhing away from the heat. Suddenly it buckled, snapped, and crashed to the ground, with Adrian still clinging to it desperately. The pipe smashed on the iron railings of the area, and Adrian was thrown across the pavement into the road. He lay where he fell, a limp bundle of smouldering rags.

Daniel knelt beside him and felt his fluttering heart. Adrian's eyes flickered open and widened with stark horror as they stared at the raging fury that enveloped the house. He struggled to rise but Daniel firmly held him down.

"Mary!" he gasped pitifully. "I've...got to go...to her. Oh, my leg..."

Daniel tenderly examined the boy's leg which was doubled under him. There was no doubt that it was broken. Beckoning to a policeman, Daniel sent him to fetch the ambulance that Howells had thoughtfully provided, which was parked at the head of the street.

Although he was in acute agony, Adrian weakly fought the stretcher-bearers who hoisted him gently into the ambulance. He kept crying hoarsely that he must go to Mary...Mary needed him...didn't they hear her calling him . . .how piteous her cries were...He must answer...He must...

Doctor Britling's eyes were wet with tears as he looked up at the window of the room in which the girl had suddenly vanished. It was terrible thing that one so young and so sweet as Mary Quail should die like that. There was no hope of saving her. No one could possibly reach her through the wild storm of flame and smoke that raged below. Mercifully, the smoke must overcome her before the flames hungrily devoured her slender body.

Suddenly, his heart jumped, as though a shout were ringing through it. Wood and glass were flying from the window to which his eyes were raised as a chair crashed through it. More smashing blows, then at the gaping hole appeared a figure in the black and white of a housemaid's uniform, but with the cropped head of a man. A figure that gulped air into starved lungs, then swept with appraising eyes the street below before disappearing again into the room.

It reappeared and pushed the limp form of a young girl through the shattered window, supporting her on the stone sill for a moment before lowering her on the end of a rope of knotted sheets.

Holding his breath Daniel watched the inert form of Mary Quail spinning slowly downwards between the mouths that spat out angry bursts of fire to destroy her. She reached the area and collapsed in a heap. Strong arms awaited her and carried her up the steps to the street. She was overcome by the fumes but seemed to have sustained no other harm.

While Mary was being carried to the ambulance, Daniel looked up and saw the black and white figure climbing through the smashed window above and swarming down the rope of knotted sheets. Below, flames were eating away the rope, and the tongues of flame from the first-floor windows were tangled together across the space which the swaying figure must pass.

For a moment, Daniel could see nothing but a leaping, whirling ball of fire, then a shapeless black bundle dropped with a thud to the area and lay still.

Daniel knelt beside the faintly moaning form.

There was great clangour of whistles and bells as fire engines raced down the streets; a hissing as columns of water rose to battle with the flames; the challenging roar of the triumphant serpents of fire.

Daniel removed his hat. Sydney Levine had atoned for whatever crimes he had committed by laying down his life for another.

Capture of Arthur Marckheim

ARTHUR MARCKHEIM STOOD on the roof ridge of the burning house, clutching the brickwork of a chimney for support, and looked down at the white faces that stared up at him from the street.

Fingers were pointing upward; a dozen flashlights illuminated his swaying figure; the hoarse shouts of the jostling crowds came to him faintly like 'noises off' in a stage play.

The scene appealed to his sense of the dramatic; the setting was more vivid than any that could be presented on a stage. Above his head the purple star-flecked sky; about him intersecting blades of light; about him the gaunt silhouette of roof peaks and chimney stacks; below the dancing glow of ravenous flame; from the street the dull murmur of the supers, who were also the thrilled audience.

He, Markheim, held the centre of the stage! The last act of his drama was drawing to a close...

Marckheim looked curiously unreal as he swayed against the skyline, clouds of black smoke eddying about him, wreathing him with curling tendrils. Almost his distended nostrils seemed to breathe out smoke and flame. He had the arched eyebrows, the high forehead, the hawk-like nose of Satan. A smile which was devoid of humour twisted his thin lips, baring two rows of white teeth like those of a snarling animal. Soon they would ring down the curtain on him but they could not rob him of the revenge he had visited on his enemies, nor this last dizzy hour of defiance.

This was his last stand.

He had hoped that the raiding party would be a small one, and that he would be able to escape over the sloping roofs, but he realised now that escape was impossible. The streets on all sides of his hiding-place were teeming with people, with eyes only for him, and already dark forms were closing in on him from the surrounding rooftops.

In the revolver that dangled from his fingers four cartridges were still unfired. Three, he decided grimly, would spit defiance for the last time at those swarming figures. The last would cheat the gallows of its prey.

Like a trapped animal he peered from side to side watching for the loophole that was an impossibility. The veneer of civilisation had dropped from him, leaving him a savage beast to whom the whole world was an enemy. The bitter years of prison had warped his brain, although they had not impaired its cleverness. Hatred had been the only impulse of his life within the grey walls. He had breathed hatred, lived hatred, absorbed it with the very food he ate. And now that his hatred was glutted with the blood of his victims, to kill was the only desire that inspired his twisted brain—to kill, and die himself in a last mocking gesture.

Through the skylight which had admitted Marckheim to the roof climbed the burly form of Chief Inspector Howells. He crouched low, for the slates were slippery and one misstep meant that he would slide down the sloping roof and topple to destruction in the street below, but his eyes were fixed with grim intensity on the man he had followed through the flames, as he slowly began to worm his way toward him over the leaded ridge.

A sound like the hoarse cry of a multitude from a bottomless pit came from the street as those below saw hunter and hunted facing each other across the peaked roof.

Marckheim laughed, and the searching blades of light revealed his white, demoniacal face.

He raised the gleaming muzzle of his revolver.

He took aim deliberately and fired once…twice…three times…

Howells shuddered as hot lead seared his shoulder—tore through the muscles of his right arm—creased his temple. He felt his strength oozing out of him, but his teeth clamped together, and sheer determination forced his numbed body to crawl a little further across the roof.

Something warm and sticky trickled down his sleeve and dripped from his fingers. In his hand was an empty revolver. Raising it, he pointed at Markheim.

"Surrender…or I fire!" he gasped painfully.

Marckheim uttered the shrill cry of a defiant animal. His hand came up and put the muzzle of his revolver to his temple…

With a supreme effort, Howells raised himself on his wounded arm and threw his revolver full in Marckheim's face.

Marckheim uttered a wild shout and swayed. He clutched at the chimney, but his feet went from under him and he plunged down the side of the roof. There was a dull echoing thud as his body landed on the stone pavement below.

The Confession

THE SICKLY ODOUR of anaesthetics had followed the stretcher on which Arthur Marckheim had been wheeled from the operating theatre. It hung heavily on the air of the little white room in which he lay.

Marckheim's eyes opened slightly and looked up dully at the kindly bearded face of Doctor Daniel Britling, who was bending over him.

The shadowy figure of a nurse hovered in the background.

"I'm going to give you another injection of morphine," murmured Daniel softly. "It will ease the pain a little."

Marckheim's lips moved slightly. "Thanks, Doctor…make it a strong one…"

He lay with waxen eyelids drooping on his ashen cheeks while the doctor's sure fingers did their work, then his eyes looked up again, with a feeble shadow of a mocking glint in them. "Patching me up for the gallows?" he whispered hoarsely.

"There's no question of that," replied Doctor Britling quietly.

"Then I'm…dying?"

Doctor Britling nodded. It was the only answer he was capable of making.

Arthur Marckheim sighed, and a tired smile curved his pale lips. "I'm glad," he said simply.

"Is there anything more I can do for you?" asked Daniel.

The wan features smiled again. "Funny," murmured the bloodless lips. "I almost killed you…only luck saved you… If there'd been time, I'd have had another try…And you ask what you can do to help me. Funny. No, there's nothing… Nothing at all."

Daniel bent his head to catch something that Marckheim

was mumbling almost inaudibly: "I don't mind dying…I've settled my score with those five rats…and Cora…Cora will settle with herself. That's all I lived for…without the prospect of revenge I'd have died in prison.

"Sydney?" he said more distinctly, his dark eyes anxiously scanning Doctor Britling's face.

"Sydney died through injuries received through saving the life of Mary Quail," replied Daniel.

The anxious face became more restful. "Poor Sydney! But he would have wanted to go out like that…I…should have kept him out of it…it was my affair…but…couldn't manage without him."

Doctor Britling took Marckheim's thin wrist and felt the feeble pulse. "The police are waiting to see you," he said. "They want you to make a statement."

The dying man almost contrived a grin although his agony must have been excruciating.

"Show them in," he croaked hoarsely.

With a quiet nod to the nurse, Doctor Britling left the room and closed the door behind him. Sir Basil Mumford, Chief Inspector Howells, and a clerk were waiting in the corridor. The Chief Inspector's head and shoulder were bandaged and his right arm was in a sling.

"You can go in now," said Daniel, "but let him take it easy, he's only got a few hours to live. And don't tell him that Levison is still alive."

The others stared in some astonishment at the latter request.

"It would be too cruel," the other elucidated. "He doesn't mind dying because he thinks he's dealt effectively with each of his enemies, but death would be Hell to him if he knew that Levison is pulling through. I'll be back presently—I'm going to see how Adrian and Mary are progressing. The last report was satisfactory, but I want to see for myself. The nurse has instructions to turn you out if making his statements becomes too much for Marckheim."

The C.I.D. men filed into the room where the dying man lay, and Daniel moved on with a slow shake of his head.

He would not have been the man he was if the shattered body of his patient had failed to move him to pity, in spite of the crimes of which Marckheim had been guilty. It was pathetic to witness the twilight of a great brain; the passing of an indomitable spirit, although that brain and spirit had turned their energies to evil. And, after all, had not the men Marckheim killed deserved their fate? Had they not by their own treachery transformed him into the ruthless instrument that destroyed them? By their betrayal of him they had written their own death warrants.

Within twenty minutes, Daniel returned to the room where Marckheim lay, having assured himself that Adrian Carver and Mary Quail were making satisfactory progress. Apart from minor bruises and burns, and Adrian's broken leg, neither of them had sustained any grave injury.

As he opened the door, Daniel heard the solemn voice of Chief Inspector Howells saying: "The clerk will read your statement over to you and I want you to try to listen and make sure there is nothing you wish to alter."

"Don't be too long," whispered Marckheim, drily. "I might not last it out…"

The droning voice of the clerk began to read: "My name is Arthur Nathan Marckheim, and I am forty-eight years old…"

"You'll find all that in the reference books for the year before I went to prison," croaked the dying man wearily. "Let's not waste time over the details."

His face was grey with the agonising pain of his mangled

body. "...I was sent to prison in 1919 for frauds in connection with the Eldorado Investment Trust. There were five men who were equally involved in it with me, but they contrived to whitewash themselves at my expense. I vowed then that no matter how long it might take me, or how great the difficulties of the undertaking, I should revenge myself on each one of them in turn, and upon my wife—who had left me for Annerley—when I was released from prison. I applied to be put in the engineering shop in prison, because I hoped that mechanical knowledge would aid me in my design. It helped to the extent that I was able to manufacture for myself the appliances with which I killed Levison and Annerley.

"When I had been in prison for three years, my plans began to take definite shape, and I sent for my mother who was living in North London. I asked her to apply for the post of housekeeper at the home of Israel Straust, in order that I might have a means of entering the house when I came out of prison. She did so, and shortly went to live at Grey Towers under the name of Levine, taking with her Sydney Marckheim, my son by a previous marriage, whom I hoped would be of assistance to me in carrying out my design. For almost nine years my mother held the position of housekeeper to Israel Straust—although she shared my hatred of him—in order that 'Mrs. Levine' would be too completely established in that post to be suspected of complicity when my plan went into operation.

"None of my associates knew my mother or my son, and my wife—now Mrs. Annerley—had never seen either of them. She was pleased to despise my relations, whom she would never agree to meet.

"A month ago, when I had been out of prison for almost two years, and my enemies had begun to feel themselves safe, I disguised myself as my mother and took her place at Grey

Towers. We are both of the same build, and somewhat similar cast of features, and prison had made me look twenty years older than I am, so the disguise was not difficult. She had coached me carefully in my duties as 'Mrs. Levine' and remained in hiding at a cottage some miles away so that she would be at hand if I required assistance.

"Some weeks later, when I was thoroughly familiar with the routine of the house, I sent warning messages to each of my enemies, and, as I had foreseen, they played into my hands by gathering for mutual protection at Grey Towers. They did not of course suspect that I was in their midst, masquerading as one of the trusted servants of Israel Straust!

"The day after they arrived, I murdered Jubal Straust by substituting a poisoned tablet for one of a vial of indigestion tablets, one of which he was required to take hourly. Jubal was a hypochondriac, and scrupulously punctual in such matters, so I was able to warn him that he would die at five o'clock—the hour when he would eat the poisoned tablet. My scheme for his disposal was accomplished without a hitch.

"Number one having been disposed of I turned my attention to Hubert Quail. He was afraid of cats, and had tried that day to strangle an orange kitten which Sydney had given to his niece, so the following morning I tipped the kitten's claws with a poisonous composition based on curare, and Sydney lowered it from above to the window of Quail's bedroom. As I had planned, Quail made another attempt to strangle the kitten, sustained several scratches, and died.

"With the death of Quail, Scotland Yard detectives were summoned to the house, and I realised that the fingerprints of all the servants would be taken. I had foreseen that, however, and was ready for the emergency. Sydney drove me to the village in the Rolls to do some household shopping, then on to the cottage where my mother was in hiding. She was driven back to Grey Towers in my stead and her fingerprints were taken in due course. They did not, of course, bear the slightest resemblance to mine, which were in the hands of Scotland Yard, so 'Mrs. Levine' was absolved from suspicion. That accomplished, she changed places with me again; she returned to the cottage and I went back to Grey Towers to finish my work.

"At this juncture I must add that my mother is out of the country with ample means to enable her to live in comfort for the rest of her life, and since I have taken great pains and spent a lot of money to cover up her tracks, I do not think you will ever be able to find her.

"Doctor Britling disregarded my warning to mind his own business, and so I prepared a little surprise for him in the nature of a glass bomb filled with cyanide gas which Sydney balanced above the door of his room. One whiff of the gas would instantly have killed him, but unfortunately, the kitten with which I killed Quail ran into the trap and died in his stead. If it had not done so, I am certain that I should now be free, for it was only the efforts of Doctor Britling which exposed me. I was annoyed by this unforeseen happening, since I had expressly threatened Doctor Britling with death, and I would have effectively remedied the error had it not been that I was occupied with the more pressing affairs of the disposal of Levison and Annerley, and the suitable punishment of Israel Straust and my former wife.

"I killed Levison by rigging up a contrivance in the drawer in which he kept his revolver. It was a simple device which fired the revolver when the drawer was opened. All that was then necessary was to inspire Levison with the impulse to open the drawer. This I did by contriving certain ominous noises in his room at the dead of night, having first switched off the electric current all over the house. Levison went for his weapon and automatically killed himself.

"A humble cuckoo-clock which kept rather indifferent time disposed of Annerley. I altered the mechanism so that instead of operating the cuckoo it fired a small revolver, and Sydney hid the contrivance in the upholstery of Annerley's car, with the muzzle aimed at the driver's seat. It was timed to fire at ten o'clock, and it was a simple matter to scare Annerley out of his wits so that at the prescribed hour he was frantically driving his car on the road to London.

"Death would have been too easy a punishment for Israel Straust, who was little more than a quarter alive in any case, so I robbed him of his dearest possession—his money. That broke his heart, and makes me, I suppose, responsible for his suicide. The robbery involved certain accomplices, so I must decline to divulge the method whereby it was contrived.

"I kept my former wife supplied with poison in a ring I gave her when we were first married. She has not tried it yet, but I die in the confident expectation that she will.

"I kidnapped Quail's niece when I made my getaway from Grey Towers because early that morning she had come to my room for company, and had discovered my secret, and because I hoped to use her as a hostage in case I was cornered. The raid on my hiding place came as a complete surprise to me, however, and when I set fire to the house as a last resource, I had forgotten that she was a prisoner in it. I expected Sydney to follow me to the roofs where I hoped we would escape, but apparently he did not forget our prisoner. The manner of his death makes me very proud of my son. I think it will count in his favour if there is a judgement beyond the grave.

"I refuse to discuss any confederates I may have had, other than my son Sydney, who is beyond mortal punishment, and my mother, whom I confidently believe to be out of reach of the law. This much I will say, I certainly had no other accomplices within the walls of Grey Towers.

"The course I embarked on was deliberately taken, and each of my crimes was premeditated and carefully planned. I do not repent having committed them. I make this statement of my own free will without…"

The dying man feebly waved a limp hand. "We'll take the rest for granted," he croaked. "Give me a pen and I'll sign it."

The statement was solemnly signed and witnessed, and as the police officials left the room, Marckheim beckoned to Doctor Britling.

His eyes had the stricken, pleading look of a tortured animal. "Doctor…for the love of God! …the pain…I can't bear it…" His face was a twitching mask with agony; his eyes like lumps of blazing coal; his forehead beaded with perspiration. "Doctor… you wouldn't let…a dog suffer…like this."

Doctor Britling prepared with steady fingers a powerful dose of morphia.

As he bent over the bed, his eyes told the suffering man what he was about to do—and the dark eyes of Arthur Marckheim thanked him gratefully.

Only One Left

"Standing at the window like Sister Ann won't do any good," observed Miss Britling, the sternness of her tone belied by the twinkle in her eyes. "I warned you they wouldn't be punctual. Men talk about women but they're just as bad themselves. Especially business men. Not," she added slyly, "not that your precious Adrian is a business man, even if Mr. Levison has taken him into his office."

Mary Quail whirled from the window with a radiant smile. "And who gave Uncle Gideon the idea?" she demanded. "You! You stern old angel!"

It was with difficulty that Miss Britling maintained the severity of her expression. "Stern I may be, old I certainly am—but an angel, never!" She shook her head emphatically.

"Yes, you are!" declared Mary accusingly. "And you know you like Adrian—yes, and uncle Gideon, too, although you treat him so sniffily—so you might as well stop pretending and be yourself for once, you dear, sweet—fraud!"

Miss Britling yielded to the temptation to smile, and was lost. Their laughter mingled and rose high above the clatter of china which heralded the approach of the housemaid with tea-things for five.

For six weeks—ever since the night of the fire—these two had been the best of friends. When Mary had recovered from the slight injuries which had kept her in hospital for a day or two, Miss Britling had brought her to the Orchard Street flat, ostensibly until her future was decided. A week later she had run off with the girl to the Riviera to spend some of the profits from her Stock Exchange speculation, leaving Daniel to the tender mercies of his club. Now they had returned, and Mary was a full member of the Britling household, and would continue to be until the day (which, Miss Britling felt, was drawing alarmingly near) of her marriage to Adrian Carver.

Adrian's broken leg had healed beautifully, and he had commenced his duties in Gideon Levison's office that very morning. It was also the day of Levison's return to the City and they were both coming to tea. And they were late. Two minutes late, to be precise.

It was almost three minutes past four when the click of Doctor Daniel Britling's latch-key in the lock of the front door was heard. Mary ran out into the hall to meet him, and drew him by the arm into the drawing room. "Late again!" she chided mischievously. "The tea will be so strong it won't run out of the pot! Must you spoil every meal you naughty man?"

"Two of 'em," sighed Daniel, rolling his eyes. "As though I hadn't enough to put up with from Eunice! It seems to be my lot in life to be surrounded by nagging women. And, on this occasion, I happen to be quite blameless. Am I responsible if women will insist on having babies at mealtimes? Can I help it if one walks into the police station and says please, she's going to have a baby almost at once, and what can they do about it? Naturally, they phone me, and naturally, I have to go, tea or no tea…"

"Daniel!" exclaimed the shocked Miss Britling. "I'm surprised at you! Before Mary!" The fortunate arrival of the guests drew a merciful cloak over Doctor Britling's embarrassment, and cut short the flow of his sister's remarks.

"We've had a busy day," Gideon Levison apologised, "or we'd have been here sooner. Blame Mary; she's responsible. I've been notified that her uncle appointed me executor of a will he made in her favour a number of years ago and I've been counting her money all day long. You're going to be a very wealthy young woman, Mary."

Mary looked thoughtful at that…

Doctor Britling unobtrusively drew Levison aside and handed him a newspaper clipping. "Have you seen this?" he whispered. "I cut it out of this morning's *World*."

As Gideon Levison read it his long, intelligent-looking face became clouded with sadness.

WEST END TRAGEDY
WOMAN TAKES POISON IN FASHIONABLE HOTEL

A woman who had registered under the name of Cora Arthur was found dead of prussic acid poisoning in her room at the Alamo Hotel at a late hour last night. Her handbag, which lay on the dressing table, contained only a few coppers and was barren of identifying papers. There was nothing of value among the dead woman's effects except a large ring which appears to be of Venetian design, and which had a secret compartment, apparently intended for the carrying of poison.

The financier returned the clipping with a sigh. "Poor Cora!" He shook his head. "So, I am the only one left," he murmured, "out of the six who were to die."

He put a hand on Daniel's arm. "I've been given another chance," he said—and there was glow of sincerity in his dark eyes—"a chance to make something worthwhile of my life. Money and brains can do much to better this old world of ours—and I'm going to have a shot at it!"

"Adrian," said Mary Quail pleadingly, "you won't let my—my money make any difference to—us?"

"Darling," said Adrian cheerfully. "I couldn't be so selfish!"

"The tea," observed Miss Britling stiffly, "is becoming stone cold!"

THE END

BLIND MAN'S BLUFF

THE DAY WAS young and fresh as Martin Longworth dressed methodically. As he used comb, hairbrush, shoe-horn, and nail file, he returned each to exactly the position from which he had removed it.

Every garment that he wore had its own place in his room, and it was without hesitation that he selected his brown suit and chose a pair of russet-coloured shoes to match.

Washing did not present any difficulties, and, as he wore a neat pointed beard, shaving was unnecessary. Within ten minutes he was fully clad.

Breakfast was next, and had you watched the deftness with which he went about the task, you would have found it almost impossible to believe that Martin Longworth was blind. Yet blind he was—had been for almost twenty years.

It is a tragedy when a young man of twenty-two, just completing his last term at Cambridge, and with the promise of a brilliant career before him, loses his sight through over-study. That was what happened to Martin Longworth, and for a time it seemed that his reason must go too. He had neither mother nor father; he had been brought up by an elderly uncle who had looked forward to his nephew joining him in his profession, and he could not hide his bitter disappointment from the sensitive youth.

There had been a girl—but 'I'm not such a miserable worm,' said young Martin, and he wrote releasing her from her promise. When she would not be released, he steadily refused to see her, and at last, yielding to the persuasion of her parents, she accepted his decision. Have you ever thought what it means to be blind—at first? The darkness, the terrifying darkness, day and night; the dread of falling; having every little thing done for you; knowing that someone has entered the room, but not knowing who, until they speak?

Martin went through the whole nightmare, and although at times it seemed as if his reason must fail, he came out of it all triumphant. It was a collar-stud that saved him, just a little gold stud that slipped from his grasp as he was fumbling for it. As it fell, he felt his terrible helplessness acutely, and a wave of despondence swept over him. Then, suddenly an idea struck him. He listened as the little stud rolled across the floor, and when it came to rest, he bent down, and without hesitation picked it up. He had discovered the first of the substitutes for eyesight—sound.

At the age of forty-one he was quite capable of looking after himself. Although he had never seen the village to which he had moved five years before, he had often accurately directed strangers to their destinations.

Breakfast over, he picked up his walking stick and hat, and went for his morning stroll. His cottage was about half a mile from the village to which he was heading.

As he stepped out of his garden and closed the gate, he heard the rumble of cartwheels. He knew it was the cart from Knowe Farm, because there was a small piece of the metal stripping chipped from the nearside wheel, and it made a slightly different sound from the other. The driver he identified by a whiff of tobacco smoke wafted to him on the faint morning breeze. No one smoked thick black at Knowe farm but Jim.

"Good morning, Jim."

"Morning, sir; fine morning."

As he entered the village, the nature of the road underfoot changed from gravel to macadam. From several of the cottage doorways greetings were spoken, and he returned them all, addressing each person by name.

The first shop he came to, he entered. He had never seen it, but by scent and sound it was familiar to him.

"Good morning, Mrs. Brown," He addressed the baker's wife. "I wonder if your daughter can give me a little help next week? As you may know, Mrs. Beveridge, who does my housework, is going to her sister's from Monday to Friday."

"Surely, sur, our Mary Ann'll be glad to oblige you," Mrs. Brown answered. "Her finds time heavy on her hands, these days. 'Baint much for her to do, round here; I'll send her up, come Monday."

The blind man smiled. "That's very good of you," he told her. "There's not much to do, I'm glad to say. The work's quite light."

"The furriner's come," she continued, delighted to have a morsel of news to impart. "You know, the man from over Bristol way, who bought Joe Willis's tobacco shop. Joe Willis gave him possession last night, and Joe says he's a real tight-mouthed sort. Didn't have much to say about himself—and you know, Joe's not easily choked off. I went up s'mornin' for the paper, and I couldn't make out much. He's got neither wife nor children with him. Well, mornin', sur. If you're going for tobacco, you'll see him yourself."

Martin raised his hat, and moved off before Mrs. Brown realised her slip. Then she could have kicked herself. "See him himself, indeed," she reproached herself. "Why, he can't see no one, the pore gentleman."

Nevertheless, the moment Martin stepped inside the tobacconist's shop, he began to get definite impressions of the new owner of the business, of whom he had just heard. When the man spoke, Martin started. The voice was quite familiar.

"Good morning, sir," said the tobacconist. "What can I do for you?"

"I'll have an ounce of Elysium Mixture," replied Martin. "It's a special mixture of Joe Willis's, you know."

The tobacconist reached back and brought down a heavy jar, which he placed on the counter. "I'm going to continue to blend this mixture," he said. "It seems to be a favourite. Willis has told me several customers won't have anything else."

When the small package was wrapped up the tobacconist stood drumming his fingers, while Martin fumbled for change. Something about the drumming, in conjunction with the familiar voice, struck a chord in Martin's memory. He decided to make a little test. "This stick of mine isn't very strong," he said. "Let me see, haven't you some ash-plants?"

"Why yes, sir, just behind you," said the tobacconist, coming from behind the counter and walking across the floor. Again, something stirred in Martin's memory. The walk was familiar.

As the man selected walking-sticks from the rack, Martin filled his pipe and lit it. They were standing close together, and as Martin exhaled the first mouthful the tobacconist began to cough.

"Oh, sorry," said Martin. "Does my smoke trouble you?"

The tobacconist backed away a little before answering. "It sounds funny, I know," he replied. "A tobacconist who can't stand smoke. If I get a real good whiff of it, it always sets me coughing."

Like a flood, full recollection came to Martin. A tobacconist who couldn't stand smoke—the familiar voice—the drumming of the fingers—the walk. He selected a walking-stick, however, and said nothing, while the man returned behind the counter to take charge.

"What about a morning paper, sir?" the man asked.

Martin smiled. "I can't read," he replied simply. "I'm blind, you know. A friend reads me the important news."

"Good God," gasped the tobacconist. "I'd never have thought it. You act as if you could see."

"Yes?" smiled Martin. "Practice, you know." He turned, as though to go out, then something seemed to strike him. "By the way," he said slowly. "I once knew a tobacconist who couldn't stand smoke."

"Yes?" gasped the man. His fingers were drumming harder on the counter now.

"Yes," replied Martin. "His name—let me see, now—his name was—Morgan, I think. No connection, of course?" His tone was quiet, almost indifferent.

The tobacconist ran a finger round his neck, as if his collar was too tight. "No, sir, no—no connection," he articulated at last. "Of course not. My name's Blaine. I've never known anyone called Morgan."

Like a tattoo, his fingers tap, tap, tapped on the counter. His eyes were going desperately from side to side, like those of a hunted animal.

"Of course not," laughed Martin. "I just wondered. Curious coincidence, though—wasn't it?"

He bade the man good morning, then stepped into the street. The tobacconist's eyes followed him, and in a moment the man walked slowly to the door, to watch him go down the street.

"He knows," the man told himself desperately. "My God, he knows!"

2

Dusk was early—at about eight o'clock, "God's time," as Mrs. Brown would insist, or seven o'clock by 'daylight saving'. The village folk were for the most part hardworking and home-loving. Few stirred out after dark.

At closing time, the new tobacconist glanced up the single street of the village, and noted its deserted appearance. Behind drawn curtains, a cheery light showed in almost every window, where the good folks were whiling away an hour before bedtime, the children with 'homework,' the women with knitting and darning, and the men with a pipe and the local weekly paper. There was a small gathering in the bar parlour of the Plough, mostly of farm labourers, and one or two bachelors who lodged in the village.

Noting that all was quiet, the 'furriner from Bristol way' disappeared into his shop, to reappear in a few moments muffled up in a heavy greatcoat, and with a cloth cap pulled well down over his forehead. From his stock he had selected a stout stick, and he swung it nervously as he walked. Guarded inquiries that afternoon had found out for him where Martin Longworth lived, and he headed up the road to the blind man's cottage.

When he was almost at the gate, he waited for a moment to regain his breath. Then, glancing round to make sure that no observer was about, he opened the gate slowly, thankful that the hinge seemed well oiled, and slipped stealthily up the path to the little cottage.

His breath, coming in short gasps, betrayed his agitation as he tiptoed to a window. He looked in stealthily, half afraid of being seen, then he remembered that the man within was blind.

The room he looked into was unlit, except for the light which three windows gave. That was sufficient, however, to allow him to make out much of what was within. One side of the room was almost entirely occupied by a large bookcase. Yes, the blind read, and their taste in fiction is much like anyone else's. Romance, adventure, love, they like to read about, with fingers that press eagerly into the formations of raised dots that make their alphabet.

In the far corner of the room, the 'furriner' could see Martin Longworth examining, some gramophone records. He was running his fingers over their surface, at last, choosing one, he placed it in a nearby cabinet which the watcher knew was a gramophone. In a moment or two the strains of 'My Blue Heaven' came to the ears of the man without.

He watched Martin cross the room, holding his breath as the blind man neared some piece of furniture in his path, and marvelling as he avoided it.

Martin settled himself into an armchair, and, reaching for pipe, tobacco, and matches, he began to smoke. Behind his head the watcher stood, his hands clenching convulsively.

When the record was finished, Martin removed it, then crossing to a bookcase he selected a volume. The man without watched him settle into his chair, pipe in mouth, and run his fingers over the first page, reading with their aid almost as quickly as a normal man would with his eyes.

The watcher waited until the man within seemed engrossed in his book, then tiptoeing from the window to the door, he stealthily tried the latch. To his relief, it raised noiselessly, and he slowly pushed the door ajar.

"Come in," said Martin Longworth pleasantly, "I've been wondering when you would!"

"You expected me," gasped the man, who called himself Blaine. "You expected me?"

"Yes," said Martin. "I have been listening to you outside there for the last 15 minutes, Morgan."

"My name's not Morgan," said the other angrily. "You're confusing me with someone else. My name's Blaine, I tell you. Blaine!"

In the dim light he could see Martin smiling.

"No," said Martin. "I'm not mistaken. You are Morgan. This

morning I recognised your voice, your walk, and your nervous habit of drumming your fingers. You're drumming on the table beside you now, by the way. It also seemed too much of a coincidence that two tobacconists should be strongly susceptible to tobacco smoke."

"Details," said the 'furriner' hoarsely, "tuppence-halfpenny details. I tell you, I'm not Morgan. Any man might cough when he got smoke right in his face, and lots of people drum their fingers."

"Exactly," agreed Martin. "And for that reason, I wasn't entirely certain of you. So, for a final test, I mentioned the name—Morgan. It caught you on the raw. You'd thought your tracks were covered. If any more proof is required, I have it."

He leaned across the table and spoke in a distinct decisive voice. "You came up here to murder me," he said, "as you murdered your wife in Birmingham, eight years ago!"

Morgan gasped hoarsely, and, swinging up his stick, he took a step forward. Then he halted, for in Martin's right hand there appeared a blunt-nosed blue metal object.

"Drop that stick and step one pace back," ordered Martin, levelling it at Morgan. "If you make a false move I'll fire. You're helpless, remember. It's dark, and in the dark you're blind. Blind without the added senses that real blindness brings. Be careful. I can fire at the slightest move. Your breathing, the rustle of your clothes, the creak of a floorboard, gives me all the target I want."

He reached for the telephone, and took the receiver off the hook. "I had the 'phone installed in case of emergency," he told the helpless man. "I think we might call this one."

He was connected with the local police station in a few moments. "Hello, Sergeant," he said, "this is Mr. Longworth. Have you a 'wanted' notice there for a man named Morgan, who killed his wife in Birmingham eight years ago?"

He was asked to hold on, while the sergeant investigated. Then the reply came: "We have sir, on our old files. There's a reward offered."

"Well, come up to my cottage, Sergeant with two of your men," Martin instructed. "I've got him here. No, it's quite alright. I have him covered." He replaced the receiver and turned to the man Morgan.

"They'll be here in about 10 minutes," he told him. "You can sit down till they come. Take that chair behind you. No, don't try stepping forward. If you do, I'll shoot. That's better. Now you can be comfortable till they arrive."

The two men sat facing each other, Morgan fidgeting nervously like a cornered rat; the blind man pulling on his pipe unconcernedly, but keeping his weapon aimed unwaveringly at the other. At last, they heard the asthmatic wheeze of an ancient motorcar outside. The door opened, and the three policemen stepped in.

"Are you all right, Mr. Longworth, sir?" asked the sergeant. "Is this the man?"

"It is," replied Martin. "After you've handcuffed this man, you can put on the light."

Morgan, realising that he was cornered, showed no resistance, and in a moment or two, the gas was lit.

"Don't tally with the circular," said the sergeant. "It says: hair red, his is black; full beard and moustache, he's clean-shaven. Nose, snub; his is fairly long and pointed. Height's about right, and eyes, that's all."

Martin smiled. "The hair is probably dyed," he replied. "The moustache and beard have been shaved, his nose has probably been broken and reset. It's your man, all right, sergeant. He won't deny it."

The prisoner did not deny it. Instead, his whole dejected bearing admitted the truth of the blind man's accusation.

"But how did you recognise him?" asked the sergeant curiously. "Beggin' your pardon, sir, but you're blind, an—"

"You mean, how did a blind man succeed in recognising a murderer, where the police have failed for eight years?" Martin asked. "Well, it's quite simple. The police were looking for a man with red hair, beard, and moustache, and a snub nose. I knew none of these particulars. His hair might have been red, or black, or even green, for all I knew. But I had a description of him that still fits and that couldn't be altered.

"I was in Birmingham for a month or two before the murder happened," he continued. "I was helping in the organisation of a home for the blind. Every few days I made a purchase of tobacco in this man's shop. It was a busy one, with customers coming and going all the time. He hadn't time to note much about any single customer. He was too busy if he noticed me at all, he certainly didn't know I was blind. But a blind man makes few contacts. He goes to the same shops all the time, and those in them soon become familiar to him. Not by their features, but by their voice, walk, and other characteristics.

"This morning, when this man served me, his voice, was familiar. So, too, was his habit of drumming his fingers on the counter. I had him walk across the floor to show me some sticks, and his walk set me searching my memory. I knew he was familiar, but I couldn't place him. When I lit my pipe, he was close to me, and the smoke set him coughing. Then I knew him. Morgan never could stand smoke.

"As a last test, I mentioned his name, and I knew if he was really Morgan he'd see I recognised him and would try to put me out of the way."

"You took an awful risk," said the sergeant.

Martin laughed quietly. "Oh, it wasn't as bad as all that," he answered. "You see, he was fighting me on my own ground—in the dark. By the way, you haven't, any of you noticed the amusing feature of the whole thing, this—"

He placed the 'weapon' he had been toying with on the table. It was a flint gun, made out of blue metal, the kind that are used in thousands of homes for lighting gas stoves.

The three policemen gaped, and from the throat of the prisoner came a long drawn-out sob.

"If I'd known," he groaned. "If I'd known."

"But you didn't," Martin answered. "After all, you people with eyes see what you think you see. If someone points an object at you and it looks like an automatic, then to you it is an automatic. You were playing on my ground, Morgan—and I won!"

THE END

Coming Soon from Moonstone Press

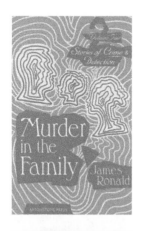

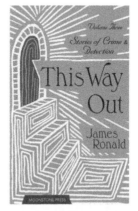